W9-BEE-405

DATE DUE
7/02   Fecha Para Retornar   02

AUG 3 0 2002			

THE LIBRARY STORE #47-0100

the lost diaries

of iris weed

FORGE BOOKS BY JANICE LAW

The Night Bus
The Lost Diaries of Iris Weed

the lost diaries
of iris weed

JANICE LAW

A TOM DOHERTY ASSOCIATES BOOK
NEW YORK

THE LOST DIARIES OF IRIS WEED

Copyright © 2002 by Janice Law

A Forge Book
Published by Tom Doherty Associates, LLC
175 Fifth Avenue
New York, NY 10010

www.tor.com

Forge® is a registered trademark of
Tom Doherty Associates, LLC.

ISBN 0-765-30273-X

First Edition: January 2002

Printed in the United States of America

0 9 8 7 6 5 4 3 2 1

For Jerry–always

part one

1.

*L*ars remembered a tree with stars caught in its hair, a strange and marvelous image that he tried to convey to Emma, visible only as a dim shape in the whitish morning light. "A tree with stars caught in its hair," he said, but the words came out as an indecipherable mumble, too soft to awaken his wife, who, had she heard him, would have said, "You're just dreaming, Lars," whereupon he would have rolled over and dropped down the cliffs of sleep.

But Emma, tired from the previous night's party, a late and happy affair, heard nothing, and Lars was left with a dim, sweetly fading sense of another world. *Classical* was the word that came into his mind, along with *sylvan, arcadian:* he had a sense of trees and stars and people dancing in flowing white garments, togas or kilts, he supposed, but which, as he came closer to real waking, he recognized as the shorts and skirts of their guests of the night before, of the children who had run about on their big lawn, calling, laughing, jumping in and out of the sprinkler behind Jake, their hyperactive terrier, and of the adults who'd danced on the big porch, first to records and then to Emma's barrelhouse piano played on her big baby grand. He himself had been singing seventies rock hits with Fred, making the children shriek and jump. The sound of music and laughter and friendly voices compounded with the smell of burgers and chicken and ribs (Lars presiding at the grill) and with the silhouettes of the big yard trees (dark as cypresses against the pink-tinged urban darkness) and the golden glimmers of fireflies (caught in a mason jar then released, to carry our wishes Lars had told the excited children)—all this distilled into a dream as lovely and mysterious as a blessing, a dream that faded as he awakened, leaving only the image of a tree with stars in its hair.

It was the Sunday after the Larsons' traditional end-of-summer party, and school would start tomorrow, early. The sun was up and yellow, Lars was awake, and a sliver of light from under the shade glowed on Emma's smooth, naked back. He turned over toward her, listening for sounds of Cookie stirring in her room down the corridor. He did not hear Jake's nails rattling along the wood floors, nor the little taps and scrapes of furniture being moved in the dollhouse, nor the quick slap of bare feet in the hall or down the stairs, nor even the soft thump of the cat, Polly, leaving her position at the foot of Cookie's bed to explore the possibility of breakfast.

Lars smiled; he was in luck. He laid his face against the small of Emma's back and breathed in the warm, familiar scent of her skin. He wanted to wake Emma, to tell her about his dream—and to suggest other early morning recreations—but he knew she'd be tired; this was the last day for a while she'd sleep past quarter to six. He dozed a little, trying to recapture the dream. Shelley, he'd been preparing Shelley and paganism for one of his early Romantic & Victorian class lectures. Was that where a classical world and toga-clad dancers came from? From the Greeks and fate and mysterious divinities? Had Shelley been the last to sense the pagan gods, or did they lurk in the shadows yet, to appear in dreams after offerings like summer parties and mason jars of fireflies?

Lars had almost fallen truly asleep again when he felt Emma stirring, a change in her breathing, a sudden restless rearrangement of her limbs. He smiled and slipped his arm around her waist and hitched himself closer to her—she had the smoothest, warmest back—and nuzzled the nape of her neck and whispered, "Emma, I just had the most wonderful dream."

"Mmmm."

"A tree against a starry sky."

"Uh-huh," said Emma, still half conscious.

"And nymphs and dryads and hamadryads, all dancing in a wood, in a moonlit field, though there was sun, too, sun on bare arms and legs."

Emma exhaled softly. "But no Apollos, no satyrs, no young shepherds?" She had, over the years, picked up more than she needed to know about pastoral poetry.

Lars hugged her; he never minded her teasing. "This was my dream," he said. "Besides, none of them was as pretty as you. But the tree, Emma, the tree was wonderful, with branches like flowing hair and stars shining through them. It was so real."

"As real as this?" asked Emma, reaching back to stroke his long, muscular thigh.

Lars laughed. "Almost," he said and pressed her close, happy and content, even though the brilliant tree was fading and the dream, its logic lost, dissolving into fragments.

S E P T E M B E R   2 — *Made Romantic & Victorian lit class today for the first time. Hurrah! Thought Professor Larson would throw a fit. Actually, I thought he wouldn't notice one way or the other, but nice fantasy to think someone would notice. Anyway, I got there late (trouble with the truck as usual), laundry bag over my shoulder because the U has no lockers, ready for hassle and set to do the woman warrior bit, when he raises an eyebrow and says, "We've been waiting for you, Ms. Weed," as if he really had been waiting. And like a wimp, as soon as he smiles, I go, "Sorry, I've got car trouble," and he says, "Best thing about the Romantic period was they hadn't invented the internal combustion engine yet."*

Which I think is probably true. Course, in the Romantic period, I would be home in the uneasy bosom of my family, I think that's what they called it, and if I wound up on the street, it wouldn't be as I am now, sleeping in the back of a truck and reading great literature. So, Iris, make a note to go time tripping rich and beloved.

Like I'd guess Professor Larson is. He's one of the most popular teachers in the department, in the whole college, really, and when you get into his classes, people say, "Oh, you're so lucky. He's so much fun and dresses up as Lord Byron and jumps on his desk to

read poetry," stuff like that. There are a lot of Larson stories about—
I guess that's how you know you've really made an impression
when people start making up stories about what you've done and
adding things on and making you better than life. That's where
Professor Larson is, Professor J. Larson, the "J" standing for Jason,
which is Greek and has reference to the Argonauts, who went after
a gold-plated sheepskin and behaved badly, as I remember from
Pokotuck H.S.

"My daddy was of a classical bent," said Professor Larson. That's
the way he talks—formal but with a bit of fun in it, a style I like
and that I am going to acquire. "My daddy was of an actuarial
bent"—how's that sound? Not as good as, "My daddy was of a classical bent, the last of an honorable line of amateur scholars," I'm
sure, but amateur scholarship is no way as mysterious a position as
my dad's, who figured life spans for a living. I used to think that
was the actual thing he did; I imagined some Mr. Jones sitting
anxiously in the office so my dad could run the figures on his calculator and say, "Presto! Your life span, Mr. Jones, best make your
plans accordingly."

One day I got him to explain life span, and he talked about
averages and populations and said the rest was "up to the good Lord
and the Fates," so maybe my daddy had a classical side to go with
his actuarial bent after all.

But back to Professor J. (Jason) Larson, who is tall and thin
with a definite face, as if his character's been settled in a good while:
a big nose and a long, thin mouth and a high, bony forehead and
deep-set eyes that are peeking out from under the overpass of his
prominent brow ridge and busy eyebrows. He's not what you'd call
handsome, but I'm keeping an open mind given his age, which is
certainly advanced. If I was interested, I could find out his exact
age when I'm in the library, because his data, actuarial and otherwise, will be up on the Web site with the faculty bios. That's if
I was interested, and I can't imagine why I would be.

Besides, what's important is the age of his heart. The age of
anybody's heart is vitally important, actuarially and spiritually. And
you can't always tell. Someone can look young outside and drop

dead, like one of those supertall basketball players who keel over in the midst of a great play, or you can look old and peculiar like William Blake, who was always young even when he was practically fossilized. Professor Larson said in class that Blake always had the rage and idealism of youth. That's how I want to grow old, full of rage and idealism.

OCTOBER 8 — *Stopped by to see Professor L today to go over my paper topic. Can't decide which poet. I love them all. I told him that I thought I'd do the best paper on Shelley because he's easiest, but I love both Blake and Byron and tried to explain why. Professor L really listened, for which I give him credit, especially since I had my laundry bag with me. The truck experiment is working out okay and saving me thousands, but it presents problems, like no running water and strictly Sterno can cuisine. Plus dirty laundry has no place to go. Still, what I save on housing I can spend on laundry and on food, preferably hot and cooked by someone other than me.*

Professor L said that he thought comedy was harder, which is why I'm having trouble with Byron and that is maybe true. We talked about comedy, and as soon as I said that comedy was more than just jokes, he brightened up the way teachers do when you say something not terminally stupid that lets them talk about what they're really interested in. (Remember, Iris, in teaching you have to talk about a lot of boring things and still sound like you're interested.) Larson said comedy can be an attitude, a way of looking at the world and not just jokes or slapstick.

"Or a kind of ending," I said, "as opposed to tragedy," and he said yes, that's what he meant by attitude. Then we talked about optimism, which is maybe why I like to be funny because it means there's hope somewhere, even if I haven't found it at the moment. I didn't say all that to Professor L, though, which is okay, because the prof began to talk about funny stories, which are one of the things he's interested in studying and classifying. Maybe he has an actuarial bent and doesn't know it.

N O V E M B E R   8 — *Stopped by to see Larson because I'd missed class. I think it's the damp weather—I keep getting colds and I've had to go to the infirmary again. Frosty weather in his office, too. Missing class suggests unseriousness and Larson takes literature seriously and himself, too. Anyway, I'm sitting there with soggy tissues and a hacking cough, trying to focus on Emily Brontë, who didn't have the comic spirit but had other things like genius for consolation, when the room begins to go dark at the edges and Larson's voice comes up from the bottom of an elevator shaft, "Ms. Weed? Iris?" He gets out of his chair, and I say, "I'm all right, I've got bronchitis."*

He says, "You should be home in bed."

And I say, "That's a bit difficult."

He goes down the hall and comes back with a big cup of black coffee with lots of sugar, and then he drives me back to the truck. He was really very nice, and I guess I'll have to explain to him about the experiment.

D E C E M B E R   3 — *Coffee again today with Lars. No date, just saw him in Joe's Joe and he came over with an extra cup and a muffin as big as a softball. "Essential to maintain your bodily resistance," he says. He likes to use nineteenth-century phrases. I've found some from Dickens to surprise him with, and then we swapped adjectives for the coffee until I tried "liquatious" which he says isn't a word but should be. It's a portmanteau word for liquid and delicious and loquacious, which sums up having coffee with Lars.*

D E C E M B E R   1 0 — *Classes ending. I was getting set to miss Lars, because he's teaching Romantic & Victorian again, but he said why not do an independent study with him and write up the experiment. He said, "Not that I'm necessarily endorsing the experiment, but . . ." and right then I saw a book with Iris Weed's name on the cover, and I went straight down to the English office and got the forms and signed up. I'm to meet Lars once a week and*

I'll turn my diary into what Lars calls a narrative, but what I'm already thinking of as MY BOOK!

J A N U A R Y   2 8 — *Long conference with Lars. Not sure my parody of Thoreau works for the start of the experiment. I still think it's funny, but maybe he's right: a bit pretentious and no point in flying too high too early. Anyway, I've been rereading* Walden *with my own life in mind. How romantic and fresh everything in* Walden *seems. That's what strikes me: new wood, new ground, new trees, though he did recycle the railway worker's cabin, gentrified it, I guess. And how few people around. That's the big difference.*

With living in the truck, everything is recycled, bought cheap, and scheduled to the city timetable: last john stop at McDonald's— 11:25 P.M. First call for coffee, juice, john—Dunkin' Donuts, three blocks away. Parking lots—one night each, McDonald's, commuter lot, Dunkin' Donuts, Burger King, Big Y, Home Depot, commuter lot again, not the cycle of the seasons but the parking lot rotation, keeping ahead of the guardians of public order. One bright spot: I've gotten to know Jorge, who's one of the beat cops; I'm never told to move along when he's on the prowl.

So is this the same as going into the woods to live off your own exertions?

F E B R U A R Y   9 — *A day of immense interest. What Lewis Carroll called a day to "mark with a white stone," like the day he told Alice Liddell the famous story that became* Alice in Wonderland. *A "white stone day" is biblical according to Lars, who does not normally approve of biographical criticism, which he says is seriously passé and, worse yet, theoretically naive. But let's admit we're curious about a man who takes little girls rowing and tells them stories of genius. We might be interested if he just took them rowing and told them ordinary stories or no stories at all, but the combination is really intriguing, and I wonder, was he interested just in them or in them as the occasion for great stories? This problem is what Lars calls the problem of audience or the knowl-*

edge community, something like that. I can't keep all the theories straight and don't need to. What's interesting is this grown man telling little girls stories.

But to get back to why this is a "white stone day": I visited the Larsarium, the inner sanctum, the home. Lars broke his ankle skiing, and when I called the office he said he was leaving early but to drop by his house with the finished chapters. So. Foggy day, thaw steaming the snow around this big brick Victorian, dark from the pines amid the bare trees on the lawn. I arrive around four P.M., just after my shift at Healthy Stuff, the food co-op, and Alice Liddell meets me at the door—just kidding, but she's the same age with the same bangs and with long, dark hair and a serious expression, and she's wearing navy corduroy overalls and a turtleneck with ruffles around the turtle that together look like a Victorian pinafore.

This is Cookie, Lars's daughter, and as soon as we go up to his study—which is just what I'd expected: books in wonderful wooden cases with glass doors and a big elegant cluttered desk with thin carved legs that bow out and in again like Victorian bloomers, and a tall uncovered window with stained glass at the top, a real scholar's study—as soon as we open the door and say hello and he jokes about being hors de combat and Cookie shows me his cast that she has decorated with dinosaur stickers and a big red Magic Marker heart, just that soon, before anything else, I can see he adores her. There is no one on earth he loves more, no one, not ever, it's not possible, and she thinks he's the greatest man on earth.

Funny how you see some things in an instant, even with looking around and his dog barking and everything else. And then there are other things you never know; you can live with the person even, and never guess certain things.

We say hello and I give him the manuscript. Cookie goes out with the dog, which is little and scrappy-looking with a coat between brown and gray. Then I notice the music playing. It's not the usual. In his office we sometimes sit and listen to Leonard Cohen after we go over my copy. Cohen's a poet with this great *deep voice, and I like the way the music reinforces what he's saying. Like in "Democracy's Coming to the USA," the beat makes the vowels heavy like feet tramping, like something powerful is marching toward you.*

But today Lars is playing some opera, and instead of getting right into the copy the way he usually does, he stops the disc and moves the control back. "You like opera?"

I shrug. "Just the Phantom of," *I say.*

"We'll have to raise your sights. What do you think of this?"

A woman, a soprano, starts singing softly, but you can feel she's got something in reserve because she holds all the notes a long time.

"It's her explanation of her life," Lars says. "Her justification. She's an opera singer and she's had lovers and given alms to the poor and said her prayers. 'Vissi d'arte, vissi d'amore': I have lived for art and love."

Without thinking, I say, "What else is there?"

He says, "I knew you would like it," and in that understanding, I was suddenly able to forget everything else I know about him.

M A R C H   2 — *Saw Lars in his office. We're on odd terms at the moment. I can tell he really likes the book—I shouldn't say "book" yet, but I think of it as the book. At the same time, he keeps pushing me for more "personal detail." He wants to know about my friends and so I wrote some pages about Jennifer, who's in my Swimming II class, which is an optional course I take to get access to the shower rooms and which is, admittedly, improving my aquatational performance in the natatorium. Anyway, I wrote about Jennifer, who's bulimic and trying to get over it with swimming and daily exercise and visits to a therapist who has these weird habits I really couldn't begin to make up. I thought the Jennifer section was pretty interesting and so did Lars, I could tell, but it wasn't quite what he wanted.*

Then the light went on—Duh! Stupid Iris!—he wants to know about men, boyfriends, sex. It's like he's interested in a different way, like he's jealous. And that's put us on a different footing.

M A R C H   1 3 — *I've been neglecting the diary for life; would Thoreau approve? The whole point of any experiment in living is to live in a more intense way, and I certainly am. I lie in my sleeping bag and think about becoming emotionally sophisticated, like a woman in a French movie. I've only seen a few French movies, courtesy of Introduction to World Film, but I've got the feel of them: clear, glareless light, big uncluttered rooms, and men with thin, white shoulders smoking naked in bed. The women are elegant even if not beautiful; they are restrained, passionate, deadly, which is maybe a tall order for Iris Weed, particularly now when there's plenty of rain and mud, and truck living is at its least elegant and sometimes scary, too.*

Winter is good in the parking lots. The druggies and prowlers stay in their cars with the heaters running. March brings out the drunks who piss on your wheels and thump on the cap over the back to see what's inside. You need to be on the alert, especially in the commuter lot mornings after there's been a late party. I like to imagine Catherine Deneuve stepping right from Belle de Jour *out the back of my truck, hair perfect, nails ditto, wearing a sheath dress and heels and stockings to ask in perfect French, "What the fuck are you doing?" Which is what I, Iris Weed, ask, or else I hide down under my sleeping bag and make not a sound.*

I've some way to go yet to achieve "that inimitable Gallic sophistication" my Introduction to World Film prof liked so much, but I've got my life satisfactorily complicated and there's no doubt that the experiment has been a success insofar as I'm now a more interesting person. Of course, I was always interesting, but now I'm interesting to other people, which is a harder thing to pull off than just being essentially fascinating, as in my essence, philosophically speaking, is fascination.

2.

*H*ow had it ever come to this? Lars was in his upstairs study, overlooking the garden still frowsy with the dead plants of winter. The unreality of his situation was increased by the familiarity of his desk, his bookshelves, the old wire-fronted cabinet that held his first editions, the framed Tenniel drawing, and a small oil Emma had done, amateurish but endearing, of Lake Windemere. His own books and monographs and the journals that held his many articles, plus the original bound copy of his thesis, stood in two close-packed rows to the left of his desk. Lars took comfort in these tokens of success, material and intellectual. His degrees were all good, his doctorate from Harvard, and if he hadn't quite scaled such pedagogical heights himself, the college was very reputable, very, and the whole university coming up. As for his own standing in the profession, he enjoyed, at forty-three, a solid reputation. Not in the superstar category, no, but rock solid. He reviewed for good journals, advised only the best students, chaired important committees.

So how had it come to this?

And more: the house and all that it contained. Bless this house! What was the old song? *Bless this house and all within, keep them free from want and sin*. Want, Lars felt, was well at bay—in today's market a brick Victorian of this vintage and quality in an up-and-coming neighborhood might fetch as much as $200,000. Could you move it a mile farther from the city line, double that, but still, a valuable commodity. And his salary was good, Emma's, too; want they had defeated on their own, leaving only sin.

Lars sometimes taught sin, that uncomfortable and unfamiliar concept, to his undergrads. Hawthorne requires an understanding of sin, sin in the classical sense as one of the ingredients of the human condition. Byron and Shelley do, too. The former had sin in his bones; the latter, modern to the core, wanted to extirpate the concept and free us for modern life and all its consequences.

Lars picked up his red pen and made a few more notes on the essay he was correcting: *dangling modifier, like comparison to "Wasteland" but note lack of Eliot fragmentation, tighten up this paragraph,* before leaning back in his chair again and staring up at the ceiling: *sin.* By some lights he, Jason Larson, was a sinner, and not just in the general commonplace sense that we are all imperfect. He, Jason Larson, had specific and particular sins, a series of them, in fact, dating back—well, quite a few years. Quite a few.

Sins by some lights, that is, but before Lars considered whether those lights were his lights, he acknowledged that he should have been warned about Iris, who preferred Blake to Shelley, and Byron to both. That should have been a tipoff. He should have examined the subtext and noticed how she'd zeroed in on the one who felt sin.

So how had it come to this? The answer was plain: He had mistaken Iris Weed for another of the pretty, ambitious, playful young women who had brightened his life by succumbing to his charm. In retrospect, he'd made his mistake the first day, the very first day, and it was bitter now to remember how complacently he'd looked over his Romantic & Victorian class. How pleased he'd been to recognize three of his students: the big dough-faced boy who wrote quite brilliant satiric poetry, the redheaded girl with the Pre-Raphaelite visage, the most beautiful girl he'd ever taught, talented, too—she offered an alternative future that would have been understandable, even excusable!—and the tall, intense boy with dark, sunken eyes who'd taken seventeenth-century drama with Lars two semesters before. Through Lars never felt easy about people with a passion for the Jacobeans, especially for Ford, the boy was a good student; they were all good students, and he, Lars, was a good teacher, brilliant, charming, and professional. Beyond temptation, without sin, so to speak, and then *she* walked in late, a vivid presence even now in his mind's eye: a tall, thin girl with a good breasts and long, untidy black hair trailing around her white face. She wore a short black dress and frayed maroon tights that ended incongruously in a pair of hiking boots, an outfit somewhere between refugee and Goth. This was Weed, Iris, seventh semester, liberal arts, who came bearing, like a dubious gift, a huge, faded green backpack with the musty smell of dirty laundry.

Here Lars stopped, as he did a mite too often, to give himself credit. He'd had a certain insight that morning, for in one sense Iris really was a refugee: She had most of her worldly goods on her back and she'd fled her old world to search for the one she needed. He should have clung to that insight; refugees are people who have known suffering and extreme conditions, and even if they love comedy like Iris, they may have hungry, rather than playful, hearts.

Lars rose from his desk and went to the long window, two lights over two with original woodwork in perfect condition. He and Emma had stripped the woodwork, window by painstaking window. The entire hall, and the main staircase, too. The back stair they'd left painted; they'd been exhausted by scraping and chemicals by that time. God knows how much lung tissue they'd sacrificed for all those yards of gleaming oak, now quietly mellowing into darker and darker shades of honey and amber. Lars wondered momentarily if he had been poisoned by renovations, if that was why he'd made such an error, if that was why he'd been led astray from the very first by that whiff of musk and genius.

He tapped restlessly on the casement. Below in the yard, the earliest crocuses were struggling to get their chartreuse noses, tender as new puppies, through the half-frozen soil of the untidy flower beds. Emma had been neglecting the garden—a subtle message to her spouse? Lars thought he might surprise her by going down and cutting back all the old dead asters and Michaelmas daisies and pulling the winter's leaves off the beds. If he did that, she would understand that his heart was in the right place, but he remained frozen at the window, mocked by young crocuses and tormented by pointless lust.

Yet how rich and juicy his desire had seemed only six weeks ago! Even a month ago, Lars had tramped the campus walks and corridors like a conqueror, full of buoyant, animal joy. Now the remembrance of happy anticipation was a tormenting yet irresistible indulgence. He allowed himself memory in small doses like a forbidden sweet: how he'd sat laughing at Joe's Joe with Iris, or in his office, a CD playing softly, her manuscript—so promising—between them, or crossing campus together, still talking about her "experiment," about *Walden*, about Byron, about anything under the sun, but really talking about each other and bringing their emotions up to the proper pitch.

At such emotional musicianship, Lars was a past master. Emma once said that he was born to be loved, and Lars was sometimes forced to admit that charm was his greatest asset. Everyone liked him: his students, his acquaintances, his ex-lovers, his colleagues. Without grace, without beauty, without a great deal of money, without fame, without notable strength or athletic endowment, he was considered the most attractive of men. He'd won Emma, who was not just an interesting-looking woman like Iris but a genuine beauty. Emma's hair was starting to gray now, but still, at faculty receptions or the president's cocktail party, at some summer barbecue on the lawn with friends, or even in a momentary separation at the theater, Lars would see her across a crowd and his heart would lift. What a beautiful woman, he would think, and then he would realize afresh that was Emma, the woman he loved.

And he did love her. Always had, always would. That was the painful thing, the fact that had hitherto made all his other romances superficial. Of course, he and Emma had their share of griefs and problems. Of course. And more in years since they lost poor Jared, who was born to live but a few hours and die, taking the joy of Emma's life with him. Lars might have blamed that and excused himself, but in matters of the heart he could be surprisingly fair-minded. There had been girls before Jared; there had been girls all along, but unlike Iris, they had been innocent indulgences, Shelleyan indulgences, Blakean indulgences: fundamentally innocent. Lars really believed that, and maybe Emma did, too, because she ignored the ones she could and forgave him the ones she discovered. She understood his nature; she understood the unique temptations of charm. She was susceptible herself.

And what harm had he done? He'd been discreet, careful, generous, fun. He'd been European, sophisticated. The proof? Where were the scandals? The tears? The hurt feelings? He'd managed everything superbly. Flirtation, romance, discreet affairs: these were his metier, his gift. And though on occasion he had had misgivings—had had more, he had to admit, since Cookie grew older—yet he had never been able to convince himself of the sinfulness, of the harm. In his heart of hearts, Lars felt that the world was poorer without pleasure, specifically that the world was poorer without the pleasure he could create.

Yet, here on a March day, full of wind and damp, he stood at his study window and asked himself, *How have I come to this?* He'd known he would have to think about last night, he'd known he would; the memory had been in the back of his mind since he woke up to the beep of his alarm. It had lurked as an ironic obbligato behind his lecture on *Leaves of Grass,* that hymn to erotic optimism, to joy. Had Whitman awakened some mornings to find *his* bed over the pit? Lars bet he had.

Then lunch, lunch with the chair and the dean, where Lars had felt a strong obligation to be amusing, charming: the English department needed another position; they were weak in Renaissance and had a shot at a truly promising young scholar. But all the time they were talking, presenting their case, impressing the dean, Lars could feel remembrance rising around him like dirty water, rising up to drowning depth.

In the afternoon, he left campus as soon as his last class was over, postponing a graduate student and canceling a committee meeting to go home and stand by his window and remember the previous night. Which could not possibly look as bad in strong light, which really was an aberration, a fluke, even, considered the right way, faintly comic, yet Lars felt sweat along his spine. He understood now the cravings of an addict.

Last night at seven o'clock he had been home and happy, joking with Emma over dinner, helping Cookie with her science project—painstakingly mounted bean sprouts in various stages of development—when suddenly the world emptied and all that was left was the need to see Iris. He'd gotten up abruptly, exclaimed about some forgotten book, something he needed from the library, a most transparent and uninventive lie, and hurried out to his car. It was only good luck that he hadn't run over the cat as he backed out.

Then off to the college. Propelled by sensual despair and crazy erotic hope, Lars had driven slowly up the hill, checking for the truck along the campus roads and in the big commuter lot, feeling emptiness falling onto his heart with the drizzly rain. Faculty parking next because Iris had written a funny section about parking tickets, her many violations elaborately and unrepentently protested. But there was nothing in the faculty lot but a blue maintenance van and growing puddles. Behind the gym, beside the stadium, no, no luck. Had she perhaps slid the truck alongside the dark theater? Worth checking there. The theater was one of the prides of the campus: a heavy turn-of-the century brownstone, dear to Lars's heart as his rendezvous with Agnes, a delectable MFA drama candidate. He'd spent all of one spring semester with Agnes. They'd seen every film shown on campus, a couple more than once, and ordinarily the theater was bathed in a reminiscent glow, but not tonight. Lars stood beside his car and watched the misty rain halo the street light and drip off the eaves. Iris's truck was nowhere in sight.

He'd crossed and recrossed the campus. He parked in the faculty lot and walked the quad, where the slick concrete paths reflecting the dorm lights should have reminded him of courting Emma and of the simpler joys of youth. He got back in his car. Where the hell did Iris park? He tried to visualize the pages of her manuscript, always slightly dog-eared from her backpack and sometimes unpleasantly scented with stale clothes or laundry detergent. Home Depot, McDonald's, Burger King, Dunkin' Donuts: that was the rota, all right, and he was set to find her if it took all night.

Lars had visited half the list when he realized that he had been relying implicitly on her truthfulness. Fool! Fool! Autobiographers are notoriously unreliable, their memoirs riddled with fabrications innocent and deliberate, with exaggerations, fantasies, outright lies. Not that it mattered for Iris, who was writing essays not a damn geography, and yet now, he, Lars, needed to know precisely: Is it Dunkin' Donuts on Tuesday night or is it McDonald's? And had she told him everything? Most likely not; most likely she'd found some safe havens that didn't write up as well, that didn't come with funny stories, that weren't inspiring; most likely.

He banged his hand on the steering wheel in rage. One more to go: the Home Depot lot, an urban savannah dotted by tall sodium arc lights, that was clear on the other side of town. The trip was futile, Lars knew it was futile, he knew he would not find her there, and yet he had to go, though the rain had become a dense grayish wall that his lights carved into soft tunnels. He had a hopeful moment when he spotted a truck, a truck with a cap, Iris, salvation, a resolution for suspense and conflict and misery—then he saw that no, this truck was dark green, not maroon, and a Dodge, not a Chevy.

Lars sat for a time in the lot, his car next to the truck, his mind going from bad to worse. There were things he didn't know about Iris, things, granted, he had no right to know, no business to know, but that he would have given, at that moment, a year of his salary to know. He wanted to know where she was—and with whom. A night like this, the rain sliding down the windows, the damp cold seeping into your bones, is the night you look for a warm apartment, a warm bed. He knew it. He knew it. And so the questions became, Whose? And, Where?

He returned to campus, a dream night of fog and aureoled lights and wet pavements washed orange, red, and green. The streets adjoining campus were full of student housing: two- and three-family houses converted to rooms, old tenements given a hasty inspection and makeover, a few single-family homes reduced to the indignities of communal living. She was here somewhere, he knew she was. Lars crawled along the streets with the old biblical names, Jerusalem, Zion, Caanan, Gilead, looking in driveways, looking along the curb, looking for Iris.

He didn't find her, though he was convinced—more, he *knew*—

25

she was there. The truck was parked in one of those dark yards, perhaps even in plain sight, protected by the dazzle of the omnipresent security spots, or else it was pulled into one of the dismal crumbling garages, or shadowed by a spider work of porches and fire escapes. She was there, all right. He just had to find her, to find who she was with, to find the truth.

Some time after one A.M. Lars wound up back where he had started, on the edge of the commuter lot, exhausted and dazed by the folly that his watch revealed. He had spent the better part of five hours prowling the campus and the surrounding area. For what, for what reason? That's what the campus security cop asked when he rolled up next to Lars's old Volvo.

"Need help?" he asked. The campus policeman had a smooth, well-fleshed face, light, alert eyes, and the short hair football players and military recruits affect to make themselves look hard and serious. Like Lars, he was looking for some anomaly to justify wasted hours cruising about the campus.

Lars shook his head.

"Mind stepping out of your car for a moment, sir?" the cop asked.

Lars rolled down his window.

"Oh, hey, Professor Larson. I should have recognized you. You spoke at the Legion banquet."

Lars nodded again, automatically. *Legion, Legionnaires, Foreign Legion, Legions of Hell* ran through his mind, before he remembered the dinner for the American Legion baseball team that had gone to the state finals and been honored with a banquet. He'd spoken about baseball, about playing as a boy, about a wonderfully awful trip to see the Red Sox at the dawn of the Dark Ages. He, Lars, had been amusing. How long ago and improbable that seemed. Yet that would save him now. He was no longer a suspicious loiterer, he was Professor J. Larson, who gave after-banquet speeches and gave them very well. Lars felt himself relax, though his shirt was torn, though he sensed there was a bruise coming up on his forehead.

"My boy really enjoyed your talk."

"Great," said Lars.

"Sorry for stopping."

"Doing your job," Lars said. And there was a pause that seemed to take on weight and moisture from the heavy, damp air, because the campus cop was a professional after all, an alert man on the lookout for irregularities.

"Having car trouble?" the cop asked.

"Heart trouble," Lars said and when the cop's face turned serious, added, "so to speak. I'm trying to come to terms with something. I hadn't realized it was so late."

"Past one," agreed the cop. "Past one."

"Time I was going home." But Lars did not switch on his motor. "There are times when life seems unreal," he observed.

The cop nodded. "Unreality's an occupational hazard this time of night."

"I understand," said Lars, who exerted himself to be friendly, pleasant, amusing, to charm. The rain was almost over and he got out of his car to stand under the light and talk. The cop was a smoker who was trying to quit. He got one cigarette a night at precisely 1:30 A.M., and Lars stayed and visited while he smoked it, enjoying the fragrant scent, the vicarious indulgence. They talked about smoking, about quitting smoking, about giving things up. Lars had abandoned his pipe reluctantly and regretfully after Cookie was born.

"Time to go," said the cop when his cigarette had become the smallest of possible butts. "Time to hit the road. Time to go home, Professor."

And Lars, meek and amusing professional, had gone home to write a fanciful apology to Emma that was nine parts persiflage and one part truth. He'd said it was just a bad night for him, and since it was close to the anniversary of Jared's birth and death, he knew that she would believe him. It was very low, Lars knew, to use the anniversary as an excuse, but perhaps his excuse was true, for what he felt when he stopped on Zion Street and saw a Chevy truck with a cap, looking dark red in the faint light, was devastation. The truck was parked behind an untidy picket fence overgrown with wisteria. From the big shingled house, a steroidal sound system pumped out a heavy bass line that reverberated along the street like a monster heart. Lars got out of his car, opened the gate, and tapped on the truck. "Iris? Iris?"

Nothing. The sound of the bass rattled his nerves. He tried the latch on the back of the cap.

"Iris?" Louder, carelessly loud.

So she wasn't there. So she was in the apartment, partying with friends, dancing, no doubt, to the monster sound, or worse, rolling on a futon upstairs in one of the seedy, sound-wracked rooms with some adolescent as treacherous as herself. Yes, he knew now; she'd been lying to him. Lars started toward the porch, as the door of the house opened, releasing a high-decibel wash of guitars and a shouted, "Hey! You!" from a tall, thin boy. Lars couldn't make out his features. The light from the foyer illuminated bare, bony shoulders, a tank top, a blond halo around the top of his head, and the silver disk of a beer can, leaving his eyes, his expression, in darkness. "What the hell you doing with my truck?"

"I'm looking for Iris Weed," Lars said, unable to grasp his mistake. "Is Iris there?"

Standing at his window, Lars flushed at the remembrance of what followed: confusion, explanations, demands, a shove, a sudden blow, then the mediation of a lanky student stinking of marijuana. Lars had gotten his shirt ripped, the boy with the tank top lost his beer. They'd jostled on the porch amid mildew and hemp fumes, a hair's breadth from violence and scandal, before he'd been saved by the common sense of a man half his age.

But that was not the worst, not those moments of humiliation and anger on the grad students' porch. No, it was the moment at the truck, a moment of such intensity that if Iris had been at home, Lars might have harmed her, shaken her, slapped her, hurt her in some undefined but horrible way. He might, and the thought terrified him, because he could find no explanation, no reason for the way happiness, pleasure, a certain careless joie de vivre had mutated into this rageful need.

The affair—call it that if you wish to be charitable to a man of a certain age—had started so pleasantly, so innocently, so familiarly.

But no, Lars corrected himself, that wasn't quite right: He had certainly not made the first moves, he could swear to that. He had not even found her attractive initially, regarding her as gawky and disheveled and undistinguished in class, where she remained silent unless called on and laconic to a fault. Iris had seemed to Lars withdrawn, almost depressed, until he'd chanced to hit upon one of her enthusiasms, asking her about Blake's poem "The Tyger." Iris's pale face lit up, a flush rose along her cheekbones, and to his surprise Lars realized that the words on the page were pure joy for her.

He'd been interested, impressed even, but then she'd been out, cutting one class after another, and Lars had written her off as one of those birds of passage who waft, bright but rudderless, through academe, their untethered imaginations making routine hateful. Would that had been the case! Instead, a damp early November afternoon, the fluorescent lights casting a greenish glow, the darkening quad brown under its coat of leaves, a knock, then her face, flushed with the chill, her eyes dull and feverish, at the door of his office. He hadn't been particularly glad to see her, but when she nearly passed out, what could he do but offer her a lift to what turned out to be a truck?

"An experiment in living," she said, "with certain hygienic downsides."

So that was interesting, and Lars had found himself intrigued by her experiment and by her accounts, which were wry and charming with real literary flair. Academic prose did not suit Iris's talents: Her class papers were adequate but not inspired. Lars saw that her gifts lay elsewhere, in her willingness to risk unusual situations and eccentric prose. She kept diaries, she said, and then reworked them. Lars sometimes saw cheap school notebooks with marbled black-and-white covers in her possession, but he'd never gotten a single glimpse inside those. "Mere raw material," said Iris. "All very boring."

In this way, she moved up in Lars's estimation, just as a student, a good student, an interesting friend, creativity in blossom. Fatal flower! She entered his mind, all right, but not his conscious mind, and here Lars stopped to think sadly about the rational delights of other academic affairs: intense lunches with talk of Derrida or Foucault before, and luxurious moments afterward, reciting poetry (impressively) from memory. Iris had only minimal interest in literary theory, though under the right circumstances, Lars knew she'd be susceptible to poetry. But basically he connected with her on a different level altogether, so that quite without consciously being attracted to her, he found her resident in his fantasy life. He blamed this on her delightful prose that returned in memory accompanied by imaginary glimpses of her breasts—large and white, he was sure—and of her long legs, mercifully denuded of her wretched frayed tights and shabby jeans.

Lars would be sitting talking to her, completely professional, discussing sentence structure or a tricky transition or whether the scene with the drunken DEKE member belonged before or after her lyrical description of a foggy night on campus, when suddenly he would be seized with longing. He wanted to pull her onto his lap and make love to her right in his office, to send their cries echoing like gulls through the quiet corridors. This was love unbidden, love as ecstasy and disaster, a passion straight out of Greek theater and threatening catastrophe.

A moment later, he would be himself again. Iris would be Iris, bright and talented but neither clean nor tidy and certainly lacking the "face that launched a thousand ships." But she'd be back, Lars knew she would, that other Iris, the woman who'd begun to haunt his dreams, who visited him like an unexpected perfume and slipped away with the dawn, leaving him restless and lonely.

Almost against his will, and certainly against his judgment, he began to exert himself to be charming, to be agreeable, to show an interest. And Iris, who craved attention, longed for an audience, needed encouragement, began to stop by the office every time Lars had conference hours. It became easy for him to say, "I have another student coming in—what about meeting me for coffee later?"

She would agree with the radiant smile that illuminated and softened her strong features, and Lars, poor deluded fool, thought that everything was proceeding smoothly and pleasantly. Secure in his charm, he'd been confident that Iris Weed would drop into his hands of her own accord.

Instead, something else happened. Lars was not sure just what, or, he amended bitterly, just who, but Iris, formerly subdued, Iris, whose wit and joy had always seemed to be struggling through some psychic cloud, became ebullient, giddy, enormously energetic, and productive, too, turning out long, ambitious chapters for her independent study project. She had a knack for meeting people: the old man rummaging through the Dumpsters at the supermarket, who told her airily that he "was in the recycling business with Donald Trump"; the woman meat cutter with the massive biceps and magnificent tattoos, who took a break every afternoon to check with her children by cell phone, the drug dealer–video artist who, like Iris, was cutting his overhead with a home base in the parking lots, plus a variety of students, faculty, and staff, all very quotable, odd, and sharply individualized, whom she somehow persuaded to discuss a quite amazing variety of topics.

With the new semester, even the accounts of her living arrangements took on a certain gusto. While the first essays had focused on the discomforts and trade-offs for money saved, now Iris presented the truck differently: It was her magic cavern, a nautilus shell from which she, lovely, radiant mollusk, emerged into the world. Her prose, a lively half lyrical, half cynical blend—like a good whiskey, she said once—fairly bubbled off the pages.

For a time, Lars had thought that he was the reason, but though Iris could be giddy and even flirtatious, whenever he had tried to move their relationship forward—or bedward—she not only refused the signals, she gave no indication of receiving them. It was as if her erotic radar was missing a few bands. Was she gay, perhaps? Certainly an explanation, but Lars did not think so. She seemed to like male company and had selected him for her independent project when she could have chosen any number of women professors, one of whom was openly lesbian.

Still, it would be nice to know for sure, and Lars had attempted, not too gracefully he realized now, to ferret out the name of Iris's boyfriend. The manuscript needed more personal detail, he told her; the character sketches were tremendous stuff, but the authorial voice needed to be stronger. Here Iris had raised an eyebrow. If young and impressionable she was not without a sturdy idea of her own talent, but Lars plunged ahead. He really thought more about her own life was needed, the life of the person who would undertake such an interesting experiment, who could engage such a range of personalities, that was what would interest readers.

In response, she produced a piece on one of her friends from swim class—as if this waterlogged undergrad was of any conceivable interest to him! Oh, it was well done, yes, indeed, with a truly queasy mix of food and water images suitable for a bulimic—"the barfing mermaid," as Iris described her. Lars had to laugh, but driven by his need to know, he had said, yes, it was good, very good, but not quite the thing he'd had in mind. "Normally with student writers"—how ponderous that sounded in memory—"normally, you're trying to extend the range, move them a little beyond their own experiences, while you have a tendency to disappear into your text . . ."

Iris had given a nervous smile, half startled, half amused; she'd seen through him in that instant, but her work was no more forthcoming. Indeed, Lars thought that she was teasing him: There was a party sequence, as disastrous as most of her social ventures seemed to be, that opened in a brief glimpse at some subterranean social life. Lars pressed her for details, the party location should surely be mentioned, a fraternity, perhaps?

"Sure," said Iris, "but with the names changed to protect the guilty."

She was already thinking of libel, of publication, Lars realized; she knew the manuscript had possibilities; she was ambitous and no fool. But he was. He was. He kissed her mouth one afternoon right on the quad, as impulsive as a boy, and saw her eyes, half fascinated, half repulsed.

"Your work is wonderful," he said by way of extenuation and apology. She took his arm and they walked all the way to her truck without saying more. He should have left it there, taken that kiss for a trophy and moved on. Instead . . .

The dog's shrill bark, the sound of the front door banging open. "I'm home! Daddy, I'm home!" That was Cookie in the hall, wild, energetic, exhilarated by her release from school, yet apprehensive, too, until she knew he was home, the house occupied, all right with the world.

"I'm upstairs, Cookie."

Then the sound of racing feet; his daughter never did anything at half pace.

"Are you ready?" she cried. "Are you ready?"

Lars tore himself from the Slough of Despond and struggled with the Ghost of Promises Past. The new Harry Potter book? No, a friend at the University of Strathclyde had become Cookie's everlasting hero by shipping the UK edition direct a month ago. Lars was canvassing the calendar of sports, music, treats, when his daughter burst into the room, dog at her heels, coat open, socks drooping, hair flying around like an angry cat, and flew to his arms.

"How was school?"

"Okay. Boring." It disappointed Lars that Cookie was such an unenthusiastic scholar.

"Homework?"

"Not much. I'll do it. But we want to get to the mall before they're all gone!" The very thought brought a note of despair to her voice, and Lars remembered: the Christmas Shop was unloading seasonal decorations, dollhouses, and miniature furniture. Prize among all Cookie's possessions, after the family dog and cat, was her dollhouse, a large and beautiful colonial that his father had made many, many years ago for Lars and his sister. Beth had kept the house, which her daughters had loved and outgrown, and it had come now to Cookie, who, inspired by their unending work on their old house, had plans for renovations.

"It's going to be mostly Christmas stuff," Lars said.

"For next year," Cookie said. "For next year, and besides, I can have Christmas in the dollhouse any time I want."

"All right," he said. "And you have money?"

She tore down the hall to her room and returned with her patent vinyl bag over her shoulder, a serious shopper, the thirst for acquisition shining in her eyes. Lars gave her a hug; she would keep him from despair. "We best take Jake out for a walk first," he said.

She hesitated only an instant, torn between greed and duty, then fetched the leash, setting Jake to dancing and leaping and giving little barks of excitement. They took him around the block, a walk that now held almost exclusively canine references for Lars: the house where the rottweiler lived, a friendly animal, bemused by Jake; the fire hydrant, a bulletin board for every dog in the neighborhood; the Sweeneys, whose battered garbage cans offered promise every collection day; the Phongs, where Siamese cats defended the lawn with yowls and snarls; the well-fenced Innocenti yard with the irresistible pickets, and the Bialouszes' distinctly unfriendly dalmatian. Cookie kept up a stream of patter to Jake, avoiding the usual chat about school, and when they finally got in the car, she fell silent. With a sinking feeling, Lars realized she must know he'd been out half the night. He did not think Emma would have said anything. That was not Emma's style; whatever happened between them, he could count on Emma to protect Cookie. And vice versa. No, she'd heard the car, heard him come in, perceived irregularity, lateness, the frightening mysteries of adult life.

"You know what I like to do?" he asked Cookie.

She shook her head.

"I sometimes, just once in a long while, like to drive around at night. It's got to be rainy. Remember the night we spent with your Aunt Agnes, who has the tin roof? Remember that?"

"Yes," said Cookie, but cautiously.

How soon she was going to grow up, to lose the transparency of childhood and gain the subtle opacity of the adult mind. Still, he must try. "It's the rain on the roof, that sound," Lars said. "Makes you feel cozy somehow, doesn't it?"

Cookie nodded, emphatically silent.

"And foggy. It's good if the night's foggy because then it's quiet. You go out, you drive around in the fog, you listen to the sound of the rain. I like to do that once in a while. It's a good way to think."

"What do you think about?" Cookie asked.

"I think about a lot of things."

"Like what?"

"Well, like Cumbersome House."

It was a little joke between them: They called the old dollhouse Cumbersome House because it had been so difficult to get upstairs.

Cookie gave him a skeptical look. She was almost eleven, on the cusp between fantasy and reason.

"I was thinking it was time to tell you that Cumbersome House has a ghost."

"No," exclaimed Cookie, but cheerfully, because now she anticipated a story, a silly story like all of Daddy's, but good just the same because created only for her.

"Oh, yes," said Lars, who was tempted to make the ghost the spirit of a roach but opted for a cricket.

This was an idea Cookie endorsed. "And the residents can hear it chirping in the walls at night."

"That's right," said Lars, "that's exactly right, so you know this is a true story."

Cookie gave him a sidelong glance but no longer a suspicious one. She thought the ghost cricket might have tea in the parlor, which reminded her that she wanted to buy a doll's dining room table, a chandelier, and a miniature wreath. "Had the cricket met a violent end?" she asked, after summarizing her shopping list.

"Oh, the very worst," Lars said, inventing an evil butler who had crushed the poor insect. "Squashed him flat! And all for nibbling a few woolens!" For the rest of the drive, Lars forgot about Iris and desperate nights, and violent longings were kept at bay in the mall, where they rummaged through a disappointing array of junk to find three treasures, a miniature Christmas tree, an ornate mirror, and a pretty wing chair.

"This is where the cricket sits," said Cookie, holding up her find.

Lars agreed it was perfect, and, since her allowance would not stretch that far, floated a loan for its acquisition. Her happiness was cheaply bought when it restored him not only to sanity but jollity. He arrived home with a kind of giddy relief, which Emma noticed when she met them at the door.

Cookie had her packages open before they were into the hall. "Look what we bought for Cumbersome House! Dad's going to put a hook on the mirror. And look at this. Isn't this perfect?"

Emma admired the wing chair while Jake circled them, barking.

"I was worried," Emma said after Cookie and the dog had run upstairs, "when neither of you was home."

"I'd forgotten about the trip to the mall. I'd promised her." Lars put his arm around Emma. "I'm sorry about last night. I went to the library and read and then I drove around for a while. It was so stupid, but I just needed to be out for a while."

"I went to bed early," said Emma, and Lars wondered if, after all, his regrets and apologies had been unnecessary. "What time did you get back?"

"Late. I don't know. Very late. I know there was hell to pay this morning when I had to get up for my nine o'clock." Would that do, he wondered. Or had she woken up, looked at the clock? "And how was your day?" Giving her a hug. Emma ran the main office of one of the local high schools.

"The usual. But you should have called me this afternoon."

"I know, I know. We took Jake for a walk and then just went. I thought we'd beat you back. I'm afraid Cookie's going to be some shopper."

Emma smiled then. "She'd been looking forward to getting some furniture for the dollhouse."

Lars said he might look for some tools and see what he could make. Maybe a dining room table; there hadn't been any, just some odd chairs, and pretty poorly made, too. He described the selection as he helped Emma in the kitchen, peeling the potatoes, setting the table, being charming and useful, aware that she was watching him and, in some subtle way, reserving judgment. She knew his habits but also that he was trying to reassure her, to cheer her up. Emma sometimes reminded herself of his kindness and of the eagerness to please that was both his great strength and great weakness. Then, too, he understood her anxiety and her fears for Cookie, fears rooted in Jared's death.

Lars had seen their daughter, rosy, healthy, unfailingly vigorous and robust, as a reprieve, as a sign of grace. The worst thing had already happened to him, and she was the rainbow, the dove, the sign of dry land after the Flood. But Emma had taken another lesson and perceived the inherent instability of the universe. The child, who should have been pure joy for Emma, had brought instead a gnawing anxiety that ate away at her ease and happiness. Compared to her fears for Cookie, Lars's peccadilloes were minor; she forgave him more easily because he had been displaced from the center of her heart.

"We'll have a decent wine," Lars said. "How about that? That bottle left over from Christmas."

"What's the occasion?" asked Emma.

Lars came over and kissed her by way of response. "You and Cookie mean the world to me," he said. And he meant it, he did. He kissed her again, made her smile; he could cheer her up and defeat her anxiety and save himself, he knew he could. They had a leisurely dinner and inspected Cumbersome House, now resplendent with its Christmas decorations and wing chair and the gilt mirror (affixed with a strip of double-sided tape by clever Daddy) over the mantelpiece.

Then time to read in the living room before bed, Emma with a new novel, Lars preparing a lecture on Elizabeth Browning, not a favorite but provocative and coming back into scholarly prominence. Marital love has its pleasures, too, Lars thought: time, ease, leisure. What a fool he would be to risk awkward amours in a truck. With an undergrad. In the commuter lot. The nearness of humiliation made him feel uneasy, and he got up to check on Cookie.

Her room was full of dark mauves and lavenders cast by the angelfish night-light swimming in the gloom, and Jake was curled at the foot of the bed, tucked against Cookie's feet. She was sound asleep, her thick dark hair swept away from her smooth forehead, the loveliest child on earth. Lars remembered Iris saying, "How much your daughter looks like the pictures of Alice Liddell." That remark had stuck in his mind, for, yes, Cookie was attractive in the same vigorous, self-possessed way. A splendid, healthy child. *I have no reason to be afraid*, Lars thought, *no reason*. He closed the door and went into their room where Emma's bare shoulders and supple back, her thick hair smoked with gray at her brow, her slim legs and strong hips all delighted him. Emma understood him, loved him, responded to him unambiguously: such are the pleasures of familiarity. *I've been saved from folly*, Lars thought when he lay, sweated and gasping with Emma's head on his shoulder. *I've been saved*.

And yet, that very night, Iris returned again—troubling, intense, erotic—as a brief, vivid dream.

3.

N O V E M B E R   2 3 — *Quick while he's fresh in my memory: a man, walking across campus early, black hair in a short ponytail, black coat, dark slacks, heavy black shoes, a black carrier over one shoulder, altogether making a dark silhouette against the worn camels and olives of the grass. Just a quick glimpse of his profile, large straight nose, high cheekbones, dark eyebrows, but, oh, there's some mysterious something in his shoulders, in his gait, some indefinable fascination. Feast your eyes, before he disappears to an early class or he's maybe a teaching assistant or someone over in computers. Yes, he's going past the English building. Unkind gods! Cruel Fate! Watch out, Iris! But if I've fallen into neoromantic clichés, it's already too late.*

D E C E M B E R   1 2 — *I've been flirting with Lars, I admit it. And dressing up and keeping my hair washed and generally being the gorgeous one, Iris Weed. Ha ha. As if he cares! Among other Larson stories going around is that he is Death to the Maidens and a general Lady Killer. Maybe I should have done my independent study on literary tropes of the predatory male, but the thing is, Lars makes you feel pretty and important and brilliant, which naturally makes you want to see him often and behave well and generally be charming in turn. Which leads to flirting, which I begin to understand now, I mean all those indirect glances and dropped handkerchiefs and erotic strategies that Lars had to explain to us in*

Romantic & Victorian. Come to think of it, he did go on about that, even including pianos, as in pantaloons on the legs of, as in cozy duets at the pianoforte. Even sheet music provided opportunities, what with those naked Victorian shoulders and down to there necklines and flattering candlelight from the music stands and your beau's mustache tickling your neck as he turns the pages. I begin to see the point of indirection, and since Lars explained it all, it seems not too unfair to try some out on him, even if we lack the props. A dropped Kleenex is just a piece of paper unless it's a disgusting germ ball and not as nice under any circumstances as an expensive little bit of lace and linen. Certainly cozying up to the CD player isn't quite like making music together, singing, say. I begin to see singing as erotic, pouring out one's soul, gazing into each other's eyes: no wonder the nineteenth-century birth rate was high, not forgetting those appalling corsets—S & M for everyman— and the bustles, the ruffles, plus those tight pants on the men, the split-tail coats over their butts, their high collars, and all that facial hair—get a grip, Iris!

Course evaluation time: I learned an appreciation of sexual foreplay in the Victorian period. Professor Larson made everything so real for us; I hadn't realized until this course how impoverished modern erotic life has become. *Probably not the best idea; he'll recognize my handwriting for sure. But it's true. Sex was so totally discouraging in high school, quality abysmal, frequency erratic, a total mismatch between the desires of Iris Weed, Remarkable Woman, and those of all desirable males. Freshman year here was confirmation of everything I'd already learned. I really thought Brian T., encountered at the frosh mixer, had put me off sex for life. Really.*

But now between Lars and a certain hopeful prospect, I'm ready to reconsider the proposition. I'm like Marianne in Sense and Sensibility; *I'm ready "to counteract, by my conduct, my most favorite maxims," like LOVE STINKS.*

D E C E M B E R 1 5 — *I realize there have been omissions in this diary. A creeping bad habit, the sin of sloth? Whatever the reason, I haven't discussed Him yet. "Repression," says my Psych I prof, who disapproved of it as a general thing. But my modus operandi is, "Don't tempt fate." If you write something down, does that make it more or less likely? If you write a wish down, does it change anything in reality? I think it does. Once you write something down, you've given a shape to what was only an idea, a little rustling in the neurons. So, Him. I know his name now, but after three weeks of Him, he's Him now and forever or at least till next month when I hope our acquaintance will improve. Actually acquaintance is not quite what I have in mind, but I'm still in the Romantic & Victorian mode, thanks to Lars I'm sure.*

D E C E M B E R   1 9 — *Met Him in the library. A reward for good behavior, because I was beating the return deadline for the commentaries on Browning I'd used for my Romantic & Victorian paper. He had a book out on the Norse sagas. "Any good?" I asked, and he turned around, surprised as if he'd been away with the Vikings, who made trouble, as I recall, from Russia to Scotland and points west.*

His eyes are very light—palest gray with a thin black line around the iris. "It's okay," he said. "Decently written but not exactly what I needed."

"Are they ever?"

He smiled and nodded. "What's your topic?" He tilted his head to look at my stack of books.

"Browning's 'The Dark Tower.' "

"I love 'The Dark Tower,' " he said with a note in his voice, a kind of sympathetic vibration, that told me he really did. "Poème Noir."

"Very noir," I say and hope he's not a French major. I know en famille and film noir and a few other tasty phrases, but the rest is terrain inconnu. But no, he's a fourth-year literature grad student and he's interested in the medieval revival and the uses of myth in Wagner and, of course, in "The Dark Tower." If I could have talked to him before the Romantic & Victorian paper, I'd have really impressed Lars. Or maybe not, because I don't remember much of

what he said about the poem. What I remember is the thin black line around the iris of his eye, like a band around an opal, and the glossy blackness of his hair.

D E C E M B E R   2 1 — *Met Him again serendipitiously, right outside Healthy Stuff. "How're the sagas going?" I asked.*

He swung one arm over his head as if he was armed with a battle-ax or something similarly lethal and gave a yell in no language I recognize. I broke up laughing.

He laughed, too. "And on and on," he said. "For centuries."

This is hard to imagine. "I suppose some people thrived on it."

"They lived lives of unique intensity—and boredom."

"Do you suppose that's the trade-off?" I asked.

And he gave me that curious, sharp look men sometimes do when you surprise them.

"Yes," he said. "Yes I think that's right, but 'The Conservation of Boredom in the Norse Sagas' would hardly do for my thesis."

"I don't know. You might become the leading expert on literary boredom."

He took off with that. He has the jargon to make any crap sound impressive. I could hardly stop laughing and then, abruptly, he said he had to run, but was I going to be around over break?

"I'll be back right after Christmas," I said, and his face lit up and all my hopes, too.

D E C E M B E R   2 2 — *Exams finished. I drive home tomorrow for Christmas en famille, which is French for only your family with no outsiders to keep things defused and running smoothly. En famille would run smoothly enough without me, of course, and I asked Mom, "Sure you want me to come home? I can stay on and work at the health food shop." And she said, "You'd never have said that to your dad," as if she was going to cry. I felt like a shit, but really we don't get along, not anymore. We needed Dad between us; then we were fine. Without him, nothing I do pleases her, and she gets on my nerves like she's just watching, waiting for me to screw up, so she can put on that devastated look.*

Well, it's not a look, that's the thing, she really is devastated, and it's my fault. So I don't see why she wants me home when Marge and Dan are so satisfactory, leading normal lives, working good jobs, having no problems, and she and Marge and Dan could be en famille with a tree and presents and everything just fine, whereas I can't hardly face going back when Dad's not there. I haven't absorbed his death yet, not yet, maybe not ever, and going back is the hardest thing in the world. Even writing about this is not good.

D E C E M B E R   2 3 — *Home and miserable but trying my best. I helped Mom set up the tree in the living room before the others arrived. Mom kept grousing about how thin the branches are and how dry, as if her heart wasn't in the project. It's not like the quality of the tree matters anyway, because the house is so hot any tree's needles would be dropping. I point that out and she says, no it's just me. "Probably," I say. "After the truck everything seems tropical." Mom says, "I'm not going to discuss the truck with you," and looks like a martyr. "You wouldn't have done anything like this if your Dad were here," which is true but which I don't want to discuss.*

She sends me to get the box with all the old corny ornaments we've collected over the years on the traditional pre-Christmas trip to the mall. This will be the first year I can remember that there are no new ornaments, though Mom's laid in a bale or so of tinsel and angel hair. The ornaments are stored in the downstairs cupboard, and when I switched on the light by the steps I realized that this was the first time I'd been downstairs since it happened. I started shaking just walking across the basement to Dad's old office. But of course there was nothing there: just the desk and the file cabinet, all empty, and the bookshelves, still with books on accounting and business and taxes, which Dan is supposed to box up this week and ship to some college in Africa. Mom is pleased about that and I should be too, but all I can think of is that they are going to be so far from home, which is the pathetic fallacy raised to lunatic level.

I sat down in Dad's chair and opened all the drawers, which were

bare and clean except for one little piece of paper that was caught at
the back: a column of figures in Dad's handwriting, very small, plain,
and clear. An actuarial projection? A life span? He didn't calculate
his very carefully, or maybe he did. Maybe he knew to the day, which
I think would be a terrible thing. To go down to your office one evening, "just to finish up some paperwork," and to know that when you
sat down you'd feel a terrible pain and never get up.

I remember the call and waking up in the dark dorm room to
my roommate's sleepy voice, "Yeah, just a sec. Iris, it's your mom,"
and I rolled over in bed with a foretaste of disaster.

My overwhelming desire was to shut the door of the office and
sit there the whole holiday, but Mom started hollering for the ornaments. "They're in the cupboard by the Ping-Pong table. Do you
see them? Big blue box."

I got the ornaments and went back upstairs. We put everything
on, every single ornament, although the tree was way smaller than
usual and looked overloaded, its poor branches drooping. We put
everything on anyway as if any omissions would be bad luck, a
concesssion of defeat and reality. Mom and I connect on some curious levels. Then we put out the house lights and went outside to
check. Surprise: there it was just like every one of our Christmas
trees always, red and blue and white and green, a magic fairy tree,
as if nothing bad had ever happened.

Mom said, "There. That looks fine. Your brother and sister will
be pleased." And I felt annoyed for no reason except the tree hadn't
been there when I arrived, late and cold out of darkness. I might
have made some crack I'd have regretted, except Mom put her arm
around me and said, "Couldn't have done it without you."

In a way I know that's true. None of this has been a picnic for
Mom, either. Just the same, I'll be glad when the others get here.
They're the grown-ups, after all, who are able to take a mature
perspective or whatever the hell you're supposed to take on life.
Dan is coming in tonight, and we're leaving momentarily to pick
him up. Marge arrives tomorrow morning with boyfriend. "Her
steady," Mom says, "so be on your best." Whatever that means.
We've spent the holiday so far talking about Marge's Mr. Right and

about the Christmas decorations, and the sad thing is I think Mom might want to talk about Dad, too.

D E C E M B E R   2 7 — *I've screwed up. The only phrase for it. Nothing planned, no malice, just a classic Iris screwup leading to crisis en* famille *and my imminent departure, which is the only positive. We managed okay till Christmas night when there was a party at one of Marge's old friends' houses, complete with something called a wassail bowl, which was totally toxic, plus lots of beer and a pretty jumping beat on the stereo. I didn't want to go, but Mom was after me to get out and see people, as if I hadn't been out caroling with Dan and some of his old Youth Group friends. It strikes me that I am without either a Youth Group or a circle of old friends, high school and all groups therein soonest left and best forgotten. But I went and it wasn't too bad, because the caroling, which really was corny, broke up in a snowball fight in the park, all of us running through the trees and down the snow-covered lawns, slipping in and out of the shadows until we reached the lighted skating rink, a gold and silver bowl among the trees. We sang on the empty ice and went sliding on it with just our shoes. Dan wanted to come back skating but not enough of his friends have their skates and just me wasn't quite enough company. Dan's social; he likes crowds around him and organizing parties. He stood around talking to his friends, trying to get them to rent skates the next day when the hut's open so they can have a pickup hockey game. I'm pretty good at skating and ice hockey. I remember Dad teaching me to skate with a little hockey stick for balance.*

That's what I need now, metaphorically speaking, after the wassail bowl and subsequent events, mostly involving Chris, who's Marge's steady boyfriend or was her steady boyfriend and now is in what Dad used to refer to as "the doghouse."

Anyway, Christmas night was an example of the danger of good intentions. I only went to the party to please Mom and to get out of the house, and Chris only started talking to me because it was obvious I didn't know anyone and was seriously out of place. That was all, that and a few trips to the wassail bowl. Pretty soon every-

one is dancing and joking around and some idiot starts fooling with the lights, and I, Iris, attain a certain interesting level of detachment that ends out on the back porch—icy cold and smelling of sand and damp and winter boots—with Chris, who's a handsome guy and not, I think, as steady as he might be. All this is hardly a federal case in and of itself, the porch being subzero and not conducive to anything more than subserious fooling around, until Marge comes out with a couple drinks in her hands and sees the previously noted Iris Weed and Chris Harke up against the family freezer.

J A N U A R Y   1 — *Major depression. Some happy New Year! Even Healthy Stuff is closed. I took a book to Burger King and sat at a table in the back and read for four hours. I don't even feel like writing. Stuff it, Diary!*

J A N U A R Y   8 — *Saw Him in Healthy Stuff, where I've been racking up the hours in order to fight the glooms. Can the smell of fennel stave off depression? Have soy products some cheering effect beyond purifying the digestive system and saving the biosphere? Wish I knew, but at this rate, I could afford an apartment if I had a congenial roommate. But to the heart of the matter: he came in, bought some of the organic rice, and said, "What about a pizza?"*

My heart rose: depravity lives. We went to this little Italian place in the south end to swap department gossip. He told me about the Norse sagas, which made me think, and I asked him, did he believe we all have an ideal era, and it's just luck if we're born into it? He said he doesn't know about eras, but he thinks it's true of families. I had to agree about that and started to cry, which is chief among all lousy strategies.

But he was very nice, and I wound up talking to him about my dad's heart attack, about the total unexpectedness of it, and how it took the center right out of our family and left us without much to say to each other. He said you don't always know who the vital person in a family is, and I nodded my head, but I was always really, really close to Dad, who was the only one in the family who understood me, despite my having no actuarial bent at all.

J A N U A R Y   1 2 — *Out with Him again. Local band, not very good, but he can dance. Why am I surprised at this? Is it the black clothes, that priest-in-training expression he sometimes wears, the fact he's serious and just a wee bit withdrawn, repressed? What's the precise diagnosis, Dr. Weed? I figured there would be a girl-friend somewhere, past, present, or sharing his apartment—the classic romantic conjugation—but no. No sign. I will ask when the time is right. Maybe he met the female equivalent of Brian T. or some of the horrors of high school. Or maybe he was just waiting for me, Iris Weed.*

Anyway, the band's some sort of weird punk-zydeco fusion normally to be avoided like a case of the zits, but this one's got a drummer who can lay down a beat. Before we even finish one beer, he's up on the floor moving his shoulders, snaking his hips, stamping his feet, and I see what I must have glimpsed that first morning, a smooth flow of sexual energy. Iris Weed's gotten lucky at last.

J A N U A R Y   1 5 — *He loves my name. I think this is a good omen. "I love the name Iris," he says. "A great literary name. Iris is the goddess of the rainbow."*

"That's me, radiant and technicolor."

"She had golden wings," he says and reaches out and touches the side of my neck, which sets off tremors throughout my anatomy and makes me regret that we're sitting in the sunny chill outside Joe's Joe and not lying in the back of my truck or snug in his apartment (which, incidently, I have not yet seen). "She was Zeus's messenger and she could travel to the underworld." He smiles slowly. He has a sensual smile. I realize that for the first few weeks when I saw him around, watched him on campus, I never saw him smile. "And then there's Iris Murdoch. The greatest."

"The greatest," I agree, though I maybe like Toni Morrison or Joyce Carol Oates better. But Iris Murdoch was a great writer and Iris is a great name. Being with Him puts me in an agreeable mood.

What surprises me is how much he dislikes his own name. I mention that I think of him as Him, and he laughs again. "Pick a name," he says. "Pick a name for me."

"You must have a favorite male name," I say.

"See if you can guess it," he says. "A little test."

"Of what?" I ask.

"Compatibility."

Oh. I'm not so sure about this and he can see that from my face.

"I'll give you hints," he says and takes my hand. He has wonderful eyes. Hypnotic. I wonder if he could hypnotize someone. I wonder if he could.

He's waiting, so I say, "It's got to be a Viking name, a Norse name, a medieval name."

And he smiles.

"Pre-Christian."

Smile again.

I try a few and reject them—Eric had red hair, Gunter sounds like a pig, and Hundig was a bad hat. "Sven," I say. "What about Sven?"

It wasn't his choice, but I can see him thinking it over. "Sven is a good name," he says after a minute. "Call me Sven from now on." Dead serious.

I laugh. "Always?" I still think he's joking.

"Of course, but you have to stay Iris."

"Iris of the Golden Wings," I say. "Will we be a good combination?"

"Oh yes," he said and took my hand and put the fingers in his mouth and nipped them just hard enough so that I could feel the sharpness of his teeth. "Sven's ferocious and Iris is immortal."

"Ferocious?"

"You'll see," he said.

J A N U A R Y   1 7 — *Significant departure: Sven met me after my modern novel class ended at three o'clock. There he was, standing in the crowd in the hall. Quick greetings, then down the stair, my feet bouncing for joy. Outside, the light was already drain-*

ing away toward the west and the shadows of the bare campus trees had reached the building. It was dark when I got up this morning and it will be dark by the time I get to work, real Nordic weather. Perhaps that's what brought Sven out.

"I want to visit your truck," he said.

This would have been a white stone moment but for my Healthy Stuff schedule.

"Sorry, but I've got to be at the store by four," I said.

"I'll drive you over to the lot and you can drive to work. How's that? I just want to see where you live."

"Okay," I said, and off we went to my present venue, the Burger King lot.

"I didn't really believe you the first time," he said.

"Iris of the Golden Wings has to roost somewhere."

"But you tease," he said, "and you have a fanciful imagination."

"You still don't believe me." Is it possible, I'm now thinking, that all he does want is to see the truck?

"No, I do," he said. "I do."

"But you want to see my truck?"

"And other things," he said.

With this promising idea in mind, I unlocked the back, moved the laundry bag, shifted the supply crate, and climbed in with Sven after me. "Close the hatch," I said. He did, but he's not used to the limitations of mobile living so he banged his head and wound up sitting swearing next to me on the sleeping bag, which is the sole and entire piece of furniture. "It's goddamn dark," he said.

"Hold on." I switch on my battery snake light courtesy of Home Depot, and there we sit looking at each other.

"You intend to live here all winter."

I nodded.

"Like a Viking on board a warship," he said.

"Yes," I said, though I hadn't thought of it that way, and if you ask me, he has the really fanciful imagination. I switched mine off and put my hand on his hair. Things progressed from there until my sweater was up around my ears and his jeans were unzipped. I'd ac-

quired this ringing in my ears and a new and genuine sense of the meaning of "the body electric," when he said, "The truck squeaks."

This is true; it does, being metal. I point out that the nature of metal is to squeak, but apparently squeaking metal, not Iris, is the messenger of the gods and it's told him something. Then thanks to my stick-on clock that hangs right over the hatch, I see the time.

"I gotta rush," I say. "To make work."

He rolls away and stretches his arms and puts his hands behind his head. "Just as well, maybe."

I look at him.

"We don't know if we're serious, do we?"

"It felt pretty serious just now," I said.

"I meant really serious," he said. "I meant for keeps."

I want to make a joke about the Viking way, but somehow I know to keep my mouth shut. Could that be my gift with Sven: to know when to keep my mouth shut? He takes my face in his hands and looks at me with those banded opal eyes. "We want to be sure," he said. "We want to be serious."

At the time I didn't know what to think. I was late as it was, and I had to get the truck over to Healthy Stuff or lose my job. Then later I was serious, as in seriously pissed off. And now, I don't know what to think. I've avoided him for three days and may just avoid him for three more. There is something a little weird about Sven even if he is gorgeous.

F E B R U A R Y   4 — Went out for a beer with Sven after work. We met at the Blue Dog, which used to be the Water Hole and before that was Keggers. You'd think a bar right next to a campus wouldn't have any trouble staying in business, but the owners never seem to do more than change the name, and the place remains dreary with its big dark bar and board floor and mirrors with beer names on them. Anywhere else it would be a working men's pub or fixed up smart as a yuppie venue. But at the moment it's just a place for students to drink who really need a drink fast, and there's a pall over the whole enterprise. Normally, I wouldn't darken the Blue Dog's doorway, but Sven called Healthy Stuff and asked if I could come by. We met out front, and he'd been waiting because his cheeks were red and his nose was turning white. As I drove along the street looking for a parking space, I saw him stamping his feet and hunching his head down into the collar of his coat. I forgave him right then because he'd been waiting in the cold for me, instead of going inside and having a quick first drink on his own.

Inside, we found a table and I ordered a beer. He had a beer and a shot, which he tells me used to be called a boilermaker but I personally think is likely to rot your boiler. Sven was restless and nervous. Apologized for not calling: crisis with his teaching assistantship, adviser on leave, prof he's working for breathing fire. I told him I understood. The start of the semester is always busy. Iris, herself, has been engaged in turning out the copy, amazing Lars who says he'll never keep up with it.

"Forget what I said. I'm trying to make excuses and it's all bullshit," said Sven, his face white, his voice strained. "I'm trying to bullshit you. I don't know why I didn't call you, when I wanted to so much, when I've missed you such a lot." He took my hands. "Why do we do things?" he demanded. "Why do we do stupid, horrid things and pretend we don't care?"

"I don't know," I said. After Christmas, I asked myself the same thing.

"Let's get out of here, all right? Let's just get out of here. I hate bars."

It was clear and cold with a bitter wind that made talking difficult. We walked fast along the street and up the edge of campus, side by side, our heads down, our ears and feet going numb, until finally I took his arm and he stopped and pulled me into his arms and kissed me and said, "Come to my apartment. Please."

He lives on the Hill, the north side of campus, and we drove there in the truck. I made a U-turn on the steep, icy street and slid the truck in the last space left. Under the bluish street light, his face was dead white. The truck door creaked in the cold.

"Watch the steps," he said. Wooden with a crust of ice pocked with halite. Door, foyer with mailboxes, narrow side stair, everything almost as cold as the truck; at least, I'm shivering, but maybe that's just nerves. He unlocks the door of his apartment, which has sad, brownish cream paint the color of used chewing gum and a big lumpy sofa that more or less matches. The overhead light casts a faintly greenish glow, and the apartment smells of cigarette smoke and french fries.

"I'll try for more heat," he said and went to fiddle with the thermostat.

There's a big gloomy kitchen, a museum of appliances, and the dark rectangle of his bedroom. The street light turns the bedroom shade a bluish gray, like an empty computer screen. I was so nervous I forgot about his name.

"Sven," he corrected. "Sven."

"Yes, Sven the Viking, who is ferocious," I said, joking. When I'm nervous, I often joke.

"Right," he said and grabbed my arms and pushed me up against the wall by the bedroom door, hard but not hard enough to hurt. "Vikings are ferocious." He pressed against me, his body all ready, and said, "Look in my eyes, keep looking in my eyes." I did. All the time he's touching me and pulling off my clothes and all the time his eyes are enormous, wild, and I can see the utility of this, how it will rewrite everything like initializing a disk. I reached out and grabbed his hair and tore it free of the band he uses for the ponytail. He began biting at my neck and shoulders and I jerked his hair until he pulled away from the wall and pushed me toward the bed. I still had hold of his hair, which must have hurt, and I felt the blanket rough and the sheets cold and he cried, "My eyes, look in my eyes!" Which I did until everything closed down into a red-tinged blackness.

This morning I discovered an amazing number of small bruises.

4.

The office secretaries were selling daffodils for the cancer fund and Lars picked up a triple order for Emma, who loved flowers. They sat in a coffee can on his office windowsill in the bright April sunshine, their cheerful yellow ruffles a reproach to his uneasy heart. Six weeks to go before final papers, exams, summer break. Lars thought he could stand six weeks the way he had his life organized. He went home every day to meet Cookie, and he took a couple afternoons off each week to play ball with her and her friends in the park or to take her to music lessons. He had even arranged an early getaway to the shore, a treat for Emma who loved the water in all weather. They'd sailed in rain and wind, the Block Island ferry heaving on the waves, and when they disembarked at the chilly, sodden, rain-swept dock, Lars feared the worst. But Cookie had been delighted by the gaudy pleasures of the bed-and-breakfast's vintage comic books, while he and Emma had lain snug under a feather quilt and joked about the moaning wind and rain outside. She was exhilarated by the wet and cold; the pounding surf, the mist blowing along the beach, the manifold discomforts of island weather that left Lars bored and shivering, swept away her caution and anxiety. She was playful with Lars, and when she asked how he was, meaning had the sudden, strange moods of winter been vanquished, he said he was fine and meant it.

On Saturday, they walked between rain showers. Cookie raced along the damp beach, while he made Emma laugh by whispering creative and indecent proposals in her ear. Sunday morning with departure imminent came a calm sound, full sun, and rafts of sea ducks and loons migrating north. Cookie stood on the edge of shore, her bright face red in the wind, pointing her little disposable camera out to sea, then, pivoting, caught the two of them arm in arm, smiling. The photo sat on his desk now, and Lars picked it up like a talisman, reminding himself that he had a lot to lose.

He'd been acting on that insight. When he woke up mornings, Lars would rehearse his day: breakfast, school preparation, morning lecture, books to read, grad students to see. Office hours were either fully scheduled or cut, a note reading *Professor Larson is in the library* pasted on the door. No vacant hours, no idle—or wandering— hands. The dean, who went on about "profit centers" and "productivity," should be pleased with Professor Jason Larson, who was clearly not a man to be thrown off stride by a pretty undergrad. No! Life was earnest and real and altogether well managed except for Thursday, the danger day, the day he saw Iris to review her manuscript.

After his humiliating night search for her truck, Lars had stopped the coffee dates, emptying noons of their promise and leaving lazy afternoons studded with deadfalls of sudden desire. He held firm, nonetheless. Thursday only was his rule, and then he saw Iris in his office, door open, with another student scheduled for exactly forty-five minutes later. Professor Jason Larson was an exemplar, he really was—if you excluded certain new habits. Perhaps there is a conservation of folly as well as of mass and energy, because Lars's day now included walks around campus just as Iris's classes were ending, and trips, morning and afternoon, to various parking lots, plus regular visits to Healthy Stuff and certain book and record stores she favored, all of which activities, cautious, quick, and deeply exciting, amounted to a kind of surveillance. Though this represented a comedown from past amorous buccaneering, Lars found satisfaction in knowing where Iris was and who she was seeing; he liked to have the parameters of her existence in hand. The difficulty was that his knowledge was never complete enough to spare him the torment of uncertainty. However reassuring it was to find Iris working away in the library or laboring at Healthy Stuff, no theory can be proved purely by negatives. She eluded him as soon as he turned his car toward home. And what of the positives? That bearded fellow who borrowed her notes from their Renaissance class, the barfing mermaid, the pale, dark boy who hung around Healthy Stuff—what of them, her friends, her acquaintances? In happy moods, Lars disregarded them; in gloomy moments, he asked himself, *Which of them has her heart?*

He looked at the calendar again. Six weeks of torture and suspense. And once she was gone, wouldn't that be worse? Never to see her again, to be beyond hope? Lars looked at the daffodils and told himself that he had to survive six weeks; then Iris would be gone. Or putting it another way, he had six more weeks before he lost her. Which was worse?

A knock at the half-open door.

"Come in." His heart was pounding. Perhaps it was his blood pressure, perhaps Iris was no more than a narrowing of major arteries, for in all his long and varied romantic life, love had never taken this form.

"Hi!" A brilliant smile, a flick of the long, shining hair. Trimmed, he noticed. Iris was spending some of her Healthy Stuff wages on good grooming. She'd dropped the ghastly purple eye shadow and black lipstick, retaining only her blue nail polish. Of course, her clothes were still wrinkled, and her svelte form was concealed in Farmer Brown bib overalls, a garment Lars had always regarded as erotically beneath notice but which, in his present abject state, suggested newly enchanting possibilities.

Iris carried her manuscript and a cardboard tray with coffees and a pair of cherry-topped sticky buns in frilly paper cups like two neat little breasts.

"I thought I'd bring a light collation—is that the right word?"

"Yes, yes, though redundant," Lars said, eyeing this Freudian offering with interest. "The original meaning of *collation* was a light snack."

"Needs the adjective."

"Indeed. Victorian linguistic excess. But they'd have had a rum punch or lemonade and fancy biscuits."

"You've got ruffled paper instead," said Iris.

I gave up too soon, Lars thought, as virtue slid away like water. Into its place rushed exhilaration, hope, a volcanic rise in spirits. Could she be beginning to see his virtues? To repent her indifference and the follies of youthful taste? "Sit, sit," Lars said. How the afternoon had brightened. "I've got your last chapters here. Just minor changes."

Her smile again. She was as tall as he was, and when she sat down in the office chair next to his desk, her long fine legs—encased, alas in the Farmer Browns—nearly touched his knee. How easy it would be to reach down. He could see the curve of her thigh, the bony mesa of her knee, the breathtakingly elegant bone of her bare ankle. He had perhaps taught Victorian literature too long.

"I suppose we ought to talk about conclusions," Lars said, though he could think of any number of delightful digressions. What conclusion? And when? And where? He had some ideas for how. "We've got, what—how many pages did you bring me today?"

"Twenty-five," said Iris, a trifle abashed at her own productivity.

"Are you eating and sleeping?" Lars teased and Iris laughed. "That's over three hundred. We don't want it to get baggy. You're going to need a strong conclusion."

Iris nodded vigorously. Conclusions were hard. She felt she needed a rounding-off incident. It might just come?

"How lucky do you feel?" he asked and saw her face darken, crossed by an almost visible shadow as if some inner light had shifted. Lars felt his heart again. Was that the attraction? That occasional Miltonian sense of darkness visible? "I mean, you might get just the right incident, but maybe not. Depends how long you want to wait. As far as your project is concerned, we've got plenty already. You know I'm pleased, impressed, even, but for a really first-rate job, you need a satisfactory conclusion, not just, 'Here's the end, I ran out of time.' You know."

"Hmmm." She caught her lower lip with her front teeth, providing a glimpse of the gap tooth that Lars adored. "I'm thinking of giving up on the truck," she said. "Would that do? I should maybe look at *Walden* again. How did he leave? Did he just leave and that's it?"

"He mentions leaving in the beginning."

"Oh, yes, I remember. 'I lived there two years' and something."

"And 'now I am a sojourner in civilized life again.' "

"That's right, that's right. You know, early on in *Walden* I wondered why he ever went back. If that was the ideal life, if he'd proved it could be done, why return to the second rate?"

"He did have suppers at his mom's on the weekends." Thoreau had always struck Lars, who didn't entirely trust rarified pleasures, as too good to be true.

"Even so. If that was the good life, why leave? I wondered."

"And now you know?" That was interesting. Giving up the truck! Moving in with mystery man? Was that it? The beard from Renaissance Literature or the other, the dark boy? Although Lars's hopes had shot up only moments before, he felt his head pounding. His good conduct, his dedication to Emma and Cookie now looked to be fatal errors. With the conviction that he had a rival, Lars felt the familiar cold surge of resentment. Hot anger, cold resentment, tormenting envy, a temptation to cruelty: Iris Weed provoked a market basket of sins.

"Circumstances change," she said with an enigmatic expression. "You find things in solitude, but they're not all good. Maybe that's what Thoreau found. Maybe he found . . ." a break, a hesitation. How much they had discussed and confided of a philosophical nature and how little of anything else. He knew her ideas on dozens of things, but her heart was a secret. Was that true of Thoreau, as well? Was *he* ever in love?

". . . maybe he found there's safety in numbers after all."

"Or diversion?" Habitually flirtatious, Lars raised his eyebrows and winked, so that Iris dropped the dark thread and ended his best chance at discovery.

"But the conclusion?" she asked with a smile.

He swiveled in his chair and slid along beside the bookcase for the big anthology, for *Walden*. He scanned the pages, recognizing afresh the tide of nineteenth-century optimism and individualism. Radical stuff in its day, but with modern scholarship Thoreau had been safely pedestaled and categorized. There were a good dozen ways of looking at Thoreau. Lars handed the book over to Iris.

"Oh, yes," she exclaimed. "I love this: 'The life in us is like the water in the river. It may rise this year higher than man has ever known it, and flood the parched uplands; even this may be the eventful year, which will drown out all our muskrats.' Hard on the muskrats, but I suppose they'd had a previous year."

Lars laughed and was saved momentarily, because she reminded him of Cookie, who would surely worry about the muskrats.

"I'm not sure I can come up with anything quite like that," Iris said.

"Not so optimistic?"

"Not so well written *and* not so optimistic. Is anyone that optimistic? But it's true there are eventful years. This has been an eventful year."

A second opening that Lars might have taken—was he losing his nerve? "At your age," he began and stopped. How had he fallen heir to that dread phrase? "I was going to say every year should be eventful."

"Lived with rage and idealism. The very first class, you said Blake was always young and filled with rage and idealism. I like that idea; I'd like to live that way. You've influenced me a lot."

Now it was Lars's turn to look away. "I hope an influence for the best, Iris."

"Do we ever know what's best for us?" she asked, denying him reassurance. There was an edge in her voice, a demand.

Lars shrugged. There she sat, wanting to live with rage and idealism, and, for all he knew, succeeding. But rage and idealism was a fatal combination for a man like him. To succeed, he'd have to corrupt her, make her sophisticated, pleasure loving—and would that be so bad? Would it? Were rage and idealism making her happy?

"Just let me look over these pages," Lars said, smooth and professorial, already planning. "I'll give you my comments as soon as possible."

Iris had afternoon classes on Friday, her day off from Healthy Stuff, the day Lars usually managed to be in the vicinity of Ricker Hall before her sociology class and in the corridors of Galloway after her Renaissance lecture. He told Emma he had a late committee meeting, arranged with Betty from next door to be home for Cookie, and right at five P.M. he set off with Iris's manuscript in search of the truck. He was in luck. She was not in the commuter lot, full of gossipy colleagues and sharp-eyed students, nor in the Burger King precincts much favored by the younger campus crowd, tattletales every one, but in Dunkin' Donuts. Lars slid his aging Volvo next to the truck, then, crafty, pulled away again and parked several rows over. The lot was almost empty; the bay windows of the doughnut shop showed a clutch of retirees trying to pass the afternoon and a couple of workmen laying in the carbs and sugars. Lars looked quickly over his shoulder, as if he'd acquired the furtiveness of an affair without the actual transgression. Then he tapped the side of Iris's truck. "Iris? It's Lars."

A rustle within before the hatch of the truck's cap opened, and Iris looked out, surprised.

"I was hoping you'd be at home," Lars said formally. "I didn't come equipped with a card."

"Bet you don't have one with an up-to-date daguerreotype," said Iris. Lars thought she looked tired and worried, despite this effort at their usual banter.

"I was just passing, and I wanted to give you the manuscript."

"Oh, sure. Thanks."

She reached for the pages, ready to disappear again, but Lars said, "There are just a couple things we need to talk about," so that she had to drop the tailgate and climb out of her den, her long hair swinging free, her Farmer Browns tight across her wide hips. What is so irresistible about her? Lars wondered: she was not as beautiful as Emma and not nearly as graceful. Perhaps it was only Iris's gleeful, rapid-fire prose, which hinted so much more than it revealed. And if she had been more revealing, if she'd included her erotic adventures, would that have been enough, would he have been satisfied? Was it the novel of her life he wanted, Lars asked himself, or just her shining hair and white breasts?

Iris perched cross-legged and alert on the tailgate. Lars, feeling foolishly exposed, asked, "Perhaps we might sit in the cab?"

"Well, the house is a mess." She gave a nervous giggle as if she understood the subtext perfectly well.

Once in the high dusty seats, Iris looked at him without taking the manuscript. "I'm getting so tired of parking lots."

"April is the cruelest month," Lars agreed. The truck smelled strongly of pizza and fried chicken and a musty combination of spices that he associated with the health food store.

"Yeah. Maybe it's just spring. New starts, new growth."

Her voice sounded indescribably bitter and weary, and Lars's hopeful, playful mood began to sour. "The manuscript," he said and handed over the folder.

Iris flipped carelessly through the pages. Normally she went slowly over his comments, testing and savoring the corrections, making quick additions and changes. "Nothing much here," she said. "I don't see what there is to talk about."

"Everything and nothing," said Lars.

Iris fished her keys from her pocket. When the motor turned over, a tape left in the deck washed the truck with a shock wave of acid guitars and pulsing drums. "Not the stuff we normally listen to," she said, reminding Lars that they were on her turf. "I need to get out of here."

"Fine, I have time. I've been thinking about endings."

"Me, too," said Iris, but the conversation lapsed after they got up on the interstate where she drove with more speed and elan than was strictly necessary. A number of awkward scenarios ran through Lars's mind and were as swiftly discarded. The drive represented a great leap forward, and he could not help feeling exhilarated. The privacy of the car, the speed of motion, the promise of intimacy delighted him, while the late April afternoon, the rose and sienna that bathed the trees and intensified the green spring grass, even the swirling clouds of starlings rising from the highway underpasses all assured Lars that the world and his prospects were new again.

Iris left the highway at one of the neighboring suburbs and negotiated a corridor of shopping plazas and corporate headquarters to reach the metropolitan reservoir district. "I sometimes come here to think," she said.

"Thoreau's sort of place."

A pause in which Iris should have made some remark about Thoreau or her paper; instead, after a long moment, she said, "You've been following me."

"I beg your pardon."

"Don't play games, Lars. You're in Ricker, you're in Galloway, you're at the stores. I see you watching me very time I turn around. This isn't about school or the book, is it?"

Lars considered denial, humor, some zany fact-entangling narrative that would evade the moment by making her laugh, then took a breath and said, "No. It's about my being hopelessly, madly in love with you."

She flushed slightly before her jaw hardened and she said, "You want to screw me, isn't that right?"

It was the first coarse thing she'd ever said, and Lars, who saw himself as a civilized lover, frowned without examining the implications. "You didn't learn such language in Victorian lit."

Again the slight flush as if embarrassed, but by his rebuke or his advances, Lars could not tell. "That's what it comes down to," she said, not meeting his eyes. "And the only questions are when, where, yes or no."

"It's not that way," he said; at that moment, he really thought it wasn't. "But all right, you're right. But yes. Please say yes. Which is it? I'm out of my mind."

Iris stared out the window at the big pond and the Canada geese grazing along the lawn. "I don't know," she said sadly. "I don't know."

She looked so miserable that Lars reached out to ruffle her hair, which was every bit as smooth and silky as he'd hoped. "Don't be unhappy," he said, "I never wanted you to be unhappy."

Iris turned into his arms then and kissed him with an avidity quite beyond his hopes. Things progressed until Lars had her Farmer Browns unsnapped and was half impaled himself on the truck's gears—a novel way to die for love!—before she tore free, wiped her mouth, and slid out of the truck. Lars followed, flushed and dazzled with visions of al fresco love, but no sooner had he started around the side of the vehicle than Iris jumped back in and started the motor. The truck lurched up the track toward the reservoir's maintenance buildings, reversed in the driveway, and rocketed toward the main road. Waving, Lars stepped onto the track, then jumped back as Iris whipped past without a glance in his direction, leaving him astonished in the middle of nowhere. So much for rage and idealism! So much for youth! Folly! Good behavior!

A faint murmur of cars from the street beyond, a birdsong as descant to his beating heart, his feet on the crumbling asphalt and gravel of the access road. Nothing else but the tidy emptiness of the reservoir works with the water and the woods beyond. Lars cursed Thoreau, who'd promoted wilderness, and Iris, who was heartless; he stamped around feeling furious and ill-used and amazed, until, realizing it was after six, he hustled up to the maintenance building where he was able to call a cab. An hour, the dispatcher told him. Lars swore again but agreed because even his ingenuity did not extend to a suitable excuse for Emma: *A misunderstanding with a student has stranded me in a suburban water company?* He didn't think so. *Cooperative research on Thoreau has landed me in woods up to my ass?* Not much better. *I hitched a lift with someone out to the reservoir to meet a student who is doing work on Thoreau but we got our signals got crossed?* Too many phrases raising too many questions and altogether too elaborate a scenario. Emma knew his habits; she wouldn't need subtle critical tools to penetrate such a feeble text.

Lars stretched his legs and walked halfway around the water, keeping an eye on the gateway all the time, then sat on a rock halfway up the access drive, not so close to the main road as to be conspicuous, not so far in that the cabbie wouldn't see him. The sun dropped, the shadows lengthened, the pond took on a purplish depth of hue, and Lars had plenty of time to ponder treachery and youth before he was ferried back to the Dunkin' Donuts parking lot by a taciturn Jamaican.

This second, semifarcical humiliation should have been the cure. There is a tide in amorous, as in political, affairs, and it was pretty clear to Lars that he had missed the crest. The tide was running out; the boat had sailed. He was later to think that had he gone to the truck a month later, even three weeks later, maybe even two, they would have been in the end-of-school rush and everything might have been different. Instead, with a couple of weeks of class left there was time for second thoughts, time to find a modus vivendi, time for Iris, who had a kind heart, to call him after dinner one night just as they were finishing their coffee. Lars guessed who it was before Emma lifted the receiver. "Just a minute," she said. "One of your students, Iris someone."

Lars stood up. He would take the call right there; there was nothing personal to say, nothing to hide from Emma; all that was finished. He'd gone over the line, but so had Iris. They were square and even, and all there was to settle was the due date for her finished project. She could find her own conclusion. Maybe even a funny narrative about humiliating the older man who loved her. Maybe that and the hell with her. He could reach out his hand for the phone and say . . . but here imagination failed him. "All sorts of boring arrangements to make," he told Emma. "I'll take the call upstairs."

In the lavender and amber glow of his study window, Iris was a vivid presence even before Lars picked up the phone. She had come one gray winter day when he was home with the bad ankle. He remembered how she'd joked with Cookie and patted Jake and exclaimed over the window: "You've got a real scholar's study!" How simple life had once been. Lars lifted the receiver and said, "I've got the phone, Emma." A click downstairs, then Iris's voice, shaky and faraway. "Lars? Are you very angry?"

He was in such a jumble of emotions that he hesitated. "I was very disappointed, very angry at the time," he said less harshly than he'd intended. "At the time, I was not happy at all."

"I know." An infinitesimal voice like a caress in his ear. "I panicked, Lars. It's so hard to understand, but I absolutely panicked."

Could she possibly be a virgin, he wondered, but, no, in those few precious, exciting moments she'd revealed both passion and expertise. He did not think inexperience was the problem. "I know," he said, his voice low, an intimate murmur. "I understand." This was a lie. He did not understand anything, except that in his dark study with her voice soft in his ear he was ready to break any number of good resolutions.

"It's been such a tough year, Lars. I just didn't know what to do. I wanted to make a fresh start, a clean break with the past, with everything."

"No harm done," Lars said. Though there had been explanations and awkwardness and he'd felt Emma appraising him ever since, but that was maybe just his imagination.

"I wanted to say I'm sorry," Iris said.

"Me, too. It wasn't all your fault. I was absolutely out of line. I was, wasn't I?" He could be sly, too.

Silence down the line then, "Well, maybe."

He was undone by ambiguity. "Come to the office tomorrow and we'll talk." And though he hung up and went straight back downstairs to supervise Cookie's homework and play backgammon with Emma, his relationship with Iris had already entered a new phase.

There were phone calls now, late, erratic, inappropriate. *Inappropriate:* tepid, bureaucratic word! Say rather *intense, rambling, flirtatious, arousing, confessional,* all those things. Iris talked about her mother, who, Lars gathered, was devoted but difficult. She talked about the manuscript, about the ending, which, really, was also about them, about ending and beginning, and about some nameless boy whom she saw off and on, who both attracted and alarmed her. His rival wasn't just a product of Lars's fevered imagination, but real, and unreal, too, for Iris never mentioned his actual name. "I just call him Sven," she said. Another Scandinavian, Lars thought, and wondered if that was a good sign. He could not read the runes for their future at all and found himself in a curious and, he suspected, unwholesome relationship where he was part confessor, part confidant, part lover—oh, yes, there was some faint progress there, a few pas-

sionate kisses, a few light embraces—perhaps she had dipped into
Whitman as well as Thoreau. Iris called up late, at inappropriate
hours; that was when she desired him, maybe loved him. At appropriate hours, times, places, she was elusive, undecided. "It's
impossible," she told him one day when he'd returned to the truck.
He became angry and accused her of not caring for him, and they
quarreled just beyond the Dumpsters in the Home Depot lot. The
next day, she called him at his office first thing, and that afternoon
she kissed him in an empty classroom in Galloway, a treasured moment of sweet incaution. That's how things went, not truly serious,
or rather, to speak to the climate of the time, not truly actionable,
but indiscreet and always on the verge of the irrevocable.

So Lars was grateful for the drudgery, for the distraction of the
otherwise loathsome piles of final papers and makeup essays that
occupied the last weeks of classes. Weekend was family time; he
had to squire Cookie to her soccer team, adorable mites who raced
around in baggy shorts and shirts after a ball half as big as themselves. Lars took her to the field early every Saturday and stood on
the damp grass with the other parents. One of the dads worried on
about age groups and traveling teams, bizarre minutiae that provided
another distraction, but, basically, Lars watched Cookie, impetuous
and agile, red faced with exertion and almost frighteningly concen-
trated right up until the final whistle, upon which, giggling and
shrieking, she disappeared into a huddle of little girls with flying
ponytails and drooping socks, then emerged to hurl herself, jubilant,
it seemed, in victory or in defeat, at Lars.

They drove back in a welter of sweaty uniforms, shin guards, and
boots for lunch, where Cookie would recount each play with a precision that surprised her parents—if only she applied herself the
same way to school! Then out for garden work with Emma, trans-
planting ever more shrubs for some ambitious but mysterious master
plan, before another round of papers and blue books: all safe havens.
It was only after dinner, work done, Cookie reading in her bed,
Emma playing softly at the piano, when domestic happiness—say
even *love*—showed its weaknesses, and Lars's mental curtains
opened onto melancholy and desire. Terrible thoughts would come,

soundings of despair: two weeks to go, week to go, a few days, graduation dead ahead, and he would make some excuse to go to his study, close the door, and call Iris's cell phone. If it rang, transports of electronic joy; if it was turned off, such foul rage and misery that he felt graduation couldn't come soon enough and his only fear was that Iris might stay on in town afterward.

It was in such a mood that Lars ventured out to campus one evening. The sky was still light despite a drizzling rain that threatened to ruin any number of pregraduation parties. He needed to turn in his grade sheets at the receptacle in front of the registrar's office. Later Lars would search his mind, trying without success to decide if he had had other plans, if he had intended to make a sweep through the parking lots, if he had been determined to find Iris. Whatever was in the depths of his mind, Lars parked in his usual place, walked straight across the quad to the registrar's, dropped off his envelope of grade sheets, and headed back toward the car, his big black umbrella raised against a now steadier rain.

He might have walked into her, they were that close in the fog and mist. He'd been looking down, keeping the umbrella between him and the driving rain, when he glanced toward the stone arcade that ran along the oldest of the quad buildings and saw Iris like a sudden apparition.

Lars turned, closed his umbrella, and entered the faux Gothic archway where Iris stood motionless, without greeting. She had no raincoat, and with her book bag hanging off one shoulder she looked subtly disheveled. In another mood, Lars would have noticed, made some remark. Instead he walked directly up to her, leaned over, and kissed her mouth, once, twice. His umbrella clattered on the flagstones; he pulled up her sweatshirt, unfastened her bra, and kissed her warm breasts; he slid his hands down the back of her jeans to explore her smooth and perfect cheeks, then loosened his raincoat and wrapped them both in its folds. Iris was trembling and her hands against his face were cold.

"Where's your truck?"

She made a vague gesture. "Near Healthy Stuff." Her hair was wet. "I was waiting out the shower," she said.

"I'll drive you back. Here, take the umbrella. I have a raincoat."
More kisses and caresses, bringing a pleasant rise in temperature,
before the umbrella was retrieved, and they ran across campus to
his car, where he kissed her again in the front seat—the back was
filled with soccer paraphernalia: practice balls and orange plastic
cones. The truck, Lars thought, the truck: paradise and salvation, a
port for this particular storm, where, like Emily Dickinson, he hoped
to row in Eden. He collected himself enough to start the car. Iris
leaned back against her seat with her book bag half on her lap and
looked out at the rain in a troubling silence.

"Ready for graduation?" he asked. He wanted to ask was she
leaving, was she staying, but he felt he could not bear to know the
answer.

"Mom is coming and I think my brother."

"Weather's supposed to be okay."

Silence. Lars switched on the motor, and the wipers sluiced off
the water streaming down the windshield. He turned onto the city
streets and headed toward the store. They were in a block of fraternity houses and student rentals before Iris spoke again. "You can let
me out here, the rain's letting up."

"It's no bother to take you to the truck. You're half frozen."

"I don't want you to drive me to the truck. You know what will
happen if we go to the truck."

"The fulfillment of my profoundest hopes," said Lars, trying to
break through her mood and reenlist her in pleasure.

"I told you the other day: It's impossible. You're not serious
about me."

"Jesus, Iris! How can you say that?" Lars elaborated on his devotion, his frustrations, the manifold humiliations he'd suffered at
her hands. He quoted Shakespeare and obscure Elizabethans and
even made her laugh a little, but at the end she shook her head.

"The thing is, Lars, I could be in love with you, of all the men
I know. You're very nice, very attractive, very lovable. You're the one
I could love and you'd only break my heart."

"Never, Iris, darling!" Lars was so distraught that he pulled over
and parked alongside one of the derelict pocket parks that had been

an enthusiasm of a previous city administration. "Why won't you let us be happy? Why, Iris?"

"Because you'd never leave Cookie and your wife."

"Leave Cookie? Leave Emma?" Lars was shocked to have misjudged Iris so seriously, to have conveyed his intentions so inadequately, to have, with all his experience, blundered so badly. "We can be happy without hurting anyone, Iris. We don't need to be melodramatic and irresponsible."

"But for me, you'd have to leave Cookie and your wife, you'd have to, that's all there is to it. I've been loved," said Iris, tears beginning to run down her face. "Someone loved me unconditionally, the way you love Cookie."

"Fathers," said Lars in exasperation, "fathers are a totally different thing from lovers. You can't expect . . ."

"What, Lars? Permanence, fidelity, honesty? What can't I expect?"

"Nothing in this life is permanent," he said sententiously.

"Bull," said Iris.

"I'm offering you happiness, pleasure, life as it can be, and don't say you aren't tempted. There aren't that many joyful moments, Iris. You either take them where you find them or you find you've missed them." He leaned toward her and tried to kiss her, but Iris was having none of it.

"All that's easy for you; you're so selfish and self-indulgent," she cried, her hand already on the door latch.

Lars grabbed her shoulder. "What about all those phone calls, those late night chats, what about all that? What was I supposed to think? Tell me, Iris, what was I supposed to think?"

She was half out of the car, but Lars grabbed the strap of her bag so that she had to face him. "You've been my lifeline," she said. "You've kept me safe. But I see now you can't help me because you're not serious."

"Help you," exclaimed Lars, furious, "I didn't want to help you, I wanted to screw you, you priggish coldhearted bitch!"

She jerked her bag out of his grasp and shot from the car. Though he called to her not to be an idiot, that he was sorry, that she'd driven him half mad, Iris made straight for the path through the park. Lars followed, shouting and pleading, but when he caught up with her, they said angry, hurtful things before she broke away again, running now, through the trees to the next street where she was lost in the shadows of the shrubs and houses.

Lars stood in the middle of the park with his heart pounding and a queer, sick feeling spreading from his stomach. He looked up at the soggy gray clouds until his face was wet from the mist and he had to blink to keep the drizzly rain out of his eyes. He returned to the car, which he'd left with both doors open and the key in the ignition—good thing urban crime was down. He was closing the passenger door when he noticed one of Iris's notebooks lying on the floor mat. He looked over his shoulder and called after her, but she was out of earshot. When Lars got into the car, he switched on the overhead light and examined the square school notebook with the classic marbled black-and-white cover and white label for name, course, and date. Inside, in assertive multicolor penmanship, was the last four months of Iris's diary.

Lars thought first that he should run the notebook back to the truck, and then he thought that everything he'd wanted to know would be in its pages. Iris owed him that much. He stuck the notebook in the large pocket of his raincoat and started the car.

5.

*L*ars wound up in the library until nearly ten P.M. He hadn't felt right about reading Iris's journal, or, more accurately, he hadn't felt right about reading it at home where Cookie or Emma or both might appear at any time and see—what exactly? His reaction? His guilty look? As he drove past student rentals festive with the lights and music of end-of-semester parties, Lars tried to convince himself that his trepidation was nonsense. A quick flip through the pages, just to find out if he'd guessed right about the Rival, maybe even to discover what Iris really thought of him. At this latter idea, Lars had a strong impulse to turn the car back toward town, to find Iris's truck, maybe even to stick the damn diary under a wiper blade, rain or no rain. That's what he might have done; instead, after driving through city streets and around the park, Lars found himself in the faculty lot adjoining the campus library.

Inside, he stopped at the pay phones to call Emma. It was 8:05, and Emma said that they were watching a *Simpsons* rerun. Cookie's voice was shrill in the background, shouting that this was a good episode, one he shouldn't miss.

"Matt mentioned a journal article that sounded interesting," Lars said. "When I was over here, I thought I'd check it out. It shouldn't take long, but I didn't want you to be worried."

He hung up and passed through the turnstile, nodding to the guard, stout, elderly, beyond boredom, who remarked that it was a wet night.

"Foggy, too," said Lars.

"But good for the gardens." The guard's eyes glistened behind his thick glasses: another lover of vegetation—surprising how many people shared that passion.

"And for shrubs," Lars said, thinking of Emma's transplanted azaleas and rhododendrons. Such matters horticultural took up a few, unconsidered minutes; Lars felt himself in a curious state, as if the normal motive powers of his body had been suspended in favor of some biological autopilot that led him into the elevator, stainless steel, gleaming, and vaguely threatening, and up to the periodicals floor where he had a small study. Lars unlocked door of the closet-sized cubicle and switched on a gooseneck lamp. The golden cone of light revealed the untidy piles of red, brown, and blue library volumes, thick bound journals, and shiny paperbacks that littered the reading desk. Through the narrow panel in the door, he could see rows of gray metal shelving under the shadowless white glare of the fluorescents and, beyond, the stacks' dark reflections in the glass wall.

The study was cramped, far smaller than his departmental office, but Lars felt a kind of affection for discomforts that could remind him so strongly of youth and graduate school, of spring passions both romantic and scholarly. Lars did nothing in cold blood. Various poems, lines of Blake and Wordsworth, certain passages in *Wuthering Heights* and *Madame Bovary* recalled a world of unique intensity, which even his quick and sensitive temperament had not managed to carry beyond three decades. Especially at night, especially late, especially under his old, nonfluorescent gooseneck lamp, the little study brought back happy memories of first loving Emma, of his first successes, and his first books. Lars sometimes thought that his romances, for all their intensity, really possessed a Proustian dimension, which raised his philandering to a more elevated plane.

He locked the door behind him and hung up his coat, taking Iris's diary from the deep inside pocket. The thin notebook was faintly damp and smelled of wet paper and the woodsy perfume she favored. This was a relatively new diary; the first date was in early April, the last—here Lars flipped through the blank pages at the

back—was yesterday. He looked at that entry. She'd found her conclusion, and in spite of his anger, Lars was pleased for her. Hers
would be the best student project he'd ever supervised. And what
else? Some sort of understanding with Sven, apparently: an amicable
parting. Here Lars felt a twinge of guilt; the Rival had proved a
gentleman at the last, unlike Lars, who'd lost his temper and his
sophistication in an overgrown public park.

He didn't want to read about the Rival's virtues and skipped back
a few pages. "I've come to a decision," he read, and though he'd
planned to be logical and chronological—which sometimes passes
as the same thing—he started to read.

M A Y   1 5 — *I've come to a decision, or I should say, I came
to a decision because I've already carried it out. This afternoon after
work, I burned the diaries. All that I had in the truck, that is.
Earlier ones at home were spared this auto-da-fé (watch the puns,
Iris) because they haven't been used for the book yet. Once diaries
have been used, they're no good; they've been supplanted by art or,
at least, by effort. I hadn't understood that when Lars and I talked
once about the relations between memories and memoirs and between memoirs and fiction. Or, really, when he talked and Iris
listened.*

Lars winced.

What he said was very true: Art consumes.

Lars doubted very much he had been so pithy, but it was nice
to think he had.

*Even a diary is not "true" in some senses. If you are honest, it's
truth as you think it is at the moment, the best you can do. Like
now, I'm trying to put down exactly what I thought and am thinking and exactly what happened and why. As best I can. Okay! If
in a month I add this to the book, I'll write today up and change
it to fit the demands of the chapter. When I'm done, if I do it right,*

*the material will be emotionally true, but I'll have emphasized dif-
ferent things and that will be another stage away from the events,
which are simple: A woman puts a stack of diaries in a paper bag,
drives them to the picnic area of a local park, named, incidentally,
for Fanny Fern, a successful nineteenth-century sentimental poet,
where she, our heroine, that is, not Fanny Fern, sets them alight
in one of the barbecue pits to burn unhappiness, foolishness, danger, the past. As usual with our heroine, Iris of the Golden Wings,
this is harder than it looks. Cardboard takes time to catch, and I
have to rip some pages out to start the flames; the ashes in the
barbecue pit are damp, delaying combustion until the matches are
almost gone. I guess the past is resistant, which sounds like one of
those heavy articles Lars recommends.*

*But after a struggle, triumph: Everything catches, flames fill the
pit. I thought I might feel bad—all that writing, all that time, all
that work—but I don't. I feel decisive, able to say, "That's done,
that's finished," which I must be able to say, because there are other
things that have to be settled.*

Lars felt a twinge, both for the loss of the other diaries and
because he realized that Iris would want this one. She would need it.
He should call her; she might have her cell phone on. He could call
her and apologize and listen to her apologize to him; they would
agree to meet in a glow of possibilities. Instead, he succumbed to a
different temptation and flipped back through the pages until he
found a truncated account of the reservoir incident, which ignited a
gust of anger, *whoosh*, like a propane stove. Writers cannot be
trusted, Lars thought. Modern critics are right; literature would be
better in some ways without authors, for what was her version? That
he, Lars, had kissed her in the truck, whereupon she'd told him it
was impossible. She mentioned Cookie and Emma (righteous prig!)
and totally omitted his abandonment in the wilderness. Liar! Treacherous, ungrateful liar! The hell with her book, Lars thought, for what
else had she distorted? What else? He went right to the first page
and began to read.

A P R I L   1 2 — *Called Him. Foolish, stupid, beyond stupid, moronic, beyond that if there is such a category (check the thesaurus, Iris, the dinosaur book). Met at his apartment for the usual: rage and intensity. He's the rage, of course, though he doesn't know why and neither do I. He suspects I'm tired of him, indifferent to him, deliberately tormenting him. Not true, but becoming true: the huge power of negative expectations. If I could resist, I'd never see him again and* be better off for it, *as Dad used to say, but I can't. With him, everything is vivid and important and the world alive with the ideas his body burns into my brain. Some days I can't wait to get back to the diary. At the same time, I can hardly bear to leave him, because with him I can forget everything else and dissolve grief with sex.*

Lars pushed back his chair, feeling older than he liked. It amazed him that he'd thought he'd wanted to know this, that he'd wanted to see this side of Iris. He should close the diary, put it in an envelope and straight into the mail, but though he closed the book and sat tapping the cover with his fingers, a moment later it was open again.

A P R I L   1 4 — *I notice I am referring to him as Him again, like a force of nature, like something beyond reason. And yet I know him now; I know he is in most ways ordinary: jealous, petty, intelligent but not excessively, more quick than deep. He worries about his dissertation, collects comic books, eats badly, drinks rarely but dangerously, and should change his socks more often.*

Lars smiled ruefully at that. Though it was faint consolation, failure had enabled him to escape her sharp observations. He was not sure now that she would have been kind. Certainly, she was not always kind in the diary to the Rival, who came across as an ardent, exciting lover but also as a high-strung, petty sadist. Petty, Lars thought, through weakness rather than inclination. For though they apparently went in for rather rough games, Iris was a big girl, not easily bullied, and the Rival was sometimes on the losing end. Brava, Iris, Lars thought. Now she just had to leave this man, to see the pointlessness of juvenile affairs, and join the civilized community.

A P R I L   2 1   (G O O D   F R I D A Y) — *He came to the truck. I recognized his footsteps, the commuter lot being extra quiet now, and I flicked off the light, hoping he'd think it was just a reflection from the light tower overhead. Then I waited in the dark. He walked over here from the center of campus. A quarter mile? A half mile? What's distance to see Iris of the Golden Wings? I put down my book and sat still. The windows were open, of course, it's getting warm, but they're narrow and the screens are dark and dirty. I resent having to sit in the dark in my own truck, but that's the breaks. I didn't want to talk to him. He tapped on the side. Softly. Lars used to do that sometimes, as if he was knocking at the door. Very civilized. Taps again. I was tempted to answer, because I could see how silence breeds fear: he's beginning to frighten me. "Iris." Very soft.*

He used to raise his voice and sometimes his hands, but he doesn't do that anymore. Iris has golden gloves as well as Golden Wings, so physically there's nothing to be afraid of. Not one thing. And yet I sat there in the truck and refused to answer. He waited for quite a while, tried to see in the windows, rattled at the latch. "I know you're in there," he said and sat down on the asphalt, still warm from the day, and talked for quite a while. At first he was positive I was inside, and he was pleading and abusive; he swore and threatened and begged and apologized. I kept my mouth shut— what was there to say to all that? And anyway, conversation was never my first priority with him. After a while, his tone changed; I could tell he wasn't sure anymore and he began to talk off the top of his head, the way you do when you talk out loud to yourself or write in a diary. The old, Dear Diary, Tonight I sat in the commuter lot and talked to a truck that might or might not have contained a woman I'm in love with. *That's what he'd write: He thinks he's in love with me. I don't think he is: He is violent, sometimes cruel. He's more like a collector, a trapper: He wants* to collect me and bend me into shape and stuff me (which has its moments) and put me up on his mantel. That's what he wants. Yes, he'd say, that's Iris of the Golden Wings, very rare, a spectacular example of the type and available only to a man of my abilities. *He wants that experience very badly, so he begs and pleads and starts to cry, which nearly gets to me. I swore under my breath and I wanted to jump out and tell him to knock it off and hold all that until he has real grief. I very nearly did, but before I could, he stood up and leaned against the screen of the window, and said, very softly, "You'll be sorry, Iris," as if he'd heard something, as if I'd given myself away. Then he left. I watched him walking across the lot into the shadows.*

I need to talk to somebody about him.

A P R I L   2 3 — *I called Mom, who complained that I don't call enough, so we got off to our traditional bad start and I didn't tell her the things I should have and maybe even wanted to. For one thing, she doesn't know I have a cell phone, so she worries about getting in touch with me "in an emergency," which makes both of us think about my dad and early morning phone calls and other disasters and depresses the hell out of me. I know she'd feel bad if she found out I have the phone and haven't told her. But if I did, she'd phone me every day at all hours and drive me crazy, because she'd feel she ought to call. The sad thing is that we want to get along, we really do, but every time one of us makes a step in the right direction, the other is on the wrong wavelength. Like today: I wanted to talk to her about coming home, about living at home this summer, which she would like. But within five minutes, I not only didn't mention coming home, I realized that it would be the worst of all possible summer venues. That's Mom and me.*

A P R I L   2 5 — *A bad day. A bad, bad day. I called him just to get out of my head. He's right that I'm inconsistent. So what? He does what he has to do to live, and so do I. Maybe that's all there is: no big theory, no ethical framework, just survival. Today my dad would have been forty-six, younger than Lars, I think, not*

*very old at all. Could I have talked to Dad about Him? Or about
Lars, for that matter? But if I'd never gotten that call in the night,
if Dad had survived the attack, if he'd gotten better, if I hadn't
loved him, I'd be a different person with a different set of problems.*

So I picked up the phone. When I got to the apartment, he
said, "I came to see you the other night."

"I know," I said. "I know all about it. I heard every word."

He grabbed my shoulders angrily, but he was already excited,
pushing his body against mine, his face flushed. "Why do you do
things like that to me?"

"It makes you ferocious," I said, because I don't talk about despair to him. What would be the point? He wants to be the center
of my universe; he doesn't want to know he's contingent. Neither
do I. He started to kiss me, his teeth sharp against my mouth, as if
he wanted to hurt me but doesn't dare. Maybe I want to hurt him,
too, but don't dare either—like the nuclear powers: MAD, mutually
assured destruction. Instead, we rip our clothes off right in his living
room despite the fact it has a big window right onto the front porch.
His couch is dusty and awkward, the floor's hard. I can't decide
now if we don't notice or don't want to notice. I make a variety of
noises, he strains into the furthest point of me, the world goes red
and black. Sometimes at this point, I have curious insights and
understand the connections between sex and ideas. Sometimes.

Afterward, we got up and Iris made omelets and he washed up
plates to put them on: domestic, friendly, but it's false: we'll never
be domestic and friendly, there's some vital connection missing.
Once when we were lying in bed, he put his fingers into my vagina
and then licked them one by one. "I want to devour you," he said.

A P R I L   2 8 — *A good conference with Lars. Can men split
their personalities easier than women? He's the perfect adviser, a
great editor, a wonderful teacher. Wonderful. And yet he's still following me around with this creepy persistence. He shows up in the
halls after my classes, he drops by Healthy Stuff, he hangs around
Record Resource. Since he never invites me for coffee anymore, I*

assume Lars is looking for Sven, but he comes out by night to the
truck though I refuse to let him in.
  Would Lars understand that?
  I'm tempted to ask.

Lars closed the diary with confused emotions. The next entry
was the day of the reservoir, a day of bungled interpretations and
missed opportunities. He did not feel he needed to read anymore;
he already knew that he had failed Iris. He put on his coat and stuck
the diary in his pocket. When he got down to the lobby, Lars was
surprised to see that it was already quarter to ten, and he drove
straight home. The house was dark except for the porch light, because Emma and Cookie started early in the morning. Polly was
waiting on the step, a miniature sphinx, her eyes aglow. Lars unlocked the door and heard the rattle of Jake's nails in the upper hall.
Lars smiled, and with this evidence of Jake's faithfulness, his normal optimism reasserted itself. He always liked coming home to the
sleeping house, to the quiet, to the sense that all he loved was safe
inside.

The diary was a record of his failure, but he hadn't made a complete fool of himself, and tomorrow he'd think of a tactful way to
return it. A flat-out lie might be best: he'd found the notebook in
the car that morning and brought it right to the truck. Lars thought
he could carry that off, though it was odd, now that he thought
about it, that she'd dropped it at all. It should have been in her book
bag. Had she left it deliberately? Could she want his advice, confirmation that she was doing the right thing in leaving, in making a
fresh start? He stood in the downstairs hall with the notebook in his
hand. Perhaps he should take another tack, confess he'd read a little
of the diary and caution her about the Rival, give her good advice.
He should, for though it was perhaps only the dark hallway and his
own turbulent emotions, Lars felt uneasy for Iris. Now that his quick
anger and wounded feelings were receding he felt an undeniable
concern. He should call. He wouldn't mention the diary. Finding it
in the morning was a good idea. But a call. I'm concerned. Stop by

tomorrow. Something like that. He went to the phone and dialed. *The number is not available. At the tone, record a message.* Lars looked at his watch. Barely 10:15—early for the nocturnal undergrads.

"Iris? Lars. I need to talk to you. Will you call me tomorrow? Take care, take care of yourself."

That would do for tonight. Tomorrow: some sort of good advice, counsel, direction. Exactly what that might be, Lars would trust to the inspiration of the morning. He went up to his study, where he locked the diary in his briefcase and told himself that there was nothing to worry about. He walked softly along the quiet hall to Cookie's room, an aqueous blue-green chamber. Jake was already back on the end of her bed. He wagged his stubby tail without lifting his bristly muzzle, and Lars gave him a pat; he felt grateful to Jake. You cannot be too watchful with children; the dangers are so many, so varied, so manifest; life is infinitely precarious. His daughter was deeply asleep, her thick dark hair over her forehead, one bare arm up against her face. What would her life be like? Would the flesh be kind to her, or would she be tormented by intense and unsuitable longings? And would he be there to protect her, to give her good advice, to listen? Iris's father must have wondered that, too, for those long, seductive limbs, the wide hips, the shining hair, the wonderful eyes and quick smile had all unfurled from a child no bigger than Cookie, a child who slept as soundly, whose face was as smooth, perhaps as untroubled. Lars watched his sleeping daughter for a moment, the night clotted with emotion, then bent down and kissed her forehead.

Emma Larson stood at the kitchen window in the early morning sun studying her new bed of azaleas and drinking a second cup of coffee. She thought a paler hue would be better against the dark house. White would be fine but timid; pink would be okay, but not if the orange hybrids were out at the same time. She would have to get a garden diary, put in the blooming dates, postpone her vision of flowery splendor for another year—too bad when she was so much in the buying and planting mood. "Patience," she said aloud and reached over to tickle the large black cat that sat beside her on the counter, sending Polly into ecstasies of purring.

Overhead came the sound of Cookie's feet on the bare wood floors. Emma could tell that her daughter was now shod, therefore dressed and approaching readiness for school. She turned her wrist and consulted her watch but without concern: twenty minutes. Plenty of time to drop Cookie at the elementary and still reach the high school with time to spare. Emma Larson never rushed. Tall and fair with a wide, placid, beautiful face, her blonde hair, calm temperament, and Scandinavian surname led to assumptions that she was Swedish. In fact, her Pre-Raphaelite looks came from the far north of Italy. It was Lars, dark, mercurial, high-strung, who was Swedish on both sides as far back as anyone cared to trace.

Emma Paoli Larson had been admired from babyhood for her beauty, and perhaps the beautiful, like Fitzgerald's rich, are subtly different. Emma ran her family and her office without ever raising her voice. Tyrannical administrators, huffy board members, temperamental staff, blustering parents, surly, disaffected, or distraught adolescents all fell under her spell. They found her calm and ever so sensible and sympathetic; in a word, they found her beautiful.

Her nature was sweet and almost excessively tranquil although she was physically energetic: a great skier, swimmer, hiker, cyclist. Emma could ride a horse, fly a plane, manage a skateboard; her serenity made all easy, and any athletic activity was quickly mastered. If she had a fault, it was an emotional calm almost amounting to passivity, a weakness counteracted by her choice of husband. Lars was restless and intense, quick to love, quick to anger. Imaginative and mercurial, he gave Emma a needed emotional seasoning, heightening her life in ways she found hard to define.

And on the whole, that life had been fortunate. Emma was not one of those people who expect cloudless skies, who see misfortune as a personal affront from the universe. Her reverses and disappointments had been absorbed stoically until she became a mother, a role she'd taken on reluctantly, as she had not really been eager for children. She liked her work, liked independence, liked spontaneous trips to the ski slopes or the beach, liked making love with Lars of a weekend morning, unhampered by the shouts and demands of small, beloved voices. It had been Lars, feckless, self-centered, occasionally unfaithful, who had wanted children, and Emma, content and easygoing, had eventually agreed.

Carrying Jared, she had been seriously unwell. Emma sometimes still wondered whether her ill health had been a symptom of the various maladies afflicting their son or of a resistance to the fetus, a covert rebellion. She had once watched a television program about birds rearing their young. With horrified fascination, she'd seen coots kill excess chicks and herons ignore their younger offspring, and realized that maternal love is by no means a pure gush of sentiment. Emma had been pregnant reluctantly, the pregnancy difficult, her labor extended, the results disastrous.

She had been devastated, ill for a long time, grief stricken, in part for Lars, who'd seen the child and held it and taken it into his heart in a way that Emma, doped to the eyes with painkillers and, later, Valium, never did. For months after she got home, she would sit in front of her mirror and study her face, because surely all this meant something, but if it did she could never read a line of the message. Her skin, her features, her hair, her teeth, her eyes were unblemished, her expression serene. It was only within that some tiny, hidden vein had been opened never to close, destined forever to drop a nameless, featureless anxiety into her system. Then Cookie was born and that anxiety had a focus, as if it had been waiting all along for Emma to bear a daughter and to love her with all her heart.

"Cookie! Time to leave!"

"I'm coming!" Her voice was muffled. She was waking Lars, who had late-morning classes and liked to sleep in but who forgave Cookie pretty much anything. Without Emma as disciplinarian of the family, Lars would have been totally enslaved by their daughter, who had Emma's looks and his enthusiasm. Yet he was a good father. He was never too busy for Cookie, or for Emma, either, which was important to remember, particularly when the currents of her anxiety roiled like water in an early thaw. Though at one time or another, most of Emma's friends had wondered, sometimes aloud, why she'd married Lars, and, having committed that folly, why she stayed with him, he made her laugh and he adored Cookie. For these things, she forgave him a host of brief, romantic peccadilloes.

"Cookie!"

A resounding clatter on the stairs, the bouncing descent of Cookie's sneakers, Jake's nails rattling on the bare treads.

"Are you all set? Daddy up?"

Yes to both questions. The pink book bag with the stuffed bear attached was strapped to her back, her wild hair was tied back with a ribbon, her socks matched. Emma got her purse and opened the door. Cookie snatched the paper from the front step and ran to put it on the table, for while Emma liked her brief, quick breakfast free from worldly distractions, Lars woke up with the news. Jake began barking to announce that the paper had come and that it was now time for his walk.

"Do you have your homework?"

"Yes." Such an unenthusiastic proclamation that Emma asked, "All of it?"

"Uh-huh. My science project's finished. The beans are this tall. We can put them in the garden after school."

"If they're not too spindly. If they're spindly we'll start new ones." Emma gave her a kiss before they got into the car. On the way to school, they talked about the beans and the garden. Emma suggested planting a tepee of vines and sunflowers that could double as a playhouse. Cookie approved. She would help with the digging, the posts, any outdoor work, for she was an energetic, athletic child. What Cookie was not good at was sitting still in school, rote lessons, pencil-and-paper homework. This sometimes worried Lars, who thought schoolwork was as important to the whole world as it was to him. Emma, having seen half a generation of indifferent scholars go on to become solid and useful citizens, had a wholesome skepticism about grades and tests. Her worries about Cookie were all existential: Emma feared the malice of the universe.

She idled in front of the elementary, watching Cookie tear up the steps. A quick wave at the door, then she was gone, off to the before-school music program where she was learning percussion, so good, as the music instructor put it, for an active child.

The high school was only a block away, and as usual, she arrived right on time. She greeted Joe, security guard and de facto counselor, and Delores, who ran the desk, before collecting the local newspaper from the counter and unlocking her office. Emma adjusted the blinds against the morning sun, checked her messages, then unfolded the paper: the obits had to be checked daily in case of a death in a school family. Outside the door, Delores's coffee maker was already perking. The earliest buses had wheezed up to disgorge the first students. Momentarily, Emma would be able to track their movements by the rattle and slam of lockers, a metallic cacophony spreading to the farthest reaches of the school. She had perhaps five minutes to scan the paper before the first wave of problems, questions, requests, phone calls.

So, the morning's headlines: "Ferry Sunk in Bangladesh," "Small Plane Missing," "More Questions About State Pension Fund Investments," and down below the fold, the story that would change her life: "University Student Stabbed." This one Emma read, as she read everything connected with the university, but quickly, feeling regret rather than alarm. A young woman had been seriously wounded just a few blocks from campus, apparently within yards of a graduation party in full swing. She had been taken to University Hospital. No other information, the story was obviously a late insertion. Emma thought she should call Lars later and see if he knew anything more. What a shame just at the end of school, just at graduation.

"Mrs. Larson."

She looked up from the paper and smiled at the principal, a shambling, soft spoken man with a grayish complexion and an aura of unspoken anxiety that aroused her sympathy. Mr. Hoffman suffered from indigestion and was not, Emma feared, really up to the high pressures of modern school administration.

"I'm having trouble with the computer."

"They have a mind of their own," she agreed. Emma could afford to be serene: She backed up all the office files. "Is it the newsletter?"

A frantic nod.

"I have a copy on my hard drive," she said and saw his heavy, prematurely lined face relax.

He wanted to insert some additional material, and Emma followed him into the long, sun-washed office. The day had started; sinking ferries and missing planes slipped below the calm surface of her attention. Only one idea remained, bobbing like flotsam: Who was the student and had she survived? What might her name be? Could it be—? But here her mind, usually so good on names—one of the secrets of her power at school—did not produce the answer. She would learn that only when she got home to find Lars sitting white and tense at the kitchen table drinking, most unusually, a large whiskey.

She hadn't seen the expression on his face more than once or twice: when he came in with the doctor to tell her about Jared, when his father took the stroke. "What's wrong?" she cried, fear surging straight to her heart. "Where's Cookie?"

"She's at Jenny's. Betty said she'd take them to the park." Lars glanced up at the clock. "They'll be home soon."

"The student," Emma said, for anxiety made her intuitive; it grasped the connections of catastrophe in a way her surface personality never would. She sat down beside her husband and put her hand on his shoulder, which felt hot and damp as if he were feverish.

"You saw the paper?" Lars asked.

The local evening paper lay on the table. "Murdered Student Identified. Iris Weed, a senior literature major who was due to graduate with honors this weekend, died at University Hospital early this morning with multiple stab wounds . . ." "Oh, Lars, how awful. She was doing a project with you. She called one night."

Lars put his face in his hands and began to weep.

6.

At ten o'clock Saturday morning, Lars was in full academic regalia: mortarboard, blue-and-white hood, dark suit and shoes, long black gown, the latter with a paperback tucked into one sleeve to while away the chancellor's remarks and trustees' greetings. Overhead, unclouded sun; below, the much coddled campus lawns lay green and immaculate. The beer cans and bottles, the paper cups and plates, and various latex remnants of youthful bacchanals all had vanished, while shorts and T-shirts, tank tops, and cutoffs were hidden beneath newly rented robes and mortarboards. Every scenic spot—the steps of the chapel, the herb garden sundial, the bronze Diana fountain—had families, proud, nervous, relieved, clustered for photographs, so that the campus was dappled in maroon and pastel with the graduates' robes and their parents' festive spring clothing. Graduation day, a day of ridiculous costumes, tedious speeches, various signs, shouts, and gestures in bad taste, endless camera flashes, and suppressed jubilation. Lars liked it. Although he always complained about the ceremony, about having to march in the academic parade, about this needless prolongation of the semester, he usually responded to the pleasures of the day. He had a secret love for "Pomp and Circumstance"; he enjoyed seeing his students graduate; he liked meeting their parents—always so full of compliments and commendations—and on general principles he approved of excitement and festivity.

But today was different. Shock had not so much lessened as

metamorphosed into a reduced alertness, a sort of emotional stupidity, interrupted by nerves. Lars had not believed the story in the
morning paper, not at all, although his mouth had gone dry and he
became aware, in a horrid and somehow unnatural way, of his heartbeat. He phoned the department and found the secretary willing to
pass on what she knew but no better informed than he was. Lars
told himself there was nothing to worry about: The college had
thousands of students, half of them female. Just the same, when he
drove to Healthy Stuff, there were cruisers in the lot and skeins of
yellow tape and two dark unmarked cars parked beside Iris's truck.
What he had known the moment he saw the story was true: Iris was
the girl who had been hurt, and it served her right. His heart leaped
with the rightness of it, with this vindication of his sufferings, then,
in the next instant, fell into devastation. In intense emotional confusion, Lars reversed out of the lot, his tires squealing.

Since then, he had existed in a curious parallel universe where
nothing looked different but everything was subtly changed. The
news had filtered around campus: "Iris, Iris Weed, you know, the
writer, with the weird clothes, the long hair, Iris, Iris Weed," a murmur like wind through reeds. The department chair stopped staff in
the halls to relay what was known: "One of our students . . . fortunately off campus . . . a meeting with the parent . . . the chancellor
will be making a statement." To Lars, he expressed sympathy: "You
were doing an independent study with her, I believe." And Lars said,
"The most talented writer I've ever taught." Still, meaning eluded
him. He went through the day, reassured some nervous undergrads,
managed, managed really well, to be a complete professional, until
he got home and read the evening paper and had to pour himself a
large whiskey.

When Emma returned, he talked about Iris's talent, about her
book, about the waste. "If I'd only known," he said. Emma said,
"Crime is random, violence is in the air." That's how Lars would like
to think of it: as a sudden eruption of violence, a natural, rather than
a moral, phenomenon. The alternative led back to the people she
knew, to the Rival, to him, to people who had loved her and let her
down. But there was no reason for him to feel so guilty. Shocked,

yes, guilty, no. However unpleasant to think that Iris might have known her killer, surely the boyfriend would be the chief suspect. And surely, surely, there would have been witnesses, or, if not witnesses, informants. Someone must have heard, must have suspected, someone would have information, far better information than Lars had. The police would discover the truth. Lars wanted very badly to believe in the police; he wanted to think they could do their job without any help from him.

Commencement at the university was always held in Buck Auditorium. Approaching the big beaux arts building with its dome and columns, Lars thought that the faculty members looked like a procession of monks, their dark robes made sinister by his gloomy cast of mind. Inside, he noticed a bouquet of white flowers on one of the seats reserved for honors graduates: Iris's place. It was true, then, that she was dead, for the school had made this small gesture of sorrow and regret. Lars realized that on some level he had expected her to march in with the rest, her Farmer Browns hidden under her rented robe, her long hair falling beneath her mortarboard, a maroon-and-white tassel swinging against her cheek, her bright eyes excited, observant, satiric. She would have smiled at him, perhaps given him a little nod, a little wave. How happy he would have been had she been saved from death.

Of course, if she had been alive and well and perfectly safe, Lars knew that he would have been tormented, frustrated, half angry, half hopeful. If you want to know how you really feel about your friends, he thought, imagine them dead, then weigh their faults and your disappointments. Death is the test, and were Iris sitting now in her appointed place in the third row of the honors graduates, this would be a happy day. No matter what.

A rustle of chairs, the hollow whine of the mike, the provost's usual joke about the mike, the usual appreciative chuckles from the audience, the spatter of flashes from besotted parents willing to record even the provost, the dullest man on campus, introducing the chancellor, a money-raising bore, who departed from his usual script to ask for a moment of silence for Iris Weed, who'd called herself Iris of the Golden Wings. Lars remembered that the classical Iris was the goddess of the rainbow and a messenger to the underworld, a combination showing that the old Greeks knew a thing or two about hope and despair, about love and death. He realized with alarm that there were tears in his eyes, that he might begin to cry as he had when he talked to Emma. Had he given himself away to his wife? He had not considered that. He had told her about the book, Iris's project, about how good it was. "A nice girl, too, odd, arty, but nice. She was living in her truck to save on housing costs." And Emma had said, "No savings are worth the risk." Then she asked if he had known Iris well. (Had there been some subtext there? Had Emma an inkling of his true feelings? It wouldn't be the first time, though with Iris he was, at least, technically, innocent.) "Well, in one way," he'd answered. "The book. Her writing. Not much at all about her personal life." If he hadn't opened her diary, he could have said that he knew next to nothing about her personal life. He wished he hadn't touched the damn thing. Though he had called. He had to remember that. For suppose he had reached Iris that night, warned her, counseled her, altered the course of events? Then reading the diary would have been the right thing, after all.

Time for the commencement address, given this year by a popular writer, a woman who looked smaller and older than the jacket photos on her ubiquitous books. Lars thought he would have to write to Iris's mother. He should maybe have the office duplicate the last version of the book and enclose a copy. The manuscript was an admirable piece of work and might have meaning for her, though he wondered what book could possibly console him if Cookie were lost. All of Shakespeare, the Greek tragedies, every nineteenth-century novel? His daughter was in another, incommensurate category.

Still, he must write Mrs. Weed, and immediately after the ceremony, Lars was back in his office, his black gown hanging beside the door, his mortarboard sitting on his desk, pen and stationery before him, attempting condolences: . . . *one of the most gifted students I've ever taught, a young woman of supreme talent and vitality, an absolute original* . . . He stopped at the last phrase. Was that going too far? Iris had been truly and absolutely original, but to a grieving parent originality might suggest risky behavior and outlandish choices. Might suggest Iris, in short. Lars was thinking this over, trying to decide on the polite phrases to convey, *I loved her. I'm sorry she's dead. It wasn't my fault,* when there was a knock.

"Come in."

The door opened on a man and a woman. Lars knew instantly that they were police, a surprising recognition that informed him that in some way he had been expecting them. But, of course, the authorities had been on campus yesterday, checking identification, asking about Iris, about her teachers, her friends, her associates. They'd come to talk to him because she had been in his class, because he had supervised her independent project, perhaps because, and here he felt hot and nervous, they had been seen around campus together. *It wasn't my fault,* he wanted to say, and the words were as real, as physical in his mouth as a round, hard candy or a spoonful of hot, spicy food. *It wasn't my fault.*

"Professor Jason Larson?" The man was tall, heavy, and remarkably, even spectacularly, ugly with coarse, uneven features, pitted skin, and a rubbery, thick-lipped mouth. "Detective Roy Harrelson, homicide." Detective Harrelson had his credentials in hand as if Lars might dispute this, as if the English department were haunted by persons claiming to be homicide detectives, as if he, Lars, were well conversant with police.

"And this is Detective Kay Paatelainen." The woman was nearly as handsome as her companion was off-putting: a robust woman of between fifty and sixty with pure white hair and a perfect pink-and-white complexion. "Sex crimes unit," she said and shook Lars's hand. "We're interviewing everyone who had Iris Weed in class."

"Sex crimes unit?" Lars asked. He had envisioned something clean, catastrophic, sudden, an arrow from the gods; he had closed his mind to the possibly sordid details.

"The commonest motivation in stabbings of young women," Detective Paatelainen said briskly. "A jealous lover, a would-be lover, they're the likely candidates."

Was it just imagination that she gave him a speculative look? Lars nodded and tried to appear knowledgeable, while wondering what a specialization in evil would be like. If Detective Paatelainen was any indication, the sex crimes unit was a mellow bunch, for she had a sweet, almost motherly smile. Her colleague, by contrast, created an aura of apprehension. *Louring*, Lars thought. Victorian writers were fond of *louring skies*. They would have recognized the atmosphere that accompanied Detective Harrelson, for although his face was so carefully neutral as to be almost expressionless, the homicide detective conveyed a cynical, almost existential, paranoia. Lars wanted to say, *I know you, you're the bad cop of good cop, bad cop; I know the semiotics of the cop show, that popular but undertheorized genre; I know the lingo.* In this temptation to be flip, Lars understood that he was desperately nervous.

"We'd like to ask you a few questions, if we might," Detective Harrelson said ponderously.

Lars told himself that he had to be careful; he had to concentrate; he must not indulge in displays of scholarly cleverness. He must not. "Of course. Please." Lars gestured to the conference chair and pulled over a rather battered desk chair. "State issue," he said by way of apology.

The detectives, who seemed quite innocent of small talk, sat down without comment. They asked about Iris and wrote the answers in small black leatherette notebooks. *R & V class*—a quizzical look from Detective Harrelson. *Romantic & Victorian.* Into the notebooks that went. *The independent project*, ditto.

"A talented student?" Detective Paatelainen wished to know.

"Very. I was just writing to her mother, trying to convey what made her daughter such a special writer."

"What sort of project, exactly?"

Lars reached into his file and brought up the three-inch-thick pile of Iris's manuscript.

"Such a long work," exclaimed Paatelainen.

"Yes, especially for an undergraduate project, but she was truly exceptional. Truly."

"And this is a story, a novel?"

"Part memoir, part reportage. It's her account of living in her truck."

The two detectives brightened at this and sat up straighter like terriers who smell a rat. But not me, thought Lars, no rodent here. He started to explain about Iris's style and method, pointing out the features that made the work remarkable.

Detective Harrelson interrupted what Lars thought was an illuminating analysis. "We'll need a copy," he said heavily.

"The office can make you one. I was going to have them run one for Mrs. Weed, anyway."

"We will do that at the station and return the original to you." Harrelson's eyes were septic, Lars thought, the exact color of dirty water. The detective's profession gave him license to stare and also to command.

"I'll need a receipt," said Lars, irritated at the idea of losing the manuscript. "This is my only copy. Have you checked her laptop? Everything should be on her hard drive anyway."

The two detectives did not answer his question, arousing another hoary cliché: *We're here to ask the questions, Professor,* and sundry variations on that theme. *Cliché in Genre Dialogue.* Could it be catalogued meaningfully? If so, *Semiotics and Clichés* might be an attractive title; maybe try that out, Lars thought, then he pulled himself back, aware that he was trying to escape the situation at hand, a situation not dangerous in and of itself, no, no, he was quite innocent, but one where he must be alert and careful. The problem was that whenever he took the detectives seriously he felt an underlying panic, manifested as guilt with a strong temptation toward confession, and when he saw them as denizens of some banal entertainment, he was prone to amusing scholarly riffs. What to do, what to tell them?

"Her friends," said Detective Paatelainen. "Do you know anything about her friends?"

"Not really. She knew a lot of people casually. She wrote about a friend in her swimming class. She mentioned a boy she was seeing—he isn't in the book."

"His name?" asked Detective Paatelainen.

"She called him Sven. I have no idea what his real name is." That was true and, feeling virtuous, Lars started again with the explanation that Detective Harrelson had so rudely interrupted. "She felt free to change names, to modify incidents." He wanted to add, *like the day in the reservoir;* he wanted to explain how she had improved her own part and made his worse. "Writers have a certain license, you know."

"Poetic," said Detective Harrelson in the same tone that he might have used for *murder one* or some other criminal abomination.

"Precisely." Lars mentioned Thoreau to try to give them an analogy, to show them Iris's model. "I don't know if you're familiar with *Walden,*" he began, and Harrelson said, "Standard college reading."

The hell with you, thought Lars, to hell with the new-model, college-educated, sophisticated copper. "Then you understand the sort of book Iris wanted to write."

"A work of ideas," suggested Detective Paatelainen. "Unusual for a young person." She had begun flipping through the pages. "And you say the names are changed?"

"Many of them. Of course, she kept diaries, too." The damn diary was in his mind and the words came unbidden. "I never saw them; I mean, I saw the notebooks but never read them." In his realization of the stupidity of mentioning the diaries, Lars almost stumbled over the words. He must beware of the impulse to teach, to explain, yet he continued, drawn into a silence suddenly charged with interest. "Iris regarded them purely as raw material."

The detectives were looking at him, as if they heard a rat in the wainscotting. Detective Harrelson wanted to know everything about the diaries, their size, shape, composition, how Lars had seen them, what they might contain.

"They'll be in the truck, I suppose," Lars said at last. Let them look: The diaries were ashes, and he had the last one, the vital one. Without that, he was out of the picture, irrelevant, just a helpful, conscientious professor, and he would stay that way—unless she had put something on her hard drive. But, no, there would be no point in burning the books and keeping the contents, would there? Would there? Who knew how Iris's mind had worked. "Unless she mailed them home," he said; he hated the detectives' silences. "She often had one in her backpack. That's all I know."

"You've been extremely helpful," Detective Paatelainen said

sweetly, bringing almost an orgasm of relief. She must be devastating
on the sex crimes unit. Your poor average pervert wouldn't stand a
chance against her. Even he, Lars, innocent as he was, felt temptation. "Now if you could just tell us when you last saw Ms. Weed?"
The smile again beneath the cloudless blue eyes.

Lars's shirt felt sticky. *It wasn't my fault,* he wanted to say. *I
dropped her off, safe and sound. A few words, a misunderstanding, you
know how young people can be. I know you understand.* Detective
Paatelainen waited, so pleasant, so pretty (perhaps his taste was ma-
turing after all)—so lethal. Lars reached for his organizer. "One moment." There was a subtle tremor in his hands. "Tuesday," he said,
"a week ago Tuesday. We normally conferenced on Thursdays but
there was a conflict." As he spoke, some little moral calculator, the
residue of many pious generations, whispered, *second lie.* Only an
omission, Lars protested. But it made no difference. *He knew nothing. He had seen Iris walk away. Safe and sound.* "She came in with
a draft of her conclusion. We wanted something elegant that would
round off the whole work. She had ambitions to publish," he added.

"A realistic hope?" asked Detective Paatelainen, who seemed interested in things literary.

"I think it would have been inevitable," Lars said, and his heart
lurched with grief and regret. "She was truly very gifted."

By the time they left, his shirt was drenched. Lars sat and stared
at the letter to Isobel Weed as at Egyptian hieroglyphics. What to
say? Modern, secular society had taken away all the satisfying explanations: God wills, fate, the malice of some deity, the violence of
an evil spirit. What had Paatelainen said? A jealous lover, a would-
be lover? What was that but an evil spirit? And he, Lars, what was
he? He got up abruptly from his desk, leaving the letter unfinished.

Emma and Cookie were in the yard, turning over the dirt in a sunny
patch for what appeared to be, from his daughter's excited and incoherent descriptions, a major bit of gardening. Certainly there
would be sunflowers taller than his head, and blue morning glories
and red flowered runner beans, all forming, if he envisioned it cor-

rectly, a bower fit for a princess. Near them, Jake rolled in the dirt in ecstasy, while Polly took advantage of the loosened soil to dig a discreet feline latrine. Lars said he would change and come down to help, but once upstairs he found himself watching them from the window: Emma in jeans and a white T-shirt doing the heavy digging, Cookie in pink shorts and a pink-and-white striped shirt breaking up the clods of earth with a cultivator, the two of them talking, laughing, safe momentarily from evil spirits, the malice of the gods, and the follies of the man who loved them. Lars went into his office and took Iris's last diary from his briefcase. Where to put it?

He dithered between a desk drawer and the bookcase. He tried to convince himself that there was nothing in it that would help the police except some more suggestions about Sven. But they had already been pointed in that direction. Lars had given them the name, the nickname, and certainly Detectives Harrelson and Paatelainen were alert and ready to be suspicious, especially about boyfriends, about lovers. What more would the diary do, except raise questions about his own conduct past and present? However harmless, even flattering it was in good times to be known for charm, erotic success, a roguish, wandering eye, with anything serious afoot, charm could be a danger and certain amatory adventures might be suspect. Would be suspect, would be enough to embarrass and involve him, and, by extension, Emma and Cookie. That must not happen. Lars had always prided himself on his discretion, his care, his consideration. Always. That must not change, not even for Iris, who was beyond help or caring, who could no longer be a priority.

Besides, the Rival's name was never mentioned. Never, though there was a description. But other people would have seen the Rival with her. His name would be discovered. Anyway, who said the Rival was guilty? The last entries in the diary had been so hopeful; even the Rival had been shown in a positive light. It was possible that Iris had been cut down by random violence. And if that was so, the diary was superfluous except to make trouble for Lars and for some young man who was most likely innocent. Most likely. One could have violent impulses, say violent things—how well Lars knew that now!—without coming to such a spectacular horror.

Really, Lars was doing his duty in preserving the diary at all, when it could so easily vanish into ashes like its fellows. And if he had to, absolutely had to, he could always "discover" the notebook in his car, just the way he had found it. In the meantime, let that fish-eyed Detective Harrelson find out what he could. Lars stuck the diary amid old binders of lecture notes and ran downstairs to announce that Captain Excavation, the Supergardner had arrived.

After dinner that evening, they went to the park, where Cookie and Jake ran madly down the walks and through the dark shadows of the evergreens to the sunlit rolling lawns: a small girl and a small dog, propelled by joy. Emma carried the now ubiquitous soccer ball under one arm; Lars strolled beside her, whistling a Puccini aria, one hand on her hip, the other in his pocket, almost content, so that when Emma asked, in marital shorthand, "And how are you," he said, "I'm all right. Today was tough, but I'm all right. I'm having trouble writing a letter to her mother, though."

Emma squeezed his arm affectionately, meaning she understood, meaning such a letter would be difficult.

"I'm having the office make a copy of Iris's book for Mrs. Weed. It's excellent. Really excellent. Do you think that will help?"

Emma considered this. "Yes, unless—"

"Unless?"

"Were they on good terms? You know how adolescents can be. They say things and figure they can revise later."

"I'll reread it with that in mind," Lars said. Yes, there were a few things, a few remarks. "On the whole I'd say she was quite a devoted child."

"And yet the whole *project*," said Emma. "Were they very poor?"

"Lower middle class, maybe middle middle class. The other children are grown. There wasn't a lot of money but hardly dire poverty. Iris felt she needed to *do* something. Something different. I didn't know until just recently that her father had dropped dead sometime in the fall. Iris was dealing with that."

"Ah," said Emma. "Poor girl. Were they very close?"

"Very. Reading between the lines, he and Iris were simpatico; he realized she was a swan. Mom saw her as more the ugly duckling."

"And maybe she was to Mom. That's sometimes the way."

"Sometimes. We're so lucky," Lars said. "We're so lucky with Cookie. She's a sweetie."

"She hasn't hit adolescence yet. There will be a rough patch. Count on it." But Emma did not sound too concerned. Her position as secretary of a large high school had given her a better perspective on adolescence than most parents enjoy.

"You're so sensible," Lars said fervently. Emma's good sense ravished him; it was a jewel of their marriage, one of her great beauties, his own salvation. He nuzzled her hair and felt, for one poignant instant, near tears of relief. Nothing could happen so long as he had Emma's good sense to rely on. Nothing.

"The police came," he said after a moment. He had not told Emma about his visit from Detectives Harrelson and Paatalainen, which had no real importance except novelty. Yet Lars knew that the longer he omitted to mention their visit, the greater significance it would acquire. And their visit must not acquire significance, it must not. To let the police and their visit acquire significance would be to awaken guilt and complicity, would be to open a demand for action. Lars had already made his decision. He had lied to the detectives, not once but twice. Not about important things, certainly, not about anything material, but just the same, there had been omissions, lies. To protect himself, to protect Emma, to protect Cookie. "They were at school yesterday and again today. They stopped by my office after commencement."

"Yes," said Emma, unsurprised. School secretaries are privy to many secrets. "They would have to."

"Disagreeable, though," Lars said.

"Very hard," Emma agreed. "Were you able to tell them anything useful?"

"Just about the book. They're making a copy. And I'm not sure they knew she kept diaries." Again! Again! He could not seem to keep the word from his mouth.

"Those might certainly be a help."

"Yes," Lars said with a twinge of regret. "If they can find them. I think they should already have found them. After all, a truck isn't a very big hiding place, is it?" Unless they were on her laptop. Unless they were all there. That was unlikely. He knew that was unlikely, yet he couldn't quite get rid of the idea.

"She may have had friends, a locker, a zip drive, you never know," said Emma. She put the soccer ball down and began to juggle it. She was like Cookie in her physical energy, an energy that sometimes betrayed hidden emotions. Lars watched the black-and-white ball and understood that she was worried in some way. She'd picked up on his anxiety.

"It will be all right. They'll find him," Lars said, anxious to reassure her. "Someone must have seen something. There were parties everywhere, people around the neighborhood till all hours. It will be all right."

He hugged her, but Emma still called to Cookie, now so far ahead as to be a mere bright dot against the evening shadows. Emma shouted, holding up the ball as a reward, and their daughter raced back, her face already intent, eager to play, Jake bounding beside her at the end of his red leash.

She's safe, thought Lars, *everything is safe.*

Lars went to campus Monday for the start of his first summer school class, and he half expected them then: just routine, returning the manuscript, thanking him for the mention of the diaries. When Lars saw Joe Katz, who taught Renaissance literature, he said the police had already visited him, too. Lars hoped Joe had not noticed how often he'd turned up outside room 311. On those days, they'd passed in the halls, said hello—he had said hello, hadn't he? Maybe not, maybe he'd been so focused on Iris that he'd wanted to avoid his colleagues, maybe that was why Joe seemed a bit distant today, not quite relaxed. Just the same, they stood in the hall and talked, unable to ignore detectives, investigations, sudden death. "I was really quite nervous," Joe said with an affected flutter. "Revenge tragedy's not my style at all."

Lars muttered something inane. Just what did Joe mean by revenge tragedy?

"I couldn't help them out. I never get particularly close to undergraduates. I mean, who does? Do you? Did you know her well?" He was curious, really curious, Lars saw. He had been noticed; Joe had seen him in the hall.

"Well, she did an independent study with me, you know. I have one or two independent study projects a semester." *I'm popular,* was what Lars was saying, *dedicated, altogether a superior teacher.* "I feel a responsibility for the undergraduates."

"Sure, but that's classroom. Outside, they have their lives, I have mine. Thank God, I'm no longer twenty." Lars was sure that age twenty had been wasted on Joe Katz.

"I couldn't help much on her friends, either," Lars said.

"Oh, she had friends," said Joe. "She exchanged notes with one fellow in class who had a tough work schedule. I think men liked Iris. I recall someone used to meet her after class. I think I remember someone." His glance was coolly opaque: Joe Katz, Commissar of Correctness. *What the hell had he told the detectives?*

"Someone must have seen or heard something that night," Lars said, anxious to leave Renaissance classes and hallway meetings. "I'd think the police would be questioning people along the street, tracking down people who were at the parties. I think they've been wasting their time on campus."

"Apparently they've found no witnesses," Joe said. "The police think she lay there bleeding for an hour or more. Bad luck for her, because the wounds weren't necessarily mortal."

"What a dreadful way to die!" Lars had a horrific image of Iris lying cold on the pavement, in the rain. She hadn't even had a raincoat. Why the hell hadn't she worn a raincoat to keep her dry? She had been standing shivering under the arcade. He should have followed her, taken the car, searched the streets. He hated Joe for telling him this terrible detail. And how did Joe know, anyway? He seemed suspiciously well informed. "There hasn't been much in the paper. The press has been very discreet."

"My son, the intern. He was in the ER that night. She was DOA, which presents difficulties with time of death. The rain, you know. A cold night for May."

How could he repeat such things without horror, with even a suppressed relish, delighted to be the bearer of inside information, of privileged news? "Either way, she's dead," Lars said. "And oh, she was brilliant, Joe. Such a talented writer."

Joe looked noncommittal. Iris had said once that he could make even Shakespeare dull. "The problem," he said, bright and pedantic, "is that with an inaccurate time of death, alibis are difficult. It's hard to rule people in or out, so expect the police to be all over us." He nodded for emphasis, grimly excited.

"Maybe you should be tackling revenge tragedies after all," Lars said.

Joe laughed. "You'll see I'm right." With a little wave of farewell or dismissal, he bustled off toward his office. *You'll see I'm right.* An emphasis on *you,* perhaps?

Lars shook his head as he went back down the hall. It didn't matter what Joe thought, and yet Lars was depressed. He'd taught in the same department with Joe Katz for twelve years. And like as not when the detectives came, Joe'd volunteered, self-satisfied and perky, that his colleague Jason Larson used to wait for Iris Weed outside his Renaissance class. Like as not, so Lars had expected some official police notice all Monday. He was alert for steps in the hall while he looked over his British Novel course notes. He checked both ways coming out of his lecture, expecting the Beauty and the Beast to be waiting for him. He worked longer than usual after class, thinking to forestall a visit to the house, and at noon when he left, he approached his car with trepidation, as if the two of them might pop up from behind the old Volvo. That was Monday when he was prepared.

Instead, they came on Tuesday just after class. There they were, standing outside of his office, patiently reading the cartoons and poetry announcements stuck up on his door.

"Professor Larson." Detective Paatelainen smiled, and uneasy as he was, Lars still thought irresistibly of Rubens, of Renoir, of Fragonard, of fleshy, delightful ladies with dimpled knees and cream-and-roses complexions. He would have thrown himself on her mercy and told her everything, if she hadn't saddled herself with Detective

Harrelson, who aroused completely different emotions.

"I expect you've brought back the manuscript," Lars said as he unlocked his office.

"Not yet," said Harrelson. "You've got your receipt." He stepped into the office and looked around, ostentatiously curious, a kind of parody of the alert, all-seeing detective, but Lars noticed that his eyes were focused on the bookcases and guessed that the diary entries weren't on Iris's hard drive. That was good, a relief. But why look on *his* shelves? What did they think?

"Just routine," said Detective Paatelainen, "but we would like you to describe how you spent Friday night."

"My *whereabouts,*" said Lars more cheerfully than he felt, because he knew that he would have to lie again. "Sure. I was home till, I don't know, maybe seven-thirty, when I took some grade sheets to the registrar's office. I'd had a late exam and one or two papers I'd been waiting for."

"You drove to campus?"

"That's right. I parked in my usual space next to Steele, this building, and I walked across to the registrar's. There's an after-hours mail slot. On my way back to the car, I decided to go to the library, and I called Emma from the lobby to let her know I'd be late."

"When was that?"

"Just after eight. I'd remembered an article I wanted to read, and when I was right on campus, I figured I'd stop in and have a look."

"Did anyone see you in the library?" Harrelson wanted to know.

"Just the guard. The door is always manned. We talked about the weather. About rain and shrubbery."

"You know his name?"

"No. Older man, glasses. He's the usual night attendant." Harrelson wrote all this down. Lars realized they would check. They were checking his alibi. *My alibi:* it had a surprising, exotic ring.

"And what time did you get home?"

"I left the library a bit before ten. Quarter of ten, maybe. I remember being surprised it was so late."

"Which the guard can confirm?"

Lars nodded.

"And you went straight home?" This from Detective Paatelainen.

"Of course. It was a miserable night. Mist, rain off and on, drizzle, cold. We were mighty lucky for graduation with the weather we've been having." Lars smiled to show that he was being obliging about this pro forma conversation, to indicate that he was completely relaxed.

"Yet you were nearly an hour on campus before you went to the library," Paatelainen observed. She had opened her little leatherette notebook and was watching him expectantly.

"An hour? No, not that long." God had he been seen? Had someone seen him and Iris? Love in the rain. *Singin' in the Rain.* The cool smoothness of her skin; she'd been chilled as if she'd been out for a while; he hadn't thought to ask. "I did wait out some rain in the arcade along the old quad. Quite a heavy shower. I don't know how long."

"It must have been a good half hour," Detective Paatelainen said. "It takes what, maybe ten minutes at the most to cross campus?"

"Ten, fifteen, yes."

"Your wife says you left the house just after seven. Ten or fifteen minutes to campus, ten minutes to cross campus, there was still thirty or thirty-five minutes left before you phoned."

"You talked to Emma?" Lars was surprised and showed it: a tactical error, he realized, but poor Emma. Oh, she'd have been a trooper, unflappable, but underneath—"I'm sorry you had to bother her."

"Sad to say, no one's word is enough," Detective Paatelainen said.

"Well, I never like to disagree with Emma. I'm sure I left the house later, but maybe I *was* under the arcade longer than I'd thought, because I came up with a pretty good idea for an article. My reason for going to the library—to check just what's done on *Norma*, the Bellini opera, and Whitman's *Leaves of Grass*. Most recent work on operatic heroines has been feminist, you know, but I think it may be time for another approach. I like to live dangerously and take on the critical pieties." Lars was in command, not spooked at all. "There are so many theoretical possibilities," he continued, and he started in on them energetically, just to show that he could keep the idea going, just to show that he was capable of standing under an arcade in a downpour and thinking.

Detective Harrelson ran out of patience—or interest. "We also asked your wife when you got home, but she said she was asleep."

"That's right. The house was dark. She and Cookie get an early start most mornings."

"So there's no one to confirm your arrival," Paatelainen said, her motherly expression shading delicately toward regret and disapproval.

"No," said Lars, aware now that they were suspicious of him. It seemed inconceivable, but they were suspicious. His innocence was not, as he had liked to think, self-evident. The two blasé detectives in front of him were trying to decide whether he was a man who could butcher a gifted student and leave her to bleed to death in the rain, the rain that made determining the time of death difficult, the rain and cold that made it hard to know where the danger lay, early or late? When was Iris stabbed? When did she die? Lars hoped it was around nine o'clock when he was safe in the library, his comings and goings monitored by the shrubbery aficionado on the desk.

"Switch on your computer when you got home by any chance?" Harrelson wanted to know.

Lars shook his head, though he remembered the phone call. There would be a record. A record from his house. The trouble was, the call was to Iris. Although they'd find out sooner or later, Lars could not bring himself to mention the call, to begin the explanations, tedious, insincere, irrelevant, for when all was said and done they'd find that Iris had walked away safe and sound. "I went right to bed."

"Too bad. It would have given us a time," said the detective, standing up.

"One doesn't often think about recording time and place."

"No," said Harrelson, as if this was further evidence of humanity's failings. "It makes a good deal of work for us. We'll keep in touch, Dr. Larson."

7.

*L*ars had never been superstitious. Fears of black cats or the num-ber thirteen or ladders across his path were all Stone Age beads and rattles stuff as far as he was concerned. He'd even missed the little rituals of academic life, being without a special pen, a particular brand of notebook, or even a lucky suit for important interviews and lectures. But Lars was superstitious about Iris's diary. The intelligent alternatives were to turn it in to the police or to destroy it. Lars did neither, though he thought obsessively about both. He stopped by the office supply store and examined shredders, imagining the bril-liant purple and green lines of ink turned to papery spaghetti. And then the remnants? Perhaps Iris's solution—and wouldn't that be appropriate—a quick fire in the barbecue pit, a quick fire that would take the pasteboard covers, too, and leave him free, out of the loop, burdened only by knowledge that he would strive to forget. *Can you afford to be without one?* asked the carton containing the shredder. *Privacy and security for one low price!* Lars was tempted. But as soon as he imagined the purchase of the shredder, his mind threw up cautions and difficulties. He heard Emma innocently telling Detec-tives Paatelainen and Harrelson, *Yes, that's our shredder. Lars bought it just a little while ago. No, I don't think we use it very often.* Or he saw a wind catching the shredded fragments of the diary and blowing them around the park, or worse, Detectives Paatelainen and Harrel-son arriving, by chance or by design, just as he lit the match.

Well, be prudent and sensible, burn it in the yard. But that conjured nosy neighbors, floating ash, unburned pages. In truth, Lars was convinced that the diary was indestructible, a cellulose telltale heart, and trying to eliminate it would only make matters worse.

But the other alternative, turning the book over to the police, depressed him profoundly. He'd waited too long. A day or two—yes, a day or two might have been all right. "I had a lot of papers in the car, blue books and folders of final essays. I didn't notice the diary immediately." Feeble, weak. "She put the folders on the floor when I gave her a lift. I must have picked them up and put them on top of the notebook. When I saw it, I brought it right in," etc., etc. Yes, very good, even public spirited, and the police, who were desperate for leads, evidence, clues, would be grateful. Momentarily. But after that gratitude would come the questions. *When did you see Iris Weed? Where did you drive her? Where exactly did you let her out of the car? What time was that precisely? Neighbors said they heard a man and a woman arguing around 7:30 that night. Could that have been you and Ms. Weed?* And then the biggest question of all, the one he'd avoided and finessed but that he could not evade if they had the diaries: *What exactly was your relationship with the deceased, with Ms. Weed, with Iris of the Golden Wings?*

Faced with this question and with an uncertain time of death and an uncertain time for the attack, all times confused by the big-eared busybodies who'd heard him arguing and pleading with Iris, what good answer could he make? "It's not the way it seems." How's that? An answer beneath contempt! Starting badly with an indefinite pronoun, introducing a second without a clear reference, and compounding those vices with that weak verb, *seems.* Oh, how he would go to town on that answer from some hapless student!

Another try, please, Professor, another try for the lounge suite, for the grand prize, for a clear conscience and an unblemished reputation. "I put a serious move on her and was rejected." Like that any better? A little slangy but suitable for the older man trying to sound young, hip, successful. And what would be the result of such candor? Humiliation and suspicion. *The most likely killer of young women is a lover or would-be lover,* according to the voluptuous, rosy-cheeked Paatelainen. No, no, not a line of thought to be pursued.

"She misunderstood me. Ms. Weed, I mean. I have a certain reputation." Nudge, nudge, wink, wink. Worse and worse: frivolous,
tasteless, altogether a disgusting display of callow self-centeredness.

So, back to the top, return to first alternative: invest in a shredder
and destroy the damn thing. Repeat all the reasons against, then
accept a stalemate. The diary remained on his bookshelf, perhaps
the worst solution of all, but Lars had become superstitious: So long
as the notebook remained there, so long as he avoided a decision,
nothing bad would happen. And as if the notebook were a sacred
object or a dangerous, capricious animal, Lars developed little rituals
about it. He read it often and surreptitiously, dipping into one entry
at a time. In this way, quite unintentionally and unsystematically,
he formed a picture of the Rival, who was sardonic, literate, even
erudite, but also insecure, adolescent, emotionally, and possibly
physically, violent.

But then, so was Iris. What did she love—or at least like—about
the Rival? What had put him ahead of Lars, who was so much more
lovable? She'd wanted the Rival's ferocity, his lack of balance and
sophistication, the very things Lars could so sweetly have offered
her, because unbalanced passion allowed her to forget her great grief.
She had been in mourning, and no one had known. Lars thought
how wise the Victorians had been with their black dresses and
mourning bands and crepe around their hats. A Victorian professor
would have understood Iris's state at a glance, while Lars had been
deceived by her Farmer Browns and blue nail polish.

But even knowledge might not have mattered, because the Rival
had helped her in a way that Lars could not. Had not. Had not tried,
he realized with a pang. She had been deeply upset the night she
died. Why had she been on campus without a coat, waiting and
watching in the arcade? Why was she sad? He had not asked, had
not, at the moment, cared. And yet, had he cared, had he gone
beyond his own imperative, momentary desire, she would probably
be alive and he'd be safe.

This sort of thinking drove Lars to shut the diary, feeling depressed and guilty, and made him vulnerable to the detectives, who
returned again and again, haunting his office and the corridor outside

his summer school class in an ironic echo of his pursuit of Iris.

Of course, they had her cell phone, and so his last call to her. Literary inspiration took care of that. How confidently he'd fielded Detective Paatelainen's query. "Just a thought for her conclusion. Something that had come to me, a last-minute idea."

"You sounded anxious, concerned," suggested Paatelainen.

"Graduation, farewells," said Lars. "Parting." He caught himself before he finished the quote. It would not do to lead the detective, who seemed subtle and quick, to *Romeo and Juliet.* "I was concerned about her future. She seemed uncertain about what she would do next. Her father's death had unsettled her a good deal."

"Yes," said Paatelainen, "that was my impression as well. She perhaps looked to you for counsel?"

"I think that is fair to say." This truth brought a heavy note to Lars's voice.

"She called you quite often." A pause. In the corridor, students passed, summery in their bermuda shorts and tank tops, their sandals and sneakers, talking and laughing, oblivious to his drama. At least, he hoped so. The detective's car was unmarked but becoming familiar.

"Yes," Lars agreed. "Quite often."

"But always in the evening. And sometimes quite late. That must have represented an inconvenience."

Lars, traitorous, nodded.

"But then perhaps you called her, too." Detective Paatelainen waited confidently. Like a good instructor, she had a long wait time. Longer than mine, Lars thought. He sometimes grew impatient with students, gave clues, hints, tried another pupil. Detective Paatelainen was relentless. Besides, Lars realized, she was not dependent on his answer. She could obtain his telephone records, if she had not done so already.

"Inspiration is capricious."

"So you've mentioned," the detective said. "Would you care to say anything more about the calls you made to Iris Weed?"

"What's there to say? We discussed her manuscript. She worked a lot of hours. Evening was sometimes convenient." And though

Paatelainen waited long enough to arouse Lars's admiration, he told her nothing more, which was probably why he was mentioned a week later in one of the by now regular and routine stories on the case as having received a great many late-night phone calls from Iris Weed.

"Goddamn it!" Lars shouted when he saw the story. "Goddamn it to hell and that damn detective with it." He injudiciously called the paper where he argued with some sensationalist hack over the meaning of truth and the legitimate range of opinion and implication, coming off, Lars admitted to himself later, like a pedant. This realization did not prevent him from calling Paatelainen, who listened within a vast silence before asking whether he wished to discuss the calls further.

"You leaked that information to the press," Lars protested. "There was no reason for you to do that except to embarrass me."

"How can literary advice embarrass you?" she asked.

"The story does not discuss literary advice," Lars protested. "It implies, strongly and inaccurately implies, some sort of inappropriate contact."

"I did not write the story," Paatelainen said, cool as some frozen treat. "Though the press can sometimes be helpful, in compensation for all the times when they are unhelpful."

"You've been feeding them information! And why me? Why haven't you turned up Iris's boyfriend? That Sven kid. He's the one you should throw to the tender mercies of the press."

"You seem to be the only person who ever heard of Sven," Paatelainen said. "Why do you suppose that is, Professor Larson?"

When Lars protested and blustered, Paatelainen said, "If *you'd* like to be helpful, Professor Larson, I'd be very glad to talk to you at any time. Otherwise, you'll appreciate that a murder investigation takes up a lot of my time."

Miserable, cold-hearted bitch! Lars hung up. It was extortion, that's what it was: terribly polite and official and hard to prove extortion. *Give us everything you know and you can be kept out of the papers. Maintain a shred of privacy and dignity and we'll get you in the press.* That was it. "I didn't expect that," he told Emma, when he called her at school. "Just so you know. So you're not taken by surprise. Some damned imaginative reporter."

On the other end Emma displayed a pretty good wait time of her own. "We'll talk later," she said. "The office is a madhouse today."

"Don't worry," Lars said. "It's a desperation ploy. I'm the only one who knew the girl at all."

"We'd be desperate, too," said Emma and hung up, leaving Lars feeling rebuked. Well, it was easier to take the high ground if you weren't being hounded and examined and made to look dubious. But the story *was* a desperation ploy, which must mean that the police really knew nothing. Not even the awkward facts of his relationship to Iris. He had only to keep that in mind, that and his essential innocence.

Lars threw out his half-cold breakfast coffee, made himself a fresh pot, and corrected the essays—rambling, incoherent, ill-researched, virtually unconscious—from his British Novel course, before heading off to lecture on Graham Greene's division between his literary works and his "entertainments." Lars discussed both via *The Quiet American,* which he considered superb as both genre entertainment and as literature.

The curse of good intentions, cynical realism, Catholic spirituality, and rampant sensuality: Greene offered so many possibilities. Although Lars was, in general, more sympathetic to the nineteenth-century novelists, he was very fond of Greene, who wrote somewhat outside of the expected categories. "A man of the world," Lars concluded, "a man of two worlds, the spirit and the flesh." He looked up expectantly, a man of two worlds himself, the intellect and the senses, but there were no questions, none of the usual comments, not even the expected little joke from G. Davis in the third row who liked to display his literary feathers for P. Gottshalk, the pretty red-head who sat next to him.

"No questions?" Lars asked.

Silence. They seemed not exactly restless but uneasy, uncertain, like freshmen at their first class. Of course, Lars thought bitterly, they aren't used to Professor as the Man in the Paper, Professor as Subject of Police Interest, Professor as Murder Suspect. Yes, he could see there were problems with etiquette and decorum under those circumstances. "I have your essays," he said. "Come up as I call your names."

They came forward quickly and did not stay to chat about the section or the character they'd enjoyed, a film version they'd seen, a book with similar theme. Professor Larson, He Who Is Suspected, handed out the last of the papers, snapped his briefcase shut, and walked briskly down the hall. The hell with them; they could make do with last year's notes for Lawrence Durrell. He was going home.

As Lars passed the departmental office, the chairman stepped out and waved to him. They exchanged the usual comments about hot weather and its effect (always negative) on students, about the dean's latest response (always moronic) to their staffing requests, and the most recent developments (always appalling) in the parking wars. Lars had just shifted his briefcase from one hand to the other, a signal that he was ready to leave, when the chair asked him to be on the Freshmen Experience Committee, that grave of time, digestion, and reputation, since his fall independent study projects had canceled.

"Canceled?" Lars asked, surprised and somewhat disconcerted. Independent study programs with Professor Larson were among the most sought after opportunities in the department. He could take only two students a semester and there was always a waiting list.

"Change in plans," the chair said uncomfortably, for he was sensitive to the awkwardness of the whole issue and to broaching the committee assignment so soon. Paul Andrews was thin, good-natured, red-faced, and beaky, a diplomatic man without strong ambitions or visionary programs. The various department politicos had supported him as a compromise candidate, and he was a nice enough guy. Lars thought of him as a welterweight, competent and intelligent but without the intellectual thrust or political ballast to make the top division.

"Have May call Judy Delgado and Tim Poirir, they were next on the waiting list—May has their names," Lars said airily. He had no intention of touching the Freshmen Experience—endless wrangling over the properly inclusive freshman book, battles to the death with the teaching assistants' organization, multivolume memos from Lydia, the committee chair, who saw freshman comp as her power base. Professor Larson had more sense, thank you very much.

"Lars," said Paul quietly, "it might be better not to have any independent projects this fall. Spring semester, when everything has settled down and all this is behind us, I'm sure there will be no problem."

"What the hell's the problem now?" Lars demanded, furious, the more so because he knew exactly what the chair was trying to say: Students and/or their parents do not trust Professor Larson at the moment.

"Come into my office, Lars," Paul said, and he shut the door once they were inside. "Look, this has been hard for us all."

"I don't see that it has been hard for *us*. It's been hard for *me*. What I see is the fact I taught Iris Weed for two semesters has made me a pariah. What I see is that people who have known me for years—as long as I've been here—are spreading God knows what sorts of stories. People who know me, Paul, are whispering. Nothing to my face, but behind my back. I can tell. It's even affecting my students. Just subtly. You know. No problems, but a subtle, negative atmosphere."

Paul sighed. They both knew the department's insatiable appetite for gossip. "Well, Lars, there are questions. The police have been here, what? Weekly, biweekly?"

"They've spoken to a lot of the staff and to everyone who ever taught Iris," Lars said somewhat disingenuously. "Everyone."

Paul shrugged. They both knew that the other interviews had been routine; Lars alone had gotten real attention.

"It's the manuscript, of course. They want to be sure there are no earlier drafts. They want the names of her friends, her acquaintances. They find it hard to believe a writer might alter names. Might think of libel. Might exercise invention. Harrelson would stop your car on suspicion of imagination. He'd have you up against the wall for a simile, never mind a metaphor," Lars said. "They're literal-minded philistines, Paul, your worst nightmare."

"I'm sure they are," Paul said, "but so are some of our parents.

Your name was in the paper again this morning. You seem to have made a great many phone calls to her."

"Of course I made phone calls to her! What is this? Paul! I was directing her independent study. If I hadn't made phone calls to her, I'd have been accused of neglecting my professional duties."

"At night and to her cell phone," Paul continued. The dean had noticed that information, too, and there had been a call from the chancellor first thing in the morning. While Lars amused himself with funny stories about the detectives, he, the unlucky chair, had to handle the police and pacify various university potentates. *One of our very best professors. Absolutely a favorite with the students and solid, very solid on the nineteenth century. His articles on the Brontës are cited everywhere, etc., etc.*

"Goddamn it, she was living in a truck. The phone company doesn't run fucking lines to Chevys!"

"And she called you," Paul continued, relentless. He was fed up with Lars, with his star professor airs and graces, with his sometimes biting humor, with his capacious ego, with his famous wit and charm, with his amorous habits: It was time Lars grew up and stayed away from students.

Lars took a breath; nothing would be gained by flying off the handle and alienating Paul. "Yes, she called me. She had troubles, griefs. We've all got them. This has been tough," he said with a rueful expression Paul found familiar. "I don't know if you can rightly imagine."

Paul laid his hand on Lars's shoulder. Either his old colleague was a complete sociopath or he was still the same charming, feckless, amusing man he'd always been. Whatever Paul had wondered and feared, he found it could not survive Lars's presence. "How's Emma holding up?" he asked, conciliatory.

"You know Emma. You'd never know she had a worry in the world, but of course . . ." Lars found he didn't have words for the hard, dark layer of anxiety he sensed in Emma or for her conviction (entirely correct) that he was concealing something. "I just wish they would wrap this up. It's been nearly three weeks."

"I suppose we were naive. We've lived sheltered lives, haven't we? I figured with the graduation parties, with so many people in the neighborhood, it was just a matter of days. I just keep thinking the uncertainty must be hell for her family."

"I don't even want to think about that," said Lars. "Not with a daughter myself."

"There are too many questions," Paul continued. "How did she get across town? Was she on campus? Why didn't she take her truck? There's nothing solid to get hold of, that's the problem. We need some resolution."

"Ambiguity is not confined to literature," Lars said sententiously, for he did not want to talk about clues, times, and witnesses. He had nothing to do with Iris's death, so what difference could it possibly make if he said, *I know where she was at seven, at seven-thirty. I let her off beside the pocket park on Jordan Avenue. That was us, the neighbors heard us arguing, not Iris and her killer. She was alive after seven-thirty, so your times aren't quite right.* How much help would that really be? And how much it would hurt him!

"Art reflects our times," Paul agreed, almost as thankful as Lars to finish the subject they could not seem to leave alone. "Think about the Freshman Experience Committee. If not there, we could use you on Tenure and Promotion."

A major threat: Tenure and Promotion could eat up even more time than the dreaded Freshman Experience. "I'll think it over," Lars said, but he had already decided that he would look at the waiting list for independent study projects, talk to May, maybe wait and see one or two students after school started. He said good-bye to Paul and strode down the hall, his head up, a bounce in his step: let them see his indifference, his innocence. There was no reason for him to feel this uneasiness—no, that wasn't the right word—heaviness, maybe? Deflation? Insecurity? Lars remembered that as a young teacher, he would occasionally feel a colossal unreadiness, a sense that he lacked the mental energy to buoy up a class, get it afloat, put the wind in its intellectual sails: an awkward mixture of metaphors that nonetheless accurately captured Lars's feeling of depletion and incapacity. That same sensation threatened him as he walked down the corridor, across the hot, sunny quad, and unlocked his stifling car.

If he talked to the police, would it help? Would it help *him?* He noticed the soccer balls, Cookie's shin guards, towels he'd forgotten to bring in for washing, and shook his head. An innocent man deserves some privacy.

Lars was home in time for a late lunch, and he was having a ham sandwich with potato chips and a cup of coffee when the phone rang: Dr. Dorwin, principal of Grasso Elementary, wanted to know if either Professor or Mrs. Larson could come over to school immediately.

"What's happened?" Lars asked, his mind flooded with images of violent falls and allergic reactions, of nosebleeds and intestinal flu. "Has Cookie been hurt? What's happened?"

"No, no, Cookie's all right, but she might have been hurt and other children, too. Anytime we find students playing with matches, we contact the parents."

"Matches? Cookie's never shown the slightest inclination—we don't even smoke," Lars protested. He had a vivid image of her crinkling up her nose at old Professor Butchvarov's house and whispering, "It smells like an ashtray."

"She wasn't smoking, Professor Larson, she set a fire. But I'd prefer to discuss the situation in person. I don't like to handle any serious matter by telephone."

"Quite right," said Lars. *Serious situation, Cookie, fire, might have been hurt.* Amazing how certain words and phrases rob one of speech, of volition.

"Can you stop by," Dr. Dorwin asked, a trifle impatiently, "or should I call Mrs. Larson? I have her work phone."

"No, no, I'll handle this," said Lars, who recovered himself when faced with the prospect of the principal's calling Emma. Though Emma would be better than he on the surface, calmly patient and understanding, she'd be worse underneath. The call would terrify her and she would blame him, Lars knew she would. "I'll come; I'm finished for the day. I'll come right away."

He threw the rest of the sandwich in the trash. Dumped the coffee in the sink. Grabbed his car keys, then went back for his jacket. He suddenly felt that he would need his professional armor.

On the way to the school, Lars met every light on red and found every geezer on wheels ahead of him, dawdling along as if there was all the time in the world, as if speed weren't of the essence, as if his, Lars's, errand, out of all the errands that afternoon, weren't paramount. He began sweating in his jacket, which had been stupid to wear. What did he need a jacket for to visit the elementary and Dr. Dorwin, whose degree was in elementary education?

Then he remembered that she held the fate of his child in her hands and whipped onto Main without checking the traffic: a horn behind him and an angry shout, trifles in the anxiety, no doubt completely irrational and unnecessary, that gripped him. There had been some mistake; Dorwin had never struck him as particularly intelligent despite the school's high reputation; he'd get everything sorted out. Cookie would have an explanation, he knew she would, and yet, with a mixture of fear, shame, guilt, and anger, Lars also knew she might not. The limits of knowledge, the impossibility of certainty, truth as construct: were not these his stock-in-trade? Who knows another? Had he not noticed that Cookie was growing up, becoming opaque, mysterious, separate? And what was developing within his darling child, what would emerge from the chrysalis? He didn't know, he couldn't imagine, and then, in the next instant, turning right just as the oncoming traffic pulled away from the light, he was sure of Cookie's essential innocence, and love set his heart pounding. Between devotion and suspicion, Lars was in a state by the time he reached the visitors' parking in front of Grasso Elementary. He hurried through the main door to the wide, sunny front hall where a noisy art class was painting a mural in mud browns and bold primary colors. Lars smelled the paint, warm childish flesh, some mysterious, pseudo-Italian lunch.

"Jason Larson," he told the secretary. "Dr. Dorwin called me."

The secretary went to her intercom and relayed his name with excruciating slowness, with unnecessary speed: Lars felt both rushed and delayed. "If you'd come this way, please."

Dr. Dorwin was a short, stout presence in the hall outside her office. Lars took in the thick glasses, thinning, permed hair, assertive lipstick. "Dr. Larson," she said and shook his hand.

"Where's Cookie?" he asked.

"She's in my outer office, but I wanted to speak to you for a minute first. She's rather upset." Dr. Dorwin led the way to her private office, where she sat down behind a large mahogany desk bordered with family and school pictures and gestured toward a black leather chair.

"Please tell me what happened," Lars said.

Dr. Dorwin took a noisy breath, punctuation for a difficult speech. "One of our custodians smelled smoke this morning. When he opened the girls' room near the auditorium, he found smoke coming from a lavatory wastebasket, and Cookie standing beside it, watching the flames. Hector put out the fire and brought her down to the office. He acted very promptly and correctly," Dr. Dorwin said, as if Lars might dispute this.

"Do we know she started the fire?"

"Cookie admitted it right away. She's a very open, candid child."

"A silly thing for her to do," Lars admitted, but he was secretly relieved. A lighted match, a moment of curiosity and carelessness. He'd speak to her very sharply.

"I should tell you that this may not be the first time," Dr. Dorwin said. "There was a small wastebasket fire in one of the empty classrooms last week and another outside near the playground."

Lars absorbed this into the vast hollow that opened beneath his diaphragm. "And you think Cookie was responsible?"

"These incidents have all been within the last three weeks," Dr. Dorwin said carefully.

"Have you asked her directly?" Lars was skeptical.

Dr. Dorwin nodded. "Most juvenile fire starting is a symptom of distress and turmoil. Often of deep-seated problems, but in Cookie's case, I think a reaction to"—here Dr. Dorwin paused delicately, to let his guilt sink in, Lars thought—"recent events."

"We've all been a good deal upset by the case at the college," Lars said, brisk, calm: *this has nothing to do with me*. Nonetheless, he found himself unable to pronounce either *murder or homicide*. "Iris Weed was one of my students."

"Yes," said Dr. Dorwin. "I do read the papers."

"There are more newspaper readers than one's led to believe," Lars said, irritated by her tone. "We have tried to keep as much as possible from Cookie, but it's difficult. I'm one of the few staff people who knew Iris well, and so there have been police questions to answer on top of everything else."

"There were fragments of the morning paper in the waste bin," Dr. Dorwin said. "You'll perhaps keep that in mind when you speak to her."

Oh, he would, he would. Poor Cookie with stories in the paper, with the breathless smarm of the TV commentators, with the jovial sensationalists that dominated the radio. And children can be cruel, are cruel, enjoy cruelty. Elementary schools are dens of vice and iniquity where cruelty is concerned. Lars had known all that, remembered all that, which was why he had said nothing, why he'd made the decision he had, why he had to be strong and keep his mouth shut a little longer. He'd been right, Lars knew he had.

"At the same time, she must understand this behavior is unacceptable. I've spoken to Cookie about safety in the strongest terms, and I think she understands. She is normally quite a responsible little girl."

"Yes," said Lars, full of relief and gratitude despite Dorwin's overbearing, know-it-all attitude: this woman was merciful. Liked Cookie. Saw his splendid child clearly.

"At the same time, I have no choice but to suspend her," Dr. Dorwin continued. "School regulations are quite clear in these cases.

"I didn't know elementary students could be suspended," Lars said. Was this legal? Had he a legitimate complaint?

"For up to three days," Dorwin said. "In Cookie's case, I think one day will be sufficient. But if there is any repetition, she will be suspended for the full time. I also am recommending she see our school psychologist, Dr. D'Ambrosia. She's often helpful in these cases. Talk is therapeutic."

"I would like to leave that up to Cookie," Lars said. He hated the intrusion, the medicalization, the professionalization of grief and trouble. Cookie had good reason to be upset. Good reason. "Now I'd like to talk to her."

Dr. Dorwin got up and opened the outer door, "Cookie, your father is here."

She was sitting on a bench—the penitential bench, Lars supposed—in the outer office, slumped against the wall, her feet dangling, her face tearstained and belligerent under her tangled bangs. When she saw him, she did not jump up, as she usually did, but ducked her head and caught her lower lip in her teeth as if she wanted to avoid his eye. What had they done to her? What had happened? "Cookie, Cookie, it's all right," he said. "We're going home now."

She slid down off the bench, still not looking at him, but when he put his arm around her, she embraced him so fiercely he caught his breath. She felt warm, her arms and hair moist, and she was shaking with sobs. "It's going to be all right, darling." He put his head against hers and made soothing noises, the way he used to when she woke from nightmares as a small child.

"We'll start fresh Monday morning," Dr. Dorwin said, but it wouldn't be her who'd have to start anew, but Cookie. The woman was an imbecile.

"We'll keep in touch," said Lars. He took out his handkerchief and wiped Cookie's face. "Chin up," he said and heard an echo of his own father. That's what Dad used to say when things went wrong: "Chin up. It's not the end of the world."

Cookie rubbed her nose. "I'm sorry," she said in a small voice.

"We all make mistakes," said Dr. Dorwin. "Thankfully, you weren't hurt and neither was anyone else." She nodded crisply and turned toward her inner office, dismissing them.

"Let's go home," said Lars, but Cookie hesitated at the door, and he knew she was thinking of the corridor, of curious faces, of the art class busy in the lobby. He brushed her hair back from her face, wiped her face. "Take my arm," he said. "Like a grown-up."

He got a sideways glance.

"Professor and Ms. Cookie Larson depart Grasso Elementary."

She put her hand on his arm.

"Good girl." Lars opened the door and walked out, head up, brisk, innocent, superior to fortune. With Cookie's small hand clenched on his forearm, they advanced down the main hallway, past the mural—an aquatic scene of fish, starfish, crabs, lobsters, and dolphins against a murky navy blue; past youthful voices, the directions of their art instructor, waving her paint-spattered hands; past the display cases, out the double set of doors, and over to their car: deliverance. And awkwardness. As Lars unlocked the side door for Cookie, he realized he had no idea what to say to her. His whole focus had been on getting out of school, away from Dorwin and official displeasure. Now he needed inspiration and some parental wisdom. "Roll down your window," he said, because she was sitting motionless in the stifling car. "We need some air."

Cookie turned the handle.

"You're to stay home Friday," Lars said after a few blocks. "Did Dr. Dorwin tell you?"

Silence. Lars glanced at her, and she nodded her head.

"Lighting fires in a school is very dangerous. That's why. You understand."

Another nod.

"You won't do that again. Promise me."

Another nod, then, "Yes. Promise."

"Maybe you'll want to talk about this later? You can always talk to me," Lars said. "You know that." Cookie's silence suggested that she knew this was false, that she recognized him as part of the problem. "Cookie?"

"What will we tell Mom?" she asked in a soft voice.

"We'll tell her the truth: You made a mistake and you're sorry. End of story." Was that too abrupt? To be honest, he did not want to know a great deal more. He did not want to hear that his troubles had infected her life, had frightened and upset her and attracted cruel remarks. "Things will be all right. You can't worry too much about what people say—or even what they write—about you."

"What's in the papers is true, or it wouldn't be printed," Cookie said, with a definite, almost Dorwinish tone in her voice.

So much for critical thinking in the elementary schools! "Well, not always," Lars said. "Everybody makes mistakes." A quick glance showed her face set, stubborn. "The morning paper runs corrections," he said, inspired. "Every day, they run a set of corrections. Every paper does. Those are just the mistakes they've caught and admitted to."

Lars felt Cookie's eyes on him.

"Haven't you seen that box on the second page?"

"No."

"We'll look when we get home. All right?" Lars asked, his voice cheerful. He could do this, raise the clouds and divert her from troubles at school and his own putative sins. "And lunch. Have you had lunch?"

Another negative.

"You'll have a late lunch. So late it might have to be called *dunch,* which is—?"

"Dinner and lunch." Prompt and with a little of her usual spirit. "Or could we call it *linner*?"

"*Linner* sounds nicer."

"*Dunch* sounds like what you get in the cafeteria," Cookie said. "Wouldn't you like some lovely *dunch* today?"

"Is it chocolate-covered and delicious?"

"No, it's not." Confident and bossy. "It's full of soy and vegetables and very good for you!"

Lars smiled and Cookie did, too.

"It will be all right," he said when they got out of the car. "There's no need for you to worry"—he couldn't quite say, "about me"—"and that's the truth. I promise."

She looked at him across the car, serious again, and for a moment, Lars thought she might ask him outright. Then she said, "They'll have to correct whatever they've written wrong."

"Yes," said Lars, with more confidence than he really felt in the fourth estate.

"Every word," she said.

Words on a page, the printed artifact, were still magic to her, Lars saw. "Yes."

She nodded and brightened. "Let's have some dunch!"

Dinner, like dunch, was late that night. Lars had planned to brief Emma when she got home from school, had wanted to set things up and control the process, but he was forestalled by his impulsive daughter who ran downstairs as soon as she heard her mother's car. Lars looked out the hall window and saw them, Cookie leaning her head against Emma's shoulder, Emma's face tight for a moment, then calm. Her voice was low in the hall, asking, Lars recalled, the sensible, practical things like where had Cookie found the matches and how it was that she was wandering about school in the morning, anyway. Emma later called and discussed these points with Dr. Dorwin and Cookie's homeroom teacher, catching one at school and calling the other at home. Lars sulked upstairs, relieved yet feeling that he should have thought of this strategy; he should have demanded conferences and corroboration. He should have talked more to Cookie. Instead, guilt, by and large unmerited guilt, had made him stupidly alarmed at first, then overly indulgent and whimsical— not properly parental at all. As a result, Lars was grumpy at dinner, and, afterward, when Emma raised the question of Friday, he felt inclined to err on the side of severity.

"Ask Betty if she can stop by," he said.

"I don't need a sitter," Cookie cried. "Please, I don't need a sitter. I'll be okay. I'll do my homework."

She was humiliated by being kept home, by having her friend's mom know, by this tremendous loss of face that could be compensated for only by some major show of trust and independence. Lars saw that, but just the same, he said, "It's not safe for you to be home alone all morning." God knows that might be true the way things were. Besides, he felt a little hurt that she had confided in Emma when with him she'd been silent.

"Please," said Cookie, flushing, her eyes shiny with unshed tears. "Please."

Emma told her to go upstairs, and after a few more appeals, she did, clutching Polly to her shoulder. Jake rattled up the stairs after her. The animals of the household were always in her corner.

Lars and Emma stayed at the kitchen table, silently watching the pink evening sky fade behind the neighbor's trees. In another week public school would be finished and the first session of summer school, too. He'd be off until fall and Emma would be able to take some days. Lars had been looking forward to the vacation, but now, testing the awkward silence that seemed to be spreading in from the shadowed yard, he found himself thinking about a summer project, library work, even a research trip somewhere.

"I don't feel I should cancel my lecture," he said, feeling defensive and subtly in the wrong. "I've been trying to avoid any break in the routine. The students, not to mention the staff, notice everything."

Emma played with her coffee cup. "This is a busy time at school for me, too. But if Cookie has a sitter, she's only going to feel worse."

"In light of what happened, it won't hurt her to feel bad for a while," Lars said, although when he'd seen Cookie sitting in Dr. Dorwin's office, he'd have shed his blood to make things better. At the same time, he was irritated, exasperated, frightened for her and a little bit for himself. Cookie's trouble lent reality to a whole range of events that he'd been working to keep unsubstantial.

Emma's impassive expression did not change, but Lars sensed her anger.

"It was a damn dangerous thing for her to do. Not that I blame her if she was burning the paper—pure rubbish—but dangerous enough so she better feel bad. And," he added, conciliatory, "she has taken it to heart, I know she has."

"They want her to speak to the school psychologist," Emma said. "They think Dr. D'Ambrosia might be able to help."

"I don't think we should make too much of this," he said, his fears retreating a little before his habitual optimism. "Too much is as bad as too little. She's hardly given us a moment's anxiety till now.

Which is why I don't see why we can't get someone in for tomorrow morning."

But Emma, usually so anxious about physical safety was now focused on Cookie's feelings. "I don't want to put any more pressure on her, and I think having her talk to Dr. D'Ambrosia might be a good idea."

They argued about that the way they argued about most things: Lars provided intelligent arguments and cogent reasons while Emma mulishly repeated what she wanted until Lars agreed she should call the counselor.

"I still don't know if I want her home alone," he said. Normally he would have gotten a concession in turn, but an underlying aware-ness that this mess was somehow his doing left him without lever-age. Emma stressed Cookie's humiliation and repentance, and Lars, so often indulgent, capitulated: if he left just in time for his lecture and came home immediately afterward, Cookie would be alone for barely two hours.

"I think that's reasonable for a child her age," Emma said, but her face was uncertain, her voice, touched with anxiety, and, as so often, she looked to him for reassurance.

"She'll have Jake and Polly for company." Lars felt that their positions had reversed again. "I'll call her from school. She'll cheer up, you'll see," he said, exerting himself to be reassuring.

"She adores you," said Emma. "She thought you could do no wrong."

Lars was wounded by the past tense as much as by that mon-strous burden of expectation. "Reputation is at the mercy of the media."

They had not switched on the overhead light, and the room had darkened perceptibly. Perhaps that is why she spoke now when she hadn't questioned him, not once, unless you count her inquiring if he'd known Iris well. "Totally at the mercy of the media?" Emma asked.

Lars felt a sickening opening somewhere under his heart. He had made no declaration, no appeal, had, in fact, operated as if his innocence was axiomatic. He had been grateful for her silence, which he took for confidence and which, he thought, might have continued but for Cookie's trouble.

"What can I say to that, Emma? Please don't think I hurt poor Iris."

She shook her head. "You are too kind," she said simply and matter-of-factly. Maybe a little coolly, too.

Lars understood he was on dangerous ground. Still, she was a blessed woman and he took her hand. "Well then?"

"What was your relationship to her? This time I need to know, Lars."

This time. As if he had not been the soul of discretion, as if he had not always protected her. *This time.* Well *this time* he'd failed, been rejected, booted out of the game, fortunately, as it turned out, enabling him to say quite honestly, "She was a student. That's it. Nothing else. Despite the phone calls, our relationship really was innocent. Really. God knows, Emma." He pressed her hand to his forehead, tempted, truly tempted, to add, *I wanted it otherwise.* He felt a need to confess to foolish desires and humiliating disappointments. He was tempted to mention the diary as proof and evidence and extenuation. But what good would that do? Presented that way, his innocence might be as bad as guilt and his omissions would show him in a bad light; both would hurt Emma. Not for the first time, Lars wished he could reel back time and relive the fall, the winter, the weeks before school ended, even the night Iris died. Even that! With the most minor of changes, he would be sitting contented with Emma, his life fortunate and happy. "As I tried to explain to Cookie—and probably didn't do very well—I'm on the spot only because the police have nothing else at the moment. People saw me with her around campus. They didn't see her with the boy I believe she was interested in. Or he has an alibi, I don't know. The police have gotten focused on what little they have."

"You know that nothing can ever be the same again if you are"—a pause in which his heart clenched—"involved."

"There is truly no reason for them to suspect me, Emma," he said, although in this matter, his guilt and innocence were irrevocably intertwined.

"She must have had other friends," Emma suggested after a moment. *Friends besides you, that is.* Had he been Iris's friend? Once he would have answered yes without hesitation. Hard to say now.

"Yes, yes, she did. But Iris was rather a solitary person in some ways. A solitary person who could get people to open up." Lars talked about Iris and Emma listened, companionably enough, the way she so often did when he was enthusiastic about something. Yet, even in the half darkness, even in her silence, Lars understood she had reservations. Could he go back? Could he go back and tell her everything? Probably not, he thought, though he could see that the price of silence was a certain cool indifference emanating from Emma. Sitting across the table from her, Lars sensed that she was withdrawing from him, protecting herself emotionally and getting ready to cut her losses.

8.

*L*ars cut fifteen minutes out of his lecture, "Philosophy and Artifice in the Novels of Iris Murdoch" and left the classroom without waiting for questions. He called Cookie from the office, relieved to hear her voice at the second ring, and appointed her chef for the day, a role she usually enjoyed. But when he arrived home twenty minutes later, he found her ruining her hearing with nuclear-strength MTV and the kitchen stinking of burning soup.

"Cookie! Cookie! Turn that down!"

"It's not loud," she shouted back.

Juggling his briefcase, Lars switched off the stove and poured the soup into another pan, rescuing some of it. He put the scorched pot in the sink to run it full of water, then went to the living room, where Cookie was rapt before a boneless young blonde with too much makeup and too little clothing gyrating to a heavy beat. Memory carried Lars irresistibly to Iris's truck, to drums like cement mixers and guitars like buzz saws, and made him more irritable than he needed to be. "I told you to shut that off," he said, and when Cookie didn't hop up as she usually did, he stepped over and flicked the switch himself. "No more TV for the rest of the day. You weren't kept home to trash out on pop videos. Didn't you smell the soup burning?"

"I *had* it on low." Indignant innocence.

"Not low enough. You get in there and scrub the pot. You know you need to watch things on the stove."

"It was only for a *minute*. Britney Spears was on."

Lars wondered if there was some hormonal change that kicked in that nasal whine. "Britney Spears should be in some secure facility," he said. "Come on. You're not leaving that mess for your mom to clean up."

Cookie trailed behind him to the kitchen, where she sloshed water around the pot and announced that she couldn't get it clean.

"Use a scrubber," Lars said.

She found one after an ostentatious search and began rubbing, her hand limp, her arm like rubber. Children are the true masters of passive resistance.

"What did you do today?" Lars asked. His anger dissipated quickly where Cookie was concerned, and besides, he hated glooms and whining and demanded good company in all weather.

Cookie moved her head and shoulders in what, with more energy, might have been called a shrug.

"Did you do your homework?"

"Uh-huh."

"All of it?" A sharp note. "You told your mother you would."

"I said I did." Just on the verge of sass.

"Hey," said Lars, "this wasn't my idea. My idea was that you'd spend a riotous morning with Betty, followed by a gourmet lunch of Betty's own peanut butter and marshmallow sandwiches. That was my idea, if you remember. Instead, you chose the serious, ascetic life of homework and a humble lunch of soup with your dad."

"I don't know what *ascetic* means," Cookie observed. She didn't raise her head, but the question itself was a concession, and Lars could see that she would come around.

"Well, for one thing, it means eating burned soup instead of marshmallow delight, and for another it means doing what you're supposed to do instead of watching trashy videos."

Cookie ignored this and asked, "Do you live an ascetic life?"

Even if she liked alien recreations and was indifferent at school, Cookie was indeed his child: she'd already mastered the subtle, loaded question.

"No, I do not." Lars rarely lied to his daughter, a habit that might eventually prove awkward. "I prefer my soup unburned and I enjoy amusing myself. How's the pot coming?"

She held it out, her lip suddenly trembling, so that Lars saw all her hidden misery.

He put his arm around her. "Listen, listen, it's not the end of the world, is it? That's what my dad used to ask: Is it the end of the world?" He gave her a little shake, and she admitted, "No," reluctantly.

"Right! Remember, we all make mistakes. You, me, Mom, Dr. Dorwin. Everybody." He gave her a serious look. Lars hoped she would remember that if worst came to worst. "Okay? Let's have lunch and go to the park. How would that be?"

Cookie shook her head energetically, a surprising reversal of form.

"You want to stay home? You want poor old dad to have to do papers?"

"I don't want to go today," Cookie said, near tears again.

"What about soccer practice on Saturday?" Lars asked, although he, personally, could miss every soccer practice ever with the most perfect equanimity. "Practice is important. You'll need to do that."

"I'll go Saturday," she said in her smallest voice. "I will."

"Good girl," Lars said, remembering, however dimly, the woes of childhood. "So what's on the docket for today?" He released her and thought for a minute. "What about painting Cumbersome House?"

Cookie had been teasing him about this project for weeks. At the prospect of the long anticipated redecoration, she began skipping around the kitchen, her usual brio instantly restored. "All right!"

"But only if your homework really is done."

"Everything but spelling and you have to give me my words," Cookie said and began setting the table at high speed. She got out the bread, found some cheese, told him a joke, became, in short, the little girl who was such fun, the one who owned his heart. They spent the meal discussing their project, and later, in the garage, they discovered some leftover oil paint in a nice shade of yellow. Cookie wanted to start right away, but knowing how strong the smell would be, Lars said they'd better try to get Cumbersome House down to the back porch first.

That was where Emma found them when she got home, led by the smell of oil paint and turpentine. She'd come home early, worried about Cookie and concerned that Lars, who'd seemed uncharacteristically severe with her, would make matters worse. Emma expected quiet and tension, a certain depression of spirits; instead, general hilarity, conveyed, from the moment she opened the door, by Jake, the household barometer, who met her with barks and jumps, as if desperate for her to witness the joy of the other inhabitants.

"Look at this, Mom!" They had the dollhouse set up in the middle of the porch on an old card table covered with newspapers. Cookie had paint on most of the exposed portions of her anatomy, and Emma was glad to see that Lars had thought to put a hat on her head and to give her one of his old shirts. Beside her, also paint smeared, Lars was beaming the way he did when he'd created some amusement, some pleasure.

I've married a frivolous man, Emma thought. She'd been fooled by his work ethic, his professional seriousness, even his professorship, but he was frivolous at heart. She'd begun to realize that there was no point in expecting seriousness or even maturity from him. Look at the way he'd handled yesterday. She was the one who'd had to straighten the school out. Yet looking at the two of them, so happy with their brushes, with mess and untidiness and yellow paint everywhere, the cat with some on her tail and Jake tracking little yellow pawprints everywhere, Emma had to admit that he had the secret of happiness. She'd talked to Cookie that morning, snatching a minute from her desk at school to hear her daughter's sad and wistful voice. But let her father come home, the source, to be honest, of Cookie's miseries, and there she was, bubbling like champagne, excited by the project, thrilled with her own handiwork. Lars had the knack of making fun out of nothing, even out of work. The evil thought came to Emma that he'd probably made his work with Iris Weed fun, too; she was sure he had, and those phone calls proved it, despite his denials. Was that all he was hiding? She thought so, yes. Yes, seeing him with a smudge of paint on his cheek, seeing his happiness with Cookie, yes, about the rest she believed him and she was half ashamed for her moments of doubt. She did believe him. At least at this moment. "It looks very handsome," Emma said.

"We're to have white trim and a red door and black shutters."

"Maybe shutters," corrected Lars. "If I can make them."

"*Maybe* shutters."

"Nice with or without," said Emma. The dollhouse reminded her pleasantly of her late father-in-law, a good craftsman and a kind, solid man. Lars had gotten his father's kindness and some of his skill without the older man's solidity. Everything about her husband was mercurial and elusive. How well did she know him? Well, she'd have said. And now? What did she think now? She hadn't had a moment's doubt until this latest story in the paper. Not one moment's.

"It should look nice," Lars said. "This is an epic project."

"Heroic," added Cookie, who shared her father's knack for stories though you wouldn't know it by her schoolwork. "Epic and heroic."

"It began," said Lars, projecting his voice to the backyards of the neighborhood, "with the lifting up of Cumbersome House. What voice, what lute can tell of heroic Daddy Lars, who lifted it upon his shoulders, or of intrepid Daughter Cookie, who guided the edifice down the back stairs? How to describe how this heroic duo negotiated the doors, avoiding the dog and frightening the cat?" He continued in this vein: He'd nearly slipped, his back would never be the same—an *honorable wound in a noble cause,* as he phrased it—and they had skirted disaster when the edifice became stuck on the turn at the landing.

"And pulled off a piece!" Cookie exclaimed, lifting a bit of the thick molding from around the base. Emma saw that the trim had been broken in half.

"Don't move the trim, the glue's not set yet," Lars said, interrupting his saga to say that glue had been applied but finishing nails must be acquired. The trim was not original. Did Emma remember when they'd made the repairs?

"There's a sort of little basement underneath now," said Cookie, who was at the age to love secret passages and hiding places, blind drawers and hidden doors: the paraphernalia of juvenile mysteries.

Emma was suitably impressed. Yes, she remembered that the elderly Cumbersome House had had sill trouble.

Lars resumed in his mock-heroic style: The back door almost stymied them—just barely wide enough—while the screen door with its spring had nearly finished the heroic Daddy Lars, who, on his knees from exhaustion, got stuck in the opening when Cumbersome House started to slip out of his hands.

Emma had to laugh, though she was glad she had missed the actual operation which would, she knew, have included a great deal of shouting and probably had left scratches in the paint and wood-work all the way down. Good thing they'd taken the back stairs. But now, unalloyed triumph, and Emma felt a few scrapes were a small price to pay for her daughter's shining face.

On the very last day that Lars had to teach, the police arrived with a search warrant. He thought that they might have waited one more day before descending with their latex gloves and evidence bags and hangmen's faces, but since their aim was to pressure him, Lars supposed there was a certain logic to interrupting his office hour and providing the staff and students with fresh and tasty gossip. This particular visit was led by Detective Harrelson, and Lars was glad. While Detective Paatelainen aroused mixed feelings of fear and ad-miration, Lars felt only detestation for Harrelson. "Blessed are all simple emotions, be they dark or bright!" wrote Nathaniel Haw-thorne. "It is the lurid intermixture of the two that produces the illuminating blaze of the infernal regions." Too right. And too bad Lars wouldn't be able to use his experience as an example for his students, because he now had not just a keen but also a visceral appreciation of that passage.

"How long will this take?" he asked Harrelson. "I have an exam to give in twenty minutes. You might have called me. I could have come in early."

"Depends what we find. We can do the initial work on your car at your house, if you prefer."

"My car?" Lars asked, surprised and not really registering the implications.

Detective Harrelson ponderously produced the search warrant again. "Office, car, house. You have a problem with that?"

"Iris was in my office, she was in my car—I told you I'd given her a lift on occasion. And yes, she came to the house once. To bring me some chapters when I was home with a sprained ankle. I believe I told you all that," Lars said quite calmly, which was surprising, considering that the whole forefront of his mind was occupied with one image: Iris's notebook left stupidly, inexplicably, among his old lecture notes in the bookcase. He had to get home.

Harrelson sighed so audibly that Lars wondered if the detective was afflicted by depression, if the career that had left his colleague Paatelainen cheerful and rosy cheeked had dropped him into some copper's cave of spleen.

"We have to check," said Harrelson. He never quite adjusted to the stupidity of the general population. Here was a man of education and supposed intelligence who absolutely refused to acknowledge that he was suspect numero uno in a homicide. Harrelson waited to see if revelation would strike the professor, then when Lars made no answer, turned back to the file cabinet and began flipping through the folders: recommendations, student papers, exams, essay questions, old blue books—"I remember those," one of the forensic technicians said, and Lars joked, feebly, Harrelson thought, "It's not an exam without them."

Then committee reports, memos, grant proposals, more essays, the professor's own productions this time, plus speeches, presentations: paper, paper, paper. "Couple hours," Harrelson announced.

Lars looked at his watch. "I can't postpone The British Novel final. Really I don't see why you couldn't have come tomorrow or Monday."

"We have schedules, too," said Harrelson in a sniffy way so that Lars had to remind himself he couldn't afford to lose his temper.

"Perhaps I can find a teaching assistant to proctor. The main thing is that Cookie will be home by one o'clock. I need to be home as close to one as I can."

"We break for lunch," Harrelson said.

"At one? Then I can meet you at the house," Lars suggested.

"Where's your car?"

"Right in the Steele lot. You can look at it now," Lars said, and he reached into his pocket for his keys.

"That's all right," said Harrelson, his dark eyes flat, watchful.

This man suspects me of murder, Lars told himself. *He is looking for bloodstains, for fibers or whatever they look for, but especially for bloodstains. He thinks Iris's blood is in my car.* Or maybe not, for now Harrelson seemed in no hurry to check the Volvo.

"We'd like to take the car into the lab," the detective said, "for a thorough inspection. We can give you a ride home."

"I don't want to alarm Cookie with a strange car in the driveway." Harrelson noticed that Lars was quite insistent about that and made sure they weren't finished until just before one. Lars hurriedly locked the office and bolted for the stairs.

"We getting lunch?" the sergeant asked as he and Detective Harrelson left, burdened with their equipment and carrying two of the victim's essay drafts and a blue exam book in a plastic evidence bag.

"You can go out for something once we get there. We don't want him to have any time alone. He didn't care about the office, you notice that? Aside from being the important professor who doesn't want to be inconvenienced, he didn't care about the office. He doesn't care about the car. If there's anything at all, it's at his house."

"His kid's getting home," said the sergeant, who was young and lanky and perpetually hungry. He'd be lucky to see even a sandwich before midafternoon.

"Kid gets home every day," said Harrelson. "What time's school out, anyway?"

"I don't know. Earlier now, though. Last few days are half days, aren't they?"

"I didn't want to know that," said Harrelson. The case was getting him down. All they had was the fact that Professor Larson got phone calls at inappropriate hours. Otherwise zilch. Zip. Nada. He and

Paatelainen chewed it over every other day. Sometimes he liked Larson for the killing, sometimes she did. Next day they would change. Paatelainen would say Larson was their man and he'd disagree. It broke the monotony.

They opened the main door of Steele Hall and threaded their way through puffing clusters of weed addicts, just as the professor's Volvo zipped out of the adjoining lot. He'd wasted no time.

"Give me the bag," Harrelson said, his suspicions confirmed. "You're younger than me. Hustle over to the visitors' lot and come back and pick me up."

Lars saw them in his mirror as he cut behind the building to the Deliveries Only road. He tooted in a friendly way to one of the campus cops and called, "Package at the Coop," and so got waved through, which enabled him to take the access road between the Coop and the old administration building, which brought him out— with at least five minutes saved—on the city streets. *Not too fast,* Lars kept telling himself, *not too fast.* Harrelson and his henchmen had to park in the visitors' lot, and thank God today for university regulations, for the much reviled parking code, for the eagle-eyed lot attendants and heartless parking services minions. Thanks to them, he had a chance. He'd get home and get the diary. Then what? Briefcase? They'd surely check that again. Garbage? First place they'd look. Under a mattress? In Jake's bed? Why hadn't he destroyed the damn thing? What bizarre reluctance had kept the book on his shelves? Maybe leave it? Hide in plain sight? Maybe that was safest. Would Harrelson go through every book? There were several thousand in the house, several hundred in his office. Would they check every one? Would they? Yes, Lars admitted to himself, yes they would. He'd seen them lift every folder, consult every binder. Harrelson had wanted everything about Iris, even last semester's blue book final with the red-ink commentary: "Very interesting on Byron. Literary criticism may be your forte after all." Poor Iris, perhaps she might have made a provocative critic or a popular professor, but he couldn't risk thinking about her now. He had to concentrate, he had to plan.

Lars turned his wrist, glanced at his watch. One-ten. Cookie would be home. She'd be waiting on the porch, or maybe she'd go over to Betty's. Yes, she'd go to Betty's and he'd get up to his office unimpeded and get the diary. Maybe. But she'd been avoiding Betty and some of her other friends, so it was more likely that Cookie would be on the porch and he'd have to explain, reassure her, spend time that should be devoted to hiding the diary. Maybe he'd better just give it to Harrelson. Or maybe let them find it and say he'd forgotten it. He'd left it in plain sight, hadn't he? And didn't that suggest the truth: his fundamental innocence? Didn't it? *Not too fast,* Lars warned himself as he rolled through a stop sign, *Not too fast. But not too slow either. They must be right behind me.*

Usually Lars enjoyed coming home, puttering with lunch, waiting for Cookie, working in his comfortable study, but today he turned onto the handsome tree-lined street with dread: He had no idea of what to do or what to say to Cookie—or to Emma, who must surely be told. And after he'd promised there was nothing. And there wasn't! That was the painful thing. There were half a dozen cases where he must admit he was guilty as charged, but the whole business with Iris had been little more than folly and hope.

He craned his neck, looking down the street, hoping Cookie was at Betty's, and yes, the front porch was empty! Lars left his car in the drive and took the front steps at a bound, setting Jake barking. He fiddled for his key, turned it in the lock, found he'd locked the door, turned the key again, and opened the door. *Careless of Cookie to leave the house unlocked.* Jake bounced onto the porch. *Good, he'd bark when the detectives arrived.* Lars ran upstairs to his office, dropped his briefcase beside the desk, and grabbed the diary. Too big for his pocket, too obvious in his shirt.

"Daddy?" Cookie called from her room, a nervous, reproachful note in her voice. She hated to be home alone.

"Right here, sweetheart." He tucked the diary casually under his arm as she came running down the hall.

"You're late," she said, catching hold of the doorway and swinging nervously back and forth.

"I was delayed at school helping the detectives." *Helping,* what a euphemism, and ill-chosen, Lars realized. Wasn't that the official phrase? So and so wasn't under arrest, he was helping the police with their inquiries. What that really meant was that your office was ripped apart by strangers so that the details of your life could be put up for forensic consumption in sandwich baggies.

"What were they there for?" Her voice was edged with anxiety.

"Just the usual." He tried to sound reassuring, as if that was possible with Iris's diary in hand. "They came to look for Iris's papers. They took fingerprints and sprinkled powder around and put her exam book in an evidence bag just like on a TV show." Lars wanted Cookie to feel that these events were unreal, fictional, the way they so often seemed to him.

Downstairs, Jake, brave and territorial, began barking, and Lars's heart jumped several gears to land in overdrive.

"See if that's a car, Cookie."

She ran to the head of the stairs. "Yes, there's a car. It's a black car. I think it's a police car." She gave Lars a look that mingled alarm and resentment.

"Go get the door. I'll be right down."

Cookie balked at this. "I don't want to open the door."

"I'll be right down."

"I don't want to open the door for the police." She shook her head vigorously.

"I just need a minute. Be a good girl." Cookie shook her head again, then they heard footsteps on the porch and Jake's high-pitched barks. "Hurry up before Jake nips one of them!"

She clattered down to the front hall, and Lars took the back stairs to the little corridor between the kitchen and the pantry where he had a mad thought of destroying the diary in the microwave. How long would it take? What would it smell like? Ashes, of course, there had be ashes! He had an impulse to make a break through the yard, to throw the diary into the shrubbery or under some of Emma's handsome bark mulch. His hands were sweating and his heart jumping and yet, still, there was a kind of unreality. When all was said and done, what had he to fear but embarrassment? He was innocent, and it was only the detectives and the gossip and the suspicion, unmerited and unprovoked, that had cornered him, panicky and undignified, at his own back door. He should turn around and face the detectives; distasteful as that might be, he should talk to Harrelson man to man.

A mumble of voices in the front hall. "Dad!"

Through the glass of the back door, Lars saw Cumbersome House, resplendently painted—with one loose piece of trim. He thought of Emma and Cookie, then he flicked the catch and opened the door and the outer screen.

"Dad!" The high note of the juvenile imperative.

Lars touched the wide molding around the base of the dollhouse; everything felt solid. The other side, it was on the other side. Yes, this was the piece; he could see a faint crack under the primer, but when he tried to lift the molding, he found it stuck with the new paint.

"Dad!"

"Coming," Lars shouted.

He dug his nails into the seam, breaking the paint seal. The trim piece came away, and Lars took the diary out of his pocket and pushed it under the lower floor of Cumbersome House, where it lodged, sticking halfway out. Was there something under the house? A joist he'd forgotten? Cookie's feet sounded in the back hallway. Lars bent the stiff corner of the notebook and jammed it out of sight, scraping his hand.

The door opened behind him as he replaced the piece of trim, his hands shaking. "What are you doing?" Cookie demanded.

Lars turned to see her flushed and suspicious face; she hadn't seen the book. She couldn't have. Lars was sure she couldn't. "I didn't remember the size of the nails," he said. "We need to nail down that last piece of trim."

Cookie's expression of astonishment reminded him a good deal of Emma's; she did not believe him. "There's this detective to see you. He's at the door and there are other people with him. What do they want?" she asked, her voice rising with fear.

Lars put his hand on her shoulder. "I told you. They're looking for any papers Iris might have left. School papers and papers from her project. The project she was doing with me when she died."

"Why didn't you give them all the papers?" An accusatory, unbelieving note, the sound of a rational woman, the sound of Emma.

"I have. I've assured them there is nothing else."

"Didn't they believe you?" Cookie asked. "Didn't they believe you?"

Lars knew that she was asking whether the police had reasons and if she should have doubts. "I suppose they did believe me, but it doesn't matter. They have to check."

"Professor Larson?" A voice from the hall provoked more barking from Jake, followed by the heavy approaching footsteps of authority.

"I'm in back," Lars called. "I'll be right there." To Cookie, he said, "You see, no one's word is enough."

"But even two or three people can lie. Like a newspaper can lie."

Lars nodded. "That's why the detectives are here," he said and turned toward the kitchen and the hallway that led to the foyer. "Come in, come in," he called, friendly and relaxed, a fair impersonation of a host with special guests arriving. "I wanted to explain to Cookie why you were here, why you need to make a search."

"Just our job," Harrelson said heavily.

Cookie stood slightly behind her father, glowering at the police from under her thick, dark bangs.

"I thought I might take Cookie over to our neighbor's house," Lars said, but she protested this at once, and with the uncanny perversity of childhood announced she wanted to put the furniture back in Cumbersome House.

"It's all dry now and I haven't been able to play with it for a week."

"We'll need to take it back upstairs first," Lars said. He tried to give her a warning look. "You don't want to put the furniture back in the dollhouse until it's upstairs, do you?"

"I want to play with it now," said Cookie, her face set. "I'll just put in a few things. I'll just put up the pictures the way we decided. They'll be glued so it won't matter if we move it."

"All right, but not a lot of furniture," Lars said, adding to the officers, "My daughter has a very fine old dollhouse."

Cookie gave them a tight, somehow knowing smile and raced away down the hall with Jake like a small rocket behind her, his nails scratching the varnished floor.

"What do you want to see?" Lars asked Harrelson, who looked around the hall, glanced into the living room, sighed again at the number of bookcases and said, "Pretty much everything, Professor."

He was as good as his word. The police team opened drawers, looked in closets, visited the attic and the basement; they lifted the tops of the toilet tanks and moved the dry goods in the pantry. Harrelson wandered around the yard for a while, too, and Lars's caution was rewarded when the detective, hands behind his back like a visiting royal, stared at Emma's bed of young rhododendrons and azaleas.

If he wants that bed dug up, I'll call my lawyer, Lars thought, and realized, too late, he should have made that call first thing in the morning.

"I like those Exbury hybrids myself," Harrelson remarked, and when Lars said the garden was Emma's domain, he added, "Azaleas need more sun than you'd think. She'll have some trouble with the ones at the back."

Lars supposed this was Harrelson's attempt at the small talk that lulls suspects to their undoing. "I'll let her know."

"What time you expect Mrs. Larson back this afternoon?"

"Around five," Lars said. Harrelson nodded without expression, and Lars understood they would not be gone before Emma came home.

Harrelson returned to the porch where Cookie was busy with the dollhouse. She had magazines spread on the floor and was cutting out small pictures to make "paintings" for the walls. Cumbersome House had diminutive siding and miniature shingles, and the detective reached out and touched the roof admiringly. "A lot of work," he remarked. "You don't often see children's toys with that kind of workmanship."

Lars smiled uncomfortably. He didn't like the eager and knowledgeable way the detective was examining the construction. If he should touch the molding at the base . . .

"Killer detail," Harrelson said. "You make this?"

"My father did," said Lars. "He was a very fine carpenter."

"I can see that."

"Course it's taken hard use. My sisters and their children had it before Cookie."

"But you've painted it up. And some repairs, right? That base trim isn't original."

"Juvenile damage," Lars said, annoyed despite his alarm.

"My dad fixed that," Cookie interrupted, jumping up from the floor. "When I was small. But now the house needs renovation. We've started repainting. The trim around the windows was the hardest," she said, directing Harrelson's attention to the front facade. "I got some of the white on the siding right here. Dad is maybe going to make shutters. Maybe." An arch look at Lars, who had a frightening preview of a truly formidable, grown-up Cookie.

She was quite the proud home owner, making even the dour Harrelson smile. "Shutters! You're a lucky girl. It's really impressive."

"My dad says Cumbersome House is a noble edifice." Cookie plumped down again on the floor and resumed work, her small hands deftly guiding the scissors around a dog food advertisement showing a terrier quite like Jake. She put the picture up on the card table beside the house and selected a square of stiff gold paper to use as a frame. Under her breath, she began humming, ostentatiously busy, Lars thought, in the way children are when they are hiding something. He hoped Harrelson did not have children, that he was ignorant of their habits, their wild loyalty, their obstinacy. Cookie's expression was hidden by the thick wave of her hair, but she couldn't have seen the diary. She couldn't have; Lars prayed she hadn't.

"We've had it outside, letting the paint air," Lars said. "Quite a struggle to get that house up and down stairs."

"Cumbersome," Harrelson said, getting the joke, and he smiled as he opened the screen door and went inside. Lars followed him, not daring to look back at Cookie.

*   *   *

Emma got home at five. She surveyed the piles of books on the living room carpet, unstable towers haloed by dust motes in the yellow afternoon sun, and saw her pantry goods set out on the counters. She found a technician in the narrow, rather dingy upstairs bathroom, where she noticed a touch of mildew on the shower curtain and some soap scum on the tiles—housekeeping demerits she'd managed to ignore until then. In their bedroom, she discovered a policewoman with a clipboard, who was somewhat apologetically rooting through the bureau drawers.

Lars was standing in the upstairs hall, looking half guilty and half supervisory. "It's better they do this and clear me once and for all," he told Emma in a low voice. "It's the only way. Otherwise, suspicions, rumors. Right? We want this over and done with." He put his arm around her. "They'll put everything back once they're done. Come look at my study. They've finished in there. You'd really never know."

He made her look at his study, which was, yes, quite neat, with only the almost geometric rearrangement of his papers on the desk and the unaccustomed tidiness of the bookshelves to indicate that prying hands had been at work. The sight made Emma feel queasy, physically queasy, as if she'd eaten something dubious, an item digestible, right enough, but unwise, regrettable. It seemed to her almost worse that they'd been so tidy and careful, that so profound and disturbing an event as a police search should leave so little trace.

"I don't like having strangers paw through our home, especially with Cookie here," she said in an undertone, without considering that Lars had been with them all day. That they'd also gone through his office. That he was the one who supposedly had something to hide.

"I hardly like it myself," he said.

She hugged him then, and he was suddenly moved, tears in his eyes. He put his chin on top of her soft hair and held her close.

"Goddamn them. It *will* be all right. I don't have anything I haven't given them." But those words brought Lars instant regret. He closed his eyes, wishing he hadn't lied again to Emma, who loved him, who would stand by him, who must stand by him. "It's hard to prove a negative," he said. "Proving you haven't done something can be damn hard."

"Hence the presumption of innocence," Emma said.

"The glory of our judicial system. But that's theory. This is the way it is in real life." He heard the bitterness in his voice. It wouldn't have mattered, he reminded himself. Nothing could bring Iris back. What more could I have added? Even a time, even a place, even the diary—how much would that *really* have changed?

"I'm going to take Cookie to the park," Emma said.

"I wanted her to go to Betty's." Lars released Emma and stepped away. He didn't want to be criticized, not when he'd had the police and Cookie and the worry of the diary, which glowed like a toxic waste site in his imagination. "She insisted on playing with Cumbersome House. She's been busy decorating all afternoon. See if you can get her away from it."

Emma patted his arm sympathetically. He knew how to defuse her anxiety, and she knew when, as now, to assume a serene face, to shed calm all round. "We'll go to the park," she said. "How long do you think they'll be?"

"I'll ask. And then we'll go out to dinner, all right?"

"I have stuff in the fridge."

"No, no, it'll keep. We'll go out. We'll go to that Mexican place Cookie likes. She's been great. A trooper."

Lars felt relief at the very thought of the restaurant, dim and cluttered with junk store oddments, busy with its casual waiters and waitresses—college students mostly—in their red T-shirts and black pants. The restaurant would be noisy with the crowded bar and the usual small children in their high chairs. There would be families and couples on dates and, at one of the gaudy, tiled tables, he and Emma and Cookie, who loved going out and treats of all kinds, a child full of delight, who had no need to guard a dollhouse or to protect her dad.

Yes, the restaurant was the right idea, Lars decided, and when the police departed with their notepads and plastic bags and evidence kits, and with Lars's old Volvo, too, that's where the Larson family went, the bon vivant professor, known to all the servers, who greeted him—yes, the same as ever, with maybe just a slight hesitation or a comment or two in their wake (that's Professor Larson, you know, the one whose student was . . .)—and the beautiful Emma Larson (capable of turning heads at past forty), and the spritely, valiant, irresistible Ms. Cookie Larson.

"We'll have a big appetizer," Lars declared. "The nachos, yes?"

"All right!" said Cookie.

"Cholesterol," murmured Emma, guardian of health and sanity.

"Growing children need fats. Plus proteins and jalapeño peppers. It's well known."

"Everyone knows that," echoed Cookie, bouncing in her seat.

"And fortyish professors?"

"I'm young at heart," said Lars.

Emma thought *that* was true, at least.

"And then what? A glass of wine for the lady and the usual lemonade special for mademoiselle?" He'd put on a French accent that made Cookie giggle.

Lars seemed very up to Emma, managing the dinner, being amusing. Of course, it must be a relief to have the search over after all this time, for even Lars, nonchalant as he'd been, must have known it was a possibility. Yes, despite the humiliation of the actual business, what a relief when Detective Harrelson and his team left empty-handed and Lars, vindicated, knew he'd passed the test. Emma had felt relieved herself, despite her confidence in Lars and her anger at the intrusion. But the search was over now, and, with it, surely, the suspicion and rumors.

She felt they ought to celebrate without quite being able to get into the spirit of the evening. Oh, she laughed when Lars told jokes and when Cookie produced the latest funnies from the elementary, but she felt, not sad or worried exactly, but watchful. In the busy restaurant with its copper lamps and pots of greenery and the decorative old toys and signs and tools that kept Cookie occupied, Emma found herself watching her husband, just that, just keeping an eye on him as if he were a stranger she was trying to assess.

"How's your salad?" Lars asked, as solicitous as if he'd made it himself.

"Good. Very nice."

"And Mademoiselle Larson? The cheeseburger is satisfactory?"

"The cheeseburger is great," said Cookie, her face smeared with catsup and melted cheese.

"Could I have one of your onion rings?" His fork hovered above her plate like a heron's bill.

"Just one," she said. Lars made a great display of selecting the largest one, while Cookie tried to steer him to the smallest on her plate.

She has an infectious giggle, Emma thought, but she heard a nervous note, too. There was something missing in the evening. Lars was like a man straining to blow up a balloon, which swelled into a buoyant pastel shell so that the people standing about oohed and ahed in admiration but did nothing to help. What are we waiting for, Emma wondered. What are we waiting for to be relieved and happy?

Our home has been officially ransacked and all the proper authorities have come up empty against our husband and father. Isn't that enough to celebrate? The unpleasant thought that if Lars had a different reputation, the police would not have been so persistent, reappeared in Emma's mind. Of course, she told herself, people are murdered even at the best schools, even ones with the best professors, and even the best professor, even a wholly unexceptionable professor, can teach a student destined for catastrophe. It's a matter of luck. But if Lars had been on a shorter leash, he'd have been safer. He'd become a target because he was flirtatious, because he was sexually venturesome, because he was unfaithful, because, in some way she, Emma, had not kept her eye on him. And now that dismal fact made her watchful.

But what about Cookie? Emma had long ago decided that Cookie was never going to be a battleground. Never. Had she ever complained about Lars to Cookie? Never. Had she as much as intimated that Daddy had a wandering eye? She had not. So there was no reason for Cookie to be alertly nervous, none, except for the search, which had clearly upset her, because she had played with her dollhouse all afternoon and had even resisted going to the park. Well, she had reasons for that reluctance, too, her mother supposed, with all the gossip and the news reports. The events today wouldn't help, either; the idea of a search, never mind how satisfactory or conclusive, would get to school, could make more trouble. At the thought of pain and difficulty for Cookie, Emma felt her face harden, though, really, she should be relieved, for she realized that if the police *had* found anything, she never could have forgiven Lars. Never.

"I thought the pictures looked great in your dollhouse," Emma said to change the topic and to get her mind back in the right place, the celebratory place. "Did you see the pictures, Lars?"

"No, but I believe they're all very professionally framed." A smile at Cookie, whose mood changed instantly.

"We need to buy nails," she said flatly.

"I thought you were going to glue them on. It's pretty hard to nail up pictures that small. The work crew's going to have a hard time getting a hammer inside the rooms."

"For the *trim*," Cookie said, irritated. "*You said* you needed nails to fix the *trim*." Heavy emphasis on *you said* and on *trim*, a good illustration of the dangers of lying to children.

"I did. I haven't forgotten. I'll be at the hardware store this week."

"You wanted them right away," said Cookie with nervous insistence. "We can go to Ames right here at the mall. They'll have *finishing nails*. We don't have to go to the hardware just for *finishing nails*."

It was curious that women could know you were lying and yet insist on what you'd said. Lars wondered if that was an overlooked, but fundamental, sex difference or strictly a characteristic of *Larsonis femalis*. "We don't have to rush dinner for nails," he said.

"They'll still be open after dinner. Won't Ames be open after dinner, Mom?"

"I thought we had nails," Emma said. "I'm sure I saw some in the kitchen drawer."

"No, I'm sure we don't. We'll try to stop tonight," said Lars, who didn't want to discuss their supply of fasteners. He'd tack that telltale piece of trim and the damnable diary would be safe overnight. Cookie had school in the morning: the last-day picnic, an all-day extravaganza with games and watermelon and class pictures. The ever popular Daddy Lars would make an appearance and join the festivities. But first, he'd remove the diary. Then all would be well and after the picnic would come the triumphal return of Cumbersome House to the police-searched, certifiably clean and innocent second floor. He'd kept his nerve, recognized his priorities, really managed things very nicely. Lars smiled at Emma and Cookie, their happiness once again safe in his hands. "So," he said. "Dessert. This is a day that needs dessert."

Cookie woke up in the darkness, felt, with one cautious toe under the cover, to be sure that Jake was on the bed, touched his warm, compact, rough-coated body, heard a doggy sigh. It was all right. Jake was with her and nothing escaped his notice. Polly would be outside, sitting on the porch or slinking through their garden or the neighbor's yard, on the hunt. If she were to go outside, Polly would be there and being in the yard with Polly would be all right, too, because it wasn't so much the dark that Cookie minded as being alone in the dark.

She sat up, as she had several times in the night, odd, confused times between sleep and waking, uncertain if this was a dream or not. There was something she had to do. Something she should have done. The first time, Cookie thought it was her math homework, those dismal columns of decimals or the grim, blunt teeth of bar graphs. But school was finished for the summer! Today was the picnic! So it wasn't her math homework, and Cookie went back to sleep.

The second time, she *thought* it was the second time, but in the dark, half asleep, numbers get squishy and unreliable, even big solid numbers like *one* and *two* and their mathematical cousins *first* and *second*. Anyway, the *second* time, Cookie thought about the soccer equipment, the cones and balls and the game towels. She was in charge of the game balls and cones, or rather Daddy was, but he said it was good for her to manage them because it "taught responsibility," which was something Daddy took seriously.

Actually, Mrs. Plattenberg and Coach Turiff had wanted Daddy to help with the team, with running along the sidelines and shouting directions and explaining things. Cookie had been doubtful about this, and sure enough Daddy had said he "loved children too much to teach them anything about athletics." Cookie had worried how to tell Mrs. Plattenberg this, even though Daddy was much better than some of the other parents. June's daddy, for example, once said very bad words when June got called for a foul, and Martha's mom yelled at everyone and made Martha so nervous she wet her pants before one game. But still, everyone was supposed to participate, because "it's your league," as Mrs. Plattenberg liked to say.

But Daddy, who really was the cleverest daddy in the world, solved the problem. He said he'd be equipment manager, and he actually did fix one pair of boots and mended one of the little practice nets, so Mrs. Plattenberg couldn't really say that wasn't enough. He and Cookie got to the field ten minutes before everyone else with the bag of balls and the Creamsicle-colored cones, and they waited after the game and collected the equipment and crammed everything into the Volvo.

Lying in bed, Cookie had a panicky moment when she remembered that the Volvo was gone with the police, who were looking, Daddy said, for Iris Weed's homework and papers and such, but also, as Cookie understood but Daddy did not mention, for bloodstains and hair and other things like the bits of lint and thread that come off your clothes without you even noticing.

And skin, too. They learned that in school. Your skin sheds off in tiny pieces, and these really gross insect things live on it and cause people like Lyddie, who was in Cookie's reading group, to have runny noses and to carry an inhaler. *Whoosh.* That was the sound of Lyddie's inhaler, which was all because of these dust mites and everybody's skin coming off like tiny snowflakes. It was an odd thing to Cookie that Iris Weed, who was dead, could leave so much behind her, even bits of her skin to get up your nose and feed the dust mites.

So that's why the Volvo was gone, and Cookie's momentary fear was that the balls and cones and soccer stuff had gone, too, but, no, they were in the garage. She and Daddy had made sure of that. And the game wasn't tomorrow, anyway! Tomorrow was the picnic and not the game at all.

At that moment of realization, Cookie might have thought about other things Iris Weed had left behind, but perhaps it really was a dream, because she only thought about the soccer balls and dust mites and Lyddie Pelligrino's asthma. It was only when Cookie woke up again and touched Jake and thought about Polly and darkness and going downstairs that her panic assumed a clear shape and she knew what had to be done.

She lay in bed for quite a while just the same, full of dread but also of a nasty kind of excitement, until she could see that the black night had turned to gray, and that the gray was about to seep away into dawn. She couldn't wait much longer. She couldn't. Cookie sat up, and Jake, who missed nothing, lifted his head as she climbed out of bed. She walked barefoot across to the door, where she waited until Jake realized that his presence was required and bounced off the bed. She would be all right as long as Jake was with her.

Down the back stair, which was all dark and angley, with scuffed treads and scary shadows. Jake went down, hop, hop from one tread to the next, gaining speed as he went to end in a scramble at the bottom. He ran into the kitchen and began drinking water noisily. Cookie felt for the doorway at the end of the dark hall and touched the light switch. She would like to have turned on the lights, but did not, because it was basically okay with Jake noisy at his water bowl. She edged around the kitchen table to the stove. The kitchen matches for the gas range were in a metal container over the counter, and Cookie reached up and took three of them.

At school, she'd had a book of matches, stolen from Betty, their neighbor, whose husband smoked a pipe. *The Bradford Grill* was printed on the matchbook in maroon letters outlined in black and underneath, in fancy handwriting, *where the whole town meets to eat.* Cookie had an image of the matchbook with its small, clear lettering and the first yellow and blue flames in the trash can. Then the matchbook turned black at its edges before bursting into a bright puff of flame that leapt up above the green metal rim, taking all the lies, all the hard, nasty words away.

Cookie went down the back hall, unlocked the inner door, and pushed open the screen. It was lighter outside. She could see the big muffled shapes of the trees and the neighbors' houses, and the white globe of a street light almost useless now with morning coming. Jake rushed down the steps to snuffle for mice and chipmunks in the mulch around Mom's shrubs. Cookie stood on the porch, her feet getting cold on the cool, damp boards, and looked at Cumbersome House. She should have brought the furniture down. It would have been better with the furniture, which she loved almost more than the house. Cookie wondered if it would work as well if there was no furniture, if she kept something back. But to go upstairs and put on the light and find the boxes where Mom had packed up the miniature chairs and tables and the pretty mirror and the darling four-poster bed would be to invite sleepy voices from her parents' bedroom. Mom would appear in the doorway with her hair down on her shoulders, or Daddy would stand in the hall, yawning and scratching, to ask, "What on earth are you doing, Cookie?"

And she would not be able to tell them, just as she had not been able to tell Mr. Hector when he came into the girls' room and shouted something in Spanish and grabbed the big red fire extinguisher; she just knew this had to be done. She called Jake softly, and when he was up on the porch beside her, eager and curious and just a little puzzled, Cookie picked up the newspapers that had protected the table during Cumbersome House's paint job, crumpled them up, and put them into the back of the house. When everything was ready, there was an unexpected problem: Cookie found that she couldn't get the big, tough coated matches to light. Then she thought of the stone steps down to the lawn. She ran a match along one of the rough treads and saw the flame leap up, the beautiful, powerful flame that would save Daddy and let everyone forget Iris Weed, who'd written so much and some of it lies. Cookie didn't have any doubt about that. Daddy had never kissed Iris Weed, he never had, no matter what she'd written with her purple pen. Jake wagged his tail and gave a little bark as if to confirm this, and Cookie stepped toward Cumbersome House, the match held in front of her like a tiny candle.

Early, that was Lars's first thought, *early*. The yellow summer dawn had lightened the pleated shades of their bedroom, turning the navy fabric an intense sun-powered cobalt. It was early and school was over, two premises leading to the lovely conclusion that there was no need to get up, not even for the sun. He closed his eyes, and perhaps he dozed a little, because when he saw the shades and the walls and the bright points of morning light again, he found the reasons that he was awake in Jake's high-pitched barking and in an acrid smell of wood smoke very close at hand. Lars sat up and said, "Emma! Emma, I smell smoke!"

She was awake in an instant, leaping out of bed, crying, "Cookie, Cookie!" She was in the hall before Lars reached the door.

"She's not in her room!"

"Call the fire department! There's smoke coming from the porch!"

He bolted down the stairs, yelling for Cookie, then stumbled along the smoky hall, his feet awkward, his legs unable to respond to the overwhelming urgency of the moment until through the screen door, he saw the blazing pyre of Cumbersome House with Jake jumping and barking frantically just beyond the range of the sparks. This was terrible, but worse, infinitely worse, was the sight of Cookie, blank-faced and motionless, close, too close, to the wavering, heat-distorted column of smoke and flames that stretched up to the ceiling. Lars banged open the door, grabbed her, and almost threw her from the porch.

"Get the hose!" Emma cried behind them.

Lars rushed among the shrubs and bedding plants to find the green rubber coils and cried, "Turn it on!"

"It is on!"

But when he gripped the trigger, there was only a feeble spray of water, and, swearing in exasperation, Lars ran back up onto the porch, where he struggled to get the trickle of water close enough to the hot, bright fire without burning his hands. Emma, the gardener, reached over and adjusted the nozzle, releasing a burst of water. The table was on fire, too, and threatening the floor. Lars heard the screen door, and a moment later Emma came running back with a bucket of water and flung it onto the table, which immediately collapsed as if the fire had been holding it together. Ash and sparks flew everywhere, glowing embers landed on Emma's nightgown and on Lars' bare feet, and bits of burning wood skittered over the porch. He doused them both with water. Underfoot, the floorboards steamed. Emma, her long hair dripping, began crushing sparks and embers with the empty metal bucket, while Lars trained the hose on the blackening shingles of the wall and the scorch mark on the ceiling.

At this point, the fire company arrived, a roaring engine and men in big sensible boots and slickers dragging a hose the size of a drain pipe, which cooled off the hot charred wall of the porch and washed away the last sodden bits of Cumbersome House.

Emma went to comfort Cookie; Lars stood on the porch, numbly watching the firemen. "We need to open this up," one told him, patting the charred wall. "You can get a lot of heat behind the shingles and the sheathing. Builds up, few hours later, you've got yourself a smoldering fire."

Lars had not thought of that, but yes. Now that they were safe in the hands of the professionals, he felt shock and dismay.

The firemen produced crowbars and fire axes and went to work on the wall and the ceiling, ripping off shingles, opening up the beadboard, and levering off the heavy sheathing boards, which parted from the nails and studs with shrieks of agony.

"Any idea how it started?" the captain asked. He was a short, stoutish man with stiff graying black hair and a bold, slavic face.

"My daughter's dollhouse. We'd been repainting it."

"Oily rags, maybe? Cool this morning, but still, oily rags can catch fire. Or children playing with candles or matches."

"All I know is I woke up and heard the dog barking," Lars said. He owed Cookie that much, because on the porch floor, almost under the captain's enormous fire- and waterproof boot was a shriveled piece of marbled black-and-white cardboard: the last evidence of Iris's diary.

Jake was still barking frantically, guarding his yard from fire and firemen and especially from the thick, snakelike fire hose that had aroused his deepest indignation. "A little dog you'd hear," agreed the captain. "Give him a special treat tonight. You were very lucky you got this right away. How's that sheathing look?" he called to the fireman with the crowbar.

"Not too bad." The man took off his thick glove and patted the boards. Warm, but not hot." He gestured for Lars, who first bent over and picked up the last fragment of Iris's notebook.

"Only in a metal trash can for those," warned the Captain. "And leave the lid open until everything is cold."

Lars nodded obediently and went to examine the sheathing.

"You lucked out on the wall. Some more boards to come off on the ceiling, though. We want to be sure about the wiring, too."

Lars agreed to everything, stupid with surprise, too dazed to have ideas of his own. One of the firemen fetched a metal trash can and Lars began putting in the blackened shingles, the shattered boards, the charred plywood fragments of the dollhouse, the last of Iris's notebook, working mechanically, unaware even that he was still in his soaked underwear and barefoot and that there were nails and splinters and grit underfoot and occasional hot patches in the floor. The captain said a couple of floorboards, too, should be lifted. It was only when Lars backed away to let them get started that he looked into the yard and left the automatic emergency mode and became fully aware.

Cookie and Emma were on the lawn, the grass dark green in the shadowed early morning. The sun was coming though the trees in bright pale yellow globs, and Cookie was standing the way she had on the porch, uncharacteristically rigid, her smooth, expressionless young face frightening in its lack of emotion. Emma was kneeling beside her, and Lars did not need to hear (which he could not with Jake barking, and the firemen yelling back and forth and dragging away their hose and attacking the ceiling) to know what she was saying, what she was asking. The fire captain might believe oily rags and spontaneous combustion or even some foolishness with a candle. Emma knew better. Lars saw her give Cookie a shake and understood the mixture of anger and fear and love and exasperation, but mostly fear, that his wife felt. She was right; of course she was right, but she was wrong, too, heartbreakingly wrong.

Lars met Cookie's eye and walked over and put his arms around her, aware that she had both saved and condemned him and that he could never be the same in her eyes. "Oh, Cookie," he said. "Cookie, Cookie."

part two

9.

A memorial service for Iris Weed was held in late September on a Friday afternoon so warm the campus had a summery feel with barefoot students playing Frisbee on the lawns or catching the rays outside their dorms. The sun struck classrooms overheated, and Lars's small office was stifling, but he had no excuse to go home early because Cookie saw Dr. Viollette after school on alternate Fridays. Dr. Viollette, tiny, gray haired, elegant, with a French accent and sharp eyes behind lavender-tinted glasses, represented another of Lars's many defeats, a token of his misdeeds and miscalculations. There was, after all, no way he could explain to Emma why Cookie was perfectly justified in incinerating her beloved Cumbersome House and very nearly burning down their real house, as well. So Cookie talked twice a month with Dr. Viollette, who seemed, to Lars, the best of a dubious lot and not unkind. Cookie could now make polite greetings and requests *en français*, skills that seemed likely to be the only permanent benefit from Dr. Viollette's prompt and exorbitant bills. And didn't the fact that Viollette encouraged conversations in French—at nearly one hundred dollars an hour— suggest a sensible awareness that there was nothing very much wrong with Cookie? Didn't it?

Still, Lars had to admit that his daughter had grown moody and temperamental. Cookie went on and off in her enthusiasm for the soccer team. She refused, then reconsidered, his offer to rebuild Cumbersome House. The plan, at the moment, was to start as soon as he acquired a better skill saw and a guide for making straight cuts. Some days, Lars thought she might enjoy learning the tools; on others, when he returned to roaring music videos and a remote, self-absorbed child with wary eyes, he wasn't so sure. But that was adolescence; everyone said so, and if it wasn't so, a fair segment of the economy would collapse. Cookie would be all right, and, in the meantime, Lars tried to put the whole matter of her therapy, which greatly interested and exercised Emma, out of his mind.

But on this particular Friday afternoon, Cookie, Dr. Viollette, Cumbersome House, night fires and alarms, and Iris were prominent in his mind. The service was set for four, and had circumstances been different, Lars would have been invited to say a few words, to read a poem or an inspirational passage. In the present situation, there had been some question whether he should appear at all, but Lars had been firm about that. To stay away would be to acknowledge suspicion, to hint at guilt; besides, he wanted to be there; he should be there. He had worked closely with Iris, had known her, he guessed, as well as anyone on the staff, had grieved for her—and here he had no doubt—more deeply than anyone else at school.

His colleagues did not know how genuinely Lars regretted Iris's death, and if they had, they might not have excused him so easily. True, he had been under suspicion, but searches, interrogations, investigations of all kinds had come up empty. Once the initial awkwardness passed, people were inclined to think that, after all, the police were hardly infallible, that Lars was still the same charming guy, that, yes, he had an eye for pretty girls, but for that very reason he was not the sort to make a tragedy out of an affair. Lars was simply too frivolous to be a plausible suspect, a characterization that would have mortified him had he known how lightweight he appeared to some of the other faculty.

Instead, Lars believed that his essential, shining innocence had been made visible, and when the chapel bells began ringing at quarter to four, not tolling, thank God, but ringing, he got up from his desk, closed the windows against sparrows and pigeons, and set off to the service with strong, but largely unselfish, emotions. These intensified when he entered the fancy Victorian Gothic chapel, nearly filled with girls in sleeveless dresses and tank tops, and boys in shirtsleeves, some wearing Bermuda shorts, their bright, casual clothing anomalous in the dim, multicolored lights of the stained glass and the brown shadows of the nave. The contrast with the molten afternoon sun pooling on the stone floored vestibule was so great that Lars had a crazy impulse to yell, "Flee darkness! Embrace sunshine! Remember Iris, youth, and happiness!"

These Blakean words were so real and the impulse so strong that Lars had to cough and cover his mouth to recover himself. Iris of the Golden Wings—poor child. He thought again of Cookie, already leggier and slimmer, who was about to face the shoals and reefs of adolescence, and felt he might weep. But there was the department chair and Madeline, the gossipy Restoration specialist with the unfortunate overbite, and Bob, Modern British, a sweet guy but a bore who succumbed to every trendy theory, and the new Americanist, Pauline, looking awkward and lost as usual, who gave a quick, shy smile as Lars approached.

"A sad business," he said.

"Oh, yes. Did you know her well?" Her tone was so innocent that Lars decided this truly was a babe in the academic woods.

"Yes. A wonderful writer, a wonderful young woman." Lars found he could not discuss Iris except in clichés and generalities.

"I'm so sorry," Pauline said and then flushed, as if belatedly remembering hints and rumors from her malicious new colleagues.

"A tragedy," he agreed and turned to greet other faculty, exchanging idle platitudes of pomp and ceremony as late arrivals flowed around them to fill the remaining seats. Lars was surprised at the turnout, because Iris had always struck him as eccentric, somehow solitary. That was the side she'd showed him, anyway: the writer as outsider, as observer. He hadn't understood her as well as he'd thought, for clearly she had touched a number of people, not all of them from the college. There was a sad-faced, rather disheveled old man with a heavy cane and a pronounced enough limp so that the walk up to the chapel must have been an effort, and a sleekly groomed Hispanic youth wearing an impressive line of gold jewelry, and another boy with pale, sallow cheeks but African-American features. Lars wondered if either was her dealer buddy, the aspiring filmmaker with the marijuana connection, or was that just inadmissible stereotyping? Perhaps she had simply invented the artistic dealer as she had doubtless invented other things—Lars had to confess he did not know.

There were campus cops in uniform, one surely her friend Jorge, who'd turned a blind eye when she parked her truck overnight, and Harrelson and Paatelainen, who must attend these melancholy events as part of their official duties. Lars recognized a couple of motherly women who worked the counter at Joe's Joe—and who might have seen him there with Iris—and a good turnout of faculty, but the bulk of the crowd was students, Iris's contemporaries, an acre of young faces, smooth limbs, shining hair, and freshly shaved cheeks smelling of perfume and lotion. They had known Iris and liked her, or had seen her casually and become curious, or had read about her and been frightened into mourning by the sudden revelation of mortality. Iris of the Golden Wings had come to them with a message, and though it was too far from the event for tears, there was a somberness in the chapel despite the light summer clothes, the warm air, the cheerfully unfunereal bunches of daisies and early chrysanthemums on the altar.

Lars sat down in a side pew behind the chairman and Nelson Pettit, who was the associate chair. I'm well positioned for innocence, Lars thought cynically, but when the college's string quartet began the Barber Adagio, his heart clenched. We can lie in words, but music, the older art, betrays us. Lars bit his lip and looked down at the dusty maroon carpet, badly frayed, and up at the gray stone blocks arching into the shadows of the ceiling, and then at the front of the chapel, at the flowers, altar, podium, at the dean and the chancellor waiting to deliver their remarks, at Iris's family in dark suits and dresses.

Thanks to the manuscript and to the diary, the Weed family had a quasi-literary reality for Lars, so that it was almost a shock to see them, as if he was going to be introduced to Adam Bede or Tess of the d'Urbervilles. But such notions were a defensive ploy, and Lars understood that he was trying to distance himself.

After the chancellor's remarks and the dean's came eulogies from
Iris's brother and from Professor Katz (the latter painful, as Lars knew
that *he* could have been much more eloquent), followed by a piece
of popular music, played with great vigor and a certain amount of
wit by the chapel organist, then the reading of a poem Iris had written
several years ago (not bad, was Lars's judgment) and finally a passage
from Browne's great *Urn Burial,* which Iris would have read in
Seventeenth-Century Literature, a curious choice, sure to puzzle the
undergrads and probably the family, but, yes, apt; Joe Katz had been
perceptive in selecting the piece that ends: "To live indeed is to be
again ourselves, which being not only an hope but an evidence in noble believers, 'tis all one to lie in St. Innocent's churchyard, as in the
sands of Egypt: ready to be anything, in the ecstasy of being ever, and
as content with six foot as the *moles* of Adrianus."

The familiar strains of "Amazing Grace" closed the memorial,
provoking a girl behind Lars to put her face on a friend's shoulder
and burst into tears.

"A fine service," Lars said to the dean as he shook his hand.
"Very well done."

"A delicate matter," the dean agreed, his face impassive. As the
dean of a college cannot be too careful or too agile politically, he
was determined to appear neutral in all matters concerning Professor
Larson.

Lars stopped Joe Katz to compliment him on the Browne selection.

"A young woman of unique intensity," Joe said, which was purest
eloquence for him. "Mrs. Weed," he added quietly, "Mrs. Weed
wanted especially to meet you."

There was a reception line at the door of the chapel, and Lars,
nodding, started toward it.

"Wait until later," Joe advised, laying a hand on Lars's arm.
"There's a little private party set up for five-thirty at the chancellor's.
She wants to thank you for the manuscript. I think," lowering his
voice again, "rather an emotional topic. You understand."

Lars did. He did, indeed, but he was still not prepared for Mrs.
Weed, who was standing flanked by her son and surviving daughter

beside a tea table in the chancellor's formal wood-paneled parlor. At the service, Isobel Weed had been a dark presence in the front pew, her face hidden by a wide black straw hat. When the chancellor bent toward her and said, "Here's Jason Larson now," she turned and Lars saw a big, handsome woman, neither as old nor as matronly as he'd envisioned, with Iris's black hair and white skin. She wore startling red lipstick and a fair amount of eye shadow. A well-cut black suit accentuated an ample figure, and her strong, slightly coarse features suggested an energetic and dynamic personality. It was as if the elusive Iris, shy, eccentric, ambivalent, had reemerged from the underworld as this formidable Juno.

Isobel Weed immediately stepped forward to take his hand. "Professor Larson. You were so kind about sending the manuscript and I never answered you. Forgive me."

Lars made a vague, dismissive gesture. "I entirely understood, Mrs. Weed," he said. "Entirely. I have a daughter myself. I just thought that the manuscript was so exceptional you should have it."

She pressed his hand and gave him a look that in a different context he would have labeled flirtatious. "We must talk," she said. "But not here, not today. This has been a very emotional day for us all."

"An ordeal," said Lars. "Though I hope also a comfort to see so many people who knew Iris, who admired and liked her."

"My daughter was exceptional," Isobel Weed said. "To have an exceptional child . . ."

Here she broke off and pressed his hand again. Her son, also big, dark-haired, and good looking, if not as distinguished as either Iris or his mother, came over to put his arm protectively around her.

"Professor Larson," Isobel said. "My son, Dan. My tower of strength."

Dan nodded curtly; Lars did not try to shake his hand.

"The dean has arrived," Dan told his mother, "and the college chaplain. We must thank him for the service." He tried to steer her away, but Mrs. Weed ignored the hint, surprising Lars with her self-possession.

"It was a beautiful service," he said.

"We must talk," Isobel Weed repeated, though her son clearly disapproved.

Half out of the goodness of his heart and half to annoy her censorious boy, Lars found himself saying that he was at her disposal, that whatever he could do to help would be his privilege.

"We're staying over tonight," she said, "and leaving tomorrow afternoon."

Lars could hardly imagine anything more awkward, but he agreed to meet her in his office Saturday morning.

Another languorous day of heat and sun; the office windows stood wide open; a grounds crew mower droned across the lawn. Without the expectation of classes and lectures, Lars found himself devoid of energy, almost without volition. That he had agreed to this meeting, which would surely go badly, now seemed incredible. But he had contrived excuses and obstacles too late, so Emma had taken Cookie to morning soccer practice in his place, leaving Lars with the gloomy awareness that his confrontation with Iris's ghost was inevitable. Was this now to be his life, Lars wondered: everything settled and seemingly all right before abruptly cycling back to Iris, to error, to some essential instability? He picked up a copy of *PMLA*, ignored for months, and began an article on Robert Louis Stevenson. Lars was attempting to look and feel casual and failing at both, until, right after ten, came a soft tap on the jamb of his open door, and Isobel appeared, svelte, almost elegant, in her dark dress.

She was carrying a large tote bag, and guilt and regret must account for the twinge of nervous anxiety Lars felt, as she stepped inside the office and opened the bag. She lifted out the manuscript and placed it on the edge of his desk. "My daughter had remarkable talent." There was not the faintest doubt in her voice.

"She did, indeed." Lars drew over a chair and motioned for her to sit down. Then he got himself safely behind his desk; there were certain disturbing things about Isobel Weed, chief among them her resemblance to her daughter and a strong suggestion of sensual competence. Perceptive as Iris had been in so many ways, Lars suspected that she had read her mother all wrong—or else had taken fright.

Isobel Weed sat down, crossed a very fine pair of legs—Lars was not immune to the charms of amplitude—and said, "I was wrong."

Guessing this was the rarest of admissions, Lars said nothing.

"I didn't realize that Iris was truly talented. I suppose you feel that I failed her, that I should have understood her better." Isobel's look was challenging.

Once that's just what Lars would have felt, but recent events had unsettled all his certainties and changed his outlook. He shrugged and murmured something about the difficulties of parenthood; there had been turbulent days recently when he was sure Cookie would break his heart.

"And yet *you* noticed her talent." A faint resentment.

"I can't tell you how many student papers I've read, Mrs. Weed."

"Isobel," she said quickly. "Isobel, please. I feel I know you because you knew Iris, you *understood* Iris."

"Isobel." A smile for punctuation: Professor Larson at his best and most charming. "Noticing talent is my job. You might say that I'm a professional noticer of talent."

She reached over to ruffle the pages of the manuscript. Lars noticed that she had carefully tended hands and red nail polish. "Professional," she said. "That must be nice. It's too bad parents are all nonprofessionals, isn't it?"

"Amen to that," he agreed.

"And there are rarely second chances." She looked up sharply as she spoke. This woman is no fool, Lars thought, and he sensed that she was preparing to ask some large and difficult favor.

"You've given me sort of a second chance, though not the sort of chance I'd have wanted. I loved Iris," she said, and for the first time Lars heard the tremor of strong emotion. "We were not close; you know that. It was in the manuscript."

"I took Iris's accounts of your differences with a grain of salt," Lars said. "After her father's—your husband's—death—"

"She adored her father. Worshiped him. And he felt the sun rose and set on her."

Was it Lars's imagination that he sensed a note of discord there?

Time to be professional, to pontificate. "Adolescence, early twenties, those are difficult years, especially for—" he started to say *eccentric* and changed to "*creative* young people."

"Do you think life is really harder for them?"

That familiar look, bright, skeptical, forthright, broke through his defenses. "You sound so like Iris," Lars exclaimed. "That's just the sort of thing she'd have asked. She never bothered too much about conventional wisdom."

"A source of disagreement," Isobel admitted. "I'm a conventional woman—in most ways."

Lars might have followed up this promising remark, but instead he thought of Cookie setting her beloved dollhouse alight. What was that but an indifference to conventional wisdom? His face must have betrayed him, for Isobel said gently, "You were fond of her."

And though it behooved him to be careful, Lars nodded.

"That has made trouble for you."

"So much so that you are kind to trust me." He could be forthright, too.

"My son thinks I am a fool to come here," Isobel Weed said. "He thinks you probably killed Iris, but I felt I'd know about that when I saw you."

Her words lay like a live grenade shocking Lars into bluntness. "I did not kill Iris. I did not hurt Iris, and I did not sleep with Iris."

Although that left certain other possibilities open, Isobel Weed was focused on the essentials. She studied him, weighing up guilt and plausibility. "I believe you," she said finally, her voice heavy, all the ambiguous flirtatiousness vanished. Lars reached across the desk and took her hand for a moment.

"Thank you," he said. He got up and stood looking out the window to conceal his emotion. "You are generous," he said. "I do not know if I could be so generous, so fair." He turned back to her. "Like your husband, I have a daughter on whom the sun rises and sets. My only child." He swallowed a lump of gratitude and grief and sat down again.

"We never know how we will react," Isobel said thoughtfully. "I fell apart when Bob died. Absolutely fell apart. I wasn't there for

Iris; I know that now, and she was the youngest, she felt his loss worst. I thought her odd clothes, the business with the truck, her 'being a writer'—I believed all that was just a phase."

"Children do have phases," Lars said. He thought of Cookie who had become disillusioned, and of the emotional space that had grown between them. He profoundly hoped that was just "a phase."

"But I was wrong and I want to do the only thing I still can do for Iris." She paused, and Lars ran over the possibilities in his mind, fearing that the price of her endorsement would be something mad and heroic. Then she patted the pile of manuscript. "I want to see that Iris's book is published."

He was surprised; that was Lars's first reaction. He'd been overly subtle, overly alarmed. He hadn't considered the great modern truth: Everyone wants a book; everyone wants to be published. And Iris's manuscript was good. What were the odds? The book market was tough at the moment, but memoirs were hot. And memoirs by young writers were very hot. What about a memoir by a very young, mur-dered writer of genuine talent? Lars guessed that given the cynicism of book promotion, Iris's violent death would trump any neat and tidy ending. He realized publication might be possible.

"I think it needs, what is the word? Something at the beginning?"

"A preface."

"A preface and a bit more at the end, about her death. I would like you to provide that—I'm not sure I could bear to—and to see about the editing. Iris wasn't the best of spellers."

"I could manage a little editing," Lars said, emphasis on *little*, because he had a full course load, and the Freshman Experience Committee was proving every bit as dreadful as he'd feared. But what choice did he have? She'd maneuvered him very cleverly. "Just the same, please don't set your heart on this. The publishing business is something of a lottery, no matter how fine the work."

"I have to do this. I feel *you* can understand. I somehow know you can."

Lars could. What would he not undertake for Cookie?

"When I met you yesterday, I still wasn't sure," Isobel said. "I felt I had to talk to you and see your reaction. Dan and Marge don't like the idea of the book. They're afraid of publicity if we succeed and of wasting money—as if it was theirs!—if we fail. But Iris wanted to publish, I know she did, and I want to do this for her."

Lars nodded.

"I'm willing to do whatever it takes."

He didn't doubt that. Isobel Weed suggested vast reserves of physical and emotional energy. Lars began to understand why Iris might have resisted her mother, eluding her plans and expectations and becoming defiant and eccentric. Stymied by her daughter, Isobel was set to take over the book. She'd be the mother of a tragically short-lived writer, and Lars suspected she'd be quite brilliant in the role. He was not sure he liked the idea or the fact that he was to be a key instrument in the project.

Perhaps Isobel sensed his reservations, for she leaned forward in her chair, her dark eyes intense, her features transformed by the pressure of grief and determination. "Can I count on you?"

Lars, whose emotions were volatile but fleet-footed, felt her voracious need as an almost physical force.

"I know that with your help I can do this."

Lars saw exhausting meetings, demands, delicate negotiations between him and Isobel, between him and agents, between him and publishers, but he also realized that the book would suggest his innocence in a way that nothing short of convicting the killer would. This was a request Lars couldn't afford to refuse, and though he saw the pitfalls, he said he would do his best.

Isobel immediately relaxed and leaned back in her chair. "It means a great deal to me that *you* will do this. Really. I have such a good feeling about working with you." She smiled for the first time in their interview. "I may be naive about publishing, but I'm so confident of Iris's writing that I wouldn't have the slightest doubt if only we had the ending. Did she—did she have time to discuss the last section with you?"

"In general terms," Lars said. "We looked at patterns, at possibilities, at what Thoreau, for example, had done in *Walden*. That was one of her models."

Isobel was not familiar with *Walden*—"I was a business major," she said, "strictly down to earth"—and he gave her a brief synopsis.

"To live a different sort of life," she remarked when he finished. "Is that what Iris wanted?"

"For a while, at least. She did hint the experiment was coming to a close."

"She would have put that in her last diary. She wrote down everything from the time she was small." Isobel paused, as if revisiting something, not forgotten exactly, but long disregarded. "Even before she could write, she used to make little books. Little books with pictures and lots of scribbles. I remember asking her, 'What are all those lines?'—you usually had to get explanations of Iris's drawings— and she said, 'That's the story.' She'd have been three, maybe, four." A wistful smile. "Then after she learned her letters, the diary was just something she did. I didn't think about it as a real writer's writing."

"She kept diaries all that time? From elementary school? How extraordinary."

"I have every one, except from this past year. The police claim her recent diaries disappeared."

Lars became aware that Isobel was watching him closely. She believed him, but he saw that she could change her mind. She would not be so softhearted—or softheaded—as to ignore evidence. He was glad that he could say with a clear conscience, "They either disappeared or were destroyed, possibly by Iris herself."

Isobel was skeptical.

"I didn't know how long she'd kept diaries," Lars said, "but I do know that Iris regarded the recent ones purely as raw material for her book. At least, that's what she said. I'd seen her carrying the notebooks, and I did ask about them." Lars elaborated, telling Isobel pretty much what he'd have known if he hadn't read the last book.

Isobel remarked that she hadn't opened the earlier diaries.

"Her presence is very vivid in all her writing," Lars said. "Painfully so, I'd expect, in something as immediate as a diary."

Isobel nodded. "Of course, the police read them. I made them take copies and return the originals."

"Did they find anything useful?" Lars asked. He was pleased to hear how casual his voice sounded, but he had no reason for worry: He hadn't met Iris until fall semester. Fortunately! Who knew what she might have scribbled otherwise.

"I don't think so," said Isobel. "They never tell me anything except that they're working on the case."

"A terrible uncertainty," Lars suggested.

"Uncertainty about who, about why, about when we'll know, if we'll ever know," Isobel said passionately. "And the damn thing is that someone must know. That's what haunts me. Someone must know."

"With all the parties," Lars agreed.

"With parties, with people passing."

"Though there was rain." The drops had beaded on his windshield and glittered in the lights.

"Even with rain, there must have been people passing. I've seen the neighborhood. I drove down by myself the week after it happened. I don't think Dan and Marge know that, I don't think they do. They were being protective at the time, but I felt I couldn't rest until I saw the neighborhood. I'm not like Iris. I have to see things for myself; I couldn't imagine the place otherwise."

There was a brief silence. Extraordinary, Lars thought, how a shared disaster promotes intimacy. Isobel Weed was not a woman he found particularly sympathetic, yet he had a vivid image of her standing in spring sunshine on unfamiliar street, a grief-stricken woman trying to understand disaster, trying to determine how this terrible thing had happened and whether she could possibly have been at fault. He could put himself in her place, oh, yes, he could.

"I stopped beside a little shabby park. Do you know the area?" she asked.

Evil coincidence! Lars again saw Iris disappearing into the shadowy trees in her damp sweatshirt. He wished he'd never seen the damn park, which still came to him in dreams and in brief, disturbing waking images. "Yes."

"I sat in the car for a while, getting up my courage. I didn't know what I'd see; I didn't know how I'd feel. I was scared, I'll tell you that, but when I got out and walked, the neighborhood seemed so

ordinary. Nice, you know. If I'd been looking for an apartment for
Iris or Dan or Marge, a student apartment, I'd have thought 'nice.'
That's what you want for your children, isn't it? Not brilliance, not
excitement but nice, you think nice schools, nice apartments, nice
neighborhoods will keep them safe. That's what you think. That's
what you hope and pray for." Tears began streaming down her face,
coursing over those white cheeks that reminded Lars of Iris and
twisting her fine red mouth and blackening the corners of her subtly
painted eyes.

"Mrs. Weed. Isobel!" Lars grabbed some tissues and came
around the desk to kneel beside her. She seized his shoulder so hard
he could feel her nails through his shirt, and he put his arms around
her and held her for a long, charged, ambiguous moment. He could
feel her sobs and her beating heart—and his own; he thought of Iris
and desire and his terrors for Cookie and his notion that Mrs. Weed
was, in some sense, a ghost. Her tears touched his face and, it
seemed, her lips did, too, but that may have been imagination, Eu-
ridyce's kiss, for she drew away and let him wipe her face.

"Nothing in this life prepares you to lose a child. It's the loneliest
feeling in the world." Her dark eyes were intense with grief and
anger. "Remember that," she said, and Lars felt a chill. Then she
straightened up, smoothing her skirt and hardening her face with
what Lars now saw as a brave determination. "We must discuss the
book. I feel I can rely on you there for everything. I can, can't I?"

Lars said she could and returned to his desk, feeling shaky and
chastened. Though he had said "just a little editing," they talked for
the better part of an hour while he made notes on a yellow pad. The
book would need both a preface and an afterword, difficult assignments that must incorporate a brief account of Iris's life and death
with something about the quality of her work and how she might
have finished it. Isobel said she would attempt the preface, if Lars
would correct her work and write the afterword.

The next matter was publication, and Lars took pains to lay out
the difficulties of securing either a publisher or an agent. Isobel had
to realize that the odds were against their obtaining either one, but
he thought they should try first to get an agent. He would ask the

creative writers on the staff for advice and recommendations; she must be prepared for a long haul.

Whether Isobel paid attention to this or not, she was decisive: She would call some agents as soon as he got the names. "Writing is so slow," she said. "I can be persuasive on the phone."

Lars thought that likely. Plus, realistically, there was the human interest angle of the grieving mother. Precedent, too: John Kennedy Toole's mom flogged *A Confederacy of Dunces* for years before it was published to celebrity and the Pulitzer Prize. "We will need photocopies," Lars said. "I can do them here, but we will have to pay for the paper."

They discussed the number of copies, a tentative schedule, how quickly Lars could put the manuscript in shape. Isobel was anxious to see the book done and done quickly, and somehow from a "little editing," Lars found himself committed to managing everything. Surely for this project, his sins would be forgiven!

As she was leaving, Isobel took his hand. "We can do this."

Lars nodded. "We will certainly give it a good try."

"It means everything to me," she said. "The book is all I have left of Iris."

She leaned forward and kissed his cheek, then gave him a shrewd, parting look, as if she knew more about him than she cared to let on. When she was gone, the tap of her heels fading down the corridor, Lars closed the door of his office, his forehead wet with sweat. He had a sense of danger and of good fortune, as if he'd had a lucky, last-minute, but perhaps not permanent escape from Isobel's grief and sensuality. Lars was troubled that he hadn't been candid with her, not really, yet what to say? It would have been in the worst of taste to have confessed a lust for Iris, and, indeed, that wouldn't have been totally accurate, either. What had he felt for Iris—lust, love, friendship, estimation, exasperation, anger, envy—a mix of admirable and dangerous emotions? Lars had skirted the edge of tragedy, and, understanding that he had no taste for that noble abyss, he wanted the whole business with Iris and her mother over and done with. Behind him.

So though his impulse was to delay, to postpone, he bundled up

Iris's manuscript and put it in his briefcase. A quick read-through, notes on cuts, a rough outline of the afterword, calls to his colleagues about agents, editors, publishing houses: He would get on with the job and get it done and so reach, as his colleagues in the psych faculty were fond of saying, closure. Lars told himself, there might even be some pleasure in the calls, particularly to the suspicious and the imaginative on the staff: *I'm helping Isobel Weed put her daughter's manuscript in order, and I wondered if you could suggest some names, etc., etc.* This would be a low satisfaction, Lars knew, yet in his present limbo, not exactly under suspicion, but not exactly Sir Galahad, either, he must score points when he could.

And would the book actually see publication? Lars thought so, he really did. Even the lack of an ending was rather a postmodern touch; our literary preference is for open-ended possibility instead of finality. He had distinguished contemporaries for whom even the notion of finality was an illusion; he would touch on all that in the afterword, which would be eloquent and provocative, which wouldn't hurt him at all.

Yes, the thing might be published, a memorial to Iris, an offering to her mother and to the gods of pedagogy whom he had offended. He would start the project right away and get his life back to normal.

10.

FEBRUARY 19 — *Interesting conversation with Sven last night—or was it early this morning? Catch that sly allusion? I've been browsing fifties novels in the town library and that's how they would have indicated how our relationship is progressing. Actually, last night's conversation represented progression of another sort, revealing the surprising philosophical Sven. I haven't been thinking of him as a thoughtful being lately: He's been in the force of nature category, very reverse stereotypical, I admit, and then, bang, revelation. He was sitting up in bed with his back against the wall and his legs draped in the sheets, looking lovely as usual, when he says, "I should become a Buddhist."*

I started to laugh, I couldn't help it.

"I mean it," he said, then like he knows what I'm thinking: "We wouldn't have to give this up."

I was still laughing.

"The world is full of Buddhists," he said. "Think of China. They must be busy all the time making more Buddhists."

"I thought the Chinese were Confucianists before and now they're Communists or that new thing—Gong something. Falun Gong, is that it?"

"The Chinese were Confuciansts and Buddhists," Sven says. "Plus, don't forget the Japanese and Thais and Vietnamese and lots and lots of Indians."

"And Sven," I said. "Sven, the Viking Buddhist." That cracked

me up again. "They'd have put you off the boat. How can you be
a Viking Buddhist? You're not supposed to kill flies, never mind
Scots and Saxons." That's sort of a joke, but Sven doesn't see it.

"Not necessarily," he says, stiff and serious. I know right away
any time Sven's annoyed, because I've realized there's a missing
layer—physical or emotional—between him and the outside world.
Plus, he's always, always serious about himself. He can joke about
other things, which misled me into thinking that he had a good
sense of humor, but it turns out to be strictly limited. I wonder is
the test of humor whether you can see anything funny about yourself? That's the latest Weedian comic theory, anyway. I should ask
Lars sometime about that without mentioning who inspired the
idea.

Anyway, Sven is going on about militant Buddhism, I think
that was it, and then Zen and the Japanese samurai, and being "in
the moment," which I guess you'd better be, if you're flailing around
with a five- or six-foot razor-edged sword. I figured that was what
attracted Sven—flailing around and sharp toys with blood imminent—but I was wrong.

"The key is detachment," Sven says. "You get yourself beyond
circumstance so that you're protected from disaster."

I found this is a difficult concept, akin to the idea of a Benev-
olent Providence.

"No, no," he says, impatiently, "disaster happens; it just doesn't
bother you, because you've reached enlightenment. If you know how
much to value the world, you become superior to fortune."

You've got to understand that Sven has an appetite for the superior, for big things and special people. We argued for a while
about whether detachment was a good thing or not and about
whether one could become detached in a productive way, instead
of becoming like the guys around the Dumpsters after dark, guys
who are detached from something fundamental.

We talked for a long time, the longest conversation we've had
since we stopped sitting in bars and cafés and started going back
to his room to bed. Is this a good development? Yes and no. He's
not boring, but I'm not sure I want to know him in this way.

Getting to know people can tell you things about yourself that you'd rather not realize, and what I realized last night talking to Sven is that I'm not sure I'm ready for the whole package. When you lose someone important, he can't just be replaced, not even by someone you love in a whole different way.

The other thing is this idea that Sven, who's all intensity and emotion and seriousness, really wants to achieve satori or whatever the Buddhists call it. He told me that Kerouac and the Beats had the same idea, as if this was the killer endorsement, as if I should agree, pronto. I said satori seemed to take them a whole lot of alcohol, and he accused me of not being serious, of not taking him seriously.

But I do, because obviously I'm still thinking about the conversation, and I'm wondering if we always aspire to be our opposites. Like Sven wants to be detached, and I want to live with intensity, which suggests I am not really that sort of person at all. Maybe I don't see myself any clearer than Sven sees himself. Maybe I'm really a detached, objective person with a cold heart. Maybe I am. That's what Lars thinks, but since he believes himself irresistible, he pretty much has to think that.

And what about Mom? What does Mom think of me, other than that I'm a screw-up and a nuisance? Or does she think about what sort of person I am at all? I'd guess not. Mom lives in a different way, emotional and direct, full of worries, full of hopes. Maybe that's why she's so fussy about clothes and about looking right and being in style and in step, even when she's not at work, even when she's not representing Maybeline and the Maybeline Face to the world. I'm not a Maybeline Face and don't want to be. But Sven? Is detachment just a fancier Maybeline Face? I wonder.

M A R C H   5 — *Minor triumph. Successful dive. Given that I find the idea of hurtling face forward horrifying under any and all circumstances, one successful racing dive off the shallow end of the pool is great stuff! I tried to explain to Sven how Viking this was, a real example of "being in the moment," etc., etc., but couldn't make contact. He does that sometimes, usually when the* subject is Iris Weed. It's as if he's rowing into some Norse gale or off on the far side of the moon—completely tuned out. Today he was all absorbed in the complicated relationship he has with his adviser, Professor Aryant, a Medievalist prima donna who's had a "major book" and never lets anyone forget it. Aryant gives brilliant, heavy-duty lectures and impossible exams and hasn't had a student measure up in twenty years. You'd think he'd know what to expect by this time, but no, he prowls the corridors like a dissatisfied Grand Inquisitor and stays up nights checking footnotes in student papers.

Sven, of course, should have used his imagination. It's not as if Professor Aryant just joined the faculty; everyone knows he's a prick and the thesis adviser from hell, but Sven never considered anyone else. He thought that he'd be the exception, the one student in a generation to satisfy the great man. On good days, he'll go on about how insightful Aryant is and how influential (which may be the same thing for Sven, who is really, really ambitious). That's on good days, when Aryant has nice comments or buys the lattes or talks up some new monograph with a cutting-edge theory. Then he's a great guy. But Aryant's like New England weather; you pay for the good days, and today he had Sven all tied up in knots. The corrections made last week now don't seem "quite right"; the tone isn't there yet, and there's some new material that just has to be considered and incorporated before Sven can even think of going further.

"It's the death of a thousand cuts," Sven says.

I've heard this before. Sven regularly gets worked up about academic politics and his own progress. I wonder if he shouldn't choose another career and once suggested that, but he can't imagine being anything but Sven the Viking professor. I imagine he'll grow old impressing undergrads and wearing a long face and sleeping around, the worst of Lars and Professor Aryant combined.

I seem to be writing an awful lot about Sven.

So, back to my own minor triumph. I get to the edge of the pool for my last attempt at the racing dive, my absolute last, because Dora, our instructor, has gotten impatient with me. I get impatient with Dora, too, because this is just swimming, an optional course, a life skill. It's supposed to be fun, but she's an aquatic Professor

Aryant. *There aren't footnotes in swimming, but she has her clip-board out and half a dozen things she's going to look for—assuming I get airborne, that is.*

I'm in no hurry. I lean over and inspect the wavering aqua-marine surface yards and yards below me; I am about to fall, to dive, from a great height. I point this out to Dora, who rolls her eyes and tells me it's six inches to the water.

Of course, I'm six or eight inches taller than she is, which means my head is, yes, a couple yards at least above the water.

Dora gets all excited and demonstrates the correct position, how your head is supposed to be low and your arms out, knees bent. "Head down, head down," she yells and toots her whistle. I think she would have shoved me in, if I hadn't figured out that this was a time for rage and intensity and pushed off and yes, hands down, head down, I anticipate the whap as my belly hits the water, but no, hands cleaving water, chlorine in nose, glimpse of lane stripes, then right into the flutter kick: Iris Weed cruises!

Toot, toot, toot! I stop and turn, treading water, to look back at where Dora stands on the deck. "Pass," she calls out. No com-ments, no footnotes, no refinements needed, so I guess Dora does know when to call it a day.

M A Y 2 — *I have written over two hundred pages of diary since Thanksgiving. More than one hundred and fifty pages since midsemester, and more than one hundred pages in the last month. Scribble, scribble, scribble, Ms. Weed, another thick notebook! I diarize (is that a word?), therefore I am. A writer, that is. And I am, I think, I hope, but at the moment discouragement: Despite a good beginning and an all right middle, the book's impossible with no ending in sight. No ending, no insight: The whole thing's an item past its sell date, and Lars is only being kind in encouraging me—or, rather, he's working on a whole other agenda.*

Admittedly, I like to be consoled, and Lars is consoling. He does say I've written a lot already this term. He says writers have fallow periods (the agricultural theory of composition?) and some-

times need to "prime the pump" (a rival hydraulic theory?). I've never had problems with writing before, and the diary is certainly unaffected. The trouble is that I just don't know the conclusion, no difficulty for a diary but a major problem for a book. Gloomy mood as a result; even Sven noticed, though he'd rather not discuss manuscripts at all unless they're his. For one thing, I'm only an undergrad and a book is hubris, which, he explains, is Greek and means tempting the Gods with overconfidence, and for another thing, I sense he's just not all that interested.

There's a big point in Lars's favor: He's a man who listens. Is that the secret of his amazing success with women? Can it be that simple: Women just want a listener? Maybe, yes, because Lars has acquired a huge reputation without many obvious assets. Now Sven, with lots of obvious assets, won't be as successful, I don't think, even though he bewitched Iris of the Golden Wings. Sven either wants to talk about what he's interested in or he wants silence. I suspect men do, in general, want to talk or want silence. I remember Mom complaining about Dad, about his never listening. I never thought before that she might have had her reasons.

M A Y   1 3 — *Odd event. Odd, minor event? I think so, but that's what I'm trying to decide.* Yesterday, I left the library around 9:30 P.M. The apple trees were blooming along the quad and the warm night was full of music from stereos and car radios. People on study breaks were smoking and talking, or fooling with skate-boards, or tossing footballs out front of the dorms. A couple guys played Frisbee with a black dog that jumped and whirled in the walk lights, then disappeared into the night shadows of the lawn. I'd have to call it a lyrical evening: music in the air, mist over the pond, the approach of graduation bringing intimations of nostalgia, as if this particular evening would be one of the things I'll remem-ber from college.

We'd had rain earlier in the day and the grass was wet, so Iris,

who was wearing a very nice pair of open sandals, was sticking to
the sidewalk. She's been upgrading her wardrobe lately, investing
in what Mom calls "decent clothes," because this Iris (a surprising,
almost unrecognizable, third-person Iris) is confronting graduation
and Life After College. We're making plans, she and I. New York?
Boston? Chicago, LA? Serious writers don't go to LA, Lars says,
but I don't see why not. LA must be full of health food stores, and
I could maybe live in the truck for very little. That's one plan.
Or I could find roommates and live in Boston or NYC and get a
job in publishing or at a dot-com. I write fast and I can imitate
anything prosewise, so why not? That's what I said to Sven a few
weeks ago.

"Somebody writes all that stuff on the Web and in magazines
and catalogs and things. Why not me?"

"You want to write for a catalog?" Sven longs for higher realms,
and this is a notion beneath contempt.

"I want to pay my bills. I want to write novels and screenplays
and have great thoughts." The latter was teasing, of course.

"You won't be able to do that if you're doing a lot of hack work."

"Right now my hack work is school papers, and I still write a
lot. All I need is an ending, and my book will be finished," I said
more confidently than I felt. I pointed out the drudgery of the health
food store and the well-known miseries of the minimum-wage life.
"Lars says there's money in business and commercial writing, if you
don't mind the routine."

" 'Lars says,' " Sven repeated in this nasty tone. "Lars says this
and that. Do you believe everything Lars says?"

"You know I don't," I said, and he said I did, which led to a
quarrel with a good deal of shouting, followed by an intense, tu-
multuous reconciliation. Not the worst of evenings, but at the end
of it, I realized two things: Sven doesn't want me to leave and I'm
going to, anyway. And this led me to suspect that a new Iris was
about to be born, because three months ago, even a month ago, I'd
have been thrilled to know that Sven saw us as even semiperma-

nent. He's an interesting, attractive man, but I'm an interesting, and maybe an attractive, woman; I expect there will be other men on my particular horizon. My alter ego, Iris, the Soon to Be Graduate, realizes this and she's started making plans. She's bought city sandals, a going-to-interviews dress, panty hose. She thinks she has some talent and she's going to put the idea to the test—she and I, I should say, because I can imagine becoming her; I can imagine becoming a different person, perhaps a professional writer or editor who earns a good living and carries a briefcase and wears heeled sandals, which go clack, clack, clack *on city sidewalks.*

I return to those new sandals, because if I hadn't been wearing them last night, I might not have noticed anything. That's the really odd aspect: how one tiny detail makes a difference. I wonder just how big a detail has to be to have an effect. Is there a limit *as we used to use in calculus? Can an important detail be infinitesimally small, or is there a moment when the trivial suddenly undergoes a change of state and becomes significant? I wonder, because last night, after months of boots and sneakers, I was aware of the* clack, clack, clack *of my sandals, which made me aware of all the night sounds around: bass chords coming down like rain, tires on wet pavement, the murmur of voices and laughter, the barking dog and the men calling to it, a bird of some sort, singing from the very top of one of the trees, and starlings and pigeons stirring on the ledges and cornices of the stonework, and then, just as I started along the arcade, the sound of careful footsteps behind me.*

Careful, that's the best word I can come up with. It's not the right word, but it's as close as I can come, because these weren't normal, casual, unselfconscious footsteps. I recognized the different quality immediately and glanced back without breaking stride, curious, not worried, and heard a sudden movement. I stopped, but there was silence and the small overhead lights did not penetrate the shadows. A trick of sound, perhaps? Someone walking in one of the corridors that pierce the arcade? " 'Twas the wind and nothing more."

Clack, clack, clack, my new sandals sound expensive, a sound

I like. I'll bet the classical Iris wore nice sandals, assuming goddesses indulge in quality footwear. More silence behind me; this side of the arcade—access roads, loading docks, parking, and delivery entrances—is quiet at night. As I left the quad, taking a narrow alley between the math and science buildings, I reminded myself of the dangers of an overactive imagination, but just past the chem department loading ramp, I heard footsteps again. I stopped in the bright security light and fiddled with my knapsack, waiting to see who was on the path. After living in the truck, I'm not overly nervous at night. Not overly—at least not until lately.

The footsteps stopped. No doubt this time. I turned the corner of the chemistry building and walked as fast as possible without actually running toward the south end of the quad, the newer part with squat brick structures—"cryptofascist architecture," according to my art history lecturer, "a cultural residue of the Second World War"—instead of atmospheric old stone buildings, which, I guess, are a cultural residue of the Wars of the Roses. Heavier fog, quieter. In the few minutes it took me to cross the old arcade, it's gotten late. The dog is silent, the smokers have gone in, the distant stereos pulse like a soft heartbeat. Lars used to show up outside my classes, at Joe's Joe, at the store. Was that "following" me? I'd see him in the hall, with oh, so casual a wave and a "Hi, Iris," or busy talking to another professor but keeping one eye for yours truly, or striding along, nose in a book, an unworldly scholar who just happens to arrive at Joe's Joe when I'm expecting Sven. That was Lars's approach; I think this is someone else.

There's a long open stretch of walkway past the chapel: a clean, well-lighted sidewalk, much to be desired. Iris, the Soon to Be Graduate, strides along a corridor of light. I look around, see nothing, and pass, without even a second glance, a blue-lighted emergency box—this is not an emergency and I'm not in danger—and head toward the Humanities and Social Science buildings. Behind them the parking lots begin. My truck is parked in D section, very far back, near the trees. Clack, clack, clack. I realize how audible I am just about the time I see a figure moving parallel with me across the dark lawn. He's visible as a momentary darkness against the gold and silver reflections in the small pond, and he stops when I stop.

Coincidence? I stand under one of the street lights. The brightness that slicks the wet sidewalk with sour orange does not extend quite far enough. Drunken refugee from a keg party? Campus survivalist practicing stalking? Local exhibitionist waiting to flap his raincoat? Notice how I omit Sven, who visits the truck and bangs on the panels, and Lars, who shops without enthusiasm at Healthy Stuff? Of course, I could have called out; I could have walked directly over to him, whoever he was; I could have been confrontational. Or, as my truck was parked only ten minutes' walk away, I could just have ignored shadows and footsteps and walked away. I could, but though I felt foolish, I fished out my cell phone, punched up the campus escort service, and requested a ride in a crisp, clear, carrying voice. Then I waited on the well-lighted steps of the Humanities building.

The escort driver's name was Matthew—for some reason a high proportion of the boys on campus are named Matthew. This Matthew had curly brown hair above a round face and black-rimmed glasses. He'd been trained, he said, in "intervention." I said that sounded good and could he possibly intervene in imagination—a stupidly pretentious thing to say, but I've had some moments of fear lately.

"I thought someone was following me," I said and felt terminally whimpy. "I was just being twitchy, I guess."

"Not necessarily. We've had incidents," he said.

I hoped he would tell me about them, but I guess he'd been trained in discretion, too.

"Which dorm?"

"Just drop me at my truck. I'm parked at the back of the commuter lot. D Lot. Not that far a walk."

"D Lot's dark. You made the right decision," he said. "Besides, keeps me employed."

He was trying to be nice, so I asked him about driving around

*campus at night with the fog and the orange and white lights, about
escorting the nervous and the neurotic. He said that he got some
of each and quite a bit of repeat business. "The ones who study
until the library closes. It makes good sense for them to get a ride.
Stuff happens, that's for sure."*

*"So I could have been followed?" I asked. Sitting on the high
seat of the escort van, I was ready to write the evening up as fantasy,
as Iris's overactive imagination, as a wayward example of poetic
license.*

"Absolutely. But who knows why?"

"Oh, secret admirer, in my case."

*He gave me a glance, checking to see if I was joking. "There
are all different sorts of admirers," he said soberly.*

*I didn't feel like exploring that issue. Instead, I asked him what
he liked about the job, and he said it paid well. And then he said
he likes the night, because it's quieter; there's not as much stimu-
lation, not so many lights, not so much color and noise. And people
aren't so bright at night. "There are people during the day who hurt
your eyes," he said, "but at night everything is quieter and calmer."*

"You must get some frightened people, though," I said.

*"But I can talk to them. I can intervene to calm them down.
I know how to talk to frightened people. Do you know how? Always
talk very slowly to people who are frightened. It works. And then,
after all, once they're in the van, they're quite safe, you know. Yes,
in general, people talk to me at night in a very pleasant, okay sort
of way."*

*I wondered how they talked to him in the daylight but we'd
almost reached the truck. "A couple more rows," I said. "There.
Right there. The red truck." I opened the door and climbed out. A
little drizzly rain was starting, which would drive all but true weir-
dos home. I could have walked fine. "Thanks so much."*

*"I'll wait until you get your truck started," he said. "We always
do that, just in case."*

"Don't bother. This engine's reliable."

"It's in our guidelines," he said. "Some people cut corners, but I like to follow the guidelines. You need the guidelines at night."

I could understand that point of view. "Actually I live here," I said. "In my truck."

He was surprised; this was clearly outside his personal guidelines, but he recovered quickly. "But maybe you shouldn't stay here tonight."

"I'll be all right," I said. "No real problem. I've made it all semester."

"But why take risks? You called the escort service, after all." The light from my open door glittered over his glasses, enlarging his reproachful eyes. "Don't you have a friend in the dorms or in an apartment?"

"Sure," I said and, because I could see that he was not going to leave otherwise, I added, "I can do that."

He waited until I started up the motor before he waved and pulled away. I followed him out of the lot and drove across town to Dunkin' Donuts, the ultimate well lighted parking place, a favorite of cops on breaks and night-driving truckers.

I could have called the barfing mermaid, I could have called Ross from Renaissance, or other people. I suppose in a pinch I could have called Lars. The person I did call was Sven; his phone rang once, twice, before I hung up. I am not going to be a prisoner of my imagination.

M A Y   1 7 — I have the ending. At last! At last! I knew I was right to burn the old diaries, which were tying me to dates and times and former habits of thought. To burn my diaries and burn my bridges was absolutely essential, and I hope Sven will come to understand that. I think he will; we talked, really talked, and I think he was listening. I don't want to stay here; I'm definitely moving out, and long-distance romance is just not for us. I told him he was right from the first, that we were insufficiently serious, and he agreed. Reluctantly, maybe, but the facts are obvious, and we've been making each other miserable. That's not the sort of love I want—and he agreed with that, too.

So. Clouds lifted. I would like us to joke and be friends. I would like that to be part of the ending: for intensity to end in laughter. I want to remember Sven dancing, rapt and wonderful and music propelled; I want to take some of his good qualities away with me, his forcefulness and energy, and the exhilaration of running with the brakes off. But writers need both energy and reflection. I learned that this semester working on the book with Lars, who really is a good teacher. I've learned to do sustained work and for that you need a mixture of resources.

I tried to explain that to Sven, and right away he quoted Wordsworth that "poetry is emotion recollected in tranquility," which is pretty close to what I had in mind. Just the same, bringing up the idea was maybe a mistake, sort of. Sven doesn't like to think of me as a writer. I'm still an undergraduate to him, a type of subintellectual, and he resents the fact that I'm serious about writing, which brought us back, inevitably, to my leaving, to my reasons for leaving. He doesn't see why I can't write here if I have to write.

I pointed out the lack of jobs, the glut of student labor, the impossibility of making a living, which I need to do and intend to do. But I think he can read between the lines: I want the city, I want opportunity, I want to get away.

All this will go into the conclusion of my book. I can feel the shape of it. It's odd, how you can feel ideas approaching, how thoughts have weight. One of my aunts used to say that such and such was weighing on her mind. Writing's like that, but it's a good sort of pressure, a happy pressure, so that you can hardly wait for the first words to come. And then when they do and all the rest follows, it's the most wonderful thing in the world.

That's where I was yesterday with my conclusion, and today it's arrived. It's good, I know it's good, and I'm so sure I'm not even going to make the usual notes. Right to the computer instead for vacuum-sealed freshness!

M A Y   1 7 — *Iris's usual luck! At the moment of inspiration my computer battery light flickers and fades down and out. "An outlet!" Iris cries. "My kingdom for an outlet!"*

So off to the uncongenial library computer carrels to finish. I want the draft of the conclusion done and printed for Lars tomorrow.

I'll be finished exactly one day before graduation!

11.

A drizzly fall rain pooled along the sidewalks and mixed the city's soot and grime with scraps of paper, crumbs of pizzas, pretzels, and rolls, and washed the resulting slurry into the gutters. The rain steamed on the grates and sluiced from the wipers of the close-packed taxis, cars, and buses. Men in clear plastic coats hauled handcarts heaped with rain-spotted cartons and muscled wet garment racks between delivery trucks at crosswalks. Bicycle messengers with their shiny helmets and spandex pants whirred by in plumes of spray, and Lars felt dampness creeping up his pant legs to meet the hot, closeness suffusing from the dress shirt, suit, and vest he wore under his raincoat. Isobel had her umbrella up, and every time she turned to say something to Vivienne, their formidable New York agent, little runlets of water drained from the ribs onto Lars's head.

"Terrific," said Viv. "You were both seriously terrific. They're going back for a third printing, and Suzie told me that it's to be a much bigger run. Ninety thousand at least."

"That's not a risk?" Lars asked.

"After today?" Viv gave a soft-throated snort, which went, Lars thought, with the rest of the package, a square bulldog face, octagonal pink-tinted glasses, and a habit of command. In their division of labor, he had been pretty much left to do the heavy lifting with Suzie, their keen but busy and overworked editor, while Isobel had found common ground with Viv. They were two of a kind, both bossy, determined, and enthusiastic, but while Isobel aroused complicated emotions, Lars and the humorless Viv were strictly business.

"You have no idea," she was saying. "You have no idea of the power of television to sell books. Not," putting her hand on Isobel's arm and causing another trickle of the city's acid rain to slide down Lars's neck, "that sales were ever your primary motivation, I don't mean that, but the power to get Iris's book before the public, to bring her ideas and talent to a mass audience—it's almost inconceivable. The media is revolutionizing bookselling."

"A brave new world," murmured Lars.

"With certain old verities," Viv declared.

Lars found their agent very positive, as if she were never betrayed by doubt. But that was nonsense; she was fifty if she was a day. In fifty years, one had plenty of time to accumulate doubts. He, personally, had acquired a great many in just the last year.

"Personality," she proclaimed now. "Personality is the key. I have authors—it breaks my heart—brilliant, brilliant writers, who are just hopeless in front of a camera. You might as well put a store dummy on the set. How can I sell them? This is a people-to-people business. You need great characters in the books and real personalities for the media. Real people!" She raised her voice over the *wush, wush* of the traffic, the tramp and shuffle of the sidewalk, the snatches of conversation, the rattle and clank of awnings and grates, the brittle sound of rain gear rubbing against parcels and briefcases.

The aftermath of the lights and tension of the studio always left Lars on heightened alert, although he was getting to be an old pro at interviews, fit for newspaper, magazine, radio, or television; fit for reporters, plain or fancy; fit for notepads, mikes, recorders, cameras. And, yes, he was good: not too talky; generous with Isobel, who was often nervous on the set; tasteful in his selections from the book. The local paper had run a flattering piece crediting Lars with bringing Iris's work to its present celebrity, and he was keeping his shoulder to the wheel with talks and appearances right up to the second anniversary of her death when he was scheduled for an academic conference titled "Memoirs and the Reconstruction of Memory."

Lars expected to be grilled there, because Iris's precocious talent had raised some questions about authorship, distasteful speculations that made him regret the loss of the diaries and even the fortuitous destruction of the very last of them. Viv and, to his surprise, Isobel were unperturbed. Isobel had proof in the form of Iris's youthful diaries (not up to the book but still impressive) while Viv had the sales figures.

"Controversy is wonderful," she proclaimed, "and, besides, you don't have any talent for fiction." This was true, but Lars would rather she had not been quite so certain.

Nonetheless, that's what he told the press, for no one wants to hear about talents and triumphs. The world wants weakness: the maggot in the muscle, the gaffs and flubs and follies—the more humiliating the better—that comprise the underbelly of success. So Lars amused reporters with descriptions of adolescent poems and with a short story he'd written in college. With every recounting, this hapless narrative grew more convoluted, and the snippets of murky clichés and high-flown metaphors always disarmed interviewers. But he assured them that the poetry—all three surviving examples of Larson verse—would remain interred. As with the great, unwritten story of Sherlock Holmes and the Giant Sumatra Rat, the world was not yet ready for *Larsonis poeticus*. He soon realized that it wasn't any harder to make reporters laugh than undergraduates.

With his funny little riffs, Lars gained a reputation for wit as well as learning. "Charming" and "humorous" were his defining adjectives, and increasingly "dedicated" popped up, as if his own diffidence were not genuine, as if he were putting aside important works to preserve Iris's talent. Though he never bothered to disabuse reporters of this idea, in truth, he had postponed a few interesting, if inconsequential, papers to become modestly famous.

At times he felt a mild guilt about his new public consequence: when he watched a replay of an almost excessively respectful interview on cable, when he heard himself pontificating on the car radio via *Fresh Air*, when he noticed that the department secretary had thoughtfully posted yet another laudatory clipping on the English department bulletin board. And yet, he deserved. Ten months of work putting the book into shape with Isobel Weed had not been a picnic, combining, as it did, difficult decisions and explanations (including grammatical explanations, for Isobel, like most of the public, cared nothing for the comma, never mind the semicolon) with a nostalgic and guilty eroticism. Isobel, robust, abundant, lonely, was both a temptation and a clear and present danger. Should he succumb to the possibilities that she had more than once hinted, she would guess more than he wanted her to know and his innocence would inevitably be compromised. It was unfair, really, but there it was. Iris had wanted a wholly unreasonable and radical commitment from him and, in a peculiar way, she'd gotten it. In exchange, he'd become a magazine intellectual, appearing on a variety of talk shows, book chats, and literary panels.

Not that any of this had hurt him. His classes were all over-enrolled and there were once again waiting lists for his independent study slots. His uneasy colleagues had swapped suspicion for envy, or boisterous congratulations. Lars had been midwife to a literary phenomenon, and his reputation for discernment and skill would certainly last until *Nite Lite* hit the mass-market racks.

And overseas outlets, too. Viv had secured more contracts: British, Japanese, and Swedish rights were already sold; the book had gone to Frankfurt for the big book fair and was scheduled for London. Viv was sure of German, French, and Italian interest. And after today! To be the first memoir chosen was truly big, big, big! "You two have no idea," she repeated, "no idea at all of the power of these new television book clubs. You'll never get better exposure."

"Oh, let's get a drink and have a little celebration," said Isobel, which sounded better than the bare fact that she needed fluid, preferably alcoholic. She felt the way she always felt after media appearances, elated and depressed and ready to jump out of her skin with nervous energy. Without a drink, she'd never sit still on the flight home, plus a drink—or maybe two—and some banter with Lars or fiscal chitchat with Viv would be distractions from the dark feelings that shadowed the pleasant rush of success and sometimes even tainted her satisfaction at having pushed the project to completion.

Give all credit to Lars for the editing, but the book would never have become a reality if she had not sat herself down in his office, put the manuscript on the desk, and declared they were going to do it. She'd done that and so secured their success, which she, more than Lars, appreciated and understood. She'd already paid off the mortgage; the cars, hers and Dan's and Marge's, would be next, and that was just with her share. Lars could educate his daughter with his. But at that thought her heart clenched, because her own daughter had lived in a truck, risking her life to save money. At least, that's how Isobel saw it now. She preferred to minimize Iris's eccentricities and rebelliousness and to emphasize her hard work, her thrift, her dedication to the arts and to her family. This was *her* Iris.

"There's a little restaurant," she said, spotting a cast-iron facade with long windows that revealed a cozy cluster of tables and chairs behind wheat-colored café curtains. "With bar. We can all have a quick drink and a quick dinner and get out of this lousy rain. My treat."

Viv stopped and consulted her watch, large and black with a great many buttons and knobs, the sort of watch, more machine than timepiece, beloved by Navy divers, mountain climbers, and polar explorers. Lars was fascinated with this touch of adventure-chic in Vivienne Gallen, master of royalties and secondary rights, who had navigated the headwaters of publishing for them and was leading them ever farther into the unchartered bush of celebrity.

"Isobel, I'd love to but I can't," Viv said. "If I don't make the train, it's a three-hour wait. I canceled I don't know how many appointments for the show, but now I really have to run."

That was Viv's style, Lars thought, half gracious, half guiltmeister. And how clever of her to speak first. Usually, it was Lars who contrived to be in a great and busy rush and Viv who was left to have the calming postappearance drink with Isobel. Well, this once he could be a gentleman.

"Go ahead, Viv, go ahead. Isobel and I will grab dinner. If I leave now, I'll just hit rush-hour traffic, anyway."

They shook hands on the sidewalk, Isobel juggling her umbrella and spraying water to every side, before Viv strode away through the rush-hour crowds, a stolid, blocky shape in a black trench coat and a round dark hat that made Lars think of ancient wars and East European generals. Viv came with certain odd quasi-military vibes.

Isobel checked the menu in the restaurant window. "I think this will be all right. It should be for the price; I can't get over what they charge for plain ordinary pasta and hamburgers."

"From what Viv said, we can go on a champagne diet."

"I'm not so fond of champagne. Give me a gin and tonic. Better yet, a double. I'm amazed you don't get more nervous," she added when they were seated inside on uncomfortable bentwood chairs at a round marble-topped table. Their sodden rain gear dripped onto the worn and rather dirty looking wood floor.

"I'm used to an audience," Lars said, "with teaching for so many years."

"Iris said you were a good teacher."

"Iris was an exceptional student. Exceptional students encourage good teachers," said Lars, deflecting the compliment. He knew that they would talk about Iris, and one part of him was willing, even eager. His other, saner side, being in the avoidance mode, signaled to a waiter, who detached himself from one of the cast-iron pillars and flipped open his order book with surly distaste. Tall with well-styled black hair and model-perfect features marred only by unsteady, dilated eyes and a twitch at the corner of his mouth, he announced that his name was Shawn. Lars hoped that Shawn's medications were properly adjusted.

Isobel ordered a large gin and tonic, while Lars opted for a Scottish import beer.

"You're too modest," she said after their waiter walked off to the bar. "I don't remember Iris talking about anyone else on the staff."

"Not everyone could see she was exceptional. I didn't see it myself for a while." Lars would rather have changed the subject but, as a topic, Iris exerted a certain gravitational force, particularly when he was with her mother. "She came in late, she dressed oddly, she had this big funny backpack with her laundry. And then she was out, sick. Bronchitis, I guess it was."

"When did you know?" Isobel asked.

"Her reaction to poems. Blake's 'The Tyger' was the first one,

I think. The words touched her soul, that's the only way I can put it. And then she was an original; the accepted opinion, the done thing just didn't mean much to her intellectually. It was as if she'd been asleep and just woke up with this marvelous brain and very few preconceptions."

Shawn returned with Isobel's gin and Lars's imported beer and a wounded air that suggested this service was an extraordinary favor. Lars guessed he was a wanna-be artist awaiting his break and compared him unfavorably to Iris, who'd toiled cheerfully enough at Healthy Stuff.

"To Iris," he said.

Isobel smiled and raised her glass. "To Iris." She took a sip before asking "Will you always say that?"

Lars found it a curiously intimate moment.

"Always, unless you'd rather I not."

"No, no. In some ways, you and I remember her best." Isobel looked away, thinking about Dan and Marge and Iris's strangely attractive professor and all the other people who had known her and about Iris herself, maddening, difficult, beloved. She wanted to weep.

Lars reached out and squeezed her shoulder, an affectionate, encouraging gesture. He knew the pattern; it was why he was usually in a rush to leave the area, why he normally abandoned Isobel to Viv, who, he supposed, talked money instead of memory.

"My husband's people would have held a wake," Isobel said after a moment. "A real Irish wake with singing and music and lots and lots of liquor. I sometimes think we should have had a wake for Iris. I sometimes think I haven't done quite the right thing yet. I haven't been able to come to terms, Lars. First Bob, then Iris."

There was a thin, hysterical note in her voice, but Lars could only shrug. Who knew what would ease one's heart? He was not sure he would have trusted himself at the sort of unbridled affair Isobel was suggesting: drinking, singing, dancing, wailing—the release of so much emotion might lead past grief to confession. "The services were nice, though," he said cautiously.

"Beautiful. Don't think I don't appreciate what the college did."

She laid one of her large, warm, red-nailed hands on Lars's wrist. "Don't think I don't. It wasn't the school's fault."

"No." Coward that he was, Lars thanked God again that Iris had been killed off campus. Fear makes one low, ungenerous, but he had his reasons: Isobel was emotionally alert, he might even have said emotionally predatory. She had some of her daughter's curiosity; she was interested in how people worked, in what they thought.

"But," she said now, "I begin to see the point of wakes, which I used to think were crude and undignified. As if grief wasn't crude and undignified. Don't you agree? Dignified sorrow's such lot of crap. Grief's made me loud and unreasonable and too fond of a drink. Speaking of which . . ." She signaled to Shawn, holding up her glass for a refill. "This is a kind of serial wake, isn't it? You and me? Or more often Viv and me." A glance, half coy, half reproachful. She knew he found these meetings awkward, and she was determined to have them until she knew why. "We meet, we do a presentation, we stop for a drink, and you toast Iris. You used to do that when we were working on the book."

"I think of her often," Lars admitted. He thought he'd have another beer. He really should have followed Isobel's lead and had gin.

"I feel I haven't reached her yet," said Isobel. "I thought I knew her; I did know her as a child, I really did." She shook her head and her face darkened. "Adolescence is a different country. Way different, foreign territory. How old is your Cookie?"

"She's twelve."

"Adolescence comes earlier and earlier," said Isobel with a gloomy resignation. "Something about the fat in our diet."

"Yes," said Lars. Cookie was growing up, changing her interests, leaving childish things behind. To his regret, the dollhouse had never been replicated. They'd gotten as far as a detailed drawing, and Lars had gone to price stock at the lumber yard. The day they were set to buy their supplies, Cookie announced she'd rather have a proper desk and a better computer. They were to pick up a rebuilt PC tomorrow, and Lars had already finished the desk. It was a handsome piece with an oak top but not what he had secretly wanted, which was, first, to challenge and honor his father's craftsmanship, and second, but more important, to revise the past, to weaken the impact of fire and charred wood, of Cookie's blank and distant eyes, of Emma's alarm. Instead, like some strange form of dark matter, the burned dollhouse remained ever present in its conspicuous absence.

"Course," said Isobel with a low chuckle, "you can hardly starve girls to keep them children, can you? That's what they did in the bad old days."

"Without knowing it," protested Lars. "That's the difference. They all had lousy diets."

"That's what we like to think, anyway."

Lars thought that in the bad old days Isobel would have been something of a witch. She was something of a witch now, a sad witch, but a witch, nonetheless. Maybe the fate of clever, determined women was to pay for power with a peaked hat and a broomstick, with an aura of magic and danger. Lars noticed that he had finished his second beer.

After their third drink, Lars suggested—insisted on, actually—dinner. He was not normally a drinker, and it did not take an awful lot of alcohol to alter reality for him. Outside, the drizzle had become a downpour; rain ran in light rippled sheets down the long windows, and the resulting dampness made the front of the restaurant chilly. Lars found the soup du jour, with its sprinkling of mystery herbs and flower petals, more elegant than sustaining on such a dank night.

Isobel ordered a bottle of red wine and began to cheer up. Lars watched the rain and listened to the unintelligible hubbub of voices around them and grew depressed. He should have gone straight home. He could have had a quick drink with Isobel at the bus station or around the corner from the lot where he'd left his car. It was going to be a lousy drive at night in this weather. He should have gone after one beer, or even two. But at that point, Isobel had blown her nose and wiped her eyes, then gone to repair her makeup. "Of course, I'm a nuisance," she'd said. "But you don't know what it's like. Maybe Dan and Marge were right; doing this is tough, remembering is tough."

"It's what Iris wanted." Loyal, foolish Lars.

"What I tell myself," Isobel said and ordered another gin.

So there he was, captive of good intentions and kind impulses, facing a long, wet drive and a throbbing head. Lars nodded whenever Isobel spoke and let his mind drift until halfway through their entrees, spaghetti alfredo for her, veal marsala for him, when she said, "My mind is made up," and he realized he'd missed something important.

He nodded again just the same.

"Evidence, right," she said. "It's amassing evidence. It's jogging people's memories."

"The book, the talk show appearances, the signings," Lars said, picking up the thread. "All those should help."

"Undeniably. Iris's *murder*"—even the word was loathsome to her, an open wound—"is now a high-profile case. Thanks to you, Lars. Don't think I don't bless you for it." She put her hand on his arm again. "But we still have to give people a reason to come forward. People, person. I think there's one person who has information. Who saw Iris, who saw her killer, who can say, *she was at this precise place at this precise moment*, who has the last little piece of information the police need. I truly believe that."

Lars nodded, but with serious private reservations. He'd been under the same mistaken confidence in witnesses, in an alert, informed citizenry. He'd gambled on someone coming forward to say, "I saw so and so," "I saw such and such a car." Instead, it appeared that the only person conscious that night had been himself, and he'd believed that his relative ignorance would excuse his silence. He wished he could explain to Isobel how little he knew. Iris had appeared out of fog and rain and disappeared the same way and left him understanding nothing: not why she'd been in the arcade, not why she wanted to be dropped at the park, not why she refused a ride back to her truck (although, honestly, that wasn't so hard to understand; Lars understood that quite well). "People do not always realize what is important."

"Just what I'm saying. So I think we do two things: get the case on one of those crime reconstruction shows and offer a reward for information, any information no matter how apparently insignificant.

We have the money," she added, and Lars realized that she meant the two of them.

"What were you thinking of?"

"Champagne. That's what you said. A champagne diet. We could put together forty, fifty thousand out of the royalties. Fifty is best, don't you think? Fifty sounds more generous."

"Fifty *is* more generous." Lars felt a certain irritation, though the reward was an excellent idea, though he should probably have been the one to suggest it, though they could well afford it out of their royalties. Just the same, he disliked semiforced contributions, and there was, of course, always the off chance that someone of lunatic curiosity or preternatural powers of observation had seen Iris in the arcade or had seen him with Iris or had noticed his car or had heard enough of their brief, sad, angry argument to remember, to identify. That was the chance—and Isobel's hope—and he was now in position to pay for half of it. Well, they'd see. In Isobel's present state, she might or might not remember the conversation and his silence which, yes, she was going to take for assent, for she took his hand and stroked it with her strong red-tipped fingers. "I knew you'd agree. I rely on you absolutely. But, of course, the actual reward must come from the family. I will let Dan do the announcement. I think that's best, don't you? And I'll contact the various producers. I'm sure Viv can get me a list, she has contacts. They will agree, I know they will."

Lars suspected they would. Isobel was a hard woman to refuse under any circumstances. As the grieving mother of a literary genius cut off in her first flowering—well!

"They'll just have to, they must," Isobel repeated. She put her hand over her mouth and started rocking back and forth in her chair. She did that sometimes after a few drinks. She'd be sitting talking and then, suddenly, sorrow overwhelmed her. She'd borne up well, Lars had to admit, but these evenings made her give way, and he wondered sometimes if she drank in order to grieve, if she needed this serial wake to release her feelings. He wondered if she didn't trust herself, otherwise, if grief for her was like an uncovered well. Lars could imagine that dark, bottomless drop, and he understood that when and where and how much you could trust yourself was important to know, a vital life skill. Iris had just been learning that. With Sven, whoever he was. He was the one the police should turn up.

"The uncertainty is killing me," Isobel said through tears. "The thought that he's out there, that he's living and breathing and maybe enjoying life. Do such people enjoy life afterward? Can they, do you think?"

A good question. Lars decided, one of the questions of our time. He thought the answer was yes. From Auschwitz to Phnom Penh to Kigali to Kosovo to good old U.S. of A., there were people who'd rolled up their sleeves and murdered their fellows, before resuming life as ordinary citizens, who doted on their pets and children, tended their gardens, mowed their lawns, played golf. If they were subsequently disturbed by justice and hauled up before mikes and cameras, they expressed astonishment and, occasionally, defiance. Perhaps the old idea that evil brings an inevitable retribution is no more certain than our hope that innocence is protective. "Killers survive, anyway. That's what the evidence suggests."

"While Iris with all her talent and all her—vitality, and—" she paused, seeking words.

"Wit," Lars suggested.

"Wit, humor. She *wanted* to live, didn't she? She was a person who *really wanted* to live."

"Yes," Lars said, "on the whole, yes."

"What do you mean, *on the whole?*" An alert, head up, Roman matron look. Should he fail or deceive her, she'd behold his body on his shield without a tremor.

"I mean that Iris was like the rest of us; she had her moments of melancholy."

"You blame me," said Isobel, and her rising voice held a keen note that cut through the background murmur. "You blame me for letting her live in the truck, for failing her when Bob died, for not understanding her *genius*. I did fail her! But at the time, with Bob's death—he was a wonderful man, a kindly, fun, wonderful man. Sensible, too. He kept me from getting carried away with things. And he kept the kids in line. He never had to raise his voice with them. Never. Not even with Iris. I have to admit, I raised my voice plenty with Iris. I miss him so much, Lars."

Lars had heard before about the virtues of Bob Weed. "I understand. I don't blame you at all. I don't know what I'd do without Emma."

But Isobel wasn't listening, or if she was, she didn't want to hear about Emma. "I didn't even know about Iris's living arrangements until partway through the semester. She could be so headstrong—it really took her father to handle Iris. It should be a girl's mother who's close to her, shouldn't it? Marge, now, Marge and I were always best friends. Iris was difficult and closemouthed. Downright secretive. But kindly, too, there's the thing, Lars. I can get so mad at her and then I remember that." Isobel sniffled again and wiped her face on her napkin. "She knew the truck business would send me up the wall, but she did it anyway and then kept it from me so I wouldn't worry. That was her excuse: 'I didn't want you to worry.' "

Lars pulled a glum face. Cookie had said nothing about her troubles at school, either. If anything, she said even less about school now than before. And less, Lars thought, to him in general. She was more cautious, less confiding; even Dr. Viollette was finding her secretive, "a charming but stubborn child." The good doctor spoke vaguely of hidden fears, and Lars guessed that she wasn't getting very far. As for him and Cookie, a secret that wasn't really a secret lay between them, and he'd never found quite the right words to talk to her about the dollhouse, about the fires. So far as he knew, they hadn't been repeated, thank God for that, but the experience had made her, like Iris, closemouthed. The suggestion of rebuilding the dollhouse had been his nonverbal gambit. Had Cookie understood that and rejected it? Or was she just growing up, becoming too old for even the most cherished toys?

"I never imagined her living like a gypsy and writing a book about it. That's hardly the first thing you'd think of," Isobel continued.

Iris had been right, Lars thought, her mother had a conventional mind.

"I'd had other ideas, other worries. When she didn't say anything about roommates, about dorm life—none of the usual complaints—I thought, Aha, there's a boy somewhere."

"There was one," Lars said. "She did mention one. But the police don't seem to think he was significant."

"Significant or insignificant: The police were all over me on that detail. Oh, you bet they were! They were surprised I didn't know, and they let me see it. 'And did you know anything about boyfriends, Mrs. Weed?' As if I could monitor her every move when she was hundreds of miles away, living in parking lots. Girls today, students, of course they have boyfriends. You start with that assumption."

"Of course," said Lars.

"And then so much was in Iris's imagination, anyway. She made up a good deal in her book. She certainly did exaggerate."

"The writing process," Lars reminded her gently. They'd had heated debates about this, yes, indeed, and about the fictive aspects of memoirs and autobiographies, and about their own roles as editors and their duty to honor the author's intentions.

"All right, she *modified* the facts," Isobel said like a good student. "Call it what you will, she *modified* a good many things in her book."

Lars nodded. He'd like to think that Iris had modified the whole Sven episode. He'd have been a lot happier if he could have convinced himself of this proposition and so freed his mind from the grasp of unsettling fears and doubts. Would that Sven himself had been a complete invention or that the police had taken Lars's hint and turned him up. But no. If anything, the detectives seemed inclined to believe Sven was an invention—Lars's, that is, not Iris's. That was an unexpected consequence of the loss of the diary, but Lars could not afford to worry about that now.

He reminded himself that the police, the experts, had questioned and eliminated all her friends and associates. The diligent investigators had done the times and places and alibis and corroborating statements and physical evidence and come up empty: Every male who'd ever been seen with Iris had an alibi. True, Lars might have corrected certain inaccuracies about the timing, inaccuracies that sometimes troubled him in the wee hours, when he awoke with a lively sense of omissions and selfishness. Then he would remind himself that professionals had been at work, because fortunately or not, everything Iris had imagined and thought about him—and Sven—was powder and ashes.

"I'd have been worried if she'd been living with someone," Isobel continued. "Worried in one way. Relieved in another. Iris hadn't had a terribly successful social life—with boys, I mean, although she was likable enough. And I think"—here, considering her alcohol consumption, she gave Lars a rather searching glance—"I think that men were attracted to her. Was she attractive? Likable?"

"She had a peculiar but considerable charm," Lars said judiciously.

"I think people, men in particular, maybe misinterpreted her and that got her into awkward situations." Isobel shook her head. Their last Christmas had been a classic Iris disaster with the trouble between her and Marge and Marge's idiot boyfriend. At the time she'd blamed Iris; now she held the boy responsible, and Marge, too. They were old enough to avoid drunken parties or not to take what happened at them so seriously.

"Iris had some growing up to do," Lars said, "but anyone can come across a crazy person. Random violence has no reason. I suppose she was in a little more danger with the truck, but she had a great deal of aplomb, and when she suggested the project, I had to admit I thought her idea was a good one."

"The project, the book! You should have thought about the dangers! I didn't know, but you did. No book is worth this." Isobel began sobbing, her face uncovered, naked as a rainwashed stone. People looked around from the nearby tables, and their formerly indifferent waiter, now vulturous and alert, drifted into the area with a quizzical look. Lars waved him away and, feeling acutely uncomfortable, patted Isobel's shoulder. He should have gone home, he should have escorted her to the airport bus an hour ago. He'd known this would happen, he'd foreseen it, and yet a few occasional drinks with Isobel seemed to be part of an elaborate—and not wholly justified—penance.

"They'll find him," he said. "They'll find him sooner or later."

"Him, him! They haven't a clue, do they?" she demanded, recovering herself a little. "They haven't a scrap of forensic evidence, no DNA, no weapon, they don't have anything or anyone, Lars, but you, do they?"

She'd taken him by surprise, and he opened his mouth to protest.

"You were the one and only suspect, simply because you worked with her on her project and had coffee with her and walked with her around the campus."

Lars found he could not read Isobel's impenetrable eyes.

She wiped her nose and, seeing his alarm, gave a faint, and faintly reassuring, smile. Lars wondered if she might not have a rather macabre sense of fun.

"Wouldn't inspire anyone to be a conscientious instructor, would it, Lars? No, no, I don't have any doubts, and, Lars, once we've issued the notice and put up the reward, other people won't have any doubts, either. You know that. This will be good for you, too."

He nodded. He felt that he was being wrapped in lead.

"I'll talk to Viv about royalties, about how soon we can expect money from the latest print run. There will have to be a joint letter. And legal advice. Tax advice. I'll let you know."

Isobel's voice sounded surprisingly crisp. She had a wonderful head for liquor and, like a singer who can leap from low-octave despair to joyous stratospheric trills, an agile range of emotion. Lars looked at his watch. "We'd better get going. You don't want to miss your flight."

Isobel reached out and turned his wrist to check his watch. "Lots of time yet. The bus goes direct to the terminal. We'll have coffee and a brandy. I need a brandy for my nerves."

"I'll leave that to you," said Lars. "I've got to drive."

"Oh, but you must," Isobel said, signaling to Shawn. "Brandy for a bargain. It's the only thing. Besides, I'm surprised you don't stay over. It's—how long back to Connecticut?"

"Couple hours if I'm lucky."

"I'd stay over and see the city if I didn't have to be at work Saturday. Absolutely, yes. Command performance at Filene's: the new holiday eye makeup. No rest from beauty."

She talked amusingly about her work, abandoning heavy emotional swells for smooth conversational sailing: She'd gotten what she'd wanted and the wake was over for this evening. Lars thought about the noisy, cheerful endings of old New Orleans jazz funerals and, in a reckless, semidrunken moment, kissed Isobel in the taxi on their way to the bus terminal. Kissed her not once, which was foolish, but twice, which was dangerous.

And he knew better; he'd foreseen all and done it anyway. Standing on the wet, light-washed sidewalk as she disappeared behind the glass doors, Lars felt depressed, even a little frightened. What good is all our caution and rationality? Were the old Greeks right that we are fated for certain predestined ends? What was he doing, why was he here, what on earth was he about with talk shows and celebrity and Isobel Weed? The city lights wavered in the drizzle, his head was throbbing. The mixture of beer and red wine was poisonous for him, and he'd had far too much of both. And then brandy! Brandy, it appeared, turned his mind to philosophy and existential questions, as well as producing a strong impulse toward oblivion. He'd never make it up the parkway.

When he called Emma, she was understanding. He omitted the taxi ride, of course, and half the drinks, to focus on Isobel's grief and the unwise consumption of brandy.

"Well, poor woman," Emma said. "Who can blame her? And just over a year after her husband."

"Tragic," said Lars.

"So you'll be home tomorrow?"

"By eleven, I hope. Eleven, eleven-thirty."

A noise in the background.

"Cookie's saying something about her computer."

"Oh, damn, that's right." They'd had the computer store put more memory in Lars's old PC and add a high-speed modem. "I think the repair department closes at noon, but I'll be up early. I can make it home in time to take her."

"Never mind," said Emma. "Girls' morning out. We'll pick up the machine after the grocery shopping."

"Terrific, thanks. Love you."

After Lars hung up, he pushed aside the inner mesh curtain to look down at the wet night, the black canyon of the alley and the mellow lights of the facing building, at the sliver of Forty-seventh Street where car lights winked red and white. He was on the ninth floor and the air system reduced the never-ending noise of the city to a homogenized rumble, interrupted now and again by sirens. Lars wasn't fond of hotel rooms, disliking equally the somehow spurious luxury of the better ones and the stale seediness of poorer. Their anonymity and uniformity depressed him, especially when, as tonight, he had no work, no business, no pleasure on tap. The particular loneliness of hotel rooms made him reflective, and, as so often since he'd first met her, Iris entered his thoughts.

He no longer missed her; time had tempered his grief if not his regrets. Iris of the Golden Wings came to him now not as desire but as warning, as a sense of vulnerability, as a reminder that he was open to attack by irrational forces without—or within.

12.

The keyboard's trashed," the young computer manager told Cookie. "I've thrown in a new one for you. The letters were all worn off," he added to Emma. "Even if you're a good typist—are you a good typist?" he asked Cookie.

She tipped her head to one side, a newly flirtatious gesture, her mother noticed. "I'm okay," she said.

"Even if you're a good typist, that old one is one tough keyboard."

Cookie gave him a quick, radiant smile.

"What do you say?" prompted Emma.

"Thanks so much!"

"No problem." He began going over the machine: the many megs of memory, the speed of the new modem, not to forget the upgraded word-processing program that he'd installed, apparently just out of the goodness of his heart, for Ms. Cookie Larson. The manager, whose name was Jack, was tall and kinetic. He had beautiful hands, like a pianist, Emma thought, and coal black hair pulled back in a ponytail and large gray eyes with a distinctive dark ring around the iris: a sleek, handsome, vigorous man. Emma registered this and the fact that the computer store seemed to attract more than the usual number of noisy young girls who drifted in and out from the mall concourse to look at the laptops and wild screen savers and new game stations, but really, Emma guessed, to scope out Mr. Jack, who ranged back and forth down the counter, answering questions, directing customers, writing up repairs, his muscular white arms visible under his rolled-up dress shirt: a prince in exile. She could understand the girls' interest: He was quite gorgeous, the sort of man who could make even a sensible woman nostalgic, nostalgic, in Emma's case, not so much for adventures past as for the delights of that earlier era when male beauty was still the stuff of daydreams and giggled conferences and the most amazing speculations.

In maturity, Emma had made other choices, selecting a man who was attractive in other ways, who joked she had enough beauty for both of them. It was true that at past forty, Emma was still noticed even by men as young as Mr. Jack. She moved through life in a cloud of admiration, an atmospheric displacement, which she was wise enough not to overvalue but which, on some level, she was always aware of, and which, on another level, she expected. Mr. Jack's smile, his attentiveness, his prompt appearance at their place on the long counter, his care with the machine, his eager explanations to Cookie—these were some of the benefits.

"E-mail," Mr. Jack was asking. "Who's your E-mail provider going to be?"

Emma told him that they'd put Cookie on their account with her own screen name.

"Good. They're all right. Good for beginners, and the addresses are easy to remember."

Emma smiled at him and then, as he turned to show Cookie how the modem worked—a demonstration far beyond the shop's usual laconic, "The instructions are enclosed"—Emma realized that his attention was really on her daughter. That made her look at Cookie, who was wearing her red team sweatshirt (soccer having come back into favor strongly that fall) and a pair of faded jeans. Her thick dark hair was tangled as usual and, Emma noticed, one of her rather dirty sneakers was untied. That was Cookie, slovenly and careless in dress, and yet the effect, Emma could see, had undergone a sea change since summer, when, in a similar outfit, Cookie had been a child, her prettiness scarcely noticeable unless you peeked under the long, messy bangs. Now, though the only real physical difference was what promised to be a pair of very long legs, Cookie had jumped forward into adolescence. Emma realized that her lively, athletic daughter might well become the femme fatale her father had always predicted, a thought that produced an odd amalgam of pride and apprehension with just a touch of indignation for she saw that Cookie's head was almost touching the manager's as they leaned over the back of the computer. *What was he about?*

"I think we can manage that," Emma said. "Both my husband and I use computers at work."

"I want to do it myself," said Cookie, sly, traitorous, irrational adolescent, giving Emma alarming visions of wild boys, fast cars, mad parties.

Mr. Jack instantly switched his interest to Emma. What system did she use? Did she like those new Macs the schools had installed? And then, too casually and slyly for her to notice, was her husband Professor Larson at the college?

One of Lars's students, Emma guessed, but no, he'd happened to see yesterday's television program.

"Wasn't he great?" asked Cookie. She loved to see her father on TV; the television appearances and his new show business glamour had done much to restore Lars to her favor. For this, Emma was thankful, for if she had sometimes envied (well, she told herself, envied was maybe too strong a word) Lars's bond with Cookie, she had been distressed when it was weakened, distressed for Cookie, distressed even for Lars, who was entirely at fault. And the results— sullenness, suspicions, the terrible business with the fires—had led Emma into anxiety and doubt. No, no, this recent celebrity was good and would have only good results.

"Terrific," agreed Mr. Jack. "I wish I'd had professors like that."

"My dad is one of the best professors at the whole college," Cookie said.

At least, Emma thought, she still sounds like a seventh grader.

"I'm sure he is," said Mr. Jack, beginning to put the tower and the keyboard into a carton. "This will give the computer some protection on the way home. Is your car in the lot?"

He carried the box for them, though they could certainly have managed, but Emma was used to these little attentions and too gracious to deny a man the pleasure of gallantry. Mr. Jack left his white fluorescent palace with its long, shiny counter to accompany them to the station wagon, which was not really the vehicle he'd expected, which reminded him again how right it was to be thorough, to give good service.

He was learning, he certainly was, and wouldn't that please George, his supervisor, who hadn't been entirely happy about his hire, who had feared that Jack, overeducated, would be too intellectual and theoretical: as if you didn't need brains to run a store, to manage computer sales and service, to cope with the daily quotient of mall rats and assorted assholes. Fortunately, Jack had all that experience on the computer help desk and doing techie work for humanities profs who were, technologically speaking, in the Stone Age. Jack not only knew his stuff, he was willing to work for the Computer Exchange's pitiful wage, a circumstance that should have raised questions in George's tiny mind but had not. And that was lucky, Jack realized, because, as this morning showed, he still needed to plan and reconnoiter. He couldn't take anything for granted. Not one single thing.

"Dad's home!" Cookie exclaimed as they turned onto their street. "Wait till he sees how fast my computer runs."

"He'll want it back," Emma teased. She pulled into the narrow drive behind Lars's old Volvo. "Groceries," she reminded Cookie as her daughter bolted up the walk. "Take those in. Your dad can bring the machine."

"Dad, Dad!" Cookie yelled, grocery bags in her arms. She used her elbow to ring the bell and sent Jake to another level of barking. "We got the computer! Wait till you see it."

Lars unhooked the screen, took one of the bags, gave her a hug. "Sorry I was late getting back."

"That's okay. Everyone saw you. Didn't they, Mom? Mr. Jack saw you. Mr. Jack thought you were great."

"Who's Mr. Jack?"

"The computer man. He showed me how the modem works and

how to log on and safe chat sites and everything. I can do it all myself. I'm going to set the machine up right away."

Bustle of groceries, bags, icebox, freezer, pantry. Dog underfoot, cat on the counter. Then inside and upstairs with the computer box while Cookie provided a stream of commentary about speeds and megs and RAM and screen names and passwords. "Never give out your password to anyone," she concluded. "You never know what they might do with it. Not even to your best friend."

"Guard it with your life," Lars agreed.

Cookie tipped her head and looked at him from under her bangs to see if he was teasing. Then she released a little bubbling giggle, as if her happiness had been bottled under pressure. "Hold the box for me. I'll lift out the tower."

"Where did she learn all this stuff?"

"They're breathing it," said Emma. "They're miles ahead of us. And the computer man really was very nice. He spent a lot of time with her. The royal treatment."

"Nothing but the best for my girls," Lars said. "Who could resist you? And together! Now if you'd been on the show, the country would have ground to a halt."

"Oh, Dad!"

"No, really. It's all about personality, Viv says. Viv also says we were very good, by the way, and there's to be another printing. Better study up, Cookie; we'll be able to send you to any school in the country."

Cookie made a face; if anything, school had dropped even further in her regard. "I'm probably going to get a soccer scholarship. Maybe I'll study computers or maybe I'll be a professional athlete."

Lars exchanged a glance with Emma, who rolled her eyes.

"Help me lift the monitor, Dad."

Connections, plugs, a whir of powerful electronics before the screen blossomed into icons like petals. Cookie's rapt face, the tweettle twittle of the connection, the plastic clatter as she typed her password. "You have to send me mail, Dad. Will you send me mail?"

"Of course," said Lars. "Every day from the office."

"But now, now so we can see if it works. You can use your school account and I'll stay on this one."

"But not for long," said Emma. "I'm starting lunch. I bet you skipped breakfast."

"Coffee and a doughnut," Lars confessed.

"I can get the weather," said Cookie, who had never before expressed interest in things meteorological. "And I'm going to find a Britney Spears Web site."

"I hope that thing has a weak speaker system," said Emma and headed for the kitchen. Lars went into his study and turned on his machine. He could still hear Cookie announcing various features and discoveries. While his head had lost the percussive throb of the previous evening, he retained the memory of folly as a dull ache. Next time, he'd leave Isobel to Viv. Or, better yet, take Emma with him or, even better, Cookie, who seemed fascinated by the whole business, who would enjoy the bustle of the studio, the lighting, the sound booth, the cameramen, the split-second timing. Yes, that's what he'd do: He'd defang Isobel by putting himself out of harm's way and cutting off the serial wake.

His mail screen came up, a torrent of subjects and addresses: *The Chronicle of Higher Education*, student queries—all, Lars suspected, relating to the paper due on Monday—another missive from the chair to the Freshman Experience Committee, the latest faculty round-robin on the journals collection, and one identified only as subject, *I Know You*. Lars realized he did not have Cookie's address and shouted down the hall. Her thunderous running feet rocked the wounded gray matter between his temples. She skidded to a stop and swung around the casement, "What?"

"Your address?"

He typed it in and added her to his address book. "Okay, here goes."

She raced back to her machine. Nice to see her enthusiastic. He and Emma had hoped the computer might stimulate her academic interests and encourage her to type her school papers. She was so bright, so careless, so—Lars stopped, shook his head. He had not previously recognized the similarities between Cookie and Iris, personal similarities, not physical: Iris was white-skinned, statuesque, often remote. Cookie, eager as a puppy, was dark with almost dusky red cheeks, but both had the kind of sturdy independence that boded . . .

An impatient cry from the vicinity of Ms. Cookie Larson.

"In a minute," he called and began typing, using the formal style that amused them both: *Dear Cookie, Your father, the quasi-celebrity and talk show habitué, is honored to be your very first E-mail correspondent. Remember to spell everything correctly and answer promptly and don't speak to strangers on line. In return, Daddy Lars promises to write you something amusing every single day. Your loving father.*

Not up to his usual standard, but the best he could do after Isobel and brandy and a three-hour drive through traffic home. A cheer from Cookie, anyway, who raced down the hall to tell him not to leave his machine. "I'm going to reply. Stay on line."

"But quick," said Lars. "Just a short, short message. Mom's going to have lunch ready."

"In a flash," she promised and was off again.

While he waited, Lars checked his mail, starting with the students' questions and excuses, evidence of impossibly complex lives. Then the chair's request for the Freshman Experience Committee preliminary report. Lars thought that their agenda for the coming months should suffice. He had no intention of being overly efficient, which might land him with more committee assignments; on the other hand, he hated to waste time when, as everyone knew, the Freshman Experience needed a radical overhaul and he, personally, needed points for good behavior. That left only *I Know You*.

"Okay, Daddy?"

Lars clicked on the newest message: *Dear Daddy, I will always look forward to your missives with the greatest pleasure. Your loving & computer litirate Cookie.*

He did not have the heart to correct her spelling but typed, *Dear Cookie, It's time for lunch!!!! Your loving and literate but not very computer savvy dad.*

The rest of the mail could wait. He deleted the *Chronicle*, which he'd seen in print, and the round-robin effusions, then hesitated at *I Know You.* It was a Hotmail address he did not recognize, probably an old student. He clicked the button, thinking he'd take a peek and answer it later with the student queries.

Professor Larson, he read, *I know all about you. You think no one knows what you did, but I know. Will I tell or will I handle this myself? That's for you to guess. Have a nice day and remember that I know.*

His first thought, quite stupid, really, was to scroll down for the signature, which was, of course, missing. His heart was racing. They had not even offered the reward yet and here came a witness, a spy, a snoop who could say, *I saw you drop off Iris Weed the night she was killed.* Or worse, *I saw you with the late Iris Weed in the arcade of the college after seven on the night she was killed.* Or absolute worst, *I saw you arguing with Iris Weed in the park. You took her arms and shook her and she pushed you and yelled that she never wanted to see you again.* And what would that do to him? To him and Emma? To him and Cookie? And to Isobel and Viv and an assortment of other professional and personal contacts? Lars gripped the side of the desk and felt pain begin pumping against the sides of his skull. This is what he had feared and dreaded. He had suffered miserably for weeks and months, before, gradually, he had come to hope, and then to believe, yes, to believe—otherwise he would never have exposed himself with book contracts and radio interviews and television shows—that he was safe. Oh, this was a betrayal of trust! He had trusted the police to find the killer, and they had not! They had found only him. And then he had trusted time, which "hath an art to make dust of all things," as Sir Thomas Browne so elegantly phrased it, but which, capriciously, had spared some fool's casual memory for his, Lars's, undoing.

He read the E-mail again, fascinated by each snake-eyed letter, feeling meaning disintegrate. *I know all about you. You think no one knows what you did, but I know. Will I tell or will I handle this myself? That's for you to guess. Have a nice day and remember that I know.*

Lars forced himself to concentrate, to get past the individual letters, the individual words. He'd absorbed the fact of a threat instantly but shock had blurred the details. What did this really say?

What did this person know? Take a deep breath and conclude: nothing very concrete! Vague, vague, vague goes the red pencil. Give me some specifics, demands the professor, who will decry the level of modern discourse in his next lecture. Was this knowledge or a guess? Some idler who had noticed him around campus with Iris and wanted to cause trouble? Or someone who'd been out that fatal night and wanted—what? A good citizen in possession of material information goes to the police. Score a point against his unknown correspondent! At the same time, Lars could scarcely wish for renewed visits from Detectives Harrelson and Paatelainen. The question remained: What was the motive? What was the plan? *That's for you to guess.* This childish cliché was followed by *Have a nice day and remember that I know*: a logical impossibility. What did he want? Or she? Lars knew he must not rule anyone out and added, *Everyone's a suspect to The Semiotics of the Cop Show.*

"Dad, Mom says you're to come," Cookie yelled. "Lunch is all ready!"

"Yes, yes. A minute."

She appeared in the doorway an instant later, and, startled, Lars hit Delete, which was his second stupid idea, because as the screen went blank he realized that he did not know the address: something hotmail, something with numbers. He was terrible at remembering numbers; he should have made a note and kept it as evidence or done some clever thing. Replied? Should he have replied? What could he have replied? The message was absurd, bizarre, a fishing expedition, a wild guess.

"We're having pizza," said Cookie. "It's all heated up. Mom says it's going to be burned black if you don't come right this minute."

Lars pulled himself away from the screen and forced a smile. He was conscious of his teeth, of the tension across his lips and at the corners of his mouth. Cookie put her arm around his waist and gave him a big hug. "The computer is so great," she said. "It's awesome."

"You'll be able to do your papers and reports on it."

"I can do cards and things if I get the right program," said Cookie. "I could write something for the team newsletter."

"You could indeed," said Lars.

Downstairs in the kitchen, he was both relieved and astonished to see that neither she nor Emma registered his mood. They chattered on about the computer, the pizza, a science project that would require a trip to the state forest, as if he wasn't sitting across from them, suspiciously silent, his head throbbing, his stomach in knots. But then he was practiced in deception. Last year, when the case was fresh, when he'd had Harrelson and Paatelainen perched on his shoulders like twin vultures, when his oldest friends were suspicious, even then Lars had managed an unclouded face at home. Calm, debonair, secure in his innocence: that was Lars, master of the deceptive arts. How he dreaded returning to that time and place, to the constant strain of a caution so foreign to his spontaneous and playful temperament.

Lars looked across at Emma's calm features and Cookie's happy expression, at the serenity he had exerted himself to preserve, and felt resentment, almost anger. How little they knew him, how little they noticed him, how little they cared. He was abrupt and snappy when Cookie suggested a ride out to the state park, then Emma reminded him that it was for the science project and he had to rein in his mood.

"Gather ye leaves while ye may, the north wind is swiftly flying," he intoned, the words like weights, so hard it was to lift his spirits and reach the comic mode. "Are we set for this botanical excursion? Are there cookies, cookies for Cookie, Emma? Sustenance for the explorers?"

When Cookie went to get her backpack and assemble a snack, Emma looked at him, the sort of slow, perceptive look he had dreaded and expected. "You all right?" she asked.

He reached out and pressed her hand. "I will never drink brandy again," he said.

"These programs—promotional appearances, whatever you call them—they're difficult for you, aren't they?"

Though in some ways Lars loved them, he said yes, they were: They reminded him of sad things and bad times. "But it means so much to Isobel and the book meant so much to Iris."

Emma smiled gently and ruffled his hair. "You've been very good,

Lars," she said, and he brightened up. Emma was his real sun; her belief sustained him, and for her he would once again embrace deception. But no need for melodrama. The poisonous E-mail was gone and good riddance; he'd taken it too seriously, or rather, too personally. We live in a confrontational society where professors can get death threats for bad grades and people pull guns over contested parking spaces. Lars thought that he might profitably write something about the rhetoric of confrontation from trash-talking athletes to the military metaphors beloved by the captains of industry. He had to say that personal stress produced a flood of useful ideas, which, if it held true across the board, meant that his colleagues' unending papers and monographs stemmed from lives above the abyss. Self-dramatization among academics might be another possibility, and, smiling at the thought, Lars embraced Emma. He'd be fine, they'd be okay.

"Let's go to the trees," he said. "Let's find some bosky dell and weave vine leaves in our hair."

Emma, that sensible woman, laughed at him, but Lars did not mind. They were safe, and things were still going to be okay.

That's what he told himself in the morning, too, when, awakened by Cookie's noisy preparations for school and Emma's coffee brewing, he had an impulse to go right to his machine and check his E-mail. He was sitting on the edge of the bed, his feet on the floor, when he realized this would never do. He never checked E-mail, never even entered his study before breakfast, and, as the first rule of deception is to appear normal, Professor Larson must stroll down just as his womenfolk were leaving, kiss them both good-bye, make his breakfast, and read the paper before troubling his mind with student pleas, faculty directives, or other possible communications. It was a matter of discipline. He might, in fact, even wait until he got to school. He might.

But in the event, Lars found he did not have quite that much self-control. He took his morning coffee to the study, powered up the PC, and went right into his mail: student messages, several on-line journals, and more on the state of the library collections, suggesting that some of his colleagues did E-mail into the wee hours. Lars felt his blood pressure receding gently and his breakfast settling comfortably into the digestive mode. Yesterday's message, as he had thought, as he had so sensibly thought, was insignificant, nothing more than cybergraffiti. Disturbing, certainly, after all these months, but to be expected. Viv had been right. He'd had no idea at all of the power of the media. In twenty minutes, millions and millions of people who'd never before known anything about him or Isobel learned that they existed and that the greatly talented Iris had written and died.

Out of all those millions, how many were nut cases, psychos, believers in Martian spaceships, black helicopters, alien thought control? The normally sobering magnitude of citizen irrationality lifted Lars's spirits. He started whistling as he dressed for school and wondered if he should warn Isobel about the possibility of crank mail. If only he'd had sense enough to keep the address—but that was hardly important now. No doubt his particular psycho had seen other shows over the weekend and was betaking himself to Milton's "fresh woods and pastures new." Lars entertained himself for a few minutes with the image of a man pounding maniacally at a keyboard, sending poison missives to the famous and the obscure alike, a crank of bardic dimensions, a demented Whitman, determined to cover folk of every race and station with spleen.

Buoyed by this fantasy, Lars was feeling positively chipper by the time he reached school, and his classes went particularly well as relief bubbled up into the witty asides and amusing anecdotes that marked the best of his lectures. He corrected some papers, typed an exam, had a long conference with a graduate student who was casting about for a dissertation topic. Lars was ready to pack up and go home when he remembered that he had not forwarded the agenda for the Freshman Experience Committee. He could print out a copy and walk down the hall, but then he'd be caught; the chair would want some more specifics, the rationale behind the agenda, Lars's thoughts on how even the most innocuous changes could be made palatable to the Precambrian minds on the staff. Quicker to E-mail.

When Lars switched to the server, he noticed that he had new mail. But E-mail was not a problem, it was from students, of course, and the day's on-line copy of *The Chronicle*, and one rogue hotmail address, subject: *Are you paying attention?* Lars clicked Read almost too quickly to feel apprehension:

Dear Professor Larson,

Are you reading your mail?

Please don't dismiss my letters as crank notes. That would be extremely dangerous for you. Repeat to yourself: someone knows. And then ask yourself, what should I do?

Have a nice day and keep this warning in mind.

Of course it was unsigned.

Lars sat in his chair, breathing, listening to his heart, feeling fear give way to anger. This was a threat, veiled and unspecific, but a threat, nonetheless. A disgruntled student hiding behind a private server? He'd find out. Lars got out a note card and copied down the address: ISPU002@hotmail.com. Better yet, he'd save the E-mail; he'd have documentation, proof. Make note of the date and time, get the department's technical whiz to see about tracking down the correspondent. He should have saved the first E-mail, too. He'd build a dossier; there were surely laws against threatening, cyber-harassment, whatever.

And yet, even as he busied himself with saving the E-mail and putting the address safely in his briefcase, Lars knew that he was not going to consult the techie or anyone else. *I know what you did. Will I tell? Someone knows.* Did he want to explain these? Did he want to remind colleagues, or even, God forbid, the police, that there had been questions, ambiguities? He had what he supposed the psychology department would call innocence issues, and he could not bear to reopen inquiries and suspicions. It wouldn't be fair to Cookie and Emma. To Isobel. It wouldn't.

Even to consider action was to fall into the trap, because what did this message actually say? *I am not a crank.* Well and good. And *someone knows.* What? If he—or she—had evidence, wouldn't something along the lines of *I saw you on the night of . . .* be mentioned? But no, there was no evidence, just the unflattering assumption that

213

Lars had such a guilty conscience he would need only a suggestion of exposure to panic. If that was it, the crank had mistaken his man! Someone who could face one hundred and fifty undergraduates with only a podium and a handful of notes or parry the combined forces of Harrelson and Paatelainen for months at a time was not so easily cowed.

This note was harassment plain and simple, and the key thing was not to get even but to keep calm. Perhaps he should just purge this letter, throw away the address, ignore the whole matter. But, no, the message was evidence. Confronting the vast Empty Quarter of Iris's death, Lars had the superstition that anything could be important: so into the electronic file cabinet, the proper place for such cyberpoisons, such toxic binaries.

He wrote a brief note to the chair about the Freshman Experience Committee, attached the agenda, and shut down his machine. He'd be home from school just after Cookie, and they'd help Emma by picking up the groceries. His correspondent might be surprised to know that Lars intended to maintain a normal life.

At first, Lars logged on every morning with a tightness in his chest and the expectation of unpleasantness, but then came a hiatus. One day passed, another. The weekend arrived with its familiar routines. Lars stood in ankle-deep mud on Sunday afternoon to watch Cookie, tireless and intent, race up and down the soccer field. Even his untutored, and largely disinterested, eye could see how her growing skill and sense of the game stood out. She'd been promoted to the travel team, and the coach had recommended that she try out for one of the area's select squads. To Lars's secret relief, Cookie seemed indifferent to this prospect. She liked the girls on the travel team; her best friend, Amanda, was the striker; she didn't want to play with anyone else.

After the game, they went home chilled and wet-footed to an early dinner, Emma's roast chicken, the best in the world. When the bird was reduced to bones, they sat around the table as Polly and Jake finished the scraps, Lars ignoring his papers, Emma, the quilt she was making, and Cookie, her new computer. They rehashed the game for Emma and swapped bad jokes for Lars, who had an eccentric taste for the schoolyard funnies with which Emma and Cookie were always well provided.

The kitchen with its old wooden cabinets, rather dark during the day, came into its own on these early fall nights when the big hanging light over the table washed the oak with gold. Emma had seen a piece of stained glass that she wanted to put into the window over the sink. Could that be done? Lars thought so; he would go with her to the antique store next weekend and take a look. There was probably a window repair shop around that could handle stained glass.

They talked about this, talking, really, about nothing, just enjoying each other's company and the web of ordinary things and topics and routines. Lars had seen the black square of the night window, the gold and sienna of the cabinets, the milky marled surface of the marble table hundreds, thousands of nights. And he'd been there, too, with them: Emma, thoughtful and relaxed, her firm, golden arms stretched on either side of her coffee cup; Cookie, mobile, alert, elbows on the table, heels balanced on the chair rail; Jake at her feet, twitching in some dream; Polly on the counter, watching them all through her yellow slitted eyes—yet often his mind had been elsewhere, sometimes disastrously absent, craving variety, change, difference.

Now it all seemed wonderfully beautiful to him: the room and Emma and Cookie and the fact of their sitting together, happily. He was a lucky man, lucky to have preserved his family, lucky to have survived suspicion, luckiest of all to appreciate what happiness he had. Sitting at the dinner table, Lars felt contented, safe in the net of ordinary things, which are, he realized, the most precious, the most protective. I must remember this, he thought, though at some point, he knew he would forget. Only saints remember the splendors of the ordinary, saints and domestic geniuses; there must, Lars thought, be geniuses of daily life, unnoticed, unsung, but happy. There must be.

"You must have some homework," Emma said finally, and Cookie conceded, reluctantly, that she had some reading. The adolescent novels (full of angst and information) favored by her English teacher seemed to hold little charm for Cookie. Lars wondered if he should try her with something more ambitious or if her talents lay entirely elsewhere. Feeling the beginnings of discontent, Lars said that he had better check his mail. "The Freshman Experience Committee calls."

"What do the freshman experience?" Cookie asked.

"Well, that's what we're trying to decide. We want them to be thrilled with learning, awakened to diversity, bonded to the community, and delighted by the arts. At least that's our program. What they want is free beer and easy grades."

"As easy to get their version as yours," Emma said.

"Easier," Lars admitted. "But fortunately we just have to talk about it, not produce it."

Cookie wanted to know what diversity was, and he sketched various multicultural rainbows before he realized she was stalling and told her to go read her book. She clattered up the stairs, Jake at her heels. Polly, too, would soon be ensconced on her bed; luckily Cookie seemed to have missed the recent plague of asthma. Lars switched on the light by his desk, punched on the computer. For the first time in a week he felt no apprehension, and so his anger and surprise were all the greater when at the top of the list, he saw subject, *Don't Think You Can Ignore Me*, and realized he had another message.

13.

Lars closed the door to his study even though the house was empty, Emma at work, Cookie at school. A new and important habit, a little reminder of how his correspondent had changed him: Now Lars never dared check his E-mail with the door open, regarding E-mail messages not as guilty pleasures but as guilty pains. He'd become cautious after Cookie unexpectedly came in one day, forcing him to hit Close.

"You get so much mail," she said enviously.

"Mostly junk," said Lars.

"You can just delete junk," Cookie said. "ISPU—I spy you! Who's that from?"

Lars mumbled something about eyeglasses sold on the Web.

"I don't get ads like that," said Cookie.

"Lucky girl. You get especially composed E-mails from Daddy Lars, instead."

She'd agreed that those were the best possible, and Lars had shut down the machine and taken her and Jake for a walk. No harm done, but a close call, and he couldn't take the chance of her spotting another ISPU message, which was the sort of thing she would notice. She certainly picked up anything to do with the computer very quickly. At the parent-teacher conference, he'd mentioned that to her math teacher, Ms. Paparelli, in extenuation for Cookie's mediocre work.

"I'm not surprised," said Ms. Paparelli, a statuesque lady with dyed, upswept blonde hair, a good deal of makeup and jewelry, and a formidable air of authority. "She's very talented. She'll learn anything she puts her mind to."

Lars immediately warmed to Ms. Paparelli, a woman of taste and perception. Still, he brought up Cookie's grades; like most parents, Lars waffled between blaming his child and blaming her teacher for academic difficulties.

"Bright children don't always make the best students at this level," Ms. Paparelli said. "Cookie is a nice child but very restless and easily bored, not unusual for a seventh grader. Unless her work drops off drastically, I'll recommend her for algebra next year. The computer is good for her, too. She needs a challenge. You might even think about one of the computer summer programs next year. Some of our students have enjoyed those." She closed Cookie's portfolio with a smile.

Lars thanked her and unfolded his long legs from the too small student chair. No wonder parents felt intimidated at conferences: These little ass grabbers took you right back to junior high; you may have forgotten, but the gluteus maximus remembers pressed wood school chairs and interminable classes. If he hadn't been on his good behavior, Lars would have asked Ms. Paparelli whether, in her professional opinion, boredom is an essential component of the civilizing process. Instead, he shook her hand, which was cool and dry and dusted with chalk. Her gold bracelets rattled: the discreet charms of the middle school math teacher. It was a symptom of his lowered state that Lars noticed her attractions without any real response.

"Don't worry too much about Cookie," Ms. Paparelli said at the classroom door. "She's getting over a hard time, and middle school is tough for everyone. For parents, too. Things get better. They really do."

Lars had been reassured at the time, had believed the worst was behind them, had foreseen smooth sailing for his darling child. Then came the correspondent with his threats and insinuations, and Lars had been alarmed, angry, curious, depressed. His modus operandi had been to feign indifference and exercise patience, a sensible decision that nonetheless frazzled his nerves. Lars hated to be dependent on someone else's good pleasure, and he hated to wait. Uncertainty made him impatient with Cookie, irritable with Emma, and he compensated with surprise gifts and treats. He went out of his way to plan special dinners and outings and half the time ruined them with tempers and grumbling. He could not help it. His mysterious correspondent haunted him, so that first thing in the morning, Lars switched on his machine to scan the mail: if no ISPU, good, his spirits rose, yet, like Hamlet, he was haunted by the thought that *if it be not now, yet it will come.*

Unless Lars kept himself well in hand, he looked at his E-mail again when he got to school, and, of course, whenever he worked on the Net, he was tempted to check. If nothing arrived by three P.M., he considered himself off the hook until the next morning, when, once again, he would look for ISPU's newest missive. Sometimes there was a break, a day or two, once nearly a whole week. But just as Lars relaxed, mentally proclaimed the business over, prepared to reduce it to an amusing anecdote, "I had a crank correspondent once, rather a philosophical chap . . . ," another message would appear.

After one of these disappointments, Lars stopped by the department's computer lab late on a wet and dreary afternoon; the faculty without classes had gone home and only a few superstudious graduate students were still mesmerized by the fertile resources of the Net or pounding out papers and bibliographies—and poison E-mails? Lars wouldn't like to think so, but you never knew. A school population this large had its aggrieved and unstable members. What about a department rival? Did anyone dislike him so much? Or, since he'd been on any number of hiring committees, a disappointed job candidate might be a possibility. There were plenty of them around these days and precedent, too; how many United States presidents had been shot by "disgruntled office seekers"?

"Question for you," Lars told Tomas, the department's technical whiz, a nice fellow whose dissertation "Euphues and Elizabethan Court Language" kept being delayed by various Web site crises and computer glitches. Tomas had a thin, white face with a little dark pointed beard that made him look scholarly in a rakish, almost Tudor manner. He was bright and reputed to be a good teacher, but Lars expected that with his computer and information tech skills, Tomas would soon head off to make real money in industry. Normally, such academic defections were depressing, but under the present circumstances, Lars found the notion encouraging; he felt he could confide a certain amount to Tomas, who, he was sure, would offer explanations, assistance. How foolish not to have made use of this resource sooner!

"Tell me about E-mails," Lars said, when Tomas left off fiddling with some balky software. "How easy is it to find out who sent one?"

"I assume you mean a blind E-mail, no address?"

"No, not a copy. I have an address. Can I trace the sender?"

"Depends," said Tomas. "Depends on whether he wants his identity known."

"I thought you could always be traced via your server?"

"Usually, but there are some good encryption programs and some new services like Anonymizer.com that let you send virtually untraceable E-mail. There's one that routes messages through a series of servers using quantum logic."

"I have enough trouble with ordinary logic," Lars confessed.

"The simplest way to remain anonymous, and quite elegant to my mind," Tomas added with an appreciation that made Lars a tad uncomfortable, "is to use a library computer to open an account through a Web-based provider. The message could be traced back to the library, but that wouldn't help very much."

"This would be an ordinary account, Yahoo or Hotmail or some such?" Lars asked.

"That's right. Pick an out-of-town library by preference, and voilà."

"I understand," said Lars, who actually saw only that the science of concealment had progressed far beyond his ability. "So as far as tracing unsigned E-mails, I'm probably out of luck."

"Probably. Unless you're getting terrorist threats, and even then tracing is problematical if the sender's computer savvy and keeps changing machines."

"Nothing in the terrorist category," Lars said. "Just disagreeable."

"Best thing if you're being spammed or flamed is to delete all unknown E-mails."

That Tomas seemed unsurprised, even unimpressed, irritated Lars. Was this a common problem, or did Tomas, like the unknown correspondent, think that Lars had trouble coming to him? I'm getting paranoid, Lars thought. "The problem is communicating with students," he said. "They don't all use university accounts." Lars prided himself on being accessible—as Tomas should have known— and on keeping in touch.

"Unless you think it is a student."

Lars shrugged. Although he had no evidence one way or the other, somehow he did not feel that the correspondent was from one of his classes. Certainly not from an undergraduate class. "I don't think this is a student."

"Try changing your address," said Tomas. "Maybe change your server, too. You can give it to your students. If it's one of them, there won't be any interruption. If it's not, you might be located eventually, but inconvenience is sometimes enough to discourage spammers and flamers."

Lars considered this without much conviction. He no longer assumed that the correspondence was a random product of malice and celebrity. More and more there was a personal tone to the notes, and the references to Iris rang true. Talking to Tomas, Lars was suddenly convinced that the correspondent was someone who had known either Iris or him or both.

"Want me to delete your E-mail address from the faculty page?"

Although it would be a nuisance to notify everyone in his address book, Lars said, "Yes, let's do that now if you have the time."

"A few keystrokes." Tomas sat down at the computer, pulled up the coded faculty page, and made the deletion.

Three days after Lars opened his new E-mail account, he received a message headed, *Your Evasion.*

Dear Lars,

You disappointed me by changing your address. And your server, too! You really are a newbie. Probably you're trying to trace these messages as well. I'll bet you are. Don't waste your time! Can't be done, not with the precautions I've taken, which are thorough. Rely on that. But maybe you just don't want to raise the issue of the Event. There's your dilemma. To get rid of me, you'll have to deal with the Event.

I don't know what you'll decide. You have that nice wife, that pretty daughter, and yet you went chasing after Iris, your student— and need I remind you of the new sexual harassment regulations?

I see you like to live on the edge. Watch you don't fall off, Larsie.

Lars sat at his desk, wondering how the correspondent had known about Emma and Cookie. The book jacket identified Lars as "living with his wife and daughter." "Nice wife" and "pretty daughter" might just be polite clichés, yet the reference took the messages to another level, upsetting Lars seriously. Even to mention them was a kind of threat. Did the correspondent expect to get away with that, trusting to technology and the mysteries of the Web, the elusiveness of the ethernet, the supposed superiority (to Lars's mind, insufficiently challenged) of the cyberworld? Well, they'd see. His father used to say that there was more than one way to skin a cat, and Lars thought that if he was blocked by technology, he would just have to apply another technique.

He switched on his laser jet, brought up the file of E-mails, and hit Print. As he watched the neat pages slide from his printer, Lars was amazed at how passive he'd been. That he'd waited for the messages to stop, that he'd wanted only to ignore and forget had been false prudence that had encouraged his correspondent. Perhaps Lars should have answered right away. Certainly, he should have done what he intended to do right now: assemble whatever he could learn about the mysterious writer, starting with the facts that the person was skilled in computer technology and connected in some way— could he deduce that?—with the college. Maybe, Lars thought; there were certain details, plus the speed with which the messages resumed. But he needed to be sure, to be precise, to see what he really had. He had to put preconceptions aside, as he always told his students, and deal strictly with the texts. Picking up his pen, Lars began to read the notes in sequence, just as if they were chap-

ters in a new novel or sections of a scholarly essay, beginning with
the first *I know all about you* message and continuing through repeated cranky, almost schizophrenic, missives, until he got to one
titled *Don't Think You Can Ignore Me*:

> *Dear Professor Larson,*
>
> *Notice the courtesy of my address in marked contrast to your
> childish attempts to ignore me.*
>
> *I understand you. You are pretending that the Event of which
> we are both daily, maybe hourly, aware did not happen. You've
> convinced yourself of your innocence, you are trying to forget.
> Worse, Professor, you are intending to forget. Why do I say "worse"?
> To forget evil is to assent to it.*
>
> *Fortunately for your morals, if not your soul—we are modern,
> are we not, and the soul is in dispute?—you have me as a reminder.
> I will be constant: memento mori.*

This is a letter I should have examined carefully, Lars thought;
it's a rhetorical gold mine. Level of diction high—and self-conscious?
He thought so; later notes were much more informal. *Courtesy of
my address* was practically antique, which suggested a specific type
of education, of reading. He should have noticed that at once, but
he had not, because it was familiar, because a certain elegant turn
of phrase was stock-in-trade around the department.

Lars put his pen down, feeling faintly queasy. A member of the
staff? One of his colleagues? Later notes had a different feel, but,
yes, put down the thought, because he had to aim for an unbiased
reading no matter how difficult, even theoretically dubious, that
might be. His writer was an educated person, well read.

There was more. The interest in morals. The equation of memory
with an ethical standpoint. The reference to the murder as the Event,
which his correspondent claimed to remember daily. Isobel? He
doubted that anonymous letters were her style and certainly not in
this style. But what about Dan Weed, that son of hers? At their first
private meeting, she'd told Lars outright, "My son thinks you probably killed Iris." Dan hadn't been sold on the book idea, either,
though he'd been happy enough with the profits. Isobel had mentioned that all was forgiven, mother recognized as a genius, etc. Still,

there'd been no mention of any new attitude toward editor Lars, who had made it all possible.

Dan Weed as the correspondent? On the plus side: his suspicion, his grief, his memories of his sister.

On the negative: the literary style—Dan was a business major and a jock—plus the disconcerting shifts in tone. "Dan's been my tower of strength," Isobel said. A direct man, too. He hadn't shaken Lars's hand at the memorial service. Would he refer to his sister's stabbing as "the Event"?

And the soul, the business of the soul. Who talked of the soul now except professional preachers and evangelicals and students of earlier literature? If he had to place a bet, Lars leaned toward a student, upper level, possibly in the graduate school. Who might that be? A snoop of particularly imaginative and malicious stripe? The unknown, yet ever expected, witness? Some friend of Iris's, someone she'd confided in, even Sven, the elusive boyfriend, whoever he was? Lars was sobered by the range of possibilities.

The next message in the sequence was from two days later. *I did expect better. I'd hoped to engage you for mutual profit; I'd hoped to discuss the Event with you. To get your perspective on it, your honest perspective, not the nauseating pap you dispense in your interviews. Have I mentioned that they turn my stomach?*

Was it coincidence that the E-mails started just after Lars's appearance on the New York talk show? That had been his original assumption, the root of the now discredited crank thesis. But perhaps there had been a relationship. The talk show and fame for him or for Iris's book—another, unexplored dimension!—might have triggered the messages from someone who had known her or who'd been jealous of her or of her writing. Lars had a funny feeling at that thought, something half remembered, something Iris had said or written. What was that?

He scribbled a row of question marks. If only he still had her last diary.

Another Try
Dear Lars,
    How's that? A little more informal, a little more intimate: what

*Iris used to call you. Surprise, surprise! You've been pretending I'm
some sort of cybercrank, haven't you? I understand. I can't say how
strongly I understand. I'd probably do the same thing myself. It's
the safest way, isn't it, to protect your precious sanity? But not in
this case, Larsie. Keeping your head up your ass is the quickest way
to disaster when we're talking about the Event.*

Significant use of my nickname? His department colleagues
called him Lars, a few graduate students, too. The undergrads
referred to him that way, though not to his face except for the
privileged Iris, who might have passed on the nickname to friends,
broadening the net. Unless this was just a lucky guess, his correspondent either knew Iris or the English department, two equally
unpleasant possibilities. The undergraduates were an innumerable
multitude, but Lars made a note to get a list of current and recent
graduate students with their E-mail addresses. He'd invent a mailing
about formative experiences for the Freshman Committee as the
excuse.

What else? Big shift in diction: *Lars, Larsie, head up your ass, cybercrank.* Any reason? Something else different, too, the more intimate
tone and the claim not just of knowledge but of understanding.

Was this just a nut, or had he or she some basis, some facts,
some observations?

Never Give Up

Dear Lars,

*You thought I'd given up, didn't you? Every time there's a break
in our correspondence, you think: the end. No way. That's the first
thing you've got to understand: I never give up. Iris didn't believe
that. She had a different outlook on life. More flexible, happier,
would you agree? I'd dearly like to get your opinion of Iris's outlook.
I see life as a fundamentally tragic business. Iris, I think, saw the
comic side. Maybe you do, too, but see, Lars, she was wrong: violent
death at age 22. Nothing funny about that, is there?*

*That's why I'll never give up. You're 43, nearly twice her age.
So Lars, if you were to die tomorrow, you'd still have had that extra
21 years, wouldn't you?*

Do you see what I'm thinking? I hope you do.

This person is dangerous, was Lars's spontaneous reaction. Perhaps he should have taken this E-mail directly to Paatelainen or Harrelson, because certainly it hinted at a threat. Explicit enough for them? Maybe.

And then the question: Was Iris's outlook comic, or just her book? The book was comic, definitely. But her grief for her father, her odd, unwholesome relationship with the boy she called Sven? Were those comic?

And why did the correspondent want to know?

Today's Question

Dear Lars,

Were you "dear Lars" to Iris? Or just a randy old guy with wandering hands? I suspect the latter, but maybe beginning as the former: She was impressionable. I myself made an impression. Oh, yes, and enjoyed it immensely.

You have a completely false idea of me, I know you do: nerd jerking off in cyberspace? Right? Quite wrong. From false premises nothing but false conclusions.

I want to avoid that fallacy. I want to get to the facts before the Event, so what was she to you that you killed her?

Or is that question in bad taste?

He knew her, Lars thought. And—though his colleague Jackie Hartemel would say this was pure gender bias—Lars knew that the correspondent was male. A man, then, who demanded respect because he had known Iris or—be careful, be exact, Lars cautioned himself—who was trying in this rather vulgar way to give the impression that he had known her. Which was more likely? And where was there evidence of anything beyond guesswork and generalities?

Reference to classical logic. Who studies that now, Lars wondered, and made a note to ask the philosophy department.

Crucial part: He thinks I killed Iris. Does this error negate everything, Lars wondered, or make the correspondent more dangerous? And something else, something Lars noticed now that he had, in the original shock of the question, passed over. The question was not, "Did you kill Iris?" The question was, "What was your relationship to Iris before you killed her?"

Reflections on Silence

Dear Lars,

Do I feel bad about your silence? On reflection, no. I can wait, and in some ways your silence gives me a chance to explore my own reactions, my own feelings. Iris was right when she said you were a good teacher.

Oops, how do I know that? Her mother mentioned it on TV, so I could have gotten that little detail secondhand, couldn't I? Still, something you'll want to think over, Lars. You'll want to weigh and assess the information, using your superior intelligence. So many decisions. I don't envy you at all, except maybe for your experience.

What's life but a collection of experiences, to be enjoyed, to be understood, to be survived.

Self-absorbed bastard! *My own reactions, my own feelings*—what did the correspondent care about Iris with all this psychobabble? Yet even in this note there was important information, namely that the correspondent had seen the television show out of New York. The talk show host was big on literacy and the impact of "extraordinary teachers." Isobel had obligingly talked about Professor Larson's influence on Iris. Had that topic come up during any other interviews? Lars thought not, not on television, anyway. So one more detail: The New York appearance was crucial, the ironic peak of celebrity and danger.

Was this the experience the correspondent envied? Interviews, talk shows, whatever went on with Iris? Be careful what you wish for, my lad! She could have abandoned you in the reservoir district. Or was what was implied more sinister yet? Lars stopped, hesitated, sensed again the peculiar atmosphere of the messages like a gust of bad drains, a draft of sewerage, accompanied always by that hint of mutual understanding, and thought, This is from a man who believes I murdered Iris.

Indeed on rereading, the messages seemed even worse than Lars remembered. Had he thought at the time: This is fiction? This is an exercise of the imagination such as I meet in my daily work? Or had he decided they represented something untouchable, beyond his ken? The creepiness of the business had sent him to see Tomas, but in retrospect, Lars could see that he had become desensitized, that he'd come to expect weird, crankish letters, that, despite nerves and anxiety, he'd been in an avoidance mode the whole time.

Seeing the entire correspondence was different. He had a sharper sense of the writer and a greater sense of control, too, because the problem was letters, and Lars was a highly trained reader. He could outwit this antagonist, who was a well-educated, computer-literate male, connected in some way to the college. He had probably known Iris, suggesting again an upper-level undergraduate or a grad student. Had he been questioned at the time of her death? It might be possible to find out.

Lars was pleased with this summary, and below it, he jotted down a plan of action:

obtain list of recent graduate students with E-mail addresses
check all articles on Iris's death for names
talk to Nate Foster in the philosophy department
explore the computer angle—ask the help desk about workers?

Lars put the printouts of the letters with his notes in a folder. He would start now by calling the English graduate office and getting a list of names. Possibly, he could get the same sort of information from the philosophy department, though there was no guarantee that his correspondent had studied either discipline. History was another possibility, or maybe the correspondent was just an omnivorous reader. Lars had a moment of trepidation at the amorphous immensity of the search: For all he knew, the writer could be a crime buff living in Texas. But to give up without trying was to resign himself to passivity or to the police.

Which was worse? To do nothing was unacceptable now, given the correspondent's snide, knowing, vaguely threatening tone, which would be harmless from Texas but might represent a genuine danger closer to home.

And the police? Did he want to reopen the whole business and bring them around to worry Emma and upset Cookie? Did he want to give them an excuse, even so flimsy an excuse as the accusations of an electronic crank, to investigate him further? And who knew what the correspondent might write next? Or might know?

Lars had to think about that, too.

14.

... *g*ives students the bigger picture ... theoretical underpinnings ... multidisciplinary concepts ..." I sound like a con-
jurer, Lars thought, a Victorian mountebank couldn't do any better.
And yes, Nate Foster was responding, pursing his thin, cautious
mouth and nodding his beaky head in a show of interest, that was
quite predictable, because if literature was in trouble, think of philosophy! The Freshman Experience, already freighted with multicultural, relevant, and gender-sensitive content, was a target of
opportunity for the desperate philosophers: Could they board this
ship and make the frosh walk the planks of existentialism and em-
piricism? Would the baby boomers' grandchildren save the grand old
discipline?

"I'd certainly like to see more interdepartmental work," Nate said,
"if we can do it without weakening the integrity of the individual
disciplines."

"Always the caveat, isn't it? But it's worked at the graduate level.
Some of our graduate students have taken philosophy courses," said
subtle, hopeful Lars, throwing out his line for a fish, a name, a
correspondent.

"Medievalists work out very well with us. Plus we've had one
Renaissance person. But the likeliest are medievalists," Nate said
and dropped ponderously into thought. Lars, normally impatient and
frankly uncharitable about Nate's lengthy cognitions, slouched farther down on the dusty office couch and cast his eyes along the gray

metal shelves filled with Kant and Husserl and Aquinas and the Scholastics. A model airplane, festooned with cobwebs, dangled from a hook set into the ceiling, and Lars remembered being told that Nate had flown Navy jets in Korea, that he'd been dashing, decorated. How far away and implausible that seemed.

"Can't think of his name," Nate said at last. "He was doing something with the sagas and needed medieval philosophy. Audited my seminar on Nietzsche afterward. Interesting student. Just the sort of person we've been talking about."

"Sagas?" Lars thought of Iris's Sven who'd wanted to be a Viking. Had his work been serious, or had things Viking been just a hobby? "Any names, Nate? We want to contact some grads, get some opinions: freshman year is really the foundation . . ."

"As long as there is no dilution of the content," Nate repeated. He had a lot to add about course integrity and the underpinnings of theory, but the precise name had slipped his mind. "Check with your own graduate division. Interesting chap," was the sum of Nate's information.

All right, Lars thought. Check with Leo, find out how many master's and doctoral candidates were in medieval studies at the moment. Get the names of recent medievalists, too. Needle in a haystack stuff, but Lars felt better when he was doing something. Accumulating files and lists, making a cross-referenced database, talking to people like Nate and Leo, reading—admittedly awkwardly and surreptitiously and only in the library—accounts of Iris's death, all these things comprised a blessed distraction from the correspondent and from Isobel's dangerous insistence on a reward. Even the letters, the nagging source of the problem, came into a different light once Lars began his investigations. While it would be inaccurate to say he looked forward to each new missive, dread had been replaced by an angry curiosity and a steadily growing conviction that sooner or later his correspondent would reveal himself with some significant detail.

Whether he was actually learning more about the E-mail writer or whether setting his mind and his subconscious to work on the problem had increased his concentration, Lars now had a sense not exactly of empathy but of contact with the writer. And the oddest thing about this one-sided correspondence was that the tenor of the messages changed with Lars's attitude. He wanted more information, and the correspondent obliged, as if, after all, confession and not concealment was his real intent.

The first indication, very soon after Lars's meeting with Nate Foster, was the writer's concern with evidence, a topic much on Lars's mind. *Probably you are wondering how I know*, the message began. *I might have discussed evidence immediately, but you will appreciate that this is an emotional issue for me. Anyway, I think that lack of evidence is the reason for your silence. You want proof, and I don't blame you, Lars. I'd feel the same way in your position, which, I agree, is not a good one: not quite cleared, not quite indictable, lucky but marked, Lars, marked for those of us who have eyes, who know.*

Now, a year later, someone sees you making money off of Iris's book, a promotion that made a bad impression on me, Larsie, that's for sure, and this individual says whoa, wait just one fucking minute. This is someone who reads the papers, watches TV, keeps apprised of current events—what would be more natural than to nominate himself for public prosecutor and tap out a note? People are looking for roles, aren't they? Try them on, take them off: the modern psychic wardrobe! I'm quoting, actually, that's something Iris once said. Was that in the manuscript? Did it make it into the book? Could this be evidence? I'll bet you'll check, Lars, because your choices are pretty limited, aren't they? Do you keep on hiding or do you confess? Simple, really.

Lars put aside a set of papers to spend all one afternoon checking the finished book and another flipping through Iris's final manuscript plus an earlier draft where, at last, he found a section headed "Choosing My Psychic Wardrobe." It was an odd feeling to see his own red-penciled opinion that this was "insufficiently developed" and an odder feeling, half apprehensive and half triumphant, to have one key question answered: The correspondent had known Iris. Whether well or casually, he knew her turns of phrase and had remembered this one vivid remark.

And even though the correspondent had dropped this information deliberately, had even predicted his course of action, Lars felt

increasingly confident. He began to devote the same restless eagerness to the chase that he once had to flirtation. Instead of creeping
to the phone at night for surreptitious calls, he would get out of bed
and go along to the study to check his E-mail.

"What's wrong?" Emma asked one night when he'd laid aside his
book and gotten up at nearly eleven.

"Nothing," Lars said and then, sensing that something more was
required, that Emma was frankly skeptical, added, "I've got such
nocturnal students this semester."

He leaned over and kissed her forehead reassuringly, which was
the wrong thing entirely, because when he had gone, quick and light-
footed down the hall, Emma, too, set her book aside. She stared up
at the dark line between the wall and the ceiling and felt a heaviness
settle around her heart. He had promised; he had promised after the
debacle with Iris Weed, and if Emma hadn't wholeheartedly believed
him, she had hoped for, even expected, an extended period of calm
and fidelity. Lars had seemed chastened and shocked and more than
once had said that he owed everything to her, meaning the now
general conviction of his innocence. She had stood by him, Emma
thought resentfully, and had gotten credit for it as if there had really
been a choice. Oh, for her, yes. But for Cookie? Impossible. To have
left Lars, to have indicated her doubts—which, to be honest, had
been small and unsustainable—would have damaged Cookie beyond
repair.

In all fairness, Emma did not think Lars had calculated that.
Where Cookie was concerned, her husband was singularly artless
and direct. But even as it was—and here the heaviness twisted up
into her stomach—things were not the same. The sulkiness, the
moods, the fears that had burned, literally burned, last summer were
diluted, if not totally gone, but Cookie, small and childish, had
vaulted, unprepared and prematurely, Emma thought, into adolescence.

And now, mysteries and self-absorption and late-night messages
began again. She must talk to Lars, bring him to reason, give him
an ultimatum: He must think of Cookie if he couldn't think of her—

as he should! As he would! Emma got up, shuffled around at the side of the bed for her slippers, and pulled on her bathrobe against the always chilly hall.

The study door was closed, and behind it, Lars, too, was feeling dismayed as he read, *Surprising how I feel I can talk to you. I wonder sometimes if I'd be disappointed if you replied, because then you'd have a different sort of reality for me. Right now, I feel I can say whatever I want, because there's nothing you can do to hurt me. I have one of the ultimate powers, Lars, invisibility, which is what you've been enjoying, isn't it?*

Fool! This man has never been a suspect, has never been accused of murder, knows nothing, nothing at all about the tenacity of the police and the remorselessness of the press. Nothing about Emma's worries or the blankness in Cookie's eyes, nothing about the doubt and guilt that take hold of even the most innocent under unrelenting suspicion. Nothing.

You got away with murder—or would that be homicide or manslaughter? Technically, we should say womanslaughter, which sounds equally bad to me. A knife, a blow, one terrible mistake, and then blood and frenzy. Have I guessed right? About the blood, the shock, the weight of your arms? Slaughter is exhausting work, Lars, as you will remember. You really have to want to kill someone to exhaust yourself so much.

The question is: How much should you be blamed? Do you have a defense ready? You'll need one eventually, because you can't run forever. For one thing, I'll always be there, your secret sharer.

Are you as pleased as I am at the way we're connecting?

The shock of the irrational and strange hit Lars like finding a snake under his bare foot. This is crazy, he thought, and then, catching hold of sense and rationality, he asked himself, If the writer really believes all this, why hasn't he come forward, even anonymously? But there had been no one around on that miserable night, Lars was sure of that, only him and Iris and whoever had killed her. And why would her killer write? Why would he take the risk of contacting Lars, the person who could most profit from his discovery? It was senseless and stupid, yet in his heart, Lars knew why: Guilt eats the

soul. Had he not been tormented by his own omissions? By his lies—
to the police, to Isobel, to Emma and Cookie? By concealing the
diary, by the cowardice that had complicated the investigation? Lars
knew what that felt like, and these were mere venial sins. How much
worse, how unimaginably much worse it would be to have a memory
of homicidal horror and violence, to be haunted by the death of
someone once loved. Only by a great stretch of his imagination could
Lars approach that point, helped by his memory of the destabilizing
effects of his desire for Iris: anger and envy and lust touched with
violence. Yes, he was acquainted with the night, a casual, passing
acquaintance, but still on that level, he and his correspondent did
connect. On other grounds, never! For this was Iris they were considering, Iris of the Golden Wings, melancholic, effervescent, shy,
outrageous. What was she to this self-absorbed idiot? Where was his
regret for charm and genius, for that beguiling slovenliness of dress,
for her plucky living arrangements, for the woman herself? His Iris
was a victim, a statistic, an occasion—at least, Lars hoped just an
occasion—for imaginative writing and morbid feelings. I feel no connection with this man, Lars told himself, and he can stick his "secret
sharer" crap right up his ass.

When Emma opened the door, she found Lars seated at his
computer, the screen glowing, the room otherwise dark. He had his
face in his hands, and when he looked around, she saw a shocked
grief in his eyes.

"Lars? What is it?"

He reached over and clicked his mouse; the screen closed. "I
don't want you to read that," he said, guiltily aware, even as he spoke,
of the mix of truth and deception in his words. "There are still some
people who believe I killed Iris."

"Lars, you mustn't read such things. You shouldn't even open
them. Is this what you've been doing locked away in your room?"

"I didn't want to worry you. I thought I might find out something.
Find who was sending them. Play Sherlock Holmes, I suppose. One
of life's lesser temptations, Emma, but, God, it makes me feel bad."

"Of course, of course," said Emma. "It's so wrong to dwell on all
this." Full of relief, she hugged him, and Lars agreed. Iris had been

in his mind, he said, with the appearances, with the book promotion, with her mother searching, agitating, talking about a reward and opening the whole case up again. And the messages, Lars told her, what was more natural than that he'd attract idle malice, and even more so if Isobel had her way?

"I know, yes, but if we were in her position," Emma began, and right there Lars knew that he could tell her nothing, not that she and Cookie had been mentioned and certainly not this latest farrago of blood and slaughter. Emma would want to go to the police; she would see evidence, if not a confession, in what Lars was struggling to see as fantasy.

"We'd never recover; we'd move heaven and earth. But Emma," he said, "we've got to think about the impact on Cookie of TV dramatizations, interviews, police statements: You know that there will be issues."

She nodded.

"In the meantime, I feel I have to look at everything. Just in case." He leaned his head against Emma's arm.

"I thought it was over," she said, a weary note in her voice.

"Now I'm almost sorry I did the book."

"No, the book is great, terrific. And nice for Isobel, for the family. No, it was good of you to do the book." Emma kissed him, because he had done the book, because he did not have a girlfriend, because he had learned his lesson. Lars pulled her onto his lap and opened her robe and promised to take her advice, with the result that he had to stop his late-night E-mail checks. He went to bed every evening in suspense, but it was the least he could do; he owed Emma.

And admittedly, daylight lent a different perspective. To Lars's morning eyes, the next missive seemed less alarming and more informative, allowing him to put aside the worst of his fears, to postpone any decision, to treat the message more as text and less as threat. Ironically, the subject was *Your Character,* and it began, *While basically despising you, I admire the way you've kept your head. I was wrong about you in that respect. I thought the ridiculous way you ran around after Iris meant that you'd hit the panic button first thing. Have I mentioned that I know all about you and Iris?*

Lars's excitement mingled with anxiety when he read this paragraph. So, the correspondent not only knew Iris, he had lived in the area a year and a half ago; he recognized Lars on sight. Probably a student or a recent graduate. Probably with his "secret sharer" crap an English major. Lars was sure of it: Who reads Conrad now except English majors? He must be on one of my lists, unless he is or was an undergraduate. But maybe it was one of her friends, one of the boys who were interviewed at the time of the murder. In any case, he's gone too far, Lars thought; he's tipped his hand; the game is getting away from him. Lars stopped reading for a moment as the idea of a game, of someone who played games ran through his mind. Sven, Lars thought, this might well be Sven, who liked rough sex and pretended to be a Viking. Do I know anything more about him? Why didn't I make notes on the diary when I had it!

You don't tell your television audience about waiting outside her classes and haunting the aisles at Healthy Stuff, do you, Lars? You never say something along the lines of, "I knew her well, having had the serious hots for her. Many's the afternoon I found myself outside Renaissance Literature, taught by the terminally boring Professor Katz. . . ." Are we in agreement about Professor Katz? I think we are. I can't explain how confident I feel about your opinions and impressions.

Possibly my confidence is the product of conversations with Iris, who wasn't always discreet. As her literary executor—a double entendre in your case, Lars—and possibly as her literary biographer (I suspect that's in the works) you'll know how writers love gossip. Their books are always their excuse, their excuse and their justification. Justification by verbiage, not by faith, eh, Lars? You and I may both need something stronger.

Very possibly, Lars thought with a pang, for there were times when the correspondent, for all his malice, touched one of the deep chords. But this message, if embarrassing, was good, because surely it suggested that the writer knew the department and had taken a class from Joe Katz. Lars felt that he was on the right track. He just had to keep working. He would add in the people interviewed at the time of the murder, with particular attention to the students. He would find out where they lived now.

Lars shut off the machine with a feeling of satisfaction that increased as he winnowed his list down to four names. Face it, he told himself, you're a clever man. He would solve the riddle of the correspondent, and perhaps of Iris's murder, too, and put himself forever beyond doubt. With this thought, the wise and ever ingenious Daddy Lars strode down the hall to see Cookie. They'd walk Jake or visit the mall or take the soccer ball to the park. He'd been preoccupied lately, his mind on the correspondent, on the case, on the past, and that had affected Cookie a little.

It seemed to him that she was less enthusiastic, less open somehow. Oh, she still came bolting up the stairs after school, still called out his name to be sure he was home, still romped noisily with Jake in the yard. But she'd been spending a great deal of time in her room E-mailing school friends and playing computer games. She was often over at her friend Denise's house, and when they were here, the two them were always teasing to be taken to the mall where they expected to be allowed to wander alone and unsupervised for hours at a time, "shopping." The big computer store was especially favored, and even a mention of this venue was enough to reduce Cookie and Denise to fits of giggles.

Lars noticed that her door was closed—like his—and he whistled softly to her before he opened it.

"Hi, Daddy."

Cheerful. That was good. And Polly on the bed, Jake sprawled watchful beside the desk, the maple tree outside turning one window to a sheet of gold and brightening the room despite the fast-approaching dusk: idyllic childhood. Yet was it really the old spontaneous Cookie cheerfulness? Don't ask. Was his the same old Daddy Lars brio? Don't tell.

"Whatcha doing?"

"E-mailing. E-mailing Denise."

Lars could not help running his eyes over the letter. . . . *would you believe that? I can't wait for the next message. Do you think I'll . . .*

"I thought you'd just seen Denise at school."

"Oh, Daddy!" Immense, surprised exasperation at parental obtuseness: Denise required hourly, nay minutely, updates, no doubt in minute detail. Be thankful she's not tying up the phone, Lars thought. He sat down on the quilt and stroked Polly's silky head. He liked Cookie's rather small room, which was cozy despite the high ceilings and long windows. He remembered painting the sky blue ceiling with an extension roller and balancing on the very top of the stepladder to cut in the white trim with a brush. The almost endless renovations meant that every corner had memories. Lars could have lain quite happily on Cookie's narrow bed and looked up at the ceiling and the egg and dart trim—not quite as neatly painted as he'd have liked—and remembered the days before they moved Cookie, still sleeping then in her high-sided crib, into her new room. Days of safety, days of simplicity! Instead, he said, "How about you finish up and we'll take Jake for a walk?"

The briefest hesitation, then, "Okay." She began typing, talking out loud as she wrote. *Daddy's just come in, so I have to go. Walkies for Jake. More later.* She hit Send. "I love my computer," she remarked. "And my new desk."

"It came out well, didn't it?" Lars heard an eager, almost supplicating tone in his voice: Let everything be well; let me be clever enough; let me keep Cookie safe always. Parenthood, he realized, is the happiest, subtlest sort of curse.

"Terrific."

"Or," he said, "we could walk Jake and go to the mall, if you like. I've finally got this semester's work under control."

"That's all right," said Cookie. "Denise and me are going Saturday. I hope. Maybe you could drop me after soccer?" He glimpsed her eyes under her bangs, darkly watchful.

"Need something special? We can pick it up today. Something new for the computer?" This was bribery, arrant bribery.

Again, hesitation, a hint of temptation resisted—when had

Cookie ever resisted a pleasure trip? "No, I don't need anything. Let's just go for a walk. Ready, Jake? Want a walk?"

Discussion ended: Human happiness is a pale and complicated affair next to canine joy. The little dog bounced once, twice, on his tough and springy shanks and bounded along the hall.

"We could make dinner for your mom, surprise her," Lars suggested when they got downstairs. "Do you know what's in the fridge?"

"Chicken parts."

"We'll do Daddy Lars's special northern fried chicken. Want to learn how to do that? It was the way to your mother's heart, you know."

Cookie gave him a mocking sidelong glance.

"It's true. I wooed your mother with northern fried chicken. You just wait until you're a thin and hungry student. Some smart fellow will sidle up to you with a picnic basket of northern fried chicken— not as good as mine, of course—and next thing you know, you'll be dating a boy without anything to recommend him but greasy fingers."

"Or," said Cookie archly, "maybe I'll tell him I can make my own just fine."

"My plan exactly," admitted Lars. "Now first we need a menu, such as you could print out with your new program, yes?"

"Oh, yes," said Cookie, noticeably more enthusiastic.

"And then we need to settle on our order of battle, who does what and when, because we need this to be perfect, or else your mother will say, 'That's not the real northern fried chicken that only Lars can make.' "

"And Cookie, too."

"And Cookie, too," Lars agreed, and in that precise repetition he felt that they'd again reached the special place where they were in harmony, in sync, in safety. He was going to do better, he really was. He and Cookie would be close again, Emma would be delighted with dinner and with him and with his confiding in her, and they'd both be astonished and impressed when he plucked the correspondent out of cyberspace and handed him over to the police, trussed up like a Christmas capon.

These thoughts were enough to keep Lars's happy mood aloft

through the preparation of northern fried chicken and a pleasant interlude with Emma after lights-out. Reality forced a sour landing only two days later, when he found a message headed, *Proof of My Existence.*

You will have noticed that I prefer the shorter modes. Odd, isn't it? The Net allows endless prolixity, an almost infinite number of links and digressions: Would such be good for you and me, Lars? Links, digressions, byways, would those be good? Would you be able to escape the blood, the thud? You can't forget the thud. It haunts your dreams. The sound of a corpse is unique, Lars, the sound of a fall without resistance. No more volition, that's the thing, hence the inanimate sound, like a sandbag, like a suitcase, an inhuman thud.

But digression is a thief of time. Do you find yourself losing time, Lars? Losing time to digression? Maybe to the temptations of the Net? The Net is long, but E-mail's short.

All this is all prologue to a proof of my existence, Are you ready, Lars? On the night of the Event, Iris was in your car. You gave her a ride from campus. You delivered her to the little park on Jordan Avenue where you began the fatal argument.

Is this something the investigating officers would like to know? I think so, Lars, I do think so.

They would be satisfied with these tidbits; you may require something more. Shall I tell you what she said to you? Shall I repeat your threats? I can, you realize, but we will save those for another letter. I find myself suddenly reluctant to end our correspondence too abruptly.

I have the feeling that this is a letter you will want to answer.

Lars swore, took a deep breath, and swore again: Suppose I've been wrong! The morbid tone of the letters had led him to suspect that this was Iris's killer. But could he be sure? The correspondent mentioned the police, surely a strong indication he was not involved. And, worse, the details were right. Lars knew that he and Iris had been seen. That was bad. Perhaps the correspondent had an alibi, an alibi for the time of death, which, of course, was not exact, which had been, Lars realized with a sudden, sharp intestinal chill, falsified by his own omissions.

At the time precision had meant nothing to him, nothing. His whole focus had been on avoiding trouble, sparing Emma and Cookie—and himself, of course. Understandable; it had been an understandable course of action, trivial, minor, an omission of what—thirty minutes tops—but the consequences had been monstrously—and continuously—magnified. Lars could hear Emma downstairs in the kitchen, the rattle of pots, snatches of classical music, Cookie calling Polly for her dinner, and over everything, the sound of his heart. He felt the contraction of the muscles of his chest—how wrong the physiologists were to dethrone the heart as the seat of the emotions! The old poets were right: The brain went on, running like a hamster in a wheel; it was the heart, the chest, the diaphragm that came to a halt with cold and terror and the apprehension of the worst of all worlds: His original assumption was correct. This man had killed Iris, and Lars himself had put him out of reach.

Could he take his carefully culled list of names to the police? Could he say, "I've been getting mysterious E-mails"? "My clearly unstable correspondent knows literature and philosophy and is or was connected with the college. He knew Iris, resents the success of her book, is perhaps her killer. I have here a list of literature students, past and present, who took the right sort of courses and who were on campus at the right time to know Iris." Oh, very impressive, Professor Larson! The public intellectual as chief investigator! Then, could he add, as he would have to, for they would soon discover everything, "And, by the way, your new chief suspect will claim that I was at the crime scene with Iris Weed"?

Could he say that? Or would that be to gamble and risk everything? With the sounds of his household around him, Lars knew the answer to that question. He was still thinking over his situation, thinking he must sit tight for a little longer, thinking he must have not names but the name, proof, evidence, something conclusive, when another, very short message arrived.

Perhaps I should have included Mrs. Weed in my list of interested persons. Interested in my observations of the night of the Event. She's a crusader, is she not, Lars?

I do not think you want me to disturb Isobel Weed.

Without hesitation, Lars hit Reply and typed, *What the hell do you want?*

"Lars," Emma called from downstairs. "Dinner's ready."

"A minute," he shouted, more annoyed than he intended, "just a damn minute," and pushed Send.

The response was waiting when he got home from school the next day.

Mission Control, we have contact!

> *I can't tell you, Lars, how pleased I am that you have reconsidered your counterproductive stance. Now that you see the wisdom of my whole approach, I hope you will be in the mood to take advice. It goes without saying that I expect and anticipate your confession. You will feel better and be a better person for it.*

> *But I understand that you will require preparation, psychological and practical, before such a step. Besides, there are so many things I want to ask you about Iris. She's on both our minds, isn't she? I do understand, Lars, I really do.*

"A better person" indeed! Lars thought irritably that the correspondent would better take some of his own pop-psych advice. Nonetheless, contact seemed to have shifted some vital balance, for while Lars answered all messages cautiously, his correspondent now seemed desperate to communicate. Again and again, he declared that only he had loved Iris; Lars, who had not loved her, who had let her down, who had killed her, must understand that. Must. And he was sure Lars did, because he knew that Lars understood him perfectly. The previous silence and misunderstandings were simply perversity, for Lars was transparent to him, and he to Lars. Surely Lars admitted that!

Lars admitted nothing and declared his innocence, but more than once his mind sprang back to that ridiculous, difficult to explain night when he had searched for Iris's truck and almost gotten into a fistfight. What might have happened to him and to Iris had he found her then? Depressed by this guilty thought, Lars postponed decision and resisted sporadic impulses to call the detectives. He would think of Harrelson or, more usually, Paatelainen, and then tell himself that, after all, the correspondence was quite different now. The most alarming messages were in the past; the correspondent, poor fellow, wanted communication, sympathy, some human contact. Well, don't we all? The rest was fantasy, such as Lars understood only too well, for who would be more plausible than some frustrated writer? Whenever Lars realized that this was the most cowardly of rationalizations, he suppressed the thought, and, though he had otherwise lost all initiative, redoubled his efforts to locate the writer.

But fortune evidently does favor the brave: His luck seemed to have run out. The list of medievalists proved a dead end: One was a girl, despite her masculine first name; one was seriously handicapped. The remaining master's candidate had been in the semester abroad program the May that Iris was killed, and the doctoral student had been delivering a conference paper in Denver. The undergraduate friends mentioned in the newspaper stories seemed to have had excellent alibis as well, and had, predictably, scattered with graduation. The only graduate student interviewed, John Mortlake, had also left the area, apparently without taking his comprehensive exams or filing his dissertation proposal.

This was hardly unusual in the present job market, but Lars took a look at his transcript: German, various nineteenth- and twentieth-century writers, medieval drama, Myth and Psychoanalysis, two comparative literature courses, plus the seminar on the nineteenth-century novel, a course Lars would normally have taught but that he had passed, in a moment of graciousness, to a distinguished visiting professor. John Mortlake had not taken Shakespeare with Joe Katz, had only one course in medieval literature, and appeared not to have dabbled in philosophy. Lars had to concede that a seat in Myth and Psychoanalysis does not a Viking berserker make and, with these dead ends, acquired a greater respect for the humble toil of detection.

Bereft of further inspiration, he saw only patience and the hope of error or of revelation, a course which fitted his low spirits nicely. In subsequent E-mails, Lars and the correspondent discussed philosophy (clearly a strong interest) and guilt (in the abstract) and error (the correspondent referred again and again to "one error"), all part of a verbal dance around what Lars suspected was a suppressed desire to confess. But any time he tried to get more information about the night Iris was killed, the messages returned to the correspondent's true (and Lars's inadequate) love for Iris and to preemptory demands for Lars's confession.

He's too clever, Lars thought, or he truly believes I'm to blame. Or else my confession will serve as his confession. Maybe that's it, as if we weren't guilty of different things, to different degrees. Maybe any guilt will do, but who could fathom the twists and turns of another's mind, especially a mind revealed not through handwriting, the seismograph of the soul, but via electronic letters, font and size sender's choice? Nothing could be decided from E-mail alone, nothing. This problem lay in the back of Lars's mind all through his lecture on Robert Browning, "Madmen's Monologues," which, in a bow to undergraduate tastes and attention spans, focused on the poet's more sensational, not to say homicidal, characters.

By the end of the discussion, Lars realized that he had set mere textual criticism an impossible task. A poet of genius seeking to reveal character is quite a different matter from a modern psychopath trying to conceal his. Lars dispatched student questions about the duke, the cardinal, and Porphyria's lover, then went into his office and tapped out a note starting, *I'm too old fashioned to feel quite comfortable in E-mail*, and suggesting a meeting.

No, Lars, no way, came the response. *You're forgetting, and I can completely understand your resistance, because wasn't Iris's mistake one meeting, that one last meeting? I will meet you only if I have despaired entirely.*

Do you believe despair is the ultimate sin? I find that a difficult concept in the modern world, where there are so many worse things than suicide. Do you think about suicide, Lars?

I can recommend it.

Even electronically, Lars felt the chilliness of this strange mind, that had, if he was guessing right, gotten away with a crime and now wanted someone else to confess to it. Just the same, this message was close to an admission. Lars sensed that the correspondent was

245

afraid, and this knowledge restored his confidence and initiative. It was time to force the issue. *We must meet,* he wrote, *or this is absolutely my last message.*

The response titled, *Lack of Understanding,* was in the system the next morning, and it was fortunate that Lars did not have classes that day, because, in a few lines, the correspondent had altered the entire situation:

> *Received your astonishing communiqué. I'm not sure I'd have the same sangfroid, especially if I had a family, a daughter of my own. Doesn't that give you pause, doesn't that make you wonder? Difference in ages—ten years maybe? Still, you should be careful. Girls are fragile; the red life runs out of them thick on the pavement, and the bones, the bones, Lars. When a knife hits bone, there's a shocking tingle at the end of your arm. Books don't mention those things, nor the smell of shit and blood, nor the stutter of your heart before the surprise of life dissolving.*
>
> *I'm sure you'll agree with me, Lars, that some experiences are beyond expectation and imagination.*

Lars felt physically sick at this display of viciousness and brutality. He sat at his desk, taking deep breaths to control his nausea. By deceiving and protecting himself, he had endangered Cookie and maybe Emma, too. He couldn't delay any longer, not even if these were just idle, irresponsible words (and Lars could no longer quite convince himself of that). *Your message today and all future communications will be forwarded directly to the police,* he wrote and pushed Send. Then, before he could waver, he reached for his phone and dialed the homicide department. "This is Professor Jason Larson," he told the operator. "I'd like to speak to either Detective Paatelainen or Detective Harrelson."

"Detective Harrelson is on vacation until next Thursday. Detective Paatelainen is out of the office at the moment. I can have her return your call."

"Please," said Lars. He left both his home and his work numbers. "She knows me. I have some information for her. Tell her it's quite urgent." He hung up the phone, his hands shaking. He had expected to reach the detectives immediately, to pass on the messages before he could have second thoughts. Now who knew how long he'd have to wait, or when and where they might call.

To distract himself, Lars went downstairs to wash his coffee cup and the breakfast dishes and take Jake for a brief turn around the neighborhood, flaming now with autumn golds and reds. When he returned, he glanced at the answering machine, then went outside to tie up one of Emma's blooming asters. He checked for messages again, just in case, but the little red light remained uncommunicative, sending Lars back upstairs. He needed to prepare something new on Oscar Wilde and to make comments on a dissertation proposal and grade some papers. He had plenty to do, plenty to fill the time, but still it was amazing that Paatelainen was so slow to respond, so disinterested, with such an incompetent staff.

What would he say when she did call? Which messages would he hand over? Should he admit the meeting, the ride, the argument? If so, how to explain, and if not, how to conceal? A dozen decisions, all important, all, Lars suspected, to be decided on the spur of the moment, as inspiration and instinct dictated. His lesser self suggested that, after all, she might not call; the message might be lost, ignored, mislaid. No, Lars told himself sharply, I'd have to call again. That would be wise anyway. Another call would indicate urgency, importance. He was reaching for the phone when it rang, and so strong was his image of Detective Paatelainen, rosy, perceptive, and pitiless, that it took him a second or two to realize this was not the detective, nor, indeed, anyone he knew.

"Lars? I thought I'd let you know the E-mail's over now. That time has passed. We've both moved on, and even if you chicken out, which I suspect—"

"Who is this?" Lars demanded, though one part of him already knew.

"Your reminder, Lars," said the voice, which was low, educated, uninflected; calm, Lars might have said, but for a buried vein of excitement like ore in rock, and certain hoarse, burry overtones as if the speaker had a cold or smoked too much or was tight with nerves. "Memento mori. Your confessor. And once you confess, Lars, I won't contact you again. Promise."

"Listen," said Lars. He felt his face flush with anger.

"No, my mind's made up. You've had enough time, Lars. Anything less than a full confession, a modern confession, I should say, reported in the papers, seen on TV, and I'll take action myself. I may take some action myself, anyway, but I'll leave you in suspense about that, which is only fair, given—"

"Understand me," Lars said keeping his temper with difficulty. "I have nothing to confess and I'm turning your crackpot E-mails over to the police."

"Not good enough, Lars, not good enough at all. And now you mention it, I'm not sure I trust the police to see the truth of the situation and not to be distracted by your lies. I know you will lie about me, Lars, just as you lied about Iris, just as you lied to Iris. I know you did."

"You're the one who's lying, you fucking creep," Lars shouted, but the line had gone dead.

15.

Mr. Jack was presiding at the long, white, gleaming counter of the computer store when he thought he saw Cookie Larson walking in the concourse, laughing and talking with a slight blonde girl. A glimpse, then they were gone, and Mr. Jack forced himself to concentrate on the task at hand: selling a new power Mac cube to a customer basically interested in home decor, not computing power. He could have been mistaken; at a certain age all young girls looked pretty much alike, but he kept alert anyway and ten minutes later, there she was, alone in the doorway. No doubt this time, and she'd ditched her friend, too. Mr. Jack smiled to himself, as the unquantifiably boring afternoon shifted toward something exciting, dangerous, and interesting. Of course, she was a mere child, just twelve, and so exactly ten years younger than Iris, whom he had loved. Mr. Jack nodded to himself, the merest little bob of his head, a confirmation of the passion that was his curse and his excuse. He'd loved Iris Weed. But the little girl, who was, yes, coming in, skittish, determined, impulsive, had certain attractions; she would, he suspected, be a beauty, would be difficult, stubborn, a treacherous bitch like Iris, would be adorable, beloved. His head was cold and he felt the sweat under his arms, because she was enough like Iris, dark and shy and clever and much loved, to be the one. He was sure Larson loved her as he, himself, had loved Iris, and so . . .

"Ready with that item, sir?"

He rang up a sale and answered a question about additional

memory, dismissing all possible difficulties with the assurance of complete instructions. All the while, smiling and patient, he was keeping one eye on the Larson girl, still half in her soccer strip, loitering beside the game display, offering opportunity. *Don't go*, Jack thought, *don't go*.

A final question, the beep of the scanner, the friction of cellophanes and polymers whispering in the plastic bags, then Jack stepped around the counter and walked over to Cookie.

"Hi. Checking out the new games?"

She waited so long to answer, he thought she might not speak at all. Had he frightened her, had he revealed too much, was the mention of Iris a mistake? That was the problem with E-mail, one wrote too fast, sent too quickly, revised too little. Not like handwriting, not like typing or even keyboarding, though he must allow that the sagas had been chanted extemporaneously, and he would not like to think what could have slipped in there.

Cookie Larson picked up the new Norwegian import. She wanted to say, "Don't write me again. I don't want any more of your stupid E-mails." She'd come into the store with just that idea in mind, but instead she said, "This good?" No greeting, no small talk.

Mr. Jack smiled. Now he knew what she wanted, why she had come in. She was beginning to understand him, and he, her. "Haven't played it yet myself, but it's supposed to be. Not so much bang-bang, you know, but with good characters."

"And the graphics?" asked Cookie, the fussy, careful shopper.

"Top of the line. That much I have seen. Tremendous." It amazed him how ordinary he sounded, how well he knew the store patter, how professional he must seem. He should have been professional with Iris, he should have had patter, he should . . .

Cookie put the game back slowly and reluctantly. "Too bad it's so expensive." She met his eyes.

Without hesitation, Mr. Jack picked up one of the shrink-wrapped boxes. "We sometimes have our good customers review new products." He walked over to the counter where he removed the alarm activator on the package and coded in a damaged item on the computer. Then he slipped the game smoothly into a store bag and handed it over. "We have a form," he said, "but you can just E-mail me your opinion. You'll do that?"

Cookie nodded and tucked the small box under her arm. The game did not seem so desirable now, because she'd given him an excuse to E-mail her again and ask. She felt like throwing the box away and maybe she would as soon as she was out the door. This thought made her feel mean and angry and fearless.

"You'll enjoy that, you really will," he said.

"How did you know Iris Weed?" Cookie asked.

Mr. Jack's lips twitched. He'd been smiling a lot, but this wasn't quite a smile, more like he was annoyed because she hadn't said thank you.

"I used to see her around." He spoke as if he had not been particularly interested, as if he had not mentioned Iris first, as if he had not guessed that Cookie was desperately curious. "I believe she worked at the health food store for a while."

"She was a liar," said Cookie. "She wrote lies about my dad."

Mr. Jack went quiet and looked puzzled. "Why do you say that?"

"Thanks for the game," said Cookie and turned away.

Mr. Jack called to her to wait and started after her, but his exit was blocked by a thin, gray-haired woman in a blazing pink windbreaker who was leaning eagerly over the counter. She wanted a scanner, she knew the desired resolution, the price. He waved toward the display models, but the woman was scornful.

"I already looked at those. Don't you have any in that nice blueberry color?"

Inwardly cursing decorator hardware, Jack had to say they'd check the stock. He called to Rhoda, shouted really, heard his voice rise and muttered something about the noise of the air system, the need to keep machines cool. But there was no response from Rhoda, who was a thorough slacker when she wasn't right under his eye and who liked to phone her boyfriend when she should have been tending the stock. He would have to look himself and get Kitty to take over the floor.

Jack glanced back toward the concourse. The Larson girl was already gone; he'd missed his chance for the sake of a color-coordinated desktop. What the hell had she meant by "telling lies"? What had she heard? What had she seen? Jack remembered Iris's notebooks, all those scribbled multicolored diaries, girl stuff, he'd thought; how was he supposed to have guessed at the talent behind those gaudy Flair pens? She'd kept the notebooks very private; he'd never read so much as a paragraph, hadn't wanted to. He'd had more to read than he could manage between grading papers for Aryant and his own class assignments and mushing though manuals at the computer help desk. But now he had to wonder what she had written about him, because surely his name would be there in green and red and purple. Would she have written enough to make him seem suspicious? To raise questions?

At the time of the investigation, at the terrible time after the mistake, after that one dreadful error, he said he'd been just a casual friend. "We went out a few times in late winter," he told the police, knowing that he and Iris would have been noticed at the coffee shop and the club and the health food store and campus bars. "Nothing serious." The police wouldn't have accepted that if they'd had Iris's diaries, would they? Ergo, the diaries must be lost, Jack told himself, without quite escaping the bad feelings he had about Iris's scribbling.

He took a deep breath: There was no need to panic. The most likely one to have something was Larson, and if old Larsie had anything in writing, he'd have given it to the police tout de suite, unless he secretly enjoyed those months of being a suspect. Of course, it was Lars who was truly at fault in everything, everything, because Lars hadn't loved Iris, not the way he, Jack, had. As he walked the narrow aisles of the stockroom, checking boxes of Popsicle-colored scanners, Jack decided that Lars must be made to understand how much he had loved Iris. It was time, he thought, to make that crystal clear to Lars, to bring the facts of the matter home to him and make him pay.

Detective Paatelainen initially suggested meeting at his house, which Lars wouldn't allow, and then at school, which was almost as bad.

Finally, she said that if it was going to be so difficult, maybe he'd prefer to come to the station. Though Lars hated the idea, hated even the thought of breathing that air, permeated as he knew it would be with the residue of suspicion, misery, and guilt, he said yes, of course. It was important, he had something for them, he would come.

"Well," said Detective Paatelainen, now pretty sure that he wasn't going to waste her time entirely, "you might prefer the coffee shop on the same block. The Kitchen Table, do you know it?"

Lars did, and he was there early and waiting. Besides his coffee, he had a folder with hard copy of the E-mails and a disk of the messages complete with their appended coding set out on the pastel Formica table. Everything, Lars told himself, that the detective required, and plenty to indicate action. But though Lars had felt confident, even ingenious, while he was sorting the messages and filling up the disk, certain omissions now seemed dubious, and the fact that Emma and Cookie were concerned, perhaps endangered, became paramount. He added sugar and a thimble of the ersatz cream to his untouched coffee, rattled the spoon against the thick white mug, and tried to convince himself that he'd included everything important.

Yes, he'd given Iris a ride, yes, they'd had an argument, but she'd walked away safe and sound and wrongheaded as ever. So that incident was irrelevant; besides, Lars told himself, for he could be exceedingly crafty in conversation with himself, nothing said he couldn't tell them eventually. If need be. Which he doubted.

Besides, the police had no complaint, no reasonable complaint; he was doing them a favor, and he might have done them other favors if they hadn't been so persistent, if they hadn't been out from the first to humiliate and harass him. Some of this was their fault, and with this convenient dispersal of guilt, Lars raised his head to the rain-spotted windows and saw the detective approaching along the sidewalk, her white hair damp in the mist, her rosy face cheerful. Of course, she had something to be cheerful about: the possibility of new evidence, a break in the case, a calamitous loss of nerve on the part of Professor Jason Larson, her present investigative target, who, standing up now, waving, making an effort, had only his fear and worry and the prospect of lies to tell.

"Professor." Her hand, cold from the walk, stretched across the table to him. She shrugged off her damp coat, smiled at the waitress, ordered coffee and inquired about the day's muffins. She would have one of the zucchini-cheese ones, which were delicious, she assured Lars, and soup, too; she'd missed lunch. "Busy, busy," she said. She might have been a jolly elementary school teacher or a saleslady in an upscale boutique or a particularly wholesome and sympathetic nurse. Instead, as Lars had to keep reminding himself, she was a detective who was measuring him for handcuffs even as they spoke. He asked himself if, after all, Harrelson would not have been the better choice with less dysfunction between image and reality.

"So," she said and waited. Lars had forgotten her long wait time.

"Sitting here, I was wondering how you got into police work. I was thinking how little you look like the stereotyped police officer."

Her handsome, open face clouded ever so slightly. "The usual mix of opportunity and impulse," she said briskly. "One thing led to another. Some day when our business is finished, I'll maybe give you the details. But at the moment," she glanced at her watch, "I just have time for whatever you've brought me."

Another busy, happy day, Lars thought, of tormenting hapless suspects and breaking down their alibis. He handed her the disk and the folder. "I printed the texts out for you."

Paatelainen put on a pair of violet-rimmed glasses and read swiftly through the messages. When she was finished, she glanced at him over her spectacles. "Not nice."

Lars agreed. "He's got to be found."

Paatelainen tipped her head, a slight, skeptical motion. "If this person is knowledgeable enough to hide his identity, that will be very difficult."

"But you'll try."

"We'll try." A long, reflective pause, in which the detective once again examined the file. "There are breaks," she observed. "Nearly a week in one case, closer to two in another."

One had been a true hiatus, the other caused by Lars's prudent deletions, but surely the difference was unimportant. "Maybe he was away, maybe he travels, had the flu, whatever."

Paatelainen shifted abruptly into some higher professional gear and asked, "Have you given me everything?"

"I wanted you to see the whole correspondence. I realize that some of the E-mails aren't important," Lars added, as if apologizing for pedantic completeness instead of significant omissions.

"And you answered none of these?"

Lars shook his head. "Not until he mentioned my daughter." Lars tapped the most sinister message. "When he seemed to be threatening Cookie, I replied that all future messages would be turned over to the police. Then I called you."

"It's possible that will be enough to discourage him."

"No," said Lars, "there's been a phone call." He described the conversation. "I'm sure it's the same man."

Paatelainen wrote down the date and time and asked him to repeat the conversation word-for-word, a difficult chore in Lars's nervous state. "I'm being as accuate as possible, but I was pretty upset."

Paatelainen nodded as if she might be reserving judgment, then wrote everything down and read it back to him. "Have you caller ID?" she asked when the phone message was accurately transcribed.

"I didn't at the time. I've had it added since."

"Good. Let us know immediately if you get a number. And, speaking unofficially now because there's not really enough here to authorize a wiretap, you might try to record the calls." Her smile was serene and worldly, the expression of a woman who had seen much and protected herself from most of it. "Of course you did not hear that from me. In the meantime, I'll see what the technical people can do and whether we'll need to have access to your hard drive."

"I hope you can do it without taking my hard drive," Lars exclaimed. "I have a lot of school material stored. And student privacy concerns aside, at this time of year, I'm on my machine such a lot." It was in the back of his mind that even deleted E-mails might be dangerous. Hadn't he read somewhere that E-mail never really disappears, that there are always resurrectable electronic ghosts? Whatever had possessed him to acquire such a succubus! "I'm concerned about Cookie and Emma. I want them protected. I don't want to be worried every time I leave the house."

Paatelainen sighed. "I wish we could help, but at the moment we have half a dozen really pressing cases, people in imminent danger, and we haven't the staff to protect them adequately."

"He's calling my house, accusing me of murder, hinting at action. He knows where I live, knows I'm married, probably knows Emma's and Cookie's names, but that's not enough to get protection for my family?"

"Professor, we've got witnesses in drug cases, we've got battered wives, we've got folks with restraining orders, and more psychos with guns than you want to imagine. This," she touched the folder, "is upsetting. I wouldn't like it one bit, but does it represent an immediate threat? E-mail, phone contact—he could be anywhere in the country."

"I thought so, too, but he knows me, knows the department— did you notice the reference to . . ." Lars caught himself just in time. He couldn't refer to Joe Katz's tedious Shakespeare class; that message was one of the dangerous ones. Lars mumbled something about the high-flown style and then mentioned that the correspondent had quoted Iris.

"Surely Iris had friends in her hometown. Unless you have something more specific . . ."

"His description of the killing," said Lars, turning the folder around. "Here it is: 'A knife, a blow, one terrible mistake, and then blood and frenzy. Have I guessed right? About the blood, the shock, the weight of your arms? Slaughter is exhausting work, Lars, as you will remember. You really have to want to kill someone to exhaust yourself so much.' Does that sound like a normal mind to you?"

"It sounds like he's accusing you of murder," said Detective Paatelainen. "There's no pleasant way to do that."

*   *   *

Lars was furious when he took his leave of the detective and still angry when he arrived on campus for a late meeting of the Freshman Experience Committee. He annoyed Lydia by announcing right at the start that he was leaving early to pick up Cookie (a blatant lie, Cookie would actually be late at band rehearsal), then compounded his offense by loitering after the meeting to chat with Pauline, the nervous new Americanist, who was making herself miserable over a nasty journal rejection.

"Ignore the arrogant bastards," was Lars's advice. "It's all political. Anything more current than close reading is anathema to them."

"My work is hardly avant-garde," protested Pauline, though Lars could see she was pleased at the notion of being ahead of the scholarly curve. "But I'm going to need a lot of articles unless I can get a second book finished. And with the course load I've got, I don't see doing very much research for a while."

Lars agreed that the system was unfair when it wasn't corrupt, then joked that he, at least, was sharing the load by being on the deadly Freshman Experience Committee, "for my sins," he said and winked.

The usually serious and conscientious Pauline took in her breath, then gave a surprisingly robust laugh. "You make it sound like some ghastly regulatory agency."

"Due to go nuclear any minute," said Lars as he caught sight of Lydia, stalking down the hall, meeting folders in hand, a thousand items still untouched on her agenda. Her anger made him feel better, as if he was still the academic buccaneer of old, feisty, irresistible, fit in every way to challenge pedants and bureaucrats and to win the hearts of fair colleagues. He looked at his watch and said to Pauline, "Let's get together for coffee, all right? We can talk over your article. Not really my specialty, but I have pretty good contacts."

"Oh, would you?" Pauline blushed and smiled, bringing a little color to her face. Though no beauty, she had a gentle, intelligent expression, and extraordinary milky skin so pale it revealed the little blue veins in her wrists and arms. Very Victorian, Lars thought. One hundred and fifty years ago those delicate wrists would have raised the ambient temperature. "I feel I need a mentor," Pauline continued. "I didn't realize how important mentoring could be."

Lars wondered how much charm he could find in linguistic monstrosities like *mentoring*. "Part of our job with junior faculty," he said, suppressing the thought that he was becoming part of the older generation, "is to console them for the presence of old farts in the citadel."

"You've made me feel better, anyway. Being new on a big campus can be an isolating experience."

Lars smiled and touched her shoulder: Occasionally inclination and duty coincide. He was set to accompany her to the parking lot when the office secretary stepped into the hall and said he had a phone call. When Lars found it was Paatelainen, he ran up to his office where he learned that his mysterious E-mails came from an account opened through the library at the University of Nebraska.

"But the actual mail could be coming from anywhere, is that right?" Lars asked.

"Yes, it could. But I'm always suspicious of anything from the academic world. It's so easy to get burned by clever college students with time on their hands. We could be looking at an ex-student of yours."

"Or someone who'd known Iris," Lars said, for he truly did not believe the writer was one of his students. The turns of phrase were odd, and the tone was distinctive enough so that he'd have remembered it. He mentioned his search through the files, his suspicions of medievalists, his application of textual criticism to detection.

Paatelainen was as noncommittal as he would have been had she announced she had some new ideas on reader response criticism.

"I suppose it could be anyone, really," Lars concluded lamely.

"Even you," said Paatelainen. "Didn't you give a talk in Lincoln last year? At that conference on 'Romanticism in the Novel'?"

"I'm flattered that you're keeping up with my vita," said Lars, who actually felt surprised and flustered, "but I'm not sending myself threatening E-mails. That's a ridiculous idea."

"You'd be surprised at the things people do," Paatelainen said, "when they're under pressure."

Lars pointed out that he wouldn't be under pressure if the police were protecting his family. He'd sure feel a lot better if they could find out who killed Iris, too. He pursued these ideas until both he and Paatelainen were shouting, then slammed the phone down with the infuriating awareness that he'd made a tactical error. His mood didn't improve when he arrived home to find that Cookie'd been at Betty's because the house had been dark when Denise's mom dropped her off. Poor Emma had come home to the empty house and no messages and a puddle on the floor from either Polly or Jake, and now the entire household was in a sour and nervous mood. Lars put the blame on Lydia's ludicrous agenda for the Freshman Experience Committee and retreated to his study to put away his briefcase and collect his thoughts. The phone rang before he reached his desk, startling him in the half dark study. It's Paatelainen, he thought, having second thoughts about her attitude and afraid he might make trouble. She'd really been out of line, and Lars answered the call in his best outraged professor voice. He was not expecting the quiet intense voice on the other end.

"I haven't forgotten you, Lars. 'The time has come, the Walrus said, to speak of many things.' In your case, Lars, just one thing, your confession."

Lars was so taken aback, it took him a second before he could say, "The police have started tracing your E-mails. They know where you are," and another second before he remembered that the caller ID display had registered *unknown*, which meant it was probably a cell phone, which could be anywhere.

"You're not taking me seriously, Lars," the voice said. "Next time I'll leave you a calling card. Iris always said you liked Victorian things."

16.

*L*ars called to Cookie as soon as he finished a sufficiently florid recommendation for one of his students. Lars wasn't sure what use rhetorical and queer theory, plus a mastery of feminist criticism and new historicism would be for handling four (or was it five?) sections of developmental English. Still, in the present job market, tenure track, full benefits, and the state pension system were nothing to sniff at, and Lars had kept Cookie waiting a good half hour while exaggerating the candidate's abilities and production as far as his conscience would allow. "Are you ready, Cookie?"

A clatter in the hall, hopeful barks from Jake, then his daughter's rosy face peeked around the door jamb.

"All set?"

A vigorous nod. "I want to get the Adidas. The red ones."

"We'll have to see what fits," said Lars. He was appalled at the prices of soccer boots and at Cookie's ability to outgrow each new pair before they were half broken in. She was going to be tall if her feet were any indication.

"I tried on Denise's brother's and they fit fine."

"I'll bet Denise doesn't have to buy boots every month or so."

"Denise is going to be petite," said Cookie. "That's what her mom says, 'Denise is going to be petite.'"

There was a satiric tinge to her voice, which was something else new. Cookie had been a rather naive, straightforward child, apt to take people at their own evaluations. Lars thought that this more critical stance wasn't entirely a bad thing where Denise and her mother were concerned. Denise Farron, already boy crazy and giggly, was allowed makeup and permitted what Lars considered excessively skimpy blouses and skirts by her mother, a self-styled beauty, who had prudently adopted her faded glamour pose quite late in life. "Denise is going to be petite," was exactly the sort of thing Mrs. Farron did say. She had talked a lot about her daughter on the few times Lars had spoken with her, and most of her remarks had been in italics.

"Whereas Cookie Larson is going to be elegant and statuesque," Lars teased.

"I'm growing so tall Coach is thinking of training me for a keeper," said Cookie, as she bent to tickle Jake's ears. "He says it's hard to find good women keepers."

Lars had visions of his darling being bombarded by soccer balls, of back-twisting leaps, dangerous dives, and tooth-shattering collisions—he'd speak to her coach about that idea! At the same time, Lars understood that Cookie would probably be a good keeper. She had her mother's physical aplomb. All the intelligence and wit that he loved and admired had physical equivalents for Cookie. It was remarkable how restless she was even doing her schoolwork. He'd come in one day when she was dancing in her room, her boom box deafening, to be told that she was memorizing her spelling words. And she probably had been. "It all depends on your grades," said Lars. "You've got to keep up with your schoolwork."

"Oh, sure," said Cookie. Her blasé expression told Lars that she was confident she need do only enough to get by. "I'll have a new strip if I'm keeper."

"With padding," said Lars, his mind reverting to the shock of combat, to injuries. "Those goalkeeper strips come with lots of padding, don't they?"

"Some. I don't know," Cookie replied indifferently. "I'll play in shorts anyway." She started down the stair, bouncing from one tread to the next.

"We'll see," said Lars.

"Mom's already said it's up to me," said Cookie, who combined obstinacy with strategy. "Shall we put Jake out back?"

"We'll take him up to the corner. Did you feed Polly?" He looked around for the cat, who usually started agitating for dinner as soon as he got home, slinking around his legs and leaping onto his desk.

"She's outside. She went out when I came in."

While Lars snapped on Jake's leash, Cookie went to the door. He heard her calling, "Polly! Come on, girl. Polly," before her voice rose in a frightened, and frightening, wail. "Dad! Dad! Something's happened to Polly."

Lars ran out onto the step. Cookie was kneeling on the grass, her hand stretched over, but not touching, Polly's limp dark body. The cat's eyes were open and Lars noticed some blood on her side and a little at the edge of her open mouth.

"She's dead! I'm afraid she'd dead!" Cookie cried. Her cheeks were flushed, but the rest of her face had gone pale and tears were already welling in her eyes.

"Hold Jake," Lars said. "Jake, no!" The little dog began whining and straining toward Polly. "Hold Jake. He's upset, too."

Cookie grabbed Jake's collar and wrapped her arms around him, trying not to cry. "She's not dead, is she?"

Lars touched the soft fur, which he had so often stroked, with the deepest reluctance. He felt the cat's throat and wrist only to show Cookie that he was doing something, for he'd had no doubt from the moment he saw the animal lying in the middle of the lawn. The spirit that had propelled Polly's effortless leaps and lunges, her cold focus on mice and birds, her flawless eye for comfort and warmth, her purring contentment, her quick, needle-tipped paws was gone, leaving soon to be matted fur and stiffening limbs behind. Lars straightened up and touched Cookie's head. "I'm sorry, sweetie. I'm sure it was quick. I'm sure she didn't suffer."

"It was my fault," Cookie said with a sob, and her face, which had seemed only a few minutes ago to be lengthening into maturity, was a child's again, distorted by grief. "I put her out the front door."

"Dear, Polly went all over. She must have seen something in the street and made a leap—you know how fast she was," Lars said, although even as he spoke he knew that made no sense. Polly lay in the middle of the lawn; if she'd been hit, surely her body would be in the street or at the curb. On the sidewalk at the very farthest. And it seemed to him now that her wounds—the one patch of blood, the trickle around her mouth—did not fit with being struck or crushed.

Cookie did not see these anomalies, being totally focused on what might have been. "I should have fed her. She wanted to be fed, but I was in a hurry. I thought I'd feed her later with Jake. What will Mom say? Polly was Mom's cat." With this Cookie burst into tears and flung herself from the grass into Lars's arms, while Jake alternately scratched at his leg and whimpered over Polly.

"She wasn't exactly a young cat," Lars said, smoothing Cookie's hair and trying to say reassuring, comforting things, while his mind raced after one idea then another: if a car, wouldn't he have heard the brakes? A thud? And also, the car stopping and a door opening as someone noticed the small corpse, someone reluctant to ring doorbells and ask, "Do you have a black cat?" Someone reluctant to say, "I'm afraid I hit it. It ran out so fast, I couldn't stop. I'm sorry," but not someone so heartless as to keep going. Instead, this someone had stopped, picked the cat out of the street—Lars conceded that he himself would have been extremely reluctant to touch it—and carried it up to the middle of the nearest lawn. "Polly was happiest hunting," he continued. "I'll bet she was after one of those naughty squirrels that try to get into our attic."

Cookie nodded, her tears making a damp patch on Lars's wind-breaker.

"She wouldn't have known what hit her. That's what we'll tell Mom."

Cookie broke away and bent over to pick up the cat.

"Let me get a towel," said Lars quickly. "There's some blood." There should be blood in the street, too, he thought. "Take Jake to the back."

Cookie nodded, but she wouldn't leave Polly. When he returned with the towel she was holding Jake with one hand and stroking Polly's head with the other. Lars spread the towel on the grass.

"I'll lift her," said Cookie.

Lars held the dog and watched her wrap Polly in the towel. The only injury seemed to be what Lars, if he hadn't been sure it was just a car accident, would have thought was a cut, a stab. But that was ridiculous; the whole neighborhood knew Polly, and the sagacious creature had known the neighborhood, known which small children would maul her fur and which old ladies would slip her a saucer of milk.

"We'll have to bury her," said Cookie.

"What about a spot in Mom's garden, would that be all right?"

"We'll wait for Mom, though, won't we? We'll have to wait for Mom."

Lars had a strong impulse to have it over, to bury Polly and his fears together, but at his hesitation, Cookie began to weep again, and Lars remembered the sovereign importance of ritual for children. He told her they'd pick the spot and dig the grave, and so have everything ready when Emma came home. At this, Cookie wiped her eyes. They took Polly around to the backyard and left her on the porch while they surveyed the yard. Lars worried a little about digging too close to Emma's prized azaleas, but, in the end, Cookie chose a piece of turf near one of the spruce trees. "She used to sit here," Cookie said. Lars agreed it was a fine place and suggested looking for a stone among the remains of the old wall along the back. They were turning over heavy lumps of brownstone when the phone rang in the house.

"Just leave it," said Lars. "It can go on the answer machine." Cookie ran back, anyway, but the ringing stopped before she had the back door open. Lars felt relieved, though of course it was just a vinyl siding company or the newest credit card offer. He levered the stone onto their hand truck and wheeled it to the grave site, where he and Cookie took turns digging in the dry, hard, root-laced soil. By the time Emma's car pulled in, they had dug a suitably deep hole and found some ivy to cover the bare earth. Cookie was dry-eyed, but she gave Lars a stricken glance when she heard the car door.

"It wasn't your fault," said Lars.

She raced around to the front, calling to Emma, who heard the news with a pang and put her arms around her daughter, who again burst into anguished tears.

Emma lingered in the kitchen that night. The supper dishes were done and put away, breakfast things laid out for the next morning. The stove was wiped and the cabinet fronts, and she even took apart the coffee maker and used vinegar to remove the mineral scum left by their hard water—busywork. Lars was upstairs; she could hear his erratic clatter at the computer, swift bursts of letters interrupted by backspaces, corrections; he was a fast but inaccurate typist. Cookie was in her room, supposedly doing homework. She'd gone up the stairs with Jake in her arms, half teary-eyed again with the thought of Polly.

When the phone rang, Emma was standing next to the kitchen extension and she lifted the receiver. "Hello?"

Silence. One of those automated dialers. Emma waited a minute, because sometimes if you hang up too soon, the machine will ring you back. Better just to wait and say no thanks to platinum credit cards or replacement windows or yet another long-distance service. "Hello?" But now she felt that someone was there. Funny how you can tell; the human ear must sense breathing too soft to register with one's consciousness. "Hello?"

Emma hung up. She'd gotten some similar calls lately, which was one reason she had suspected Lars, unjustly, she now believed. But if not a lover or an obsessive student—and Lars had had both over the years—maybe a burglar? The town was prosperous enough so that burglaries were common, and crooks frequently called ahead to see if anyone was home. Yes, that might have been a burglar checking up.

Emma looked out the window. The conifers made their yard dark at night, muffling and diffusing the neighbors' security lights with their thick, furry branches. She carried her coffee cup to the back porch and stepped out into the chill. It had been a rainy fall, and the gray sky, tinged pink and orange with city shine, promised more. She could just make out the little patch of raw earth and transplanted ivy. Poor Polly!

Emma leaned against the wide, cold porch railing. Polly would have been up beside her in a minute, purring, rubbing her head impatiently against Emma's hand or setting her soft paws on her shoulder. All that affection had been ended in a moment by a speeding car. That's what Cookie thought, though Polly was a wise old cat and cautious; her hunting ground was their own large yard, the crumbling wall and mess of shrubbery at the back. But perhaps she'd been chased by a dog, by another cat; it was no great mystery. Just the same, Emma thought she'd ask Lars later, because she'd noticed him examining the street and the sidewalk, trying to work out how it had happened.

She picked nervously at the peeling paint on the railing. How many bad nights had she sat with Polly, petting her silky coat, listening to her purr, that most soothing of sounds? How many things had she whispered to those soft, dark ears? Cats were supposed to be witches' familiars, to keep their secrets. Emma half smiled at the idea: Polly had a good many of mine, she thought, and felt the loss. Of course, pets die; only parrots and tortoises have real longevity, and outdoor cats face a thousand deaths. Yet any attended death brings memories of all the rest, so that the loss of Polly reawakened other griefs. That must be it, that and her pain for Cookie. There was no reason, otherwise, for the deep tide of anxiety that she felt rising, slowly but inevitably, around her.

The phone rang while Lars was printing out the next month's soccer schedule for Cookie. He'd showed her how to make calendars and a simple spreadsheet with dates and opponents. She now kept all the games and times straight for Coach, who, consequently, gave Lars credit for more than his share of "parent involvement."

"Hello? Cookie Larson speaking." Her expectant face grew puzzled. "Hello?" She hung up. "Another dumb wrong number. They could at least say sorry."

Lars agreed that was very rude and took the sheets from the printer. Cookie, so careless, even slovenly about her appearance and her room, was fussy and eagle-eyed when it came to printed matter, taking pride in perfectly aligned columns and snappy headlines. He'd even noticed some improvement in her spelling. "Satisfactory for mademoiselle?"

"Very satisfactory. I'll show Mom," she said, which both she and Lars understood was an excuse to speak to Emma, to see how she was, to talk about Polly. She was, Lars thought, as he heard her noisy on the stair, a sweet child and sensitive.

He closed out the page with Cookie's calendar and ejected her disk. He thought he might check his E-mail or start on the graduate student evaluation forms that sat in his briefcase. Then he considered reading some journal articles, before deciding that he'd join Emma and Cookie downstairs. Hot chocolate was the idea. Daddy Lars would preside, would perform miracles with cocoa powder and whipped cream—had they any cream? If not, a quick run to the Dairy Mart, then out with the special thin porcelain chocolate cups. Emma would complain they needed a wash, but he would not be deterred by such a trifle. They'd put the milk on the stove to heat, Cookie would whisk in the cocoa powder, he'd whip the cream, Emma might be pressed into shaving some chocolate for the top. Lars had them in his mind's eye, sitting around the kitchen table with mustaches of whipped cream, when the phone rang again. He knew immediately that it was for him. The caller ID display read *unknown*, and Lars switched on the tiny tape recorder half hidden under his papers and lifted the receiver.

"Lars?"

"What do you want?"

The caller spoke quickly, as if his words were under intense psychic pressure. "You know I can do damage, don't you? I'm like you, Lars, capable of killing. So you see, nothing's safe, no one, unless you confess. Can't you understand how fucking important it is for both of us that you confess now?" His voice had risen to a shout and tension leaped from the wire to tingle the bones of Lars's ear and slide down his spine.

"You killed our cat," said Lars. The idea had come into his mind when he'd combined the blood on her fur with the spotless street and sidewalk, but it had seemed fantastic. "You killed Polly."

"What's a cat?" The voice cried. "You killed Iris."

"If you really were there that night, you know that's not true. You know it's not."

"You didn't love Iris," the voice said, suddenly calmer and more confident. "Admit that."

"I didn't love Iris," said Lars.

"She died because you didn't love her." There was some truth in that, Lars thought. Had he not given her a ride, had he never kissed her, even had he been the sort of man to throw up everything he loved for romance, for sex, instead of being a civilized human being with pleasure in its place and duty, too—yes, everything might have been different. But this was no time for ethical inquiry; to think along such philosophical lines was to play into the caller's hands. And that reminded him of something . . .

"I think she died because you didn't love her, because you were jealous, because you were afraid she was going away." And then, because he was both angry and frightened, Lars added, "Sven."

The response was immediate and furious. "You will fucking regret saying that, Lars. You fucking will. You've had your last chance. Do you realize that? There's no way you can protect them now. No way at all."

"Who?" asked Lars, his heart jumping in spite of himself.

"Oh, Lars," the voice was calm again, even amused; the caller seemed sometimes literally to be of two minds. "Why, those you do love. That's fair, isn't it? You killed Iris, whom I loved. Now it's turnabout."

Lars interrupted, tried to keep him on the line, but the voice was already wishing him "a pleasant evening," and the line went dead.

Lars was breathing through his mouth, as if he had been running, as if he couldn't get enough oxygen. What had he said? "If you really were there that night . . ." Paatelainen would have questions about that. But what about Sven? Surely after this tape, she'd know Sven was real. And then the question would be, *Who is Sven?* Lars hummed, "Who is Sylvia, who is she, that all our swains commend her?" under his breath, but it was no use. He couldn't escape into Renaissance poetry. Not this time. The only way to protect Emma and Cookie was to confess everything. And then, Harpy, Medusa, Sphinx that she was, Paatelainen would want proof. And he'd have to say it was in the diary. The diary that burned. But she'd have to believe him, anyway. She'd have to.

How many different ways of being brave are there? Lars wondered as he punched in Paatelainen's number. Had he been a complete coward in keeping silent, in protecting Emma and Cookie? Was he really braver now, exposing himself in an effort to keep them safe? And would it have mattered, Lars asked himself, if he'd acted differently from the start? He now knew the answer to that last question was yes, things might have been different if the police had had a more precise time, if they'd had the diary, if they'd been convinced that Sven existed.

A cheerful, slightly singsong recording announced, "Detective Paatelainen is not available. Please leave your message at the beep . . ."

Lars swore. He should have gotten one of those movie detectives who are always available, who work round-the-clock and eat Chinese takeout and ruin their health with doughnuts and coffee if they're cops and with whiskey and beer if they're private eyes. What did Paatelainen do in her off-hours? Weed her garden, work needlepoint, spoil grandchildren? The voice mail signal beeped, and Lars heard a quaver in his voice when he said, "Jason Larson calling. I must speak with you. I have a tape. He's threatening my family and he's killed our cat. This is serious." Lars hung up and dialed again to leave a somewhat more detailed message for Harrelson, who was doubtless engaged in some gloom enhancing activity. Taxidermy, perhaps, or serious drinking.

But Lars had the tape, proof of a sort. Worse for him, better for Cookie and Emma, because the police would see that this was serious. They would. He'd be serious, too, and right now seriousness required hot chocolate, a united home front, a brave face, and an end to anxiety. Though it was an effort, Lars pushed himself away from his desk, straightened his shoulders, and breezed downstairs.

After much wizardry with whisks and beaters, with piles of shaved chocolate and pots of hot milk, the Larsons sat down around the kitchen table with cups of hot chocolate. While Cookie buried hers under an Everest of whipped cream, Lars sipped the hot, sweet liquid and thought about how he would tell Emma, what he would say, how the words would feel. How should he start? Should he confess a flirtation, or should he attempt the truth, which was more subtle, more painful, much harder to define. *I just loved her writing; she was not all that attractive to me, but her writing entered my imagination.* Emma might find that hard to understand, even though anxiety entered her imagination, unwanted, as Iris had entered his.

Yet it was innocent, he'd say. *Oh Emma, it was innocent mostly: I've gotten too old.* Maybe she would be half sorry about that and deny the premise. Or maybe she would be angry and say, *Don't expect any sympathy about that.* Lars looked across the table at his wife's lovely, even features, her serene expression. What had Iris written about her friend, the barfing mermaid? That she'd been sketched by an artist of genius. So had Emma, though tonight her face was pale and she looked a little tired, her clear skin dulled, and when she glanced at Cookie, Lars saw the anxiety look out.

Cookie ran her finger along her cup to catch the overflow of whipped cream and grinned at Lars. "This is the world's best hot chocolate," she said and slipped a dollop to Jake, though it wasn't particularly good for him. A taste of cream had always been Polly's treat.

The thing is, Lars would have to say, *I saw Iris that night. Yes, I know, I should have admitted it, but I was worried about how it would look.* He felt the sweat on his forehead as he tried to imagine telling Emma about the argument, those raised voices in the park. And yet, had things turned out differently, how amusing it might have seemed, how contrite he could have been. *She slapped me down, Emma,* he'd have said. *I realized then: no fool like an old fool.* There were clichés ready-made for just these situations.

Of course, if things had turned out differently, there would have been no need to confess at all. Iris Weed, a young writer of genuine talent, would have packed her bags and left for the city, probable success, and possible fame, leaving him with bittersweet memories that would shortly have transformed themselves into the amusing recollections Jason Larson did so well. He would have been restless and unsettled for a time, prone to the glooms and to semiserious reflections, a psychic penance that would have softened Emma's heart, producing consideration and forgiveness, another phase of the Larson erotic cycle. Gradually, life would have resumed its steady, normal current, and sweet nights like this, which seemed at the moment poignantly precious and precarious, would be taken for granted.

Cookie got whipped cream on the end of her nose and began to giggle. "Denise has a tattoo," she announced and let Lars and Emma react with appropriate horror before adding, "Just a paste-on. I wanted her to put it on the end of her nose. A big fly or a butterfly." Cookie crossed her eyes to focus on the end of her own pert nose.

"And what would you like?" asked Lars.

"Don't even ask," cautioned Emma.

Cookie tipped her head and considered. "A cat with a soccer ball," she said. "I saw a real cute one."

"No room on your nose for that!"

She giggled again and licked cream off her fingers. Her cholesterol count would be off the scale, but Lars told himself she was a well-adjusted child, a happy child again. Nothing must disturb that. Iris and his own folly had been dangers, how serious he had barely realized at the time, but that was all over and done with and it was important not to let Polly's loss awaken old fears. Very important. He had to be careful with the police and with Emma; he'd have to be on the alert, always. And Cookie and Emma, too. But how to warn them without alarming them?

"Time for you to get to bed," Emma said.

"Oh, Mom. One more cup. Just one more."

"You'll have a bellyache," said Emma.

Cookie tipped up her cup, ostentatiously licked up the last drops of cream and chocolate, then got up and kissed her mom and dad. "Night."

They heard her feet on the stair. Lars was casting about for a starting point: *Something I should tell you? I don't think it was a car that killed Polly? I've had another phone call?* when Emma stood up and collected the cups. She took them to the sink, half full of their various pots and implements, and began running the water. Lars came over to help, thinking that the routine of washing and drying dishes, the click of the cups and spoons in the sink, the monotonous swipe of the towel might bring inspiration.

"That's all right," said Emma so quickly Lars knew she did not want to talk. "Go finish your papers."

"Graduate student evaluations. I hate doing those."

"The more reason to get them done quickly."

Lars put his arm around her. "I'm so sorry about Polly."

"It seems odd without her. We'd had her for years."

"Just a year younger than Cookie."

"Cookie will want a kitten."

"Cookie shall have," Lars said cheerfully. "We'll get her a kitten. There will be kittens in the spring. We have room in the house for a kitten." He leaned over and nibbled at her ear.

"Go do your papers now," said Emma.

Lars went upstairs to his study, telling himself that she would be fine, that Cookie would be fine; they'd get a kitten in the spring, a new black kitten that would mark the end of anxiety, because surely by then everything would be settled. And he would tell Emma, he would. She just wasn't quite ready; he could sense that. She'd finish the dishes, maybe putter with some other housework—he knew her habits and the physical restlessness that betrayed her unease. Then she'd come upstairs and he would tell her, simply, outright, so she'd be careful and alert, not a necessity but an extra precaution, because now the police would realize the seriousness of the matter and take appropriate measures.

He opened his briefcase, resolved to do the brave and sensible thing. After he had typed up half a dozen assessments and printed them out on department stationery, Lars switched off his computer and turned out the light. It was later than he'd thought, past ten. Cookie and Jake were already asleep, her tousled head and the dog's shaggy mass just visible in the night-light. Emma, too, might be abed, though to hope that was cowardly. He switched off the hall light and eased open their bedroom door. Lars felt his way in the darkness, until his knee touched the chair to the left of the door, a reliable landmark. He took off his sweater and was unbuttoning his shirt, when his eyes, adjusting, detected motion. The pale rectangles of the pillows were empty and there was a dark shape at the side of the bed. Emma was not asleep. She was sitting hunched in her nightgown, her long hair loose, rocking silently back and forth. Some essential support dropped from beneath Lars's heart, creating an emptiness that took him right back to the smell of the hospital, to Emma's stunned, terrified face, to their son's small, flaccid, devastated body.

"Emma?"

No answer.

"Emma, what's wrong?"

"Something's wrong," she whispered, like an echo.

He sat down and put his arm around her and laid his head against her shoulder. Her neck felt hot, feverish, and she could not stop rocking back and forth. "Tell me," she said, "tell me what's wrong."

And Lars, who wanted, who intended to tell her, said, "You're just upset. When I saw Polly lying there, it brought back memories for me, too. But you mustn't let yourself become anxious. You know you have to fight that, Emma."

"There's something wrong," she persisted, turning slightly, so that he picked up his head and met her eyes, very black in the little dim light that filtered through the conifers and the pleated shades to reach their bed. "You know there is."

"We have to be careful, Emma. We mustn't jump to conclusions. We have to think of Cookie, of not upsetting Cookie."

"I don't want her to see me like this," Emma said, gripping his arm. "I don't want to be like this." She began rocking again, back and forth as if demented, and somehow that simple gesture was more frightening to Lars than if she had been weeping or shrieking with fury.

"You'll be all right," he said. "Take deep breaths. In, out, in, out. Just think of breathing. Not rocking, just breathing. Today was a shock, on top of all those months of strain, but you'll be fine. I know you will." He put his chin on the top of her head and held her close to him. "You know I love you, Emma. You know that, don't you? Tell me that you know I love you for keeps."

"For keeps," Emma said in a weak, strained voice, as if the words were stones that had to be lifted from deep within her chest.

"Did you take your medicine?" Lars asked after several minutes. She shook her head.

"I think you should."

"I haven't needed it for so long." Emma's voice was remote.

"And that's good. And you won't need it for long. But tonight . . ."

"It makes me groggy," she complained but without any real resistance. "I'll hardly be good for anything tomorrow."

"You can call in sick if need be." Lars got her Xanax and watched her take the tablet. She lay down in bed, and Lars pulled the covers over her. He was changing into his pajamas when she said, "Someone killed Polly deliberately, didn't they?"

"I—I don't really know. We couldn't tell. Why do you say that?"

"Because it could have been Cookie," she said. "It could have been Cookie."

Lars went back into his study and dialed Paatelainen's number. "For God's sake, call me," he said. "I'll tell you everything."

17.

W ell," said Kay Paatelainen, "well" as in the interrogative mode, demanding an answer, ideas, some cogent analysis. She was sitting behind a desk cluttered with case folders and interrogation transcripts and pictures of her grandchildren, her grandnieces, and Timo Paatelainen with their two portly Labrador retrievers. The department-issue digital clock behind her registered 7:56 A.M., the lower depths of the day.

In response, Roy Harrelson lifted his shoulders, then slouched farther down in his chair. She'd called him in as soon as she'd heard the voice mail messages from the professor, and they'd both thought, This is it. But, as usual with the Weed case, an initially promising situation soon morphed into confusion. "I'll tell you everything" had certainly sounded definite, and, indeed, they'd learned a bit more. But though they'd hashed everything over and slept on it and were set to go all through the evidence again with the chief in another hour, Roy still did not know what to conclude about the case except, "Larson hasn't told us everything."

Kay nodded briskly. "He hasn't told us everything. Instead, he's spun us a fine fairy tale about a diary. Did you believe him about the diary?"

Roy shrugged again. He was not at his best first thing in the morning, whereas his partner, who had fifteen years on him, was all bright and fresh. Evenings, their positions were reversed, and Roy Harrelson sometimes thought that their successful professional relationship rested on that fact and on their unspoken agreement that he would defer to her opinions in the morning and she to his in the evening. Afternoons were the tricky time, when they were apt to argue and disagree. "I contacted the fire department," Roy said, struggling to haul his mind into gear. "They were called to a residential fire at the Larsons' late last spring."

Kay made a face and nodded. That was corroboration of a sort, though she remained skeptical. The professor, if a patently foolish man, was intelligent. She had no doubt he was capable of inventing a diary and a perpetrator—and of fabricating E-mails and perhaps even the admittedly alarming phone messages, too. But why should he indulge in such antics now when the case had gone cold, when an assumption of police failure had been in the air—and in the press—for at least a year?

And what about "Sven"? What was *his* motive? Just to make trouble for Larson? Most likely, because if the caller, the E-mailer, had really killed Iris Weed, he'd hardly want to refocus attention on the case. By the same token, if Larson was the killer, why would he bring the messages to police attention? But perhaps he really was worried about his family, perhaps everything was simpler than it looked. Kay Paatelainen tapped her pen on her desk and told herself she could not let disagreeable, inconclusive interviews with the professor prejudice her mind.

"The captain who'd gone to the Larsons' was out on call all yesterday," Roy said.

"Probably for that truck fire on the interstate."

"He's supposed to get back to me today."

"Try him now," suggested Kay. "Of course, Larson could have used that fact, too," she added as Roy dialed the fire department. "If I only felt that Larson was being completely candid about even one thing, just one . . ."

Roy held up his hand. Kay watched his heavy, impassive features as he listened. She'd worked with him long enough to read his face. What she saw now was interest, interest sufficient to pull him out of the morning doldrums.

"Really? And the fire was definitely centered on the porch? So what did you think? I see. If you could put something in writing for us . . ." When Roy's always brisk pleasantries were concluded, he hung up and said, "There was a fire on their back porch, centered on the kid's dollhouse. Remember the dollhouse? Big, beautiful thing, terrific craftsmanship with lovely joinery, a quality item."

Kay looked up at the ceiling the way she did when she was trying to remember something. "I seem to recall that the little girl—Cookie, is that her name?"

"Elizabeth, I think, but Larson never calls her anything but Cookie."

"She was playing with the house the whole time we were there, wasn't she?"

"So?" It was a shame it had been burned. Really a shame, Roy thought.

"I don't know. I just remember that very clearly. She must have loved the house."

Roy opened his cigarettes and put one in his mouth without lighting it, because Kay hated the smell. "The fire lieutenant thinks she set it on fire. Playing with candles, maybe."

"Possible," said Kay. "Isn't it?"

"The call came in at four fifty-seven A.M."

"You'd need a candle if you were up at that hour," Kay said drily, but her face had turned serious. "The time bothers me."

"The whole thing bothers me. We ripped the house apart that day, didn't we?"

Kay nodded. "But we didn't touch the dollhouse."

"The dollhouse where Larson claims he hid the diary. If there was a diary."

"Let's suppose there was," Kay said. "Just suppose."

"All right. There was a diary. Don't ask me why he'd have hidden in it the kid's dollhouse. I don't know."

"We don't need to know that," said Kay, who felt that overly subtle psychological explanations were as apt to be distracting as enlightening.

"No. What we do need to determine is would she have known about the diary? Could she have seen it?"

Kay picked up the interview transcript and searched through the copy. "Here we go. He says, '*There was a loose piece of trim around the base that I hadn't had time to fix. I stuck the diary underneath the lower floor . . .*' Kids can't resist fiddling with anything loose or broken."

"So she might have known, probably would have known—and read it?" Roy asked. "Suppose she'd read it. And hadn't liked what was in it."

They sat for a moment, thinking this over and wondering what might have been in Iris Weed's last diary. "We'll have to ask her," Kay said finally. "She's the only one who can corroborate his story."

"But just for the fact of the diary. As to the content, who knows? Plus, she's not a reliable source, because open to parental influence."

"Her father may resist the idea of our questioning her." Kay nodded her head vigorously. "He could pull out all the stops. You know," she added, "the one thing that suggests he's innocent is that his lawyer has been almost out of the picture. But if the daughter's involved . . ." She sighed, "I will say for Professor Larson that he's protective of his family."

"Somewhat after the fact." Roy was less inclined to cut the professor any slack. At the same time, he felt the crank caller was significant. "Larson seems in a real panic about this."

Kay shrugged. "He's convinced himself it's Iris's mysterious old boyfriend."

"Sven. The guy no one knows. We checked out everyone Iris knew. No one had ever heard of Sven, not even the name."

"Except for Larson."

"Except for Larson, and how reliable has he been?"

"Even the unreliable tell the truth occasionally—that's my worry."

Roy gave a skeptical grunt.

"The caller, whoever he was, did react to the name. Strongly."

"I'd agree with that. But what's it prove?"

"Maybe that Larson was telling the truth. Some of it, anyway. Maybe 'Sven' was the boyfriend's nickname, a pet name."

"It doesn't sound much like a pet name," Roy said. "It sounds Scandinavian."

"Scandinavians must have pet names, too."

Roy lifted his hands in resignation, then opened his notebook. "We check again, yes? We go back and ask everyone once more about Sven?"

"I think so." Kay put Larson's tape into her recorder and they listened to the conversation again. "Another question," she said when the message ended. "When did Larson get this supposed diary?"

"Close to the time of her death," Roy said immediately. "Otherwise, she comes looking for it."

"He might have denied having it."

"He might," Roy agreed. "He probably would have."

"But if he'd acquired it much earlier, she'd have started another one, wouldn't she? She wrote compulsively. That's the one thing we do know for sure."

"Unless her killer took it."

"Another possibility," Kay admitted.

Roy took the cigarette out of his mouth and tapped it on his knee. He'd have a quick smoke before they went up to the chief's office. He thought better on nicotine. "We call the prof in again and squeeze him. On his own admissions, we can charge him as an accessory after the fact."

"I like that," Kay said, thinking that Larson, despite a certain charm, was evasive, smart mouthed, and demanding. All too much the professor for her taste. "I like that very much, but the chief may not. We grilled Larson spring, summer, and fall and got nowhere. The chief's going to want us to have some pretty strong evidence if we're to have another go."

"All right, all right, let the chief decide," said Roy, because he knew the politics of the situation as well as Kay did. The college administrators had screamed for action on the case but gotten huffy when the focus turned to one of their distinguished faculty. Mrs. Weed kept up a drumbeat in the press but was cozy with Larson: The whole thing was delicate. "We present what we've got with emphasis on the latest interviews with Larson, the tapes he's made, the threatening E-mails."

"And do we raise the matter of interviewing Cookie Larson?"

Roy nodded. "The chief will also want to know what we're doing about the threats."

"We're still trying to locate the source of the E-mails, we've applied for a wiretap, we're trying to find someone called 'Sven' who knew Iris."

"Plus we've got all the local patrol cars on alert. They go by the Larson house every couple hours."

"We'd better take their reports with us, too," Kay said, adding them to the already bulging folder. "I think we're ready to see the chief."

Roy hesitated. Kay felt that they were close to a break, but he had a bad feeling about the case. He had a nagging sense that they'd overlooked something without being able to imagine what that something was. "There will be maybe a question if we're doing enough regarding protection."

"Where's the personnel to come from?" Kay asked rhetorically. After more than year, the Weed case had been quietly downgraded. There had been seven other murders since January—one, a child. The police had plenty to do besides checking up on crank calls and E-mails, no matter how unsettling. "Besides, we agree that Larson is still lying. If he was really as worried as he wants us to think, he wouldn't hold anything back, would he?"

"Who the hell knows what that man might do?" Roy asked. Or any man. Or woman. Until he had a cigarette, Roy didn't feel he could give guarantees for anyone, himself included.

Cookie liked working on her computer at night. She liked to see the blue-tinged screen swimming in front of her in the dimness of her room with her angelfish light reflected in one corner. She wrote to Denise about how the screen looked and about the fish lamp, because it was the sort of silly thing she could write to Denise and to no one else. Denise was the repository of Cookie's small secrets.

And her big secrets? Big secrets belonged to Jake—and sometimes to Mom and Dad. She'd told them about maybe becoming a keeper, which Coach had said was to be kept quiet for the moment. Cookie knew why. Brenda and Jocelyn were the present keepers and purely awful, but between them they represented a high level of "parent involvement," which wouldn't end until spring when they moved up to the fourteens. So that was a big secret entrusted to Mom and Dad. Cookie repeated this to herself in an effort to feel better about another secret, which was Jake's alone.

Nite, nite, she wrote to Denise and pushed Send. That left only Mr. Jack's letter in the New Mail, and Cookie had an impulse to hit Delete and not read it and never read another one from him ever. At the same time, she knew perfectly well that she would push Read instead. Maybe that was what bothered her about Mr. Jack—not anything he said or did but the bare fact that she sensed she was doing something unwise and yet felt impelled to do it.

Mr. Jack had been writing regularly, almost daily, to ask about the game, which she'd kept after all. Instead of throwing the box away, she had resisted playing the game, which was silly—she might as well have discarded it. Cookie had put off his questions with tales of too much schoolwork and then, with the truth, that Polly had been killed on the street and she didn't feel like playing anything.

He'd been very sorry about Polly. He'd asked what sort of cat and what color and taken a keen interest in the burial arrangements. And then tonight, another message, though Cookie felt that there was really nothing more left to say. She clicked the button and read:

> *Forgot to mention that I have a friend with kittens at the mo-*
> *ment. Four: three gray striped and one female that is mostly black.*
> *She has a little white on her tummy. Would that be acceptable?*
> *You could get her as a surprise for your mom, since you let Polly*
> *out. I think she'd like this little kitten a lot and, otherwise, Cookie,*
> *I'm afraid they'll have to go to the animal shelter because my friend*
> *is moving at the end of the fall semester. Let me know soonest!!!*
> *Your friend Jack*

Cookie thought about this for a few minutes, but there was never any doubt what she'd write back.

> *Dear Mr. Jack,*
> *I'd like a kitten very much. Where does your friend live? Could*
> *I get there on my bike?*
> *Cookie*

She must have been on his buddy list, because the message came right back. His friend lived on the other side of town. But he, Jack, could pick her up. *What about after school on Friday? It will be a real surprise for your mother that way.*

Lars's red pen moved swiftly down the quiz, jabbing here and there, heronlike, to spear jumbled syntax, spelling errors, dangling modifiers, lapses in logic. It was a very poor paper, product of what had been a very poor class, a boring class, a class when Professor Larson's mind had been fixed not on Keats's lush imagery and poignant existence but on the stupidity and willful torpor of the police. A squad car every few hours! The best they could do with current manpower levels, etc., etc., as if it was his responsibility as the aggrieved and frightened citizen to raise a petition for more police funding. He marked the quiz even lower than he normally would have and reached for the next one in the pile.

The phone rang. His first thought was Sven, and his next the police, so that he was surprised, even a little puzzled, by the throaty voice on the other end.

"Lars?"

"Jason Larson speaking."

"Lars! Isobel. Don't you know my voice yet? Has your check come through?"

"No," Lars lied. A very handsome check for their royalties and foreign rights had come through a week earlier, an event completely overshadowed by other matters.

"Better call Suzie, call Viv—small fortune, Lars. And soon as you get it and it clears, cut me a check."

A silence from Lars, who disliked writing large checks for any purpose, particularly his own destruction.

"For the escrow account. The reward money should be placed in escrow. I'll have my lawyer contact you, all right?"

"Yes, yes, great," said Lars.

"I'm going to organize a press conference. I think you should be here, Lars."

That was impossible. To leave home, to leave Emma and Cookie for even a day—impossible. "Would it not be better here, Isobel? I mean, someone with information is more apt to be in this area." Lars saw himself exposed to an army of snoops and troublemakers. Still, if there was a reward, it would affect Sven, too, wouldn't it? So was this perhaps a good thing? Should he send a check soonest and maybe scare Sven off? Or was he only going to buy trouble for himself?

Isobel ran though the pros and cons of the college as venue with her usual enthusiasm, then said she'd speak to the chancellor; the appalling woman was on good terms with both him and the provost. Yes, it was an excellent idea, she decided. Iris had been part of the college family; the whole university was involved. She hadn't seen that, being focused on her own problems, her own sorrows. The little catch in her throat both irritated and moved Lars: He knew how she felt, he did. And he'd feel for her, too, if only she'd go away and leave him alone, accepting his many hours of work on the book as full and complete payment for what had been a trifling folly. "Lars, you don't know how much I've come to rely on you," she said, and Lars interrupted that he had a class and he'd call her back as soon as his royalty check arrived.

When he hung up the phone, Lars found he couldn't return to the unintelligible, handwritten scrawls before him, the day's ration of a life sentence of papers. He got up from his desk, put on his jacket, and sashayed down the hall to Pauline's office to propose coffee at Joe's Joe. "I've got to get out of here," he told her. "Paperitis is setting in."

Her desk, like his, was a jumble of books, essays, and class notes. "I shouldn't," she said, but something in her eyes told him she wanted to just the same.

"You should," he said. "You most certainly should, for your professional development. Bring that article and we'll develop a plan of attack."

Her face brightened; she had a certain appeal despite her gauche and timid manner. And once, yes, once, Lars would have exerted himself. Now, of course, he was so sunk in despair and nerves that amorous delights were almost out of the question. Almost. Just the same, there was no reason not to give Pauline a hand; he'd sort out her article and provide them both with a welcome distraction from the school routine. She's a nice enough person, he decided, as they sat in the clear November sun, and her article isn't bad, not bad at all, and once he finished with it—he smiled at her across the table. He couldn't help it, just a conditioned reflex, and saw her cheeks flush. The old Larson charm hadn't entirely faded. But he was on his good behavior. He didn't take her hand; he didn't amuse her with department gossip. Instead, he uncapped his pen and made some notes on the article, showing her where to cut and whom to cite more prominently. They debated several potential journals for the revised version, and Lars underlined some ideas that he said could be developed and submitted as separate articles. "Only way, you know, to run up your publications. You've got to milk every idea for all its worth. Waste of trees basically, but it's you or them. The survival of the fittest."

Her laugh was soft and high-pitched, the other end of the scale from Isobel Weed's throaty chuckle. To blossom, Pauline just needed attention, admiration, as we all do, Lars thought. "You really think there's enough material?" she asked.

"With scholarly apparatus? Of course. You've got oceans." Just then, he spotted Gus Aryant standing at the take-out window. When Gus ambled over with a latte to join them, Lars said, "I've been telling Pauline that a little idea can go a long way in the journals."

"Too damn far. I haven't read a decent article in I don't know how long."

"Since the flood," teased Lars, who didn't take Aryant's stratospheric standards too seriously.

"Still, publish we must," said Pauline, emboldened by Lars's interest and anxious to join the conversation.

Gus cast a cold and gloomy eye on her. His head was overscaled for even his large and heavy torso, and he had bold, rather battered, features; strictly old Roman, Lars always thought, decadent emperor or intelligent gladiator—probably the latter, for Gus was an academic combatant of the first rank. "So long as you know it's rubbish," he said, "as I'm sure it will be."

This was rough even by Aryant's standards. Lars was taken aback, and Pauline's eager smiled vanished. "Ellen Glasgow is a perfectly valid subject," she said, reaching nervously for her coffee cup.

"Take no notice of Gus," said Lars with a warning glance. "He hates everybody's work. He hasn't liked anything since Ruskin."

Pauline ducked her head but persisted. "Glasgow's been seriously neglected," she began.

Gus drew his lower lip up and the corners of his mouth down like a dissatisfied walrus. He did not wait to hear her defense of Ellen Glasgow. "I'm a great believer in neglect," he said and swung his heavy head toward Lars. Such gnats as Pauline and Glasgow, and whatever one might write about the other, were clearly beneath his notice.

"Don't be a bear," said Lars, on the verge of anger. He could see that Pauline was painfully thin-skinned, and after he'd spent a half hour trying to bolster her confidence, he wasn't about to let Gus undo his work. Especially not when he knew that Gus would never have been so ham-handed a couple of years ago. Never. His own professional standing had definitely slipped. "Every department needs one," he said to Pauline, "an *ursus horribilis*—is my Latin right, Gus?"

"Such as you know of it. No one knows Latin anymore."

"For an Americanist," Pauline said with a little show of spirit, "Spanish is going to be the essential language."

"Thank God I'm near retirement," said Gus, declining to look at her and turning ostentatiously toward Lars. "I've got to speak with you about next fall's schedule. We need a united front with the college."

Pauline stood up abruptly. "I didn't realize the time. I'd better run." As she pushed back her chair, her purse swung against the table, spilling her manuscript, jiggling the cups. Lars grabbed at the loose pages, getting coffee on several of them, while Gus, that connoisseur of discomfiture, watched impassively. "Sorry, stupid of me," Pauline said. "Thank you so much, Lars. And for going over the manuscript."

"It will be fine. Really. I'll read the final draft if you want."

"Oh, that's kind." She smiled again, hope returned, an awkward, lonely, determined person, and thinking the hell with Gus and department politics, Lars started to leave with her. "No, no, finish your coffee," she said. "My class is on the other side of campus. Literally. I'll have to run to make it."

She looked so flustered that Lars sat back down. He watched her hurry back toward campus; her long, thin legs and flying hair making her look like one of the students. Could he possibly suggest a haircut to her? She needed some more stylistic ballast, a little sophistication . . .

"You're not doing her any favor, you know," Gus said.

"What do you mean? You were pretty rude to her, by the way, even by your usual low standards of courtesy."

"She's not going to make it, articles or no articles, so why waste your time? She'll be here for three years and then out. You know that. She'll never get tenure."

"I think that's too harsh," said Lars. "Her article is fine. And she seems very conscientious."

"Listen to you," said Gus. "Conscientious is the kiss of death. Forget tenure without a trendsetting book or a really exotic ethnicity, preferably both. You know that. Besides, it's cheaper to hire a new person every three years, anyway."

"You're right about that."

"The old order passeth, Lars." Gus's tone was glum, his habitual arrogance shaded with depression.

"And the new one passeth understanding."

"Oh, you're wrong there; everything's downhill from this point. Entropy, Lars, entropy. Especially at the graduate level. I've got only two people signed up for my spring seminar; it's not going to fly. And my last decent doctoral candidate left the program to work at a computer store. Can you believe that?"

"Really?" Lars was not particularly interested in Gus's troubles, most of which were his own doing: witness his treatment of the sweet, harmless Pauline! Still, it was interesting that his seminar enrollments were off so much, and his admission of the fact was more interesting yet, an indication that even the formidable Augustus Aryant wasn't to going to be a Young Turk forever. Strictly to keep the conversation going, Lars asked, "Who was that?"

"John Mortlake. Know him? He had a quite interesting notion about the Norse sagas and the mythic revivals of the nineteenth century. Balked at the work, though. No German and slight French. I had to insist on German . . ."

"The sagas?" Lars asked, his senses suddenly on the alert. He perceived the bright, cool day, the student voices rising above the traffic, and the sweet bracing smell of coffee hanging over the sticky tables. "Viking legends and the Ring of the Nibelung?"

"He needed a clearer focus, of course," Gus continued, as indifferent to Lars's concern as to his previous disinterest, "but the proposal was going very nicely when he disappeared. Not a word, of course. He was a tad embarrassed when I saw him, as well he should have been."

"When was this, Gus? Just lately?" Lars realized that his shirt was damp, that the November breeze was chilly.

"Last week. He's working at that big computer store in the mall. For all they pay, he might as well have stayed a graduate student," Gus said, but Lars was already out of his chair. His only thought was to get to his office where he scrabbled through the Yellow Pages for computer dealers: Computer Depot, Computer Discount, Computer Shed, computer, computer, checking the addresses, yes, yes, there was the one in the mall. He dialed, heard the preternaturally cheerful voice of the phone system, reached a human voice, which was not nearly as cheerful or as mellifluous, and asked for John Mortlake.

"You mean Jack?"

"Yes, Jack, of course. Is he in this afternoon?"

She would see, but he'd have to be put on hold. A synthesizer began an uptempo medley guaranteed to prolong any wait, and Lars began straightening the piles of corrected papers on his desk and flipping through the ones yet to be done—ten, eleven, twelve— another hour's work.

"Computer Connection, Jack speaking. Can I help you?"

It was the nightmare voice, the dream echo of the E-mail messages. Lars caught his breath, fighting down the temptation to say, "It's over; I've caught you; I know who you are and I'd like to break your neck."

"Hello? Have we been disconnected?" A note of irritation.

So how do *you* like crank calls, Lars thought as he hung up. He dialed the police immediately, but he was leaving for home before he connected with Paatelainen, who was more interested than she let on. She warned Lars to stay away from the computer store under all circumstances and promised to talk to Mr. Mortlake "as soon as possible."

"Today," Lars demanded, "today. This man's been harassing me all fall and threatening Cookie and Emma. This is not some harmless computer hacker, some prankster."

"So far, we have only your word that this is your caller," said Paatelainen, who became suspicious every time Lars pushed too hard.

"He was Gus Aryant's doctoral student. He was researching the sagas—Vikings, the Ring cycle, axmen in the mist just like Sven, Iris's Sven. She didn't make that up. And she was a bit afraid of him. That comes through in the diaries. You said yourself, 'The most frequent killer of young women is a lover or would-be lover.' This is it, this is him."

And it might be. It really might be, Kay Paatelainen thought, but she wasn't going to tell Larson that. "So you say," she reminded him, "based on a diary that no one else has seen."

Lars was insistent, demanded action, provided more details; he really was frantic. He demanded that the police go right to the mall and arrest Mortlake. Hell, he could do that himself straight from school! At the same time, he wanted to go home, to be home early, to be home already, for he couldn't be late for Cookie, not now, not today. He should call Emma, too, for how could he have forgotten, they'd shopped at the store, gotten Cookie's computer set up there, and something else—

Paatelainen, who'd just started on a new and terrible case, a child raped and mutilated, interrupted to say that they'd take care of everything, that she had other pressing matters, that they'd get back to him as soon as possible. Furious, Lars hung up on her, grabbed his briefcase, and hustled down the stairs, anger erasing the thought, fugitive, unsettling, that had been linked to the computer store, to Cookie's computer.

Lars looked at his watch every two minutes all the way home, though he had plenty of time, though the middle school got out later than the elementary, though he had, as compared to the previous semesters, an hour-and-a-half margin. They'd go to the park, take Jake for a really long walk, have a talk, the precise content of which Lars found indefinable. But she'd get home, they'd walk, maybe talk about the dollhouse and the diary, for she might be the only other person who'd seen it. Lars would explain mistakes, their prevalence, the importance of correcting, leading to his chance now to correct a big mistake and possibly her chance to correct a small one. Would that do? He didn't know. Perhaps he should pick her up at school, or did that suggest too much seriousness, too much of a break in the routine? Besides, Cookie enjoyed the bus, the chance to see friends after a day without recess, and Lars did not much like serious talks when he was driving in traffic. So home as if an ordinary day instead of the day that had given a name to anonymous calls and bizarre E-mails. No wonder "Jack" had been surprised to see Gus Aryant! But if John or Jack or Sven had really wanted to remain anonymous, why had he returned where someone was sure to recognize him sooner or later? E-mails could have been sent from anywhere; no, no, he would have come back only if he had something more in mind. When Lars got home, he called the police again and pointed this out at length.

It was quarter past three by the time he got off the phone, no happier than he'd been before. The school bus usually stopped on the corner by three-thirty, never later than twenty to four, which meant that Lars just had time to check his E-mail and put away his school things. He tied Jake out on his line in the backyard, an indignity the little dog felt keenly, then went upstairs to his computer. While he was waiting for the machine to boot up, he noticed Cookie's disk and thought how much she'd learned in a short time. She was bright, perhaps exceptionally so, and it was just too bad that things academic held so little charm for her at the moment. Lars was afraid that she might neglect school until she got seriously behind. To reassure himself, he picked up the disk, and as he turned it over, he again felt the stirrings of the idea that had arisen while he argued with that terminal idiot Paatelainen. What was it? Computer, setting up the computer, setting up Cookie's computer . . .

His screen filled up with icons, prompting Lars typed to type in his code and browse his E-mail: a colleague looking for a citation, a student with a question about their assignment, another with a family crisis who needed an extension on a paper, the usual. Lars read the *Daily Chronicle* bulletin and checked out some grant listings before noticing that it was three-thirty, bus time. He imagined the bus at the end of the street, the peculiar sound, between a squeal and a creak, of its downshift and brakes, the noisy thump of his daughter's feet on the metal stairs, her shouted farewells to her friends, the characteristic wheeze of the engine as the driver pulled from the curb with a fart of foul-smelling exhaust. Lars could see Cookie on the sidewalk, adjusting her book pack before taking off for home, hair flying, socks drooping, backpack bouncing. This reassuring picture was so clear to him that he pulled out a handful of papers and began working on the first of them, expecting any minute to be interrupted by the sound of the front door, followed by, "Dad! You home?"

The realization that Jake was silent and had been silent for some time caused Lars to looked up at the clock, three-forty. Traffic, he thought, or that pothole filling crew he'd passed on the way in, or just Cookie, in one of her moods, loitering, shifting her heavy book bag this way and that—didn't those middle school teachers ever consider the children's spines? Five minutes, ten minutes late—he was getting as bad as Emma, who worried at the slightest deviation, who had gone with Cookie to the computer store, who had mentioned . . . The thought arrived, full-blown, freezing Lars behind his computer, as he heard Emma say, "Mr. Jack. Mr. Jack had been so kind, had set up everything for her, had had all sorts of Web advice and promised to E-mail her a list of sites." Mr. Jack!

Lars picked up Cookie's disk, as if that was to be his excuse, and went right to her computer. While the slow old machine rumbled and clucked, he checked his watch, then ran downstairs to open the front door and scan the sidewalk: only the Innocentis' two-year-old banging on the pickets of their fence. Another few minutes and he would call the school to ask if Bus 12 was late, but first back to Cookie's machine. Lars connected to the server, typed in her password—listening always for the sound of the door, of her voice, of her feet running upstairs to guilty, suspicious Daddy Lars. He pulled up her old mail, found nothing, and went to Sent Mail. He recognized Denise's Yahoo address—her "cutedenise" moniker was an object of Cookie's envy—but who was this other correspondent? Lars selected the most recent reply to the unknown recipient, and the message flashed onto the screen.

Dear Mr. Jack,

Okay, you're right. It wouldn't be a surprise otherwise, but it has to be the black kitten. I'll meet you right on the corner at the front of the school. 3:10.

Mom will really be pleased.

Cookie.

"Oh, dear God!" Lars cried. "Oh, God, Cookie!" His hands were shaking so much he could hardly bring up the two previous messages, but it took him only a moment to see what had happened and to understand that Mr. Jack hadn't been kidding at all.

Lars sat in front of the screen, paralyzed with dread and memory and a terrifying guilt. Mr. Jack, Sven, his correspondent had Cookie in his car. For a moment Lars couldn't breathe, literally choked by images of hurt and disaster, then he ran to call the police. He cut through the usual bullshit by screaming that his daughter had been

picked up at school, that this person, John Mortlake was not au-
thorized, that he was the late Iris Weed's lover, that he'd been sending crank messages, that if he, Lars, found him first, he'd kill him.
No, he didn't know the kind of car. No, he didn't know where they
might go. A friend's house, a promised kitten, the need for extreme
speed blended almost incoherently. Lars gave the name and address
of the middle school and hung up. He stood for one awful moment
of indecision, then stumbled downstairs to grab his car keys and
lunge for the door, because a little park, dark and neglected and
dripping with rain, suddenly filled his mind: the night park where
he had dropped Iris, argued with Iris, abandoned Iris. The park, Lars
thought, it has to be the park. He had to get there, he alone, it had
to be him.

18.

Although Jack usually drove nonchalantly with one elbow on his open window, he pulled away from the Alison P. Homewood Middle School with both hands on the wheel and his eyes fixed on the street traffic. It had been so easy, that's what astonished him. He'd pulled up to the corner, tense with excitement and beset by a strong sense of unreality, and there she was, waving, her dark hair blowing around her face, her thin, childish legs running from oversized white sneakers to a short, pleated navy skirt. A few lines of E-mail, a little imagination and persistence, and the princess had been delivered into his hands. What Iris used to say when she was teasing him: "a Viking moment."

But really Iris didn't know anything about that. Jack felt vaguely sick, that's what he felt, and so nervous he could smell his own sweat, a telltale sourness issuing from beneath his cheap poly store-issue shirt, his sweater, and leather jacket. He was afraid Cookie might notice, because she seemed alert, even wary; of course, she'd have been taught never to accept rides, to be careful of strange men. Strange men bearing candy, that was the classic inducement, and Jack smiled at the thought: Modern life required something a little different.

"Is it a boy or a girl cat?" Cookie asked, as they rode down the wide, busy street, dodging buses and double-parked cars.

She was wearing just a fleece jacket and her face was flushed with the cold. Jack again had the sense that she was destined for beauty, that she *had been* destined, that is. His hands turned slick on the wheel and he gripped it more tightly. He felt a great vulnerability, as if he'd picked up a bad-luck charm that might attract the disaster of a careless pedestrian or a damaged fender. He hadn't expected that feeling, and he reminded himself that he just had to be careful.

"I don't know," he said. "Does it make any difference?"

"Well, Polly was female." A glance, which Jack had trouble meeting, from under her thick bangs.

"I don't know how you tell with kittens, but it's very pretty."

"That's okay. And if it's black. Mom likes black cats. It will have to be fixed anyway, you know." She looked out the window and was silent for a time. "Where are we going?" she asked as he drove up onto the highway.

"My friend lives in the south end of town. This is quicker."

Jack was tempted to come right off again and go to the park. What was he waiting for? It had to be; he'd made up his mind; life would be intolerable otherwise. He glanced at her, sitting so still, so upright. Nothing ever comes out quite the way you plan, but if you don't plan at all, like with Iris, that's worse yet, that opens you to impulse and error and terrible mistakes. He switched lanes impatiently, then pulled back again; they had to get the kitten, even though it would mean more complications and something else to dispose of, because the kitten was part of the plan.

Besides, Jack told himself, after today, after the park, everything would be settled. It wasn't going to matter if Selena saw him with Cookie, if Selena gave her the kitten. There was going to be no more need for concealment, for lying, not after today. Jack could feel pressure building up behind his right eye and repeated to himself, not after today.

"I've wanted a kitten for a long time," Cookie said, interrupting his thoughts and jangling his nerves by bringing him back to the car. "Polly was always a grown-up cat."

Jack wondered what she'd do if he were to say, casually, "I killed your precious Polly. Just like your precious father killed Iris Weed." What would she say to that? He'd like very much to say that right now; the words were bubbling on his tongue, but they were running at sixty-five mph in the center lane of the mixmaster around the city center. This was not the time or the place. The damn cat had scratched his arm. Jack told himself that he might not have gone through with it if she hadn't made those two long, shallow gashes that had swelled up and might still be infected. It wasn't his fault; the whole Larson family was bad luck.

But nothing was inevitable at the present moment. Maybe they'd just go by Selena's and pick up the kitten and that would be it. In the gray, unreal afternoon, the last leaves brown and golden yellow, the slate-colored clouds soaring above the city, the improbable presence of Cookie Larson, dark hair and fidgety and brilliant crimson jacket, beside him, and the possibility of revenge and resolution riding with them both, Jack felt how certainty can dissolve into dream and illusion, and the very fabric of the universe into electronic pulses. He could feel his heart beating, a contraction and expansion best unnoticed, and told himself he had to get control. He would follow the plan without deviation, for the plan had, so far, brought brilliant, almost unimaginable success. He would not have envisioned doing this a year ago, a month ago. Even a week ago when the plan first went into action, it had seemed strictly virtual like one of the store's computer games; now it was real and had moved in certain important ways beyond his imagining.

Jack took the Vine Street exit, and Cookie looked around with interest at the Spanish-language signs on the little markets and bodegas. She was learning Spanish in school, she told him, but it wasn't very interesting because there was no one to talk to except Denise, who couldn't say anything. She imitated Denise's struggles until Jack laughed. It might have been a normal day, when Mr. Jack, who was turning out to be an excellent computer store assistant manager, did a nice favor for a young customer and so "built community trust and good will" as the company manual advocated. Yes, he was doing that, and then he planned to take advantage of said accumulated trust and withdraw all of the good will at once.

"Here we are," he said. "See a parking space?"

The narrow street was parked solid, and he finally made a U-turn and came down the opposite side where they squeezed into the last space, right at the edge of a driveway a good block from Selena's. "We'll have to walk back," Jack said, anticipating doubts and resistance. He envisioned Cookie Larson bolting through the backyards to safety and freedom, but she just smiled. She was interested in a grape arbor they passed and a car with a soccer team pendant and a privet hedge shaped into topiaries on either side of a front walk. Jack, struggling to keep control of the day, said that he thought she played soccer herself.

Bright look, how did he know that? Well, the soccer shorts and socks. Cookie began to talk about her team. She was maybe going to be moved to keeper, but that was a secret. It would be all right with him, though, wouldn't it, because he didn't know anyone on the team.

"On any team," Jack said.

"Do you play a sport?" she asked.

"I used to fence."

Amazement and enchantment. She wanted to know all about the swords, about how it was done, about how you were protected and if anyone got hurt. Satisfying this eager interest occupied them until they reached Selena's apartment building, a triple-decker sheathed in pale green vinyl. Jack rang the bell. Selena's voice, distorted and tinny, issued from the speaker, then the door buzzed. Cookie and Jack squeezed into a cramped entry facing a steep, narrow stair. Selena was waiting at the top, cigarette in hand, her long, furry brown hair pulled back by a wide violet band that emphasized her high forehead, dark, protruding eyes, and sharp features. She looked tired and her apartment smelled of cigarette smoke and cats. Jack sniffled and started to sneeze.

"Sure you want one of these?" Selena asked.

"It's for Cookie, Cookie Larson. This is Selena Dayton."

"I'm very pleased to meet you," Cookie said formally, and Selena, good-natured and friendly, reached out and shook hands. When she gave Jack a little pat on the shoulder, he felt how easily everything might be different. And yet he'd gone this far. He'd made a plan and stuck to it and done things and now it was too late to stop.

Selena led Cookie into the kitchen where the cat, white with patches of tiger striping like a photo not completely developed, lay in a basket. The kittens were climbing in and out of the basket and playing about the legs of the chairs.

"Oh, there's the black one," said Cookie. "It's darling!" She knelt down and extended her fingers. The kitten sat back on its haunches and then swung at her hand with one tiny paw, its round blue eyes fixed in wonder.

"I'd have had her spayed if I'd known the nuisance kittens would be," Selena said.

"Can I really have this one?" asked Cookie. "It looks so like Polly!"

"That's a female," said Selena. "Cost you to get her altered."

Cookie had already picked up the kitten and was cradling its soft wiggling body. "This is the one I want," she said firmly.

"All yours," said Selena. "Three more to go. Find me some more cat lovers, Jack." She poked him playfully in the ribs, startling him so that in his state of nerves and tension, he wanted to strike her. At the same time, he was reassured by the familiarity of the apartment, by the piles of dishes in the sink, the pot of spaghetti sauce on the stove, and the book-strewn living room that had the closed-up atmosphere of too many late nights. Which was real: Selena's apartment and kittens and a favor for a young customer, or his plan, which moment by moment threatened to dissolve into absurdity and madness?

"How are you going to get her home?" Selena asked.

The kitten had now escaped from Cookie's grasp to clamber up onto her shoulder, where it was exploring her hair and sampling the binding on her jacket. "Maybe I better not just hold her," Cookie admitted.

"A box," suggested Selena. "We'll get a cardboard box."

"We don't want her to smother," said Cookie. "She'll have to be able to breathe."

"We'll make some holes." Selena disappeared into the back of the apartment where doors opened and closed on the sounds of rustling and rearranging, before she returned with a beat-up cardboard box. Selena pulled a carving knife from a kitchen drawer and punched holes in the sides with a *thuck, thuck* and a wheezing sound on the out stroke that made Jack's chest contract.

"We'd better put some paper in the bottom," Selena advised. "In case she has an accident."

Jack watched as she and Cookie folded up a newspaper that was lying on the kitchen counter and squeezed it into the bottom of the box. Then Selena decided that in the cold the kitten would need something more and got an old towel. It gave Jack an odd feeling, at once detached and superior, to see all this purposeless activity. At the same time, he wished they'd hurry; he wished everything was over. With Iris it had been different. Nothing had been planned; emotion had risen like a tsunami and overwhelmed him.

"All right?" Selena asked.

Cookie put the kitten into the box, and Selena closed the top before the animal, mewing plaintively, could scramble out.

"Better put a piece of tape on it."

More delay. Jack stood sweating in his leather coat. His eyes began to water from the cats and the cigarette smoke.

"Thank you so much," said Cookie, her face radiant. He thought again how vivid she looked, how she was one of those people with a technicolor personality. "We'll give her the very best home."

"You're doing me a favor," said Selena. "Enjoy." She turned to Jack and said, "You look like death warmed over."

"I may be getting a cold," Jack said.

"It's stray electrons," Selena said. "Unshielded radiation from all those computer screens."

"You're a Luddite," said Jack. "Listen, we've got to go. Thanks, Selena." Open the door, down the stair; Jack first, quickly, his long legs knifing down, clatter, clatter, clatter. Cookie behind him, stepping carefully, keeping the box level and talking softly to the mewling kitten.

Forget it, Jack wanted to say. *Everything's been decided against you. It's already too late.* That knowledge, which had been so exhilarating earlier, now made him feel depressed. True foreknowledge, he saw, would be the most terrible curse. Was the most terrible curse. Was thrilling. He held the outside door for Cookie.

"Mom's going to be so surprised," she said as they walked back to the car.

"She certainly is," Jack agreed.

He wanted her to put the kitten in the trunk and then on the backseat, but Cookie wouldn't hear of it. "She'll be so frightened," she cried. "She's frightened now. Just listen to her. Poor kitty. I'll hold her on my lap. It'll be fine."

Jack had a strong impulse to grab the box and throw it into the street and rewrite the script right then and there, but instead he opened the passenger door for her and waited until she had her seat belt fastened, then handed her the box.

"I'm thinking what to call her," Cookie said after a considerable silence in which Jack had maneuvered the car from its tight parking space and threaded the maze of residential streets back to the busy commercial avenue.

"Maybe you should let your mom name her."

"Mom will ask me and I'll say Polly II. But that sounds like a boat, doesn't it? There must be a lot of boats sunk for there to be so many This II's and That II's."

Jack allowed he had not considered the number of sunken boats.

"What about Polduo—*Polly* plus *duo?*"

"But she's female," Jack said. It amazed him that he could discuss such a thing when he had so much pain in his head, when his emotions were in such disarray.

"Oh, that's right, masculine ending," said Cookie. "What about Poltoo?"

"That sounds French," said Jack.

"My dad speaks French," Cookie said, "whenever we go out to dinner."

Jack smiled then, or at least he showed his teeth. She'd said the wrong thing, mentioning Lars. The plan was going to work out after all, because she'd made that one little mistake, and everything that happened now was going to be her own fault. "I want to show you something before I take you home," he said and turned off the main street toward the college and the park.

Lars cut around a sedan at the intersection, put one of the Volvo's wheels up onto the curb, and lurched back into the busy afternoon traffic to the dismay of a trucker beginning to turn from the opposite lane. Lars ignored the hollow rasp of the semi's horn and reached into his glove compartment, hoping to find the cell phone. Emma usually took it with her, but Lars swore anyway when it was missing; he could have called the police from the car. He shifted swiftly through another changing light then checked his watch. School let out at three. She'd planned to meet Mr. Jack at three-ten. He'd waited, wasting time until nearly quarter to four. There was no time to stop, not even to call for help. Lars slammed on his brakes in time to avoid rear-ending an oversized minivan, which trapped him for agonizing minutes on red. Beside him, a helmetless youth with a dirty black bandanna and straggling fair hair revved his motor scooter, ready to tear off through the double line of traffic. That's what I need, Lars thought, a vehicle nimble but dangerous. Be careful, cyclist! And Cookie! Would she be careful? Could she be careful? All this for a kitten! Why hadn't he suggested picking one up right away from the animal shelter? Well, it had been too soon, of course. But he could have said, "We'll get another cat in the spring. Why don't we get a kitten sometime when you're ready?" And she would have written back to Mr. Jack that they'd made other arrangements.

Lars honked at a car straddling two lanes, then made an inspired turn into the Burger King lot, which had two exits. He zipped through the parking lot, gaining the cross street before the light changed, and was up to fifty-five before the next light. But if he was stopped, he'd have the police, Lars thought fatalistically, and if he wasn't, he'd make the park in time. He had to. He had to get to the park in time. He couldn't think about failure, about anything happening to Cookie, about Emma, about having to tell Emma. Those blowtorch thoughts ignited the tissue of his brain; he could feel the hot rustle of their flames whenever he thought of Cookie and Mr. Jack, thoughts to avoid because he couldn't afford mistakes. And when he did make one, scraping the rear bumper of a sporty convertible as he careened through an intersection, Lars gripped the wheel and did not look back. He heard horns and shouts and put his foot on the gas.

He took the steep hill up to the park as fast as the old car could go, bounced over the crest, and slid the Volvo behind a No Parking sign. He scrambled out onto the cracked and uneven sidewalk and ran into the park without bothering to close his door. This was the place, wasn't it? Lars was breathing heavily, his chest starved for air. It was here—or, no, was it farther? Had he been mistaken? It had been so dark that night. Please, God, don't let me be wrong! No, there was the path. He remembered the path. But where were they? He couldn't be too late, he couldn't be! Lars could see distant houses through the mesh of bare branches and the thinning brown foliage of the oaks. They must be here somewhere. He knew they were. "Cookie!" he called, "Cookie!"

Then he remembered that he'd left Iris here. He'd argued with Iris just about where he was standing; his feet, unforgetting, unerring, had brought him to the spot. But she'd gone farther into the park; it had happened elsewhere. Lars hesitated as if to go back to his car, then sprinted down a diagonal path toward the other side of the park, stumbling on roots and loose stones, catching himself on the saplings that lined the path, calling, "Cookie, Cookie!" as he ran.

If she put her eye right up to the biggest hole that Selena had cut in the box, Cookie could get a glimpse of black fur and a shiny eye and the unhappy open pink mouth of the kitten, which squeaked piteously and scuffled with its tiny paws against the cardboard. "Poor kitty! It's all right," Cookie said and clucked softly the way her mother used to call Polly. It was hard to keep her eye in the right place, especially when Mr. Jack went around a corner fast, but Cookie wasn't paying attention to the road or the neighborhood. She was focusing entirely on comforting the kitten, which was, indeed, an adorable creature. She couldn't wait for Denise to see the kitten. She began mentally composing a very long E-mail to Denise, which she would send as soon as she got home.

She would get home soon, very soon, Cookie hoped, because she was going to be later than she'd expected. Daddy would be worried and not pleased at all until he saw the kitten for Mom, which would make even being so late from school, even getting a ride from Mr. Jack, okay. Cookie began to imagine what she would say. She would have to ask him how to spell Poltoo the proper French way. She wondered if she should mention to Mr. Jack that she really, really had to get home soon. He'd been very nice about the cat and giving her a ride, yet now she had the same nervous, uneasy feeling she'd had waiting out front at school for him, the sense that something wasn't quite right, like that cheeseburger she'd had at the Old Farm Shoppe that hadn't tasted exactly as usual and had made her throw up all over the car on the way home.

The car bounced in a pothole and Cookie lost sight of Poltoo and took a look at Mr. Jack, who was holding the wheel with both hands the way Nonna Paoli used to when she was still able to take Cookie out in her ancient apple green Cadillac convertible. Cookie guessed this was not the way Mr. Jack usually drove, and the idea added a little to an anxiety that she somehow knew must be concealed. She began to talk to the kitten again, because she didn't want to think about the questions she had about Mr. Jack or the fact that this was not the way home and that they were in what Mom would call a "dubious area." Cookie had not previously had a clear idea of the meaning of *dubious*, but now she thought she did.

She looked again at Mr. Jack, who'd gone very quiet, and then at the big bare trees that arched overhead and were reflected in the car windshield; they were elms, Cookie realized, probably the last anywhere in the city. She would have to tell Mr. Shapiro about seeing them and also that she'd recognized an outcropping of rock as basalt, thanks to Earth Science I. Would there be an Earth Science II? Could that be called *Scitoo?* "Where are we?" she asked and not very politely added, "I've got to get home right away. My parents will be worried sick." That's what Denise always said, "My mom will be worried sick." Cookie hoped the phrase would add the right emphasis.

"I'll bet they will," said Mr. Jack in a kind of mean and snide voice. "Don't worry, this will only take a minute."

"But where are we?" Cookie persisted. She was beginning to wonder how she could get home from this rundown, overgrown

neighborhood and away from Mr. Jack, too, who was fine, she was
sure, and meant well and all, but who made Cookie wish that she
had Jake with her.

"We're not very far from the college. Haven't you seen the little
park on this side? It's famous. I should have thought your daddy
would have brought you to this little park."

"We have a much nicer park near our house," said Cookie primly.
Although it was hard for her to believe that anyone did not like her
father, something in Mr. Jack's tone of voice told her that at least
one person did not. "We can walk to our park."

"This is a special park, though. Do you know what happened in
this park?" He slowed the car down and pulled it to the curb but
left the motor running.

Cookie didn't answer. She put her eye up against the cardboard
box and clucked to the kitten. "Kitty's frightened," she said. Cookie
did not want to look at Mr. Jack at all. She wanted to pretend that
everything was fine, because sometimes if you act like everything is
fine, it really turns out to be okay.

"You're the one who was so curious about Iris Weed," Mr. Jack
said. Something had happened to his voice to make it sound strained
yet unemotional, almost like the voice on her computer. Cookie
could not tell what this voice meant. "Step out of the car, and you'll
learn all you'll ever want to know about Iris Weed."

Cookie wasn't sure about leaving the car, but she didn't want to
sit beside Mr. Jack, either. She unfastened her belt and released the
door latch, clutching the box under one arm. Mr. Jack reached for
the carton. "We'll put the kitty in the back," he said.

Cookie shook her head. "She'll be too frightened." She moved so
quickly that though he had his hand on the box, she was able to
push her car door open and slide out with the kitten.

"Put the cat back in the car," he said, "or we'll have to put her
in the trunk."

"No," said Cookie. "And I don't want to talk about Iris Weed,
either. I want to go home. My dad will have called the school."

"You're right. Your dad won't like your being late." Mr. Jack had gotten out of the car and was standing beside it with his door open. His handsome face looked sallow and not nearly as nice as usual, and his rigid features told Cookie that she should never have come with him. "Your father especially won't like you being in this park. And do you know why?"

Cookie gripped the carton with both hands without speaking. She could hear the kitten; no one else was around. There was a big rock outcropping half covered by scraggly sumac bushes on one side of the road and, on the other, the empty park with its long grass and overgrown paths. But she'd seen houses just a little way back, where there would be people, cars, traffic. Would she be silly if she put down the box and ran? Cookie was a little afraid of looking childish; at the same time, something told her that she must get away from Mr. Jack. And though he was bigger and older, she was a very good runner, the best runner on the whole soccer team, and if she had a head start . . . Cookie held the box tighter; she thought she'd better not leave the adorable kitten with Mr. Jack. She was wondering how fast she could run carrying the box, when he said, "This is where your father killed Iris Weed."

"That's a lie!" Cookie cried. "That's a stinking, rotten lie." Tears of rage came into her eyes. "You can get out of here," she said. "I'll walk home. I'll find my own way." She took a step backward.

Mr. Jack pivoted around the open door of his car, an oddly easy, graceful gesture, and Cookie thought, I'm going to have to run. She shifted her feet, because fear was making her legs heavy and her muscles tense. "I don't think you understand the situation," he said. "I loved Iris Weed. So your father owes me something, don't you think? What do you think I should take from him in exchange?"

"Iris Weed didn't love you," Cookie said, reckless with fear and anger. "Iris Weed was scared as shit when you used to come and bang on her truck. I know about you and Iris Weed. You're 'Sven,' aren't you?"

"You little bitch," Mr. Jack screamed. He lunged around the car, and Cookie bolted down the walk, just as someone shouted, "Cookie! Get away from him!" She glanced back to see her dad racing out of the woods toward the car and Mr. Jack.

"Dad! Dad, I'm here!"

Mr. Jack spun back around the front of his car and slid inside and put the motor in gear. All Cookie's blood rushed straight to her heart: Daddy had only to appear to send Mr. Jack and all his lies packing. She had started running up the walk toward her father, the kitten crying as the box bounced against her hip, when Mr. Jack's car jolted over the high granite curbing with a bang and a rattle. Cookie screamed as he accelerated down the sidewalk, then, as Daddy dove away, the unimaginable happened: Mr. Jack swerved and hit him with an awful thump, half hard, half soft, and a cry like the loudest gasp ever, and flung him against some saplings at the side of the walk.

Mr. Jack reversed so fast that Cookie had to jump out of the way, then the car lurched forward again, the engine roaring through its torn muffler. Cookie screamed, "Stop, stop! Oh, please stop!" The car was aimed straight at Daddy, who somehow landed behind the tree that reached out and ripped a fender from Mr. Jack's car with a shrieking crunch. Cookie was stumbling toward them, crying, "Stop that, stop that!" when the car reversed by her again, revealing Mr. Jack, his livid face blood streaked, his hands frozen on the wheel. Cookie put down the kitten's box and jumped into the middle of the sidewalk. She started waving her hands, shouting and crying, and possibly she distracted Mr. Jack just a little, because this time the car thumped back down over the curb, squashing what was left of its undercarriage. To regain momentum, he gunned the motor, sending the car back across the street and into the path of an oncoming sedan that hit the driver's side with a terrible mash and tear of metal.

Cookie ran to where Daddy was lying on his side with his legs at a bad angle. His slacks were torn and there was a slick, pulpy blue, white, and purple mess showing through the rent. He had blood all over one arm, blood that was coming right through his shirt and his tweed jacket. His face had a bluish tinge, white around his lips. "Don't touch me, Cookie," he gasped. "Get help. Get help!" His voice rose as if he was terribly angry, but Cookie knew it was pain and that this was bad, very bad.

She ran to the street where cars were stopping and a police car with its lights flashing and siren on was coming up the shoulder on the wrong side of the road.

"Get an ambulance for my dad!" The words were a whisper. It took Cookie several tries before the scream came out that cut through the noise and the cars and the shouts and the confusion: "My dad has been hurt! My dad has been hurt! Call for an ambulance right now!"

The policeman was an older traffic cop, alone on a routine patrol, and it took Cookie several desperate minutes before she could convince him that it was not Mr. Jack she meant, not Mr. Jack, who was crumpled in the collapsed front seat of his car with his mouth half open and a stunned expression, nor the stranger who was standing with one side of his face flayed open, saying over and over again to anyone who would listen, "He just backed the hell right out in front of me. He just backed the hell right out in front," but her own father, Daddy Lars, lying badly hurt and in terrible pain just at the edge of the trees. "He ran him down," she screamed to the patrolman. "He tried to kill Daddy. He hit him with his car."

The cop radioed for second ambulance, and a shrieking police car arrived with two officers, a man with a thick mustache and a heavy yellow face, who jumped out and began work with a crowbar on Mr. Jack's door, and a woman, tall, skinny, and dark, who ran into the trees with a medical kit and began doing frightening things to Daddy with bags of fluid and an inflatable cast and who yelled at Cookie when she got too close. An ambulance screamed up, then another. Cookie ran back to wave one of them over and stumbled over Poltoo's box, which she kicked across the walk. The ambulance bounced onto the sidewalk and rolled past her to disgorge an EMT crew that jumped out with oxygen and a red plastic stretcher and shouted back and forth to the policewoman.

Cookie sat down on the long dry grass. She was very cold and her panties were wet and her legs wouldn't support her weight. All around her people were yelling and hurrying and complaining and two-way radios were beeping and squawking. She felt horribly alone.

Daddy was so badly hurt he might die. She started and shook her head violently at the thought, which was terrible even to have imagined. He can't, she thought, but really she knew he could. She'd seen how it could happen, how quickly disaster could come, how easily an ordinary day could change into something horrible. The grown-up world was a strange, unknown, *dubious* neighborhood with rules she didn't understand. In the grown-up world, Daddy could die.

Cookie wiped her eyes and nose on the sleeve of her jacket and noticed, as if from very far away, that the cardboard box was dented and tipped over on its side. She wasn't sure whether the ambulance had hit it or not. But if the wheels had run over it, the box would be squashed flat. Was the kitten still alive? Cookie crawled over to see. Maybe poor, frightened Poltoo was all right. Maybe. And Cookie told herself that if the kitten was alive, Daddy would be all right, as well.

She clucked to the kitten, scared to open the box, scared at what she'd see, because if the kitten was all right, Daddy would be, too. And if it wasn't, if the ambulance had hit it, if she'd kicked it when she kicked the box out of the way . . . Cookie's hands were trembling, as she turned the carton right side up, then ripped open the tape and lifted the flap: The tiny black kitten, streaked with vomit, was cowering in one corner of the box, shivering violently. Cookie burst into tears of relief, touched its head, said, "Poor Poltoo! Poor kitty!" then wiped its fur and wrapped it in the towel. She cradled it in her arms, though it smelled bad and clawed at her hands, because Daddy would live. Please, please let him live! If he lived, she'd never be bad again, Cookie promised the universe. Never. Because this was her fault, this whole thing. She'd thought she could make it better, but everything she'd done from burning the diary to getting the kitten had been a disaster.

An ambulance pulled away with a rising shriek. One of the cops was yelling into his radio for "jaws of life," which sounded even worse to Cookie than needles and IV bags and inflatable casts and almost as bad as Daddy groaning in the terrible, uncontrollable way that hurt her to remember. He was being loaded into the other ambulance now and Cookie ran over, Poltoo in her arms. "Let me go with him," she cried. "I'm going with him."

"You can't," said the policewoman, who'd sounded so angry and impatient. Her uniform was wet with sweat under her arms and she was wearing latex gloves that turned her dark hands a milky gray. "They'll have to be working on him the whole way," she said, pulling off the bloodstained gloves.

"I'm his daughter and I want to go," cried Cookie. "I was just trying to get a kitten for Mom. It was to be a surprise, that's all." She began to sob without being able to stop, without being able to explain why she had to go, how she wouldn't be in the way. The doors of the ambulance slammed shut and the big vehicle eased back along the sidewalk, then it pulled out with its siren growing into a high-pitched howl. The policewoman set down her emergency kit and put one arm around Cookie's shoulders. "Who can we call? Is your mother home?"

Cookie shook her head. After a struggle, she managed to say, "At school. Madison High School."

"Can we call your mother there?"

Cookie nodded.

"We'll do that and tell her your father's gone to the hospital," the woman said kindly, "and then we'll take you and this cute fellow home."

Cookie put her face down against the kitten's head. "Don't say it was my fault," she pleaded. "I'll tell her how everything happened."

"Honey, you're not to blame for all this," the policewoman said. "This was attempted vehicular homicide."

She spoke in a very definite and official way that was scary yet made Cookie feel the slightest bit better, brave enough to ask, "Is my dad going to be all right?"

The woman hesitated. "He has a chance," she said. Then she picked up her medical kit and gestured for Cookie to follow her to the patrol car.

19.

I think you should try ten pounds," said Athena.

Lars groaned aloud and declared her a heartless sadist.

"You're doing fine," she said. "Just fine. But if you don't want to walk with a limp . . ."

"My limp is distinguished," Lars said, sweating as he struggled to lift his battered right leg. "My cane is dashing, my whole silhouette says, Here is a man of heroism and elan."

Athena made a face. She was short and busty with a fine complexion and clean, symmetrical features. When he was working with Athena, Lars exerted himself to be amusing and tried to keep down his complaints. "Think of your back," she said. "Your back does not like the limp."

Lars nodded. His back did not like the limp, neither did his hip, which had sustained a hairline fracture and a great many contusions. His newly mended ribs did not like it, either. He bit his lip and raised his leg, up, straight out, down. Up, straight out, down.

"All right," said Athena. "Take a rest and we'll get you on the bicycle for a while."

"My treat for the day," Lars said, and she rewarded him with a pat on the shoulder. While he stretched and caught his breath, he watched her in the big mirrors that lined the therapy room—all the better to catch flaws in gait and posture and to keep wretched clients conscious of their errors. Mirrors have replaced the eye of God, Lars thought, and also that Athena had very handsome calves. He made much better progress with Athena than he did with Amy, who was knowledgeable and businesslike but whose square silhouette, gray hair, and brusque manner did not inspire the same devotion.

There was another mirror facing the bikes, and Lars was often surprised by the gaunt-faced cyclist who confronted him. The amber Victorian lamps in the Larson master bathroom evidently had a softening effect; in the combined daylight and fluorescents of the physical therapy room, Lars could see the effects of an attempted vehicular homicide only too clearly. There was a large rope of scar tissue on his arm, concealed at school by his long-sleeved dress shirts but revealed as a painfully visible bluish purple ridge by the complimentary red T-shirt from the therapy center. The scar was a match for the triangular patch on his upper right thigh, very nicely stitched he had to admit, that concealed a myriad of nerve and muscle damage which, with a multiple fracture of his lower leg, had put him in the hands of, make that *the control of*, Ms. Amy and Ms. Athena, the Double A Twins of the Deerwood Physical Therapy Center.

The unforgiving light showed some more subtle effects as well. His face was definitely lined. The flesh on either side of his nose had contracted in a moment of horror, leaving two deep grooves, and months of pain and PT had left vertical marks between his eyebrows and a spray of tension lines at the corner of his eyes and mouth. I look older, Lars thought; he would like to have seen a face of suffering and wisdom, but even his uncritical scrutiny could not go quite that far. His face was deeply tanned, thanks to Emma's insistence on a few weeks in Florida, and his light eyes were amused. I'm not finished yet, Lars thought, and pedaled faster, the rotation burning his damaged leg muscles. I'm not finished yet, he repeated over and over to the rhythm of the gear and the chain. I'm putting my leg and life in order, leg and life in order, in order.

Ms. Athena came over to interrupt this semihypnotic state and to check the gear setting, which Lars habitually set low so that he could zip through his distance quickly. She reached over and raised the number by two. "Try it there," she said, and Lars dutifully bore down on the pedals, creating the steady rumble he knew so well. What was that old Talking Heads number? "I'm on the road to nowhere." That was the stationary bike, another therapeutic device that Lars saw as basically penitential, providing time to consider his progress and the many ironies of his position. He glanced down at the dial: seven-tenths of a mile; he had thought two or three miles at least and temporarily redoubled his efforts. The bike's gears made a satisfying *whir, whir,* and Lars looked up to see that, in addition to everything else, the mysterious cyclist facing him had a nimbus of white hair. Surely just the effect of the overhead lights, but certainly from this angle, the lock of hair that fell over his forehead was, if not white, very gray. Very gray, indeed. Won on the field of battle, Lars told himself. He hadn't had any gray, not any noticeable gray, before Mr. Jack Mortlake had aimed an elderly Honda Civic in his direction. The doctor said it was coincidence; Lars knew better. Marie Antoinette had gone white overnight, the chronicles said, and he doubted the Paris mob and the shadow of the guillotine were any more terrifying than the sight of Mr. Jack running after Cookie or the rapidly approaching hood and grille of the accelerating car.

Lars had been back to see the providential tree, a white ash, according to Cookie. It had been odd to sit bundled in invalid sweaters with his leg awkward in the cast and look out the car window at the tree with an obscene swath of naked wood the exact white-yellow of fat where the bark had been stripped away. Lars still didn't know how he'd managed to get behind it. Apparently, shock had anesthetized him and instinct had done the rest. He was a lucky man and would do honor to white ash trees for the rest of his life.

He remembered telling Emma and Cookie about luck and ash trees and the blessings of fate while he was still in the hospital. Cookie had been distraught, feeling frightened and guilty about Mr. Jack. Lars had shaken his head against the pillow and explained, rather incoherently, he guessed, that he was the luckiest man on earth. And he was. Of course, some of that luck was his own skill, Lars conceded as he discreetly slid the gear back a notch. He'd made errors: Iris for one, lying about her for two, and delaying about "Sven" for three. But set against those were mercies and blessings. The clouds had lifted from Emma and wasn't that in part his doing? Weren't they happy? Didn't she know now, if she hadn't before, that he would do anything necessary to keep them safe?

And Cookie! So tall and straight and grown-up looking, especially in the flaming red nylon shirt and long black pants of her goalkeeper strip. Automatically Lars looked over his shoulder to see if she was in the waiting room. Not yet. Her coach, a man Lars considered limited and fanatical, was in ecstasies over her performance: "So focused, Dr. Larson! Such speed, such agility."

Sooner than he should have, Lars had stood on the sideline with his leg aching inside its inflatable cast, his ribs complaining of the cold wind around the field. He'd noticed several boys lingering near the back of Cookie's goal, their expressions half wistful, half predatory. They applauded when she bounded off her line, aggressive and graceful, to scoop up the ball and clasp it furiously to her broad, flat chest, but she took no notice until she'd punted far downfield. Then she said something quick and sharp over her shoulder. Lars saw the boys laugh and the saucy flip of her thick dark hair in reply: They were right to adore her.

Yes, Cookie and Emma would be fine, the result of grace, surely. But other matters were skill, and, yes, he might give himself credit as well as blame. With gray hair and a lined face had come a certain dexterity. Case in point: Isobel Weed, who'd called a dozen times before Emma relented and put him on the line. He'd just had a dose of Percocet and the multifarious pains in his leg, arm, hip, and ribs were gently receding, sluicing away like water over a spillway. Emma left the room, and Lars said weakly, "Isobel?"

"You knew all along," she said.

He denied it. There had been other cranks, she surely had some, too: psychics, dreamers, sadists. They all have phones, Isobel!

But she meant the mistaken times, his omissions and lies, the delay and obstruction that had torn up her heart, that had almost allowed Iris's killer to escape.

"If everything was as innocent as you claim, what would have been the harm of telling the truth? Tell me that, Lars."

He had murmured apologies (quite sincere) and given explanations (quite elaborate). He blamed shock and momentary panic and the difficulties of his position (quite true) and hinted, with a delicacy and tact remarkable, given his pharmaceutically altered perceptions, that the Weed women were irresistible, even if only worshiped from afar. However uncomfortable, even painful the conversation had been, Lars could not help smiling at his ingenious flattery and put on a burst of effort with the cycle that made jolly Ms. Athena give him a thumbs-up sign of approval: Good work, Lars!

And with Mrs. Weed, too. He had groveled and pleaded and explained and cajoled, until she had been sufficiently mollified to drop the worst of her threats and accusations. Still, more in sorrow than in anger, Lars sensed, she told him that he would not be editing the early diaries.

"Not appropriate," she said. "I would not feel comfortable."

Lars murmured his regrets and understanding. She was entirely correct; his convalescence was apt to be prolonged. No, no, a good prognosis, but at his (he almost slipped and said *their*) age, everything took longer to heal. He did not mention the legal issues. Paatelainen had all but said he was out of the picture. Mr. Jack, despite a temporary insanity plea, was being cooperative and had produced the murder weapon. The detectives were happy.

Lars told Isobel that she would certainly be able to find someone suitable, but he almost laughed aloud when she mentioned Joe Katz. Not Joe the Dull! Oh, poor Iris; what a fate for her lovely prose! If Lars'd had any choice, he would have fought this suggestion, protested and implored, but desperate times require a desperate resolution. He must not think about the predictable questions and gossip or the insufferable airs of Joe the Elect! "I think Professor Katz might be ideal," he said.

It was only when he was saying good-bye that Lars slipped into sincerity. "I just loved her writing," he whispered. "Her prose entered my dreams."

Isobel Weed had paused, as if taken aback by this unexpected and eccentric truth. "I will ask Joseph Katz in any case," she said and hung up, leaving Lars exhausted, his face sweat slicked, his pillows damp. He felt, insofar as he had strength to feel anything, shame and relief. Since that day, he'd often thought of Iris. Whatever her mother believed about him, Lars thought of Iris with tenderness and regret. Toiling away in the PT room, churning off the boring miles on the stationary bike, he often thought of Iris and, sometimes, of Isobel. Though she was an irritating woman, and satire his best weapon, Lars could not laugh at Isobel. He thought he'd understood her before, through his fears for Cookie, but he'd known nothing, nothing at all, until the terrifying trip across town, until he broke from the trees and saw the strange car and a man in black and Cookie, running, brilliant in her crimson jacket. Had he been five minutes later, three minutes: What was the margin for disaster? Had he not given Iris a lift, had they not argued, or argued longer or shorter, had he insisted on dropping her at the truck—oh, yes, he understood Mrs. Weed and the torments of alternate futures now, he really did. Lars leaned down, raised the gear back to where Ms. Athena had set it, and pedaled on.

"I'll park the car," said Emma. "You go on in and see if Dad's ready."

Cookie unsnapped her belt and was out the door before the car was well stopped. How quick she was. Her fast reactions had saved her, Lars said. He was newly proud of her athletic abilities, which he recognized without much understanding. But understanding, Emma thought to herself, is not always necessary, is maybe an over-rated quality that we try for after failures of sympathy. Lately, Lars had worried less about Cookie's indifferent grades and her lack of interest in school. He dutifully went to her soccer matches and stood about uncomplaining on his aching leg. "She's quite wonderful," he said to Emma. "I don't know the first thing about it, but I can tell you she's quite wonderful."

Yes, he appreciated Cookie as she was, not just as she might be—add that to Lars's account—and Emma had to admit that he was brave. But even his courage on the day had surprised her less than his stoicism afterward. Lars had always been a grumbler, a man who needed attentions and loved comfort, who groused about petty inconveniences with a multitude of funny but heartfelt complaints. So it had come as a revelation when he'd proved jaunty and indomitable in the hospital.

"I'm so lucky," he told her. "I've been so lucky. I feel I should never complain again. Of course, I will," he added ruefully, and she laughed for the first time since Delores ran through from the outer office and said, "Pick up on four, it's the police."

Lars reached over slowly, his bandaged arm awkward, and patted her hand. "I'm an awful fool, but I love you."

"A fool for love," she joked, and he smiled and pressed her fingers.

Emma pulled into a parking space at the end of the PT center lot and thought of the old cliché, the bitter with the sweet. She'd tried to explain that to Cookie, whose passions fluctuated between hero worship and fury.

"He kissed Iris Weed," she said, almost weeping with anger.

"I suspect he did," said Emma. But not, she thought, much else. Lars had not been quite happy that spring, for Iris Weed had her other, fatal lover. The fact of the matter was that Lars's age was showing, and Emma's chief hope must be that he wouldn't make a serious fool of himself in the future.

"You shouldn't put up with it!" Cookie cried, passionate and thoughtless.

Emma had narrowed her eyes and given her a cold, hard look. "He never hesitated a moment," she said, and Cookie's face changed, for she'd said that a dozen times after waking up with a shout, stirring Jake to bark and Poltoo to skitter out of the bedroom and tangle Emma's feet in the dark hallway.

It was always the same: She found Cookie sitting up in bed, white-faced, tear-streaked, her breath coming in great gulps. She'd been running, running from something, sometimes a car, sometimes a faceless person, sometimes a mysterious, formless something. And then the sound of branches rustling and breaking (there was always that sound) before her father crashed out of the trees and shrubs and ran directly at Mr. Jack, at the car. "I thought he was going to die," Cookie said, gasping, weeping.

And he might have, he almost had, Emma knew, and that was the other side of her frivolous, even reckless, husband, the side she had sensed, though others had not, though her friends had been

skeptical and, sometimes, pitying. Yes, Lars had lied to her and betrayed her trust, and during the business with Iris Weed, Emma had
come closer than ever to withdrawing from him. Had, in fact, withdrawn somewhat, had found a different point of balance, had kept
her eyes open. But then, just at the moment when coolness began
to erode their happiness, he'd managed this heroic, surprising thing
that confirmed Emma's deepest hopes of him and lifted her anxiety.
It was odd that events that should have been the proof of all her
fears had radically diluted them, as if, by gaining substance, terror
had moved to the world of real things and left the darker places of
her mind.

Cookie swung open the heavy glass doors of the PT center and
waved to Nancy, who had her ear to the phone and was saying yes
and no and what times were available and, simultaneously, was writing up an appointment card for a shaky old woman with a walker
and a great many details about her niece's wedding. Cookie knew
all the staff and a lot of the patients. When her dad was first started,
when PT was really bad, she'd come along whenever she wasn't in
school. While Daddy was having grim things done by the physio,
Cookie had worked her way through the center's eclectic periodicals:
People, Better Homes & Gardens, Time, a variety of orthopedic journals, and an assortment of publications on wellness, diet, and
spiritual growth, illustrated by drawings of women with flowing hair
surrounded by crescent moons and wolves.

With these and the intermittent companionship of Nancy and
of Kristen, the masseuse, Cookie had whiled away the tedious hours
of her dad's rehabilitation.

"You don't have to come," he'd say. "I won't sneak out the side
door."

But Cookie knew very well that he'd relied on her coming, and
she rather relied on going, on doing what she could to make up for
secret E-mails and Mr. Jack and things she'd known weren't right at
all. Mom approved of her going, felt she should, and Daddy enjoyed
the company while he waited for Emma to pick them up. He liked

to describe every little bit of progress: how far he'd walked without his cane, how many minutes he'd gone on the stationary bike, how many leg lifts and how much weight he'd managed. Sometimes, when the center was quiet, Cookie was allowed to ride the bike next to him, to speed along imaginary highways at the head of some invisible peloton. If she looked into the mirror, she would see that Daddy's face was pale and know that his leg was sore.

"You're leaving me far behind," Lars would say, and he'd promise that in the summer, when his leg was really healed, they'd go out for long bike rides. "In the country," he'd say. "Or all round the city. We'll do a city tour." Sometimes he would list places they'd visit; other days he taught her bike songs, which, Lars explained, were variants of bus songs, now a dying art.

"It's your generation's fault with your Walkmans and portable CD players. The great tradition of the American bus song is dying. Is dead. Is done for." He began singing *Valeree, valero, valer-aha, ha-ha, ha-ha, valeree . . .*" until Ms. Amy pointed out that other patients had to concentrate.

Daddy made an elaborate, mocking apology. Ms. Amy was not impressed. Ms. Athena, now, would have laughed. She laughed a lot when she worked with Daddy and smiled at him in a way Cookie didn't much like.

Cookie opened the front door for the old lady with the walker, then went to the desk. "My dad almost done?" she asked Nancy, a massive, benign presence in a flowery smock with a darling Scottie dog pin.

"Should be. He was in right on time. Take a look."

The PT room was a long glass, brick, and mirrored rectangle with rows and rows of blue and dark red mats. The walls were lined with weights and Nautilus machines (a better grade of torture implement according to Daddy) and stacks of light blue plastic balls half as big as herself. There were treadmills, a StairMaster, mysterious wedges and inclined planes, and a big balance disk like an alien teeterboard. Daddy was at the far end on one of the row of exercise bikes, chatting with Ms. Athena. He was leaning over toward her in this quite disgustingly intimate way with one hand on her shoulder, telling her something that made her smile. Probably just like that mouthy Iris Weed had smiled.

Daddy lifted his head and saw Cookie in the mirror—he always noticed her so quickly that she knew he'd been waiting and watching just for her, a fact that gave Cookie a funny twinge, especially when she felt disgusted by the silly, embarrassing things he did. Yet he had raced out of the woods, shouting, careless of what might happen, indifferent to Mr. Jack and everything else except her. It was difficult sometimes to put those two things together, to accept the two sides of Daddy, or of anyone really, even of herself, as Cookie had learned the hard way. Mom said that some people had to learn everything *the hard way* and she was afraid that Cookie might be one of those people. Daddy, on the other hand, never talked about learning the hard way or the easy way, and Cookie had begun to suspect that there were some things he didn't intend to learn at all: just look at how he was laughing with Ms. Athena.

"Hey!" he called, waving, his face joyful. Then to Ms. Athena, "Tell Cookie I did nearly five miles today!"

"Well, over four. Which is very good."

"It's better than good. It's prodigious!" Lars exclaimed.

"You're improving my vocabulary, anyway," said Ms. Athena.

"You ready?" Cookie asked. Over the winter, there had been days when she'd wanted to kick sexy, flirtatious Ms. Athena right in the pants.

"I'll just change," Lars said, struggling off the bike.

His shirt was streaked with sweat, and Cookie smelled the sourness of exertion that had run into pain. She hadn't asked to know about pain. It somewhat surprised her to remember that she'd wanted to know about Iris Weed and the grown-up world. What she'd learned was that it was mostly mysterious and disgusting and dangerous. Mostly. A month ago, she'd have said *entirely*, but since Jed Tyler kissed her after the New Haven game she was keeping an open mind about adult things and had extended a certain tolerance even to Iris Weed.

But she didn't discuss any of this with her dad. When they reached the changing cubicles, Lars said, "Tell Mom I'll be out in